DAVID W. BURNS

HEART OF STONE

BOOK ONE OF THE MEDUSA CHRONICLES

HEART
ST⊙NE
OF

DAVID W. BURNS

woodhall press

Woodhall Press | Norwalk, CT

woodhall press

Woodhall Press, 81 Old Saugatuck Road, Norwalk, CT 06855
WoodhallPress.com

Cover design: Germancreative
Layout artist: LJ Mucci

Library of Congress Cataloging-in-Publication Data available

ISBN 978-1-954907-82-9   (paper: alk paper)
ISBN 978-1-954907-83-6   (electronic)

First Edition
Distributed by Independent Publishers Group
(800) 888-4741

Printed in the United States of America

This is a work of fiction. Names, characters, business, events and incidents are the products of the author's imagination. Any resemblance to actual persons, living or dead, or actual events is purely coincidental.

To my amazing wife, Kate, who makes the dream real.

CHAPTER 1

Killing Marco Delgado should have been easy.

When he came into the bar, I was waiting in a formfitting red dress that was slit up to my hip on one side—the side I made sure was showing toward the front door. Marco glanced around, surveying his kingdom, then made a beeline for the stool next to mine. I'd kept it empty for the last two hours with a rather inspired string of insults and put-downs.

No bodyguards, no entourage. Marco was on the prowl tonight. Like I said: easy.

I adjusted my hair ever so carefully as he settled in next to me. Every golden curl was in place. No worries there. For now, at least.

"Knob Creek," he told the barkeep. "And one for the lady."

I gave him an appraising glance, then let a slow smile play across my glossy lips.

"You might want to spare yourself," I said, which was probably going to be the last honest thing I said to this man. "I don't think I'm very good company right now." Marco always looked for the damaged ones, the birds with one broken wing. He liked playing the gallant. It was all part of his ritual.

"Misery loves company," Marco grinned. He raised his tumbler. "To starting over."

"I'll drink to that," I said, and knocked the bourbon whiskey all the way back. Why the hell not? We all have our impossible dreams, right? Mine was being able to look myself in the mirror without wanting to smash it. Marco's—though he didn't know it yet—was being able to live through the night.

"So what's your name, sweetheart?"

"Kyra," I said, extending a hand.

"Marco Delgado," he said, taking it. Then he slipped his fingers under my palm and raised my hand to his lips, kissing it gently. I felt a ripple of agitation over my scalp, like ants crawling across my skin. I drew my hand back, a little too quickly, and his black eyes narrowed for a moment.

"So," I said, to get back on script, "what do you do, Marco?" When you're not out breaking people's legs and cutting off their fingers for your boss, I could've added. But that would have been rude.

"Oh, you know, this and that," he grinned. He liked that grin. You could tell.

"A man of mystery," I teased. "My mother warned me about men like you. How do I know you're not going to try to take me off somewhere and do bad things to me?"

His gaze dropped to my cleavage, and his wide nostrils flared like a racehorse. Yeah, he'd sized me up pretty fast: young girl, probably just getting over a bad breakup, wanting to feel some connection with somebody, even if it was the wrong guy. Two drinks. Three, max.

Except Marco had arrived an hour later than his routine. And I had a long-distance call to make tonight. I wanted to keep the chitchat short.

Marco leaned forward, dropping his voice to a husky whisper. "You looking for someone to do bad things to you?"

2

He really should've brought a wingman. But enforcers are used to being their own muscle.

"Buy me another drink," I smirked, "and maybe we'll see how bad you can be." Which was, if the local Vietnamese business community was any indicator, pretty bad. Otherwise, they'd never have become desperate enough to pool their money and hire my agency.

The drinks came and vanished. I laughed at all the right jokes and put my hand on his arm at the right time. In less than fifteen minutes, we were stumbling out together into the frigid Chicago night.

"You got a car?" he asked. The next line would be some variation of "mine's in the shop." "Mine's at the shop."

Not much for originality, this Marco.

"Over here." I led him to the parking lot around the corner and the red Ferrari I'd rented for the occasion.

"Sweet ride," he said, and the next thing I knew, he had me pinned against the side of the car and was clumsily planting his mouth over mine. This is never my favorite moment on a job—I generally prefer to keep people at cattle-prod distance—but a girl's got to make a living, you know. So I pushed back with my lips just enough to keep his motor revving.

I was about to break contact when Marco jerked his head back, his eyes narrowing, and scanned the cars around us with a suddenly alert gaze.

"Did you hear that?" he said. "Sounded like . . . hissing, or something."

I blinked confusion at him. "That, maybe?" I pointed to a nearby subway grate from which clouds of vapor were gushing.

Marco's brow furrowed in doubt or confusion. He had the instinctive sense of danger that every natural predator possesses. When he turned back to me, I could see his lust had been dampened somewhat by unease.

"C'mon," I said, bouncing up and down helpfully. I hadn't bothered to button up my jacket in case I needed to call in the reserves. "I'm freezing out here."

Marco's breath steamed out of his nose. Good boy. Then his hands were on me, roaming around inside my coat. I gave him a minute, then pushed him back with breathless effort.

"Not here," I panted. "Too many people. Let's go somewhere we can be really bad."

Marco scowled, but the fish was on the hook by now, and when I scampered around the car, he got in the passenger seat quick enough.

"Don't forget your seatbelt," I giggled, and then we were heading downtown along Lake Shore Drive. The industrial park just outside Gary/Chicago Airport would be best, I'd decided. Isolated, with easy access to Lake Michigan. Adding in disposal time, I should be home by ten at the latest.

Then Marco's cell phone rang. I stiffened, but he didn't notice. Just checked the caller, then grunted.

"'Scuse me, sweetheart. Gotta take this." He tapped the phone. "Hey, Celeste. How's it going, beautiful?"

Seriously? He was hitting on some other chick while I was supposedly driving him back to my place? I felt vaguely insulted.

"What? Nah, don't worry. I got it all taken care of. I'm tellin' you, don't worry. I know a guy, okay? You can tell Little A I'll pick him up at noon." He hung up, then went back to tracing his fingers up and down my arm as though nothing had happened.

Something had, though. I had pretty finely tuned antennae for when things were off, myself.

"Who's Little A?" I asked, keeping my tone light. "Your boy?" I already knew the weasel had no children, nieces, or nephews. Maybe this was part of his act, coming across as the wrongfully separated dad.

"Hm? Nah. My godson, Antonio. I'm takin' him to the White Sox home opener tomorrow."

"His dad's not a South Siders fan?"

Marco's gaze drifted out the passenger side window. "Ain't got no dad. He had a, uh, accident at work."

I could guess what kind of accident that had been. The kind where you fell backward onto a lot of knives.

"So . . . you guys close?"

4

Marco's tone conveyed a shrug. "I take him to the games sometimes. He likes those black caps. Always brings his mitt, thinks he's gonna catch a fly ball." He chuckled. "Eight-year-olds."

I ground my capped teeth together. Goddamn it to hell. I had a strict policy against marks with close ties to kids. Somebody at the Agency had slipped up, big time. I was going to have to chew that somebody a new one in the morning.

Not to mention what a pain it was going to be refunding my portion of the fee. Literally. It didn't help that I was already behind on my rent and that a few items in my fridge were beginning to acquire sentience; there was no way I could finish this job now. Damn, damn, damn.

"Hey, Marco," I said, easing my foot off the accelerator. We'd just gotten onto South Shore Drive and were racing past Calumet Park. "Why don't you and I do this some other time? I think I'm developing one of those headaches we girls get."

"Now, don't be getting cold feet, sweetheart," said Marco, resuming his attentions to my arm. "You don't have to worry about where I'll be spending tomorrow. Like the lady says, all we've got is tonight, right?"

He reached for my hair. I couldn't help it; I flinched.

"Hey . . ." There was nothing playful in his tone now. He squeezed my arm, hard. "Let's remember who came on to who, kid. You wanted to be bad, right? You're gonna get your chance."

"Marco, please listen—"

"No, you listen," he said, dropping his hand to my leg. "You're gonna—" He stopped, his probing fingers snagging on something.

Oh, shit.

"Is that a gun?" His voice had become a guttural snarl. He fumbled for a moment with the thigh holster, then ripped the weapon out. "You bitch! Are you setting me up?"

"It's just for protection," I yelled. "It's not even loaded—"

"Pull over," he snapped.

We were on the Skyway, which ran south along the city, carrying inter-state traffic to and from the industrial parks and the airport. Not where I'd have chosen to make a pit stop, but the grip on my arm was insistent.

Marco directed me into an empty lot and steered us around the lone brick building away from the freeway's lights. He tossed the gun into the back seat, then yanked the keys from the ignition, clenching them in his fist.

"Marco, don't be this way," I said, trying to salvage the mess things had become. I needed to get him out of the car, fast. "We can still—" A back-handed blow to my face brought stars to my eyes. I tasted blood in the back of my throat. Then I sensed more than saw the knife coming out of his jacket.

Okay, enough. The situation had become unmanageable. I fumbled for the door handle and tried to shove hard enough against it to tumble out. Only Marco was too quick. His hand snagged my hair, yanking my head back, exposing my throat. But only for an instant. Then the stays ripped loose and the lovely mass of blonde curls that had cost me three hundred bucks came off all at once.

"What the—?" Marco had time to say, and then the car filled with angry hisses.

All my serpents, fully roused, reared up from my head, snapping at the air. Marco shrieked and jerked back, out of their reach. Before he could do anything else, I turned and fixed him with the power of my Gaze.

As his eyes met mine, they went from terror and surprise to something else, some deeper mixture of revulsion and incomprehension that he proba-bly wasn't consciously aware of: the reaction of a man used to dealing death who couldn't believe what it was that was killing him.

I'd let the snakes grow out nearly a week, and tonight my Gaze was potent. The transformation caused his limbs to stiffen first, turning them from flesh and blood to inanimate rock in seconds. Marco gave out a choking gasp as his heart became stone in his chest. The pallor of his skin stole from white to gray.

"What . . . are . . . you . . ." He gurgled, the words coming out like gravel. Then the Change reached his lips and his eyes went dead.

6

My hands were shaking from the adrenalin surge. I swung my legs out onto the tarmac and sucked in fresh air. The serpents shuddered and twisted around one another, recoiling from the cold. When I'd gotten my breathing under control, I tapped out a cigarette and lit it. They hissed and bit at the curling smoke, disapproving. Screw them; they'd be dead by morning anyway.

I waited there, shivering, until I felt it, the familiar sensation of a brittle shell—like invisible ice—cracking and falling off me soundlessly, all at once. *Ektos plasma*, the fury and pain and despair of Marco's victims, molded into a compulsion by an Agency spellcaster. Gone now. As compulsions go, this one had been pretty weak; if I'd bailed on the contract, I'd probably only have spent a week in bed, throwing up every other hour. To do worse, the *geas* needed more power behind it, and these clients hadn't had the bucks for that.

So . . . contract fulfilled. Good for me.

Marco's dying question echoed in my head. I supposed he deserved an answer. But I didn't turn around. I never liked to look at them afterward. I didn't need to see that horrified expression frozen for eternity on their faces. Like I didn't already know what I was.

"I thought you'd figured that out, Marco," I said over my shoulder, looking up at the frozen stars, each one flawlessly, eternally beautiful. Those same stars had shone down on the land of my ancestors, had watched over the Parthenon and the Temple of Apollo in their grandeur. They never changed, never suffered, never had to get their dainty white light dirty making a living in a land not meant for them. I drew blessed nicotine into my lungs then blew a cloud up at the distant twinkling lights, erasing their damn perfection from my sight. The serpents were making my head feel too heavy for my neck. I dropped my gaze to the detritus of the parking lot, to the casual debris of mortal lives. Would that I could just let my head sink between my knees, into the ground itself, and be swallowed up by the earth.

"I'm just a good girl gone bad."

Or a Mythic, if you want to use the popular term for folk like me, people who—for whatever twisted reason—look like, or actually are, the beasts and monsters from the world's legendary past. If you haven't read about us in a travel guide, don't feel bad. We inhabit the dark and abandoned pockets of cities like Chicago, skulking in the shadows, for the most part making our meager living picking over the refuse of what ordinary humans take for granted. Some of us—those lucky enough to be able to hide their deformities—work among regular people every day, or so I hear. But most Mythic stick to the fringes of society, doing the jobs nobody else wants to do, to lessen the risk of exposure. We take out the trash, clean the industrial tanks and machinery, dig the graves so that the human world gets to keep humming along, content and oblivious.

And speaking of trash . . .

I couldn't stick around here, not with a life-size statue of a local good-fella in the passenger seat. I ground out the cig with real regret and fitted my wig back in place. The serpents were already sluggish after expending their power; I only got nipped twice as I shoved them back under cover.

I hunted around the front seat for the car keys, then realized they were still in Marco Delgado's fist. His stone fist.

Son of a bitch. This night just kept getting better and better.

After spending a futile three minutes trying to fish them out, I gave up and popped the trunk with the manual lever. From my duffel bag I took out goggles, smock, and gloves then selected one of my ball-peen hammers. I opened the passenger side door and wriggled in next to the statue. Ferraris are not designed for multiple front-seat passengers. I had to wedge myself against the dash to get the angle right, but one swing was all it took to split the stone at the knuckles and get the keys free. In one respect, I'd been lucky: The keys were technically only mine by virtue of the loaner, so they could have just as easily been petrified along with all the other inorganic parts attached to Delgado's body. But evidently a rental contract was enough of a bond for the magic to consider the keys as belonging to me.

The ten-minute drive to Indiana Harbor felt longer, partly because I was running late and partly because every flashing or blinking light in my rearview mirror made me think I was about to be pulled over by the cops. I hadn't meant to take care of business with Delgado until I'd gotten him to one of my usual disposal sites, and I definitely hadn't wanted him to be in the car when I converted him into more than 250 pounds of deadweight. I wasn't used to advertising my abilities to anybody who happened to pass me on the freeway, and it made me sweat until I pulled into the steel mill's parking lot and parked under the shadow of the access ramp.

I needed another cigarette pretty bad by now, but it would have to wait. Nighttime security was usually lax this far from the harbor's vital points, but it still wouldn't do to get caught here. The air was still and quiet except for the gentle sound of Lake Michigan slapping against the breakwater fifty feet to my left. Over to my right, great mountains of iron ore and limestone rose up into the night sky, the bounty of quarries in south and central Indiana, all bound for processing and use in construction sites around the Great Lakes. Ordinarily, I'd have been happy to give a worthless piece of trash like Delgado a chance to give something back to the community.

But he'd really done a number on my arm; I could feel it starting to bruise. And it was nearly ten o'clock already. I still had a long night ahead of me.

I got my gear on again and tried to tip Delgado's body out of the car. No go. I was strong enough, but the head and torso of the big lug were just never going to fit under the doorjamb. I could rock it back and forth all night, but there was only so much headroom there, and no amount of wishful thinking was going to change that. I'd already scraped the rubber molding in a few places. I wasted a few more moments cursing Delgado's parentage, then decided it was time to get out the big guns.

Back to the trunk. This time I took out my pride and joy: twenty-three pounds of corrosion-resistant, non-sparking German carbon steel, fitted onto a re-gripped, three-foot fiberglass handle. A sledgehammer that could bust an eighty-pound boulder down to pebbles in minutes, as long as there was enough room to let it loose.

Which, of course, there wasn't, as I saw immediately when I tried to line up for a swing. Unless I wanted to dent the side door or smash in the windshield, I couldn't get at him. Unbelievable. I was fast getting fed up with Marco Delgado. I wished I could kill the bastard all over again, just this time out of the damn car.

In the end, I had to clamber onto the roof, hang the sledgehammer between my knees, and swing it at a forty-five-degree angle to get the job done. I almost pitched over onto my head twice before I connected solidly, but when I did, the statue broke apart with a satisfying crunch. One arm detached from the shoulder and bounced out onto the ground. The torso took two more hits before it cracked along the left scapula, sending the entire upper body, head and all, sliding off.

Panting, I pulled the rest of the statue out onto the concrete and dragged it away from the Ferrari. Three overhead swings blasted the lower body into chunks I could carry. But I didn't stop until nothing was left bigger than the size of my fist. Then I scooped the rubble up with a snow shovel and heaved it out onto Lake Michigan, where it disappeared into the froth of the breakwater.

All that remained now was Delgado's head.

It was still staring blindly up at the unforgiving stars as I stepped over it, sledgehammer in hand. The features were contorted with the same fear and agony its owner had doubtless visited on countless victims during his too-long existence. It didn't make him any easier to look at.

I wish I didn't have to see their eyes when it happened. But unless the serpents were at full growth or I held my victim's gaze right to the end, that end could take hours, even days. Death by slow petrification was agonizing; better to make the suffering quick. I'd learned that a long time ago, when I was still young and stupid enough to think I could lead a normal life.

Left to nature's devices, he'd wear that expression for a thousand years or more before wind and rain softened the sharp edges, blurred the sight in those horrified eyes, reduced him to an unrecognizable nonperson, robbed of any definite identity.

I didn't have time for that. And, like I said, the son of a bitch had hurt my arm.

The sledgehammer reduced him to scattered fragments in half a dozen blows. I took perhaps more than my usual care grinding the rocky bits of his face into dust. Each swing made my arm throb a little more, but I chalked it off to karmic payback. Marco's last hurrah. Hope he was enjoying it in Hades, or Hell, or wherever it was that people went now.

I swept the pieces into the scoop of my shovel and trudged down the slope from the cement platform to where the massive boulders of the break-water were piled up, the bulwark against Lake Michigan's unpredictable fury. High tide was rolling in, and the black rocks were already slick and gleaming under the distant lamps. With a great heave, I consigned the last of Marco Delgado's mortal remains to the deep. The muscles of my back and shoulders were burning knots by now, but only sand remained to mark that he had ever walked the earth. The wind would scour even that off the stone before dawn.

Heading back to the car, I stopped at the edge of the platform and looked back. For a moment I had the disquieting sensation that eyes were upon me, and I half-expected to see Marco Delgado's ghost hovering over the black waters.

What are you?

Spray leapt up from the rocks, cold and stinging like needles. I shivered. First week in April, and spring still had not come to the Windy City. Tomorrow morning an eight-year-old boy would wait a long time for someone who would never arrive to take him to his favorite team's home opener. Maybe he'd hear there'd been an accident, or that his godfather had to go somewhere far away. Maybe he wouldn't be told anything and would be left to conjure up his own explanation of monsters that had taken his grown-up friend from him.

I scrubbed the wetness from my face with the back of my fist. It wasn't my fault he'd lost his dad—or had drawn a killer and psychopath for a godfather. And monsters don't care about things like that anyway.

It was nearly eleven o'clock by the time I got back to my apartment on the South Side. I parked the Ferrari in the back lot and slung my duffel bag over my shoulder, groaning at the weight on my sore muscles. I just wanted to go to bed, but my night of fun wasn't over yet. The freight elevator was the only one working again, and as I rode it up to the thirteenth floor, I could feel the last of the serpents slithering around the dead bodies of its siblings, searching in vain for another survivor. For some reason, there was always only one of them left after they'd loosed their full power. If I waited till morning, it would have systematically consumed the bodies of its brethren and then died itself. God only knew where all the bones and muscles and scales went; it was more than I had ever wanted to think about. The only thing worse than knowing that would be lying in the dark and listening all night as it slowly swallowed the rest of its kin.

I wasn't waiting till morning.

I locked the triple dead bolts on my door and dropped the duffel bag by the kitchen sink. I'd clean off all my tools in the morning. After a quick cigarette or three to calm my nerves, I changed into a heavy cotton bathrobe and warmed a mug of méli in the microwave, setting it down on the counter. As the sweet smell of the diluted honey wafted up, the remaining serpent came out from among the dead coils under my wig and slithered down my cheek, its tongue flicking out. When its wedge-shaped head passed my breastbone, it paused, as though contemplating how to proceed further if I didn't bend down. I obliged, leaning toward the cup, and then seized the snake just below the jaws, yanking its body taut. In the same motion, my other hand found and drew the cutlet knife from the wood block. The serpent hissed once before I split it in two.

I tossed the head into the trash and waited for the stump to settle down and realize it was dead. When that was over, I pulled my large salad mixing bowl out from under the sink and set out my tools, which included one quart of homemade topical anesthetic in a plastic container, a pair of vintage straight razors, a box of twenty-five gauze pads, a ten-foot roll of gauze bandages, and a bottle of bourbon.

The anesthetic ointment was a carefully measured mixture of ketamine and other off-market analgesics; using oven gloves, it took ten minutes to make sure I'd worked it all through my scalp. When the tingling above my forehead had faded into complete numbness, I unlatched the razors. After sterilizing them with a splash of rubbing alcohol, and allowing myself a fortifying slug of bourbon, I bent over the bowl and began cutting.

I found the trunk of the nearest serpent and traced it down to a point just a few centimeters above my head. Holding it firmly, I sawed through the body and let it fall into the bowl with a thick, gloppy sound. Just like chopping vegetables. Except these vegetables bled a noxious black ichor that smelled of pine resin. A giggle slipped past my clenched teeth; that'd make a swell cookbook recipe: (1) Hold snakes firmly; (2) detach with razor and arrange in bowl; (3) serve chilled with capers. I bit my lip to clamp down the bubble of laughter rising in my chest. If I gave in to it, I'd be laughing until I was hysterical.

After half a dozen serpents were in the bowl, the stuff had begun trickling like molasses from the stumps down onto my brow and along the sides of my neck. If it got in my eyes, they'd sting something fierce and the skin around them would be puffy for days. I swiped it away with the collar and sleeve of my robe and kept on.

By the time I was finished, I was sweating and feeling light-headed. My hands had begun shaking from reaction, which meant that I'd metabolized too much of the ketamine and was going to have some particularly vivid nightmares tonight. The bowl looked like it was full of glistening slugs

13

marinating in dark syrup, an incongruous and oddly beautiful image. Another reason I didn't entertain much, I suppose.

I put the medicated pads over the wounds, winding the gauze around my head to keep them in place. They'd scar over in a couple of hours, the stumps sinking into the skin.

Into the trash bag went the contents of the bowl, the robe, the blonde wig, and the slinky red dress. I gently tied a bandanna over the bandages on my head and slipped on my blue sweatpants, an oversized T-shirt, and my pink bunny slippers and took the trash down to the basement.

The incinerator was something from another century, with a heavy iron grate for a mouth that was more than big enough to accept my offering. For a minute after, the hot atmosphere reeked of pine resin, stinging my eyes. Then I was alone again. Finally, blessedly, alone.

Quarter to twelve. I had maybe another twenty minutes before the topical anesthetic started wearing off.

Now for the hard part.

~~~~~

The time difference between Chicago and the eastern isles of Greece is eight hours. As I lit my candles to Hecate, I kept a careful eye on the clock. Four minutes to twelve. Just enough time. I should have felt glad; but to tell the truth, I was more nervous than anything else.

I'm not an especially religious person, but in many faiths, midnight is considered a propitious time. It's the moment of transition, when one day miraculously becomes the next. A crossroads of sorts, a place where the seams between our world and the unseen worlds are at their weakest. In ancient Greece, three-faced Hecate was worshipped as the guardian of the crossroads. I was hoping for a little divine help for this call; the last one had not gone well, and that had been three months ago.

14

I'd taken all my usual precautions to ensure the line stayed private. My candles hadn't just been dedicated to the triple goddess; I'd also gotten them enchanted with screening spells to deflect any attempt at scrying. And I had my trusty hourglass on the coffee table, between the overburdened ashtrays, ready to go. It always took precisely ninety-two seconds to pour all the sand though, which was two seconds shy of the shortest time even the Feds needed to trace a rerouted cell call.

You don't survive in this business all these years without learning the tricks of the trade.

I dialed the number, cursing the unsteadiness of my fingers; I'd have to toss that jug of topical and mix myself a new batch. The wait seemed interminable, but then the line clicked. I turned the hourglass over.

"Hello?" The voice was faint, submerged in a susurrus of static, but I knew it at once. I just wished I could still trust the face I placed with it.

"Um, hi. It's me."

We never used names. Maybe she thought it was to protect me. She thought a lot of things that weren't true.

"You are not sick?"

Was that an accusation? I hadn't called since New Year's because—because I hadn't. Maybe it was just honest concern. But her tone was so stiff, so formal. Had it always been like that? I thought so, but memory is a treacherous thing.

Was this just a chore now for her, a ritual to be endured? What else could it be?

"I'm fine." Aside from nearly having my throat slit tonight. I tapped out a cigarette and lit it with one of the candles. Hecate wouldn't mind; with three heads, the odds were at least one of them smoked.

"You are . . . tending to them?"

By "them," she meant my slithery friends. Not that she'd ever say so. Among all the Unspeakable Topics between us, that was the Mount Everest of them. The one thing I had always needed most to talk about had long ago been established as forbidden territory. If I asked or said anything directly about the serpents, she'd hang up in an instant. Small wonder the conversations felt so forced; they *were* forced.

"Sure," I said, trying for banter. "We're peachy."

"You make joke? Is this how it is in America? You joke of this now?"

Dammit. I didn't need this right now. My nerves were still jangling from my close call with Delgado and too much ketamine. I needed—I didn't know what I needed. *Something.* I drew in a comforting cloud of smoke. "No, of course not. I— No; they're not here."

A frosty silence followed. The sands tumbled down, just as silently filling the bottom of the hourglass. I took another puff, exhaled.

"You are still smoking?"

How the hell had she known that? I stabbed out the cig, then instantly regretted it. "Um, yeah. But I've cut back. I'm down to only a few a day now." What was one more lie on top of the rest?

"Mmm." Even five thousand miles away, I could hear her skepticism. "How are your classes?"

It was a game effort to change the subject; I should have been grateful. But even this topic was a sore point. In addition to the lie about my living in a posh, oversized luxury apartment like all Americans, I was supposedly also an associate professor teaching Greek Studies to the ignorant West. "Great," I answered. "I'll be eligible for tenure next year."

"What is 'ten year?'"

"It's—" Crone's blood, why did I say that? "It's when they say your job is guaranteed. You know, for life."

"*Tch.* This is the famous work ethic of the West? To tell you that you do not need to work to keep your job?"

Oh, gods be good. Couldn't we talk about something—anything—real? The top of the hourglass was half empty already.

The shadows in the apartment shifted. It happened so briefly that for a second I thought I had imagined it. Then I noticed the candles were guttering as though an unfelt wind had just passed over them. That had never happened before. Did it mean something—?

16

Shit. I'd let myself get distracted. The sand was nearly gone. And we'd said nothing. Nothing.

"Okay," I said, though it was anything but. Again. "Well, I—I gotta go." I worried at my lip, then blurted in a rush: "You're still putting the flowers out?"

There was a long silence. Too long.

"Of course. I do not forget."

Or forgive.

I cleared my throat. "All right. Until . . . until next time."

"Goodbye."

The line went dead. The last grains of sand tumbled to the bottom of the hourglass.

"Goodbye," I said, "Mom."

I put the phone down. Why did I keep torturing myself like this? What was the point of calling her? Did I really think she would ever welcome me back into her life, this woman who had put a helpless child on a ship for a far-off land and never even stayed to see it sail off? She'd cut me out of her life the way you removed a tumor. And here I was, still trying to worm my way back into her good graces, hunting for some sign of affection across a chasm as unbridgeable and vast as the hole in my heart.

My head was beginning to throb. I touched the gauze over my temple, and my fingertips came back dabbed with blood. I must've cut too close to the scalp. Sometimes, with my skin numbed up, it was hard to tell where the serpents ended and I began. I go through a lot of gauze because of that. The bleeding would stop in a little while. It always did. Hurt though.

Guess that's why I was crying a little when I went to bed.

Really.

The worst thing about my nightmares is that they always start the same way: I'm with Pietro and we're happy—briefly, dizzyingly happy. We've run away, with nothing more than a pair of rucksacks and the shirts on our backs, to be free, to be together forever. When we come to the crest of the last high hill, we don't look back, not even to say goodbye to the village we both grew up in. We look only ahead, at the vast expanse of rocky terrain that winds down to the western cliffs and the glittering cobalt of the Aegean Sea. Far off, a wisp of blue cloud hovers over the distant island of Santorini, where I have never been.

"From there, we will take a ship to Thera," Pietro says, pointing as though he can already see the vessel that will bear us away to our new life. "And I will find work in the trade shops."

"I love you," I say, with breathless adoration. They are the only words large enough to contain how I feel. Able to have the favor of any maiden in our village, Pietro has eyes only for me: the shy, awkward girl who hides the scars on her bald head with faded woolen wraps.

"I love you, *hriso mou*," he says. *My golden one.* Then he bends to kiss me and I fling my arms and legs around him so hard, we tumble down the hill together in a jumble of limbs until we roll to a stop, breathless with laughter.

"Am I beautiful?" I ask, soaking in the scent of him as I nuzzle against the open collar of his shirt. He's told me so many times, but I am always eager to hear it again.

"You are beautiful," he says, stroking the nape of my neck in a way that sends shivers of excitement through my young body. "When I see you smile, I think it is Aphrodite come again to Earth."

I prop myself up on his chest, letting his hands wend their way down the small of my back to find the place where my cotton shift fails to cover my sun-browned skin. My heart is pounding against my ribs. "Yes?" I tease. "And what do you see when you look in my eyes?" My pale green eyes, flecked with brown, have never been a source of pride for me, but Pietro has sworn he sees gleams of gold in them, like bits of buried treasure.

He stares, and as he does, something goes through me, like an electric shock. I feel the force of it leaping out but don't understand it. "I see—" Pietro begins and then his almond eyes widen and I feel his whole body go rigid, his fingers digging into my flesh like claws. His breath comes out in a horrified whisper, "—*Atë.*"

It's the last time he ever speaks, ever can speak. By the time my mother catches up with us, the sun has gone down and twilight has cloaked the land in its soft, velvet hues . . . and Pietro is dead, having gasped his last as his lungs slowly turned to stone. Without a word, my mother takes hold of my ankles and drags me out of the embrace of my love. The rough folds of his now-petrified shirt leave a bloody weal on my cheek, and his once-tender fingers trace bruises along my back. My mother makes me help her drag the body to the edge of the cliffs, where it is dashed to pieces on the rocks that jut from the crashing waves.

It is my first murder. I will do ten more by the time I am fifteen.

Atë is the Greek word for "ruin."

CHAPTER 2

My head was pounding so hard when I woke up that I thought it was thundering outside. Then I saw the dusty sunlight slicing through my gray window shades and realized that someone was rapping on my door, hard.

"Kyra Anastas? Open up please. Chicago PD."

Fear slammed adrenalin through my system and I was halfway to the fire escape landing when I stopped myself. I was still wearing my fuzzy white robe and gauze bandages. I wouldn't get far out on the street half-naked. Clamping down on my panic, I went to the door and peered through the eyehole.

Two males, one in a faded gray winter coat, the other in a dark jacket. The closer one was portly, with an unkempt mop of ash gray hair. He glanced at his watch then banged on the door again. "Ms. Anastas, we know you're in there." He sounded bored. "Your rental's still in the lot. Please open up."

I slipped the dead bolts and pulled the door open a crack.

"You woke me," I said, half as apology and half in accusation. "What do you want?"

The portly man flashed his badge. "Detective Schober, ma'am. This is Detective Druison. Can we come in?"

"Could you hold that a little closer? My eyes are bad."

Frowning, Schober leaned in. As he did, the lining of his coat parted and I made out the weapon he had in his shoulder holster: a Beretta, 92 F Series CFS from the look of it, a semiautomatic with good stopping power. The leather holster was worn—he'd know his gun and how to use it.

I turned my attention to the ID. Looked legit, with none of the over-bright hues you get with a fake. Bureau of Detectives, OCD, Area 5. Organized Crime Division, but Area 5 was north of the city. Why—?

Delgado.

Shit. *Shit-shit-shit.* I'd screwed up somehow. But when? How?

"Ms. Anastas—"

"You boys are a long way from home," I said, stalling for time. The snakes wouldn't start growing back for a few hours; that meant I'd have no Gaze for another day at least. I was on my own.

A flicker of disquiet came and went in Schober's eyes. Now he was wondering how I knew that. Sloppy, Kyra.

"Can we come in, ma'am?"

I had to get focused. I smiled meekly. "What's this all about, Detective?"

The younger detective leaned forward. "It might be better if we discussed that inside."

They weren't giving anything away. I would have to take my chances. Nodding, I slipped the chains off. "Please come in." I stepped back and let them survey the place, taking in the clutter.

Schober jabbed a thumb at the pegs in the wall. "You sure got a lot of wigs."

"Girl wants to feel pretty. Especially after chemo." I gestured to my bandaged head. Let's see how far the sympathy card took me.

"Cancer, huh?" grunted Schober. "My sister got that. A real bitch."

I didn't know if he meant his sibling or her condition, so let the remark pass. We weren't here for the witty repartee.

"I'd offer you a seat, but my cleaning service seems to have taken the day off."

"That's okay, Ms. Anastas," piped up the other detective. He had a gentle face under his wavy black hair, and his gray eyes regarded me with keen interest but no suggestion of hostility. "We won't take up much of your time. We just have a few questions."

Was this going to be the Good Cop? He was so young and clean cut, I was sure he couldn't have earned the rank more than a few years ago. If he tried any harder not to stare at my head, he looked like he might have an aneurysm.

For some reason, I found myself wishing I had put a wig on before opening the door. "About what, Detective?"

"Marco Delgado."

"Who?"

The cops glanced at each other.

"Don't play dumb, Ms. Anastas," Schober said. "We have witnesses saying you left the bar with him last night around 10:30. Street cam shows him getting into a car with your license plate."

I'd had a few seconds to consider where to take this.

"Oh," I said, working a little nausea into my expression, which wasn't hard. "Him."

"So you *were* with him?" Schober asked.

"Yeah. Not one of my better decisions." I wedged myself into a less-cluttered spot on the sofa, lit a cigarette. Time to up the ante. "Is that why you're here? The son of a bitch swear out an assault charge or something on me? That'd be just my luck."

"Why don't you tell us what happened?"

I shrugged. "I was stupid. I could see right away he was a jerk. But I was feeling pretty low with, you know, everything." I gestured vaguely at my bandages. "Anyway, he said some nice things at first and so we left. I thought we'd go to his place, but he's got us cruising on the Skyway like he's picking out a spot. I started getting antsy and told him let's just head back. Next thing I know, he's getting rough with me." I shrugged down my robe a bit and brandished the fresh bruises on my shoulder. Good Cop's eyes lingered on the bare skin of my shoulder before nodding. Druison, right? I let him have a good look; there was no harm in it, and it made me feel vaguely better. Even though it was probably an act, it was nice to see that look of interest in a man's face. "So he has me pull over in the middle of nowhere, and I just knew I was in real trouble. As soon as I could, I jumped out and ran like hell."

"Your bandages are bloody," said Druison.

He'd given me an opening so I took it.

"He . . . got kind of rough in the car. Grabbed my hair. He didn't like it when the wig came off." That was true enough. "Said I'd tried to make a fool out of him. That he'd show me what he did to people who did that. I didn't stick around to see what he meant. I got out of the car and ran."

"He didn't chase you?"

Careful here. "I didn't look back to check. I just hid. After a while, I sneaked a look. Another car had pulled up. He got into it. When I was sure he'd gone, I went back."

"You went back?"

"Well, I sure as hell wasn't going to hitchhike home. My cell phone was still in my purse in the back seat. When I saw the keys were still in the ignition, I beat it outta there."

"This other car," Druison said. "Can you describe it?"

I grimaced apologetically. "Sedan, maybe? Sorry; I was more concerned with not being seen myself, you know."

"Of course," said Druison, offering me a smile that would have made most girls dream of puppy dogs and wedding bells.

"What did you do after you drove away?" asked Schober, still making his study of the room. At least *he* could take his eyes off me.

"Drove around for a bit. To calm down. Then I went home."

Schober flipped open a little notebook. "Rental company says the GPS on your car puts you at the shipyard last night. What would you be doing way out there by yourself?"

Goddam rental company. Of course they'd have GPS tracking on a luxury sports car. But how the hell had the cops moved on this so fast? Delgado wouldn't even be a "Missing Person" for another forty-eight hours. Why was there such urgency?

"I'm a sculptor. Sometimes I get pieces of block from the harbor to work on in my studio. I thought it might settle my nerves. But it was too dark." I had to be cautious; right now, the cops were two steps ahead of me. I skirted as close to the truth as I dared. "I ended up just smoking a cigarette and going home." If they'd been out to the scene, they'd already know that much.

"You steal rock from the harbor?" Schober challenged.

I grimaced. "I'm a sculptor on a budget."

"Who drives around in a Ferrari."

"Rents one," I said. "I got some money from an aunt in Corfu recently. She told me to indulge myself, in case . . ." I winced, tapping my bandaged head, and let the implication hang there.

Schober nodded. I took it as a good sign when he flipped his notebook closed. "Sculptor, huh?" He glanced around. "Where's your stuff?"

I hesitated, then went over to the sofa and lifted a small clump of stone from behind it. I presented it to the heavyset detective.

The rat had slipped into my apartment a month ago. No amount of broom swishing had persuaded it to scat. When it made a run at me, I'd had enough. Stupid little thing. It should've just run when it had the chance.

Schober turned it over in his hands, touching the tiny claws and staring into the fierce, dead eyes.

"That's, uh, that's something," he admitted, simultaneously repulsed and fascinated. "Really . . . realistic. You even got the little hairs goin' there."

"You like it? Keep it."

Schober put it down. "Nah, that's okay."

"Where are your other pieces?" asked Druison. He was keeping himself back, as though making sure he stayed near the door. To block my escape? I almost felt hurt.

"I've got a space in a studio I share down on 54th," I said. True enough. "I could give you the address if you like. Some of it's for sale."

"That why there's so much dirt in the front seat of your car, Ms. Anastas?"

They'd already been inside my car? I'd almost demanded to see their warrant when I caught a sidelong glance from Druison. He seemed to be tensing, as though expecting me to react. I instantly chilled, forcing myself to appear unconcerned. They could've seen that much from a look through the window. Schober was still just fishing, probing for some flaw in the story.

I shrugged. "I guess. Is that why you're here, detective? Violation of my rental car agreement?"

He scowled. "Why didn't you report all this to the police, Ms. Anastas?"

"Detective . . . I already got enough troubles. I don't need to go looking for more, know what I mean?"

"Of course," put in Druison with a smile. Was he really this warm on me? It seemed unlikely. But his sheepish grin was infectious, like smile-inducing bacteria. I found myself giving one back that wasn't entirely fake.

Time to find out what I could. "So, like, what's going on, detectives? Why all these questions? Is this guy a criminal or something? Am I in danger?"

Now Druison was practically beaming at me. But Schober's expression remained dour. "Nah, nothing like that," he said. "We're just trying to find the guy, is all. He's a . . . person of interest."

"Oh." I could play as dumb as he wanted. "Okay."

Druison reached in the pocket of his jacket. It was a measure of just how high-strung I was feeling that the unexpected movement nearly cost the guy his life. But he was just hunting for his contact card.

"Take this," he said, offering it. "Call me if you remember anything else. Or if you see him again."

Not very likely. I took the card, though, noticing for the first time that Druison was wearing black shooting gloves. Our choirboy was either a marksman or hiding eczema. Neither thought was particularly attractive.

Schober was already at the door, disappointed his promising lead hadn't panned out. Druison sketched a nod at me and moved to follow. Guess I'd passed inspection.

I was reaching for the door when Druison turned. "One more thing, Ms. Anastas. We'll need to take your vehicle down to the impound lot, have Forensics look it over. Might help with our investigation."

"We already got the rental company's okay," put in Schober.

I felt like someone had punched me in the stomach. It's just dirt and sand, Kyra. Right? There was nothing to worry about. But an inchoate unease settled over me, like a poisonous cloud. "Then why tell me?"

Druison blinked. He had slow, heavy-lidded eyes that seemed out of place with his boyish face. "Just didn't want you to be surprised."

I smiled tightly. "What's life without a few surprises, Detective?"

Besides survivable.

"Kyra!" Phil's voice on my cell phone was a mixture of relief and apprehension. Per usual. "You should have checked in hours ago."

Phil was my case worker at the Agency. Right now, he was probably wishing he'd never gotten the job. If I was him, I would wish that a lot. There were quite a few Mythic in the employ of the Agency, but I could guess that I had the rep of being one of the hardest to work with. I'd gone through half a dozen handlers over the years, and each one had eventually asked to be reassigned to another agent. Something about not liking the constant abuse. Like death threats were such a big deal.

I don't even know why they got so worked up. It was Agency policy that you never knew who or where your handler really was, even though they had you on GPS at all times through your phone. To even find one of the bozos, I would have had to devote weeks, if not months, of time to the task. When I wanted to get rid of one, it was more efficient to just get them to quit. I didn't like it when they started to get attached anyway. It made them think they could ask questions about things that were none of their beeswax. Like if I ever dreamed about the things I'd done.

Phil had lasted two years now, a personal record. But only because his capacity to absorb grief from me seemed limitless.

Still, I'm a gal always up for a challenge. And I felt especially motivated today.

"Somebody screwed up, Phil," I said. I took another nip at my fingernail, which was worn down to the quick. I'd tried to quit doing that—just like I'd tried quitting smoking—about a dozen times. But I'd had a hell of a night, okay?

"What do you mean? Were you able to remove the mark?"

"Of course I was." I decided to edit part of the evening. I had made enough amateur bungles with Delgado to have been killed half a dozen times; not the sort of thing you advertised in my business. "But Delgado had a godson he looked after. You know my policy about marks with kids."

"Yeah, you know I never did understand that—"

"You don't need to understand it. You just need to make sure it never happens again."

"All right, I'll look into it. I'll tell Acquisitions to widen the scope of inquiry. Feel better?"

Not really. But what else could I do? There was no catharsis in haranguing Phil; he was already too much of a worrywart. "Yeah—no. Listen, there's something else too. Delgado: Why would the cops be looking for him so soon after he'd gone missing? He's supposed to be just another hired goon for the local mob."

"The police talked to you?"

I swore to myself; this was just going to be my week for sloppy mistakes. Maybe Delgado had cursed me with a case of the Stupids. But everything had felt off since I'd ki—since he'd been removed.

What are you?

I took a drag on my cigarette. At this rate, I was going to have to go out for another pack by noon. And I hated going out.

"Yeah," I admitted. Phil's ever-marshmallowish ability to absorb my ire seemed to blunt the edge of it, allowed me to unclench a degree. "Two came by this morning. They'd pulled my address off the plates on my rental. Wanted to know the last time I'd seen Delgado."

"What did you tell them?"

I snorted out smoke. "Oh, you know; just that the last time I'd seen him was when I smashed in his stone face with a mallet."

"Kyra!"

"What do you think I told them, Phil? I said he got rough with me and I got away. They believed me." Well, one of them, anyway. Baby Face Druison was harder to read. I couldn't tell if he wanted to date me or throw a net over me. Or both. "That doesn't concern me. What concerns me is why they're so hot on the trail of lowlife muscle like Delgado. Guys like him are a dime a dozen. Unless there's something else about him you didn't know, Phil."

"I've got nothing on him except his profile and what the client gave us," said Phil. I could hear his busy fingers tapping away, sending his invisible spiders out onto the Web. While I'd never know for sure, I always imagined Phil to be a chubby, bespectacled geek sitting amid stacks of pizza boxes and soda cans, surrounded by monitor screens in his mother's basement. I liked that image; it made my own situation seem comparatively better. "But I'll look into it." He paused. "How soon will you be operational again?"

I blinked at the phone, which was admittedly pointless. But I usually didn't get more than one assignment every three or four months. "You have something?"

"As soon as you're up for it."

Maybe that's what I needed to focus past this debacle. But the snakes wouldn't be at full power for days. And I'd been looking forward to a few weeks of bald-headed peace and quiet. Without . . . them . . . there were times I could pretend I was almost normal.

I shook the distracting thought aside. In my line of work, distractions got you killed.

"Who's the client?"

"Anonymous."

"Anonymous? How the hell can they be anonymous? What if it's a trap?"

Phil was unperturbed. "We get these from time to time, Kyra. Proxy clients. As long as they pass the filters and foot the bill, they're okay."

"Like Delgado was okay?" This last bit of info had helped me make up my mind. "I think I'll pass. Find someone else for this."

"Well, . . . they asked for you."

"They want someone disposed of by petrification?" My specialty, of course, but usually the request was only that a body be impossible to find. Others could do that. My curse simply made it practical.

"No . . ." Was Phil squirming? It sure sounded like it. "They asked for you. By name."

The pause that followed could have chilled ice. The only thing—the *only* thing—that made it safe to live in the heart of the mortal world was my anonymity.

"How," I grated, "Did. They. Get. My. Name. Phil?"

"I don't know!" sputtered Phil. "Maybe you . . . have you been . . . advertising?"

The chubby kid of my imagination just got another twenty pounds tacked on. And a fresh set of braces for his overbite. "Sure, Phil," I snarled. "I took out a billboard on 5th and Wichita: 'Kyra Anastas, Gorgon—For All Your Petrification Needs.'" Maybe it was time to start looking for another agency; I'd run into rival operatives from time to time. Maybe the ones I'd let live could put in a good word for me.

30

"No, no!" said Phil. "I just mean—I don't know how they got your name, Kyra. Honest. It was an anonymous listing."

"Read it to me."

Tap, tap, tap. "It's short," said Phil. "'Priority request for removal of Elspeth Rougnagne, care of Miss Kyra Anastas.' That's it, other than the address and payment routing information."

"Who the hell is Elspeth Rougnagne?"

"Checking." More tapping. "Whooo, okay; fifty-eight-year-old female, no husband, no children. No living relatives, and no godchildren. Ranked one of the wealthiest women in America. Made her first million buying in on Lexcomm when it went public and then selling just before the tech bubble burst. Good timing. Used the bulk of these profits to buy into certain less-than-transparent hedge funds, turning a massive profit there just six months before the curtain was pulled back on their activities. Remarkable timing once again. And . . . last, but definitely not least, she was deep into real estate for nearly a decade but sold all her holdings at their peak just two weeks before that market began to implode in '06. That's . . . epically good timing."

"She had help," I said.

"So thought the Feds," Phil said. "She's been investigated by the SEC and the Justice Department a total of fourteen times for suspected insider trading. Never got past a grand jury."

"She got help," I repeated. "And not from any inside trader. Nobody's that good at predicting the future. At least nobody mortal. She's got ties to black magic."

"If she does, they're not with anybody we know. But get this, her estate is located on a major convergence of no less than three ley lines. Ley lines are natural conduits for supernatural energy—"

"I know what ley lines are."

"Okay. I'm just saying if she is hooked up with magic, there'd be no way to tell. With that much interference, you couldn't scry or send into there from the outside."

That wasn't likely to be a coincidence. "Camouflage . . ."

"Could be. But she's not depending just on that. Online records indicate that she made a long-term contract for around-the-clock security when she built the place. She's got a cadre of more than twenty armed guards, surveillance webs, the works. Lady likes to feel safe."

"She has to come out of there sometime."

"I wouldn't count on that. According to her accounts, there hasn't been a single offsite purchase in . . . more than fifteen years. Articles in *Forbes* and *Money* have called her the 'Reclusive Multimillionaire.'"

"She's hiding. Odds are, whoever she made her deal with wants her to pay up. That's probably your 'Anonymous' right there."

"So . . . you taking the contract?"

"What's the kill fee?"

"At 10 percent, your cut would be . . . one hundred thousand dollars."

I let out a whistle. Somebody wanted Rougnagne bad, all right, to fork over a million bucks; the standard contract amount was only fifty thousand. Still, stock market manipulation wasn't really the kind of sin I felt compelled to punish. And I liked to know there was at least something less than sterling in my mark's character before I took on a job. This wasn't usually hard: Very few saints found their way onto a Kill List.

Plus, there was the little matter of going into a heavily-armed encampment with a Gaze that could barely stun a half-dead lightning bug. I doubted "Anonymous" was expecting to hire a Gorgon assassin that would dud out.

Tempting, but . . .

"Pass," I said. "I'd better lay low till the cops get bored."

Phil sighed. He could probably see his commission wafting away on fat, lazy wings. "Okay, it's your call."

"No shit." Turning down the prospect of a hundred grand gave me fresh fodder for feeling outrage. Why couldn't Delgado have been a reclusive multimillionaire? Other assassins had all the luck. "Now do something to make up for last night's screwup. Look into the detectives who graced me with their presence this morning. See if there's anything I should know."

"Names?"

"Schober and Druison, Chicago OCD."

"Schober...that name's popped up. He's a CPD vet. Don't know Druison."

"He might be a recent transfer," I mused out loud. He moved and held himself like a man, but that face was all boy. "Check that."

"My dear Kyra," sniffed Phil, in a rare and ill-timed stab at humor. "I check everything."

The image of a little kid standing by the door with a baseball glove surfaced in my mind's eye like an uneasy shipwreck. Beneath that, a memory: Brienne's arm lolling down from on high, limp hand beckoning.

I shuddered, and shook free of the cobwebs.

"Tell that to Antonio," I snapped, covering my unease with vitriol. "Call me when you have something."

"Who's Antonio—" Phil began, but I'd already hung up.

There's basically only three things that could drive me out of my warren: getting a contract, the roof collapsing, or running out of booze. Everything else I get through various delivery services—groceries, supplies, whatever. Even my cigs come to me through an online service now. It's easier that way: I don't have to worry about the looks people give me—the strange, tall woman who goes around hooded, even in the brief but intense Chicago summer heat, or who wears the bandages on her head to cover some awful disease that might be contagious. I could just wear one of my wigs all the time, I guess, but it's bad enough that I have to pretend to be someone else when I'm on a job. If I had to be a pariah, I could at least have the satisfaction of letting them know I knew I was one. I'd learned to live with it.

But the only place in the neighborhood that carried good retsina was a little Greek restaurant down on 19th; when I had a hankering for the wine of my homeland, there was no substitute.

Only I couldn't go in there myself anymore, not since the proprietor's ancient grandmother had once caught a glimpse of me standing at the counter with my oversized shades and hat sloped down over my brow. She'd muttered under her breath and made the sign of the Evil Eye at me. After that little stunt, I was persona non grata there.

Like everywhere else.

So now I always had to get some kid from the skate park to go in for me while I cooled my heels on a bench under the trees. Pickings were slim today on account of the lingering chill, and patience was not a particular virtue of mine. But after a while, one of my regulars drifted over, a boy who called himself Quick Donny; he had a premature bit of fuzz on his narrow chin and a knack for ingratiating himself with adults. He kicked his board into his hand with an air of self-indulgent skill and grinned at me like a carnival barker.

"Retsina?"

"Retsina."

I gave him two twenties—enough for a box of the stuff—and settled back with the collar of my gray raincoat pulled up to my ears. My elaborate scarf covered my bandages but was still letting the cold nip at my ears. The air was crisp today, the sunlight weak, yet it was enough of a break from the dismal weather that the Mom Brigade was coming out in force, pushing their parade of strollers along the walkways. Here they would swarm like locusts, drinking their enormous cups of steaming coffee from Intelligentsia, Asado, and Starbucks while they vociferously debated the latest achievements and tribulations of their newborns and toddlers and consoled one another over their own ridiculous problems. I scrunched deeper into my raincoat, with my head down as they marched by, serene and oblivious to the snake sitting in the middle of their urban garden paradise.

"—so advanced for her age; the other kids at her day care can't even sit up yet—"

"—I know, I know; I was just saying the same thing to Kristen about my Catherine Rose during my yoga class—"

34

"—another big project, my ass; I know why he's working late. It's that new girl in his group—"

"—swear I've tried everything, but the weight just won't come off. My personal trainer says it's stress—"

"—your hair? Look at mine: It's a crow's nest—"

Crows, I thought. If I could just have a crow's nest for hair, I'd light a candle to the gods every night in thanks. Even actual crows would be an improvement. I wanted to lurch up and yell in their faces; none of them knew how lucky they were. Let one of them spend a day with snakes crawling over their stupid skin, and they'd really have something to complain about. For a moment, the fantasy of railing at them provided some cold comfort.

But who was I kidding? They weren't the freaks here. I was. This was their park, their sunlight, their world to enjoy. They *belonged* here. Me? I was always going to be the outsider, the cruel joke of Mother Nature, the thing that should never have been born, the misfit whose own mother had rejected her, sent her away. I felt a sudden burning sensation in my nose and ground at it with my knuckles to keep the weakness of my eyes back. It's not my fault, I wanted to tell them. I didn't ask for this. I'd give anything to be like you—to have a home, a family, something besides death and horror. But I knew the reaction I'd get; I'd seen it too many times in the faces of my marks.

It did no good to dwell on such things. So I closed my eyes and did my best to shut out the constant droning. It didn't matter what they thought of me. Soon I'd be back in my apartment and could just blank all this out, go back to not feeling anything . . .

"Which one is yours?"

Startled, I opened my eyes and found standing in front of me a smiling young woman with a long braid of golden hair and pink-colored sunglasses. She was literally festooned with children: one clung to her side with his thumb jammed in his mouth, another was tucked into the gigantic stroller she was steering with one hand, and a third was pressed against her chest in some sort of pouch.

"What?" I asked, mentally scrambling for focus as my worst nightmare proceeded to sit down within inches of me. "What did you say to me?"

"Your kid," the apparition said, gesturing to where a knot of children was screaming and running around the grassy playground area as though they were on fire. "Which one's yours?"

"Oh, I—" I stopped abruptly, considering how it would look if I admitted I was slouching here like some sort of stalker; the fertility goddess would probably pull out a whistle and rain the Mommy Police down on me.

"Um, that one," I said, pointing to a heavyset kid in a purple parka who was off on his own on the far side of the swings. He looked like he knew how to handle himself.

"Ooh, he's cute! Christian, go play with him! He's all by himself."

The woman's child dutifully unplugged his thumb and ran off to join the fray.

"Isn't it glorious to get off your feet for a minute? God bless the City of Chicago's Parks Department! I'm Natalie."

I took the proffered hand. It was that or risk getting poked in the eye. "Um, Kyra."

"Oh that's lovely! Is it Irish? Like Celtic or something?"

"Greek," I answered, if only to halt the woman's steady stream of words. "It's Greek."

"I haven't seen you here before, have I? Are you new to the area?"

Yes or no? "No."

"Where does—what's your son's name?"

"Uh . . . Pietro."

"Is that Greek too? Where does Pietro go to school?"

I hesitated. I hadn't prepped for this level of interrogation; in fact, I didn't think there was a prep for this level of interrogation. And why in the name of the gods had I used Pietro's name? "He's, eh, homeschooled."

"OhmiGOD!" shrieked the woman. For half a second I thought one of the serpents had slipped out from my wrap. But they were barely more than wavy green polyps right now; I'd decided to grow them out just in case, but they wouldn't resemble anything more than strands of seaweed for nearly a day.

And the woman was staring at me with something very different than horror or fear. It almost looked like . . . admiration? With an effort, I pulled my hand back from my concealed gun.

"That is *so* awesome," she gushed. "I'd kill to be able to do that! You must be so organized."

"Yeah, I guess," I said, out of sorts but absurdly pleased at this unexpected praise. "It's . . . not that hard."

"Says you!" laughed the woman while she rocked the stroller back and forth with one foot and patted her pouch absently with the other. I half expected her to start juggling next.

The little human in the stroller was buried under so many blankets, I could only make out its nub of a nose and soft lips. But the other one's head, complete with knitted cap, was turned toward me, close enough to touch. I found myself staring with morbid fascination at the way its rounded cheeks puffed up with each short, shallow breath, like a diver preparing to take a deep plunge. There was something oddly beautiful in the smooth features of its face, the uncomplicated serenity of its sleep. No nightmares had yet come to etch lines of worry and doubt into its countenance; no guilt or pain troubled the primitive thoughts in that developing brain. I felt a sudden stab of envy for that innocence.

"How . . . how old is it?" I asked.

"Four months," the woman said. "He's so good, isn't he? I can take him anywhere like this. Not like with Christian; boy, the colic! Isn't that the worst? Did Pietro have that?"

I had no idea what colic was, but it seemed safest to agree. "Sure."

"What did you do for it?"

Great; now I was hip deep in it. I shrugged. "I told him he had to deal with it."

The woman's eyes bugged. "You told your *baby* to *deal* with it?"

Right; babies don't talk. I felt a flush blooming in my cheeks. If this was a job, I'd have half a dozen hostiles on my back by now. Normally I deal with stressful situations by blasting my way out, but as tempting as that felt right now, I had to consider the consequences of shooting up a park's worth of civilians. Besides, I was still waiting for my runner to come back. What was taking him so long, anyway? For someone who called himself Quick Donny, he was sure taking his time.

"I'm joking," I said and was relieved to see the woman's expression soften.

"You're funny," she laughed, and I was surprised to find there was no mockery in the sound, just honest delight. I couldn't remember the last time I'd laughed like that—if I'd ever laughed like that.

The baby in the pouch stirred at the sound and started mewling. Abruptly its eyes opened, staring directly at me. I couldn't believe how blue they were, like two chips of sky pulled down from the heavens. While the woman's attention was turned toward the playground as her oldest child zoomed by, the infant's puffy little fingers rose out of the pouch, pawing at the air, searching for comfort. If I just lifted my hand a little, it could touch me. I'd never felt a baby's soft skin in my life, and I was surprised to realize how much the idea scared me.

Lepers weren't meant to mix with the healthy. But what harm could it do just to feel the skin of this tiny human, this thing with no fear in its eyes, that was too young to understand that it was death sitting so close? Torn between fascination and repulsion, I hesitated. But nerved by the steadiness of the baby's gaze, I started to raise my hand—

And the woman got over her distraction with a sudden start, looking down at her charge. At once she pulled a small cloth sheet out from some secret alcove of the gigantic stroller. She draped it over her shoulder, shifted the pouch, and unzipped the front of her jacket.

I stared at her, aghast. "Oh no, you're not—seriously?"

The baby's head disappeared under the cloth like a rabbit going back into a magician's hat. Amazingly, none of this interfered in the slightest with the constant flow of words coming out of the woman's mouth: "God, it's

"We're still investigating the disappearance of Marco Delgado," Druison said, digging out his notebook. "So everyone who had any contact with him during the last twenty-four hours before he went missing is being reinterviewed."

"I'm impressed at the police department's diligence." More like *de*pressed. "I thought someone had to be missing for a few days before the police got involved."

Druison's smile was unflappable. "Mister Delgado's kind of a special case."

"Really? Why?"

Was that a twinkle in Druison's eyes? It was almost like he knew I was testing him and was somehow enjoying the sparring.

"We believe he has some information important to another ongoing investigation," Druison said.

"Wow," I said. "And here I thought he was just another guy with a good pickup line. What kind of investigation?"

The smile turned sympathetic. It was quite versatile, really. "I'm afraid that's confidential—police business, you understand."

"Of course." So, Delgado was mixed up in another case. Not a surprise. I shifted in my seat, trying to nonchalantly dig behind my back to remove the offending bag of chips.

"I can only tell you that it's a very serious matter," Druison said. "The department is making a particular effort to locate Mister Delgado as quickly as possible. All methods of investigation have been authorized and are being set up right now—you know, surveillance, wiretaps, that sort of thing."

I stopped digging for the bag. For a few seconds, I think I stopped breathing. Druison's manner couldn't have been more easygoing, but his eyes were focused on me with an intent gaze. Why would he tell me that? Was he . . . trying to warn me?

"I . . . see," I said, though I certainly did not. "That does sound serious. So, what was it you wanted to ask me?"

Druison nodded and flipped open his notebook. "Just a couple of questions that have popped up. You've, uh, led a pretty solitary life."

"Have I?" I was suddenly glad to have the low coffee table between us. I don't like people in my personal space. Have I mentioned? "Have you been investigating me, Detective?"

"Gotta do my job, Ms. Anastas." That charming grin again. "Otherwise they don't pay me." He glanced at his notes. "Graduated 2016 with a bachelor's degree in computer science from DeVries University. Online courses only. No human contact."

I fought to keep my nails from my teeth. "Lots of people do that now." I hadn't much liked how he'd tossed in the word "human."

"Sure, sure," he said agreeably. "Only . . . it's hard to tell just what you do for a living now, Ms. Anastas. Other than your . . . sculpting."

The sparring was getting serious. But the Agency had long ago set up my legend, a cover story so intricate that it was rock solid. So to speak. "I've been on disability for a while now, because of my condition. I haven't sold any pieces for . . . geez, probably two years. But I still do some software debugging for private companies."

"Oh, yeah? Like who?"

"Mostly biotech companies: Kilectics out in San Francisco has me on retainer; Vellatorx Pharmaceuticals in Malvern too. I do piecework for a few others; lets me work from home."

Druison nodded agreeably. "Who's your oncologist?"

"Burt Pearl, over at Loyola. Such a nice man."

"I'm sure he is," said Druison. "Stay in touch with any family in the Old Country?"

"Just my mother's sister," I said. He liked to change topics fast, see if he could catch me off guard. I wondered if this was what flirting felt like. "Althea Constantinos. I think I mentioned her before."

"Right, right," Druison nodded. "Boyfriend?"

"Excuse me?" That threw me. "What?"

"Boyfriend," repeated Druison. If his expression grew any more sheepish, I was going to have to hang a bell around his neck. "It's a standard follow-up question, Ms. Anastas."

44

"Really."

"Sure."

At least he hadn't said "gosh." I hesitated, pulled toward conflicting responses. "Not at the moment."

His goofy grin widened, which immediately infuriated me for some stupid reason. "How is any of this relevant to your investigation, Detective?"

Druison shrugged. "That's the thing about follow-up interviews. You never know what might be relevant."

"Uh-huh."

"Do you own a gun?"

Only about fifty, though most were in my storage lockers around the city. And to find the three I had here, you'd need a bloodhound with a metal detector strapped to its head.

"Sure do," I said, covering my sudden uneasiness with a tight smile. "God bless the Second Amendment."

"Got a card for it?"

"In my purse. Want to see it?"

"That would be great."

I rummaged through my bag, grimacing at the accumulated debris I had to dig around, and handed him my CFP and FOID.

"A Browning Hi Power. That's a pretty big gun."

"Yeah, well, you can never be too—"

And just like that, it hit me, like a punch in the gut. I'd left it, left it where Delgado had tossed it, in the back of the car. With everything that had gone on two days ago, I had forgotten to recover it.

Stupid. Stupid, stupid amateur. How the hell could I have forgotten that? That wasn't like me at all.

But right on the heels of that, I realized that it didn't matter: The gun had been empty, just a prop I'd brought along in case things went sideways and I needed to coerce Delgado to come with me.

Druison was starting at me, hard.

"Oh, my god," I said, taking my dismay and harnessing it. "I just realized: my gun."

"What about it?"

"It was still in the car," I said in a rush. "When they impounded it. I forgot: He saw it and threw it in the back seat. Please tell me you found it."

There was something like frank admiration in his gaze; it was very disconcerting.

"We found it," he said. "Glad to hear it was yours. But you didn't mention that before."

"Sorry," I said. "I totally forgot. When can I get it back?"

"Ballistics will have to check it, dust it for fingerprints and all. If it checks out, you'll get it back."

"Oh, good."

"You sure you know how to handle a gun like that?"

With my preternatural eyesight, I could pick the wings off a fruit fly at fifty meters using the Browning. Of course, I was more accurate with the Glock. But now didn't seem the best time to bring that up.

"I've . . . had some lessons."

"When Delgado got, uh, rough with you, he got hold of it?"

"Yes."

"And you say he threw it in the back seat?"

"That's right."

"Did the weapon accidentally discharge?"

"No," I said. "It wasn't loaded."

"It wasn't loaded?"

Was there an echo in here? "I always keep the bullets in my purse."

"Why take a gun with you if you're not going to be able to fire it?"

"It's mostly for target practice at the range. But I had a friend who got carjacked once and it spooked me. I figure I could scare someone off if they see I've got a gun."

"What range do you practice at?"

"Openlands, Upper West Side. Heard of it?"

46

"Sure. Owner's name is . . ."

"Big Bill," I said. It was actually kind of pleasant to give him a real name—of someone who was more than an Agency plant.

"So . . . you forgot the gun was still in the car. Sure you didn't maybe forget that you left a bullet in it last time you unloaded?"

"No, I'm fanatical about gun safety," I said. My strange lapse notwithstanding. "I'd never—" I stopped, suddenly struck again by the queer notion that Druison was trying to warn me.

But the truth will keep your ass out of jail, or something like that. And I'd been trained a long time ago that you keep your lies as close to the truth as possible.

"No," I said with finality. "It was empty."

"Fair enough." Druison snapped his notebook shut and stood up.

"We're done?"

"We're done." Was the puppy smile fractionally less wide? It seemed impossible that I should notice even if it was, but I found myself troubled by the idea as I led Druison to the door.

"I'll be in touch, Ms. Anastas."

"I—okay," I said, flummoxed with myself.

He paused at the threshold. I waited, churning with uncertainty. Every instinct told me to get his tight butt out the door as fast as possible, but I found myself wishing against all sense that he would stay.

"So, what was the line?"

I blinked. "What?"

The easy grin was back. "The pickup line Delgado used," Druison said. "You said it was a good one."

Oh. I hesitated, abruptly wanting to say something that met that smile halfway. But now I felt like I didn't deserve it. And old habits are hard to break.

"'Don't you hate people who pretend to be something they're not?'" I said, closing the door in more ways than one.

∿∿∿

"But, it's a story, um, without an ending," I murmured. "What about now?"

For the thousandth time, I heard her say that she didn't know. But she knew she couldn't leave me again. I asked her about her husband, that noble drip. She wanted me to help him. *Why should I?* I wanted to rail. Nobody ever helped me. But her eyes held me, stilled my protest; those magnificent, glittering eyes that didn't kill but only wounded you, hurt you in a way that you never recovered from and never wanted to.

She thought he lived for his work. I knew better. I told her the truth. And still—still—she chose me. *Me*, over him, over everything. I let the immortal words tumble past my numb lips, promising I'd look after her, come what may. The music swelled . . .

Pizza with feta cheese, olives and chicken toppings, a bottle of retsina and lip-synching to Humphrey Bogart on the TV. What else could a single girl need on a Saturday night?

Right?

∿∿∿

After listening to the line ring twenty times, I lost count and started to drift. I had just begun a dream where an angry macaw was squawking in my ear when the noise stopped.

"Kyra—?"

The voice on the phone sounded bleary. That was okay; after two bottles of retsina, I was pretty bleary myself.

"You don't like me." I felt like I was pushing the words out past a mouthful of mud. Maybe that was just the fact that my tongue lay like a limp snake across my teeth. Or maybe it was all the bile I'd been chewing with nowhere to spit it all night. Enter Phil, my personal spittoon.

"What? Kyra, it's the middle of the night . . ."

Christ, he was dense. Why were men always so dense? "Tell me you don't like me," I growled.

"I—I don't like you."

"Geez, Phil!" I snapped. "Could you be any less convincing? Say it like you mean it next time." I drew in a shuddering breath. Against my cheek, the couch stank of stale Fritos and spilled booze. "We're not friends. Get it?"

"Of . . . of course."

"I don't have to talk to you, you know," I said, irked by this submissiveness. Why did he always have to be so goddamn agreeable? "Except about work."

"I understand."

See what I mean? "How come you never ask?" I demanded. "All the others did. Aren't you the least bit curious?" The last word came out thick: *cureeush*. That made me laugh a little.

"What's funny?"

"Nothing. What's your favorite movie, Phil?"

"Kyra . . ." Oh, the angst in that tone. You'd think I was proposing we get married and make babies.

"C'mon," I said, "throw me a bone here. What can it possibly matter if I know your favorite movie? It's not like it tells me where you live."

There was a long silence, so long I opened my eyes to check my watch. Big mistake, as the apartment was still in spin cycle all around me, the floor and ceiling wrestling to change positions while the sofa bobbed like a cork between them. If I kept staring, I was going to get reacquainted with my dinner. I closed my eyes and tried to ignore the sensation that I was still spinning out of control.

A few miles or maybe half a world away, I could still hear Phil fidgeting. "Hey," I mumbled, "is there anybody out there? You don't have the decency to answer one—"

"*Star Wars*," Phil blurted out. "The original one. Before all the new CGI."

Star Wars. Gods give me strength.

"Now you ask me one," I said. "Go on, ask."

"Uh . . . what's—what's your favorite movie, Kyra?"

"Easy," I said. "*Casablanca*. Greatest film in *cin-neh*—um, *cin-num*—" I scrubbed at my stupid numb lips. "Ever."

"Really? I've never seen it. Why is it your favorite?"

I started to shake my head in disbelief, but it felt like my brain was sloshing around inside a great, heaving tank. How could you have lived on this planet and not seen Michael Curtiz's masterpiece?

The words were hard to find, dredged up from some place deep and dark. "He gets it back," I said. "In the end."

"Gets what back?"

"A reason," I said. "For living."

"Kyra . . ." Phil sounded pained.

"Hey, got a joke for you," I said, trying to ignore him. "Why don't gorgons have babies?"

"What? I don't—"

"'Cause they don't make cribs for little snakes!" Was I shouting? I couldn't tell. A chorus of angels, or demons, was shrieking in my other ear. For some reason they all sounded like my mother. "Get it, Phil? They'd just *suhh*—slip through the bars. *Izz* for the best, see? Can't have them flopping all over the rug, making a mess everywhere. It's better for—for everybody."

"Kyra, it's late. Nearly three in the morning. No more drinking, please? Just—just try to get some sleep. Okay?"

The idea that he would hang up and leave me alone with the screaming meemies filled me with cold dread. "Is it nice where you live? Is it warm?"

"It's . . . warm. Kyra, listen, sometimes they monitor these calls—"

"Oh, will you *stop*? Gods, Phil, do you worry every second? Do you really want to live forever? You that afraid of death?"

"Aren't you?"

I shook my head, or more like wobbled it. "The gods couldn't be crueler on the other side than they are here. If they even exist."

"You don't believe in the gods?"

This was a little weightier a matter than I was currently equipped to debate, what with the drool soaking the fabric under my chin and the choirs of Heaven or Hell banging on my eardrums. And I was tired; I was just so tired. I couldn't have lifted my head off the couch if the place were on fire. But I still couldn't bear the thought of hearing the connection go dead.

"Maybe there were gods, once. How else do you explain freaks like me?" I chuckled, but there was no mirth in it. It had never been a particularly funny joke. "But they must've left a long time ago."

"Why do you say that?"

I snorted. "Seriously? Do they have windows where you live? Have you seen the world outside? S'all fulla murderers and rapists and monst—every kind of scum. Nobody's out there anymore, if there ever was, looking out for this world. You live, you die. . . . Nobody notices. Nobody cares. Nobody loves—" My throat clenched. Ah, gods, why was I telling him this stuff? I didn't want to tell him; I didn't want to tell anybody.

"I'm probably going to kill you one day, Phil," I said, with as much vitriol as I could muster in my defense. But I was barely able to hear my own voice through the mist filling my head.

Was that a sigh? "Probably."

I tried to rouse myself. "You think I couldn't do it?"

"No." Phil's voice was soft, resigned. "I know you could."

"You don't sound very scared."

"Kyra . . . you won't even remember this in the morning."

I fumbled for the phone, but my fingers were off somewhere else. Sleep closed around me like the hands of a strangler. An abyss was opening beneath me.

"You bastard . . ." I mumbled into the cold, wet sofa as we tumbled down the well together. "What the hell . . . makes you think that?"

"Oh, Kyra." Phil's voice, fading into the immeasurable distance, sounded as though he were grieving. "You never do."

Most people work off a hangover with a bottle of aspirin and plenty of coffee. I find ballistics more engaging. Which was why the next day after my late-night binge, I dragged my aching head to the indoor shooting range at Openlands, busting a few caps into a target sheet. There's just something soothing about the sharp recoil of the pistol in your hands, the muffled report of the discharge through the cute little blue earphones Big Bill's crew gives you, the faint ammonia smell that lingers in the cramped atmosphere.

I'm in my own space while I'm here, rimmed off from the intruding world by my plugs and safety glasses, silently communing with my past and future marks. No one talks to you while you're on the range; nobody asks you how you're doing, or how was your damn date last night, or what your friggin' family is up to. Thank the gods, you can be out of your apartment and still be left alone—

As I reloaded my rented Beretta, a finger tapped on my shoulder.

"*Seriously?*" I snapped in disgust, slapping the magazine into the pistol grip. Tearing off my plexiglass visor, I wheeled around, ready to give some asshole holy hell for breaking range decorum.

Except it wasn't some staff newbie or ignorant shooter. It was "The Man" himself, Big Bill.

I've always thought Big Bill must have had ironic parents, because his head barely came up to my chin as he stood there, his thumbs stuck in the pockets of the faded blue jeans he habitually wore. The only thing truly big about him was his gut, which was even now straining the tensile strength of the buttons on his collared red shirt. There was always a strange sense of dislocation with Big Bill; despite being a ubiquitous presence at the range for all my time here, he looked like he'd have been more at home on a dude ranch or in a prairie town than the urban jungle. The impression started with the tufts of curly bleached hair crowning his sun-weathered head, was reinforced by the deep cracks that made his ruddy face look like baked mud, and continued all the way down to the worn Stetson boots he

52

liked wearing. You could practically smell it on him too, a heady cocktail of dust and sweat and aftershave.

As usual, Big Bill's rheumy blue gaze wasn't looking directly at me. Instead he seemed absorbed by the motes of dust drifting under the lights around us. It was either a Zen thing or ADHD; I'd never been sure.

"Someone was by here this morning asking 'bout you," he said with his usual laconic drawl. You always got the impression there wasn't much Big Bill hadn't seen. "Chicago Police detective."

That wasn't really a surprise, given yesterday's interview. But I still felt my stomach give a little preparatory flip. "Catch a name?"

"Gave me his card. Tossed it. Druisomething."

Druison. My guts immediately began doing cartwheels.

Which was just stupid, I reminded myself trenchantly. So, okay, maybe it *was* true that I'd come here with half a thought that I'd bump into the detective again, get back on better footing with him somehow . . . maybe. But that was a dangerous, self-destructive impulse, trying to win the good graces of a man charged with bringing in Delgado's killer, especially since that killer was me. I'd shut the door in his face for that very reason, right?

And why would I want to see him anyway? Just to see him give me another of his goofy, puppy dog grins? That was truly idiotic. How many perps had been suckered into confessing to Druison because of that disarming manner of his? I was smarter than that.

But this morning I'd woken up with the unsettling feeling that I'd been trying to get someone to listen to me all night. And for some reason, it was still nagging at the back of my mind, like a loose tooth.

"What'd you tell him?"

Big Bill shrugged. "You pay your bill. Don't cause trouble."

I nodded carefully. "Thanks."

"You in some sort of trouble?"

"Nothing I can't handle."

"Thought you'd say somethin' like that." Big Bill surveyed his concrete kingdom, chewing his thoughts the way a cow chews cud. "Get hundred people in here every month, y'know. Folks from every walk of life, good an' bad." He turned his gaze back to me. "But ain't never seen nothing like you."

I tensed. Big Bill was a decent enough guy; he'd given me some good tips over the years on sight alignment and trigger control. But if he suspected anything about my true nature . . . "What do you mean?"

"You're best shooter comes here," Big Bill said. "Use firearms like you were born with 'em in your hands."

"Thanks."

"Wasn't a compliment." Big Bill looked away. "Remind me some of m' daughter. 'Bout your age when she died."

I didn't know what to say to that. I'm not good with chitchat. So the silence stretched out. "Listen," I finally said, struggling through a skein of feelings that had me simultaneously flattered and alarmed by this much attention, "I miss the bull's-eye half the time."

Big Bill made a thick, disparaging noise deep in his throat.

"You miss when you want to miss," he said flatly, as though I was making him angry. He jerked a thumb up over his shoulder, toward the camera set in the rear corner of the range. "Watch you on the monitors. Insurance made me put 'em in a ways back." He nodded downrange. "Same pattern, every time: heart, head, liver, spleen, then the soft spots in between. Like you're practicing when to use or not use a kill shot. Bet you could do the same from fifty yards, maybe more. Am I right?"

I worried at my lower lip. "What's your point?"

Big Bill shrugged again. "People come here for their own reasons. None of my business, as long as they take their problems with 'em when they go. You're different from most. Treat your guns like they're natural . . . like they're a part of you."

"So?"

Big Bill stared at me, hard. There was something in his faded blue eyes I couldn't fathom.

"Show you something." He stepped closer, and I had to resist the instinct for fight or flight. Big Bill had never registered as a threat to me. Sidling around me, he raised my left arm to aim at the silhouetted target. I tried to steady my breathing; even though they weren't fully mature, the snakes under my beret were already capable of delivering enough venom to kill the old guy in seconds if provoked. And this was the closest I'd let a man be to me without planning to give him a shiv in the gut in longer than I could recall.

I had expected Big Bill to comment on my grip or something, but he only closed his thick, stubby fingers over mine at the pommel and pressed them against the hard metal. "Feel this?" he grunted.

I nodded expectantly. Big Bill's hand slid to my bare wrist. He squeezed it once. "And this?"

Now I was confused. "Y—yes."

"Not the same thing," he said in my ear. "Not meant to be neither."

I twisted my head to look sidelong at him. From this angle, there was something fearful about his steady gaze. "I don't—don't understand . . ."

Big Bill grimaced.

"Gun ain't a thing o' nature, kid. Just a tool. For you to use. Not the other way around." Abruptly, he released my wrist and stepped back. "Try an' remember that."

And then he just left me standing there, standing like an owl caught out in the daylight.

I like being schooled about as much as I enjoy getting root canal surgery, and now I'd had the pleasure two times in as many days—first at the park, then with Big Bill. So the rest of the day passed in a slow seethe where I just knew the next person to piss me off was going to end up in a dumpster. In order to avoid a bloodbath on Michigan Avenue, I retreated to my apartment and spent the afternoon watching old John Huston movies with a furious concentration, as though I were waiting for one of the characters to start accusing me so I could pounce on the screen.

Why did everybody think they could tell me how I should live my life? I had my mother for that, didn't I? It seemed like it was "Gang Up on the Gorgon" weekend in Chicago, and I was already sick of it. I spent enough time hating my life on my own; I didn't need amateurs weighing in.

I still had the taste of pine resin stuck to my gums, so another night of the retsina blottos was out. Besides, that vague sense of uneasiness that always followed a bout of binge drinking was still with me; I needed a better way to settle my restless nerves.

Half a dozen cigarettes and some vigorous channel surfing whittled away the hours. Cold pizza leftovers furnished an answer to the grousing of my stomach; after that, all that was necessary was to flop on the couch and wait for Jimmy to start getting funny.

I was finally beginning to doze when I suddenly had the oddest sensation that someone was in the apartment with me. I bolted up, throwing off the pizza box I'd been using as a blanket, and scanned the room, hunting for any hint of movement.

Nothing, except for Jimmy, prattling on the screen about something with his usual smirk. But I didn't doubt my instincts. Something had triggered my adrenalin rush, and it wasn't the witty monologue. I held myself still as stone, waiting . . .

There. A faint shimmer in the air, at the corner of my sight. I turned toward it, but even as I did, it vanished. The sense of another presence ceased as swiftly as though a door had closed.

I found myself breathing heavily. I sat down, trying to gather my thoughts. Three times now. Three times in as many days I'd picked up the vibe of something spying on me: on the shore of Lake Michigan, then when I'd called my mother, and now when I'd been falling asleep.

Something was hunting me. No, worse; it had already found me, which meant this place was no longer safe—

The braying of my cell phone under my butt kicked me up from the couch like a catapult. I dug out my phone.

"Phil," I panted, and winced at the unsteadiness in my voice, "I'm right in the middle of something—"

"Kyra, you're in trouble. You've got to get out of there right away."

Just like that, I was done with shadow hunting. I made for the hall closet, fishing my tiny earpiece out and jamming it in to free up my hands. "Why? What's happened?"

Phil sounded close to panic. "I was poking through the Chicago Police mainframe, looking for info on your detectives, when a cyber flag popped up—"

I was already shrugging my sturdy leather duster on and pulling my gear bag out from a high shelf. "English, Phil, English."

"Right, right. Sorry! I'd set up flags in case there was any activity with your name on it while I was searching the database, and something came up. Kyra, did you shoot Delgado?"

I felt like I'd just taken a sucker punch to the head. "What? No! What the hell are you talking about?"

"The ballistics analysis came through on your weapon an hour ago. It says your gun was fired within the last forty-eight hours. There's blood spatter inside the muzzle, indicating it was fired at close range."

"*Skor!*" I said under my breath.

"What?"

"That's bullshit!" I snapped, wriggling into my sturdy boots. "I didn't shoot the son of a bitch. Phil, this is a setup."

"Well, they issued a warrant for your arrest twenty minutes ago. Dispatch shows a unit is on its way now."

I was still wearing my blue jeans and an old sweatshirt. It would have to do. "How much time?"

"Accessing their GPS . . ." The flurry of tapping had never sounded so slow. "Oh, crap; they're pulling up to your building now."

"Who?" I popped the latch for the window and slung my bag over my shoulder. "Who is it? Druison?" If it was Druison, maybe—

"No, it's . . . the other guy. Detective Schober, riding with two uniforms."

Not good, not good. I scanned the alley below just to be sure it was empty. I climbed out onto the fire escape and eased the window shut behind me; that should buy me a few minutes while they searched the place. Then I swiftly made my way to the bottom platform and jumped onto a dumpster, landing as lightly as a cat. A trot down the alley brought me out to Diversey Parkway. I found an older Chevy along the curb and fished my slim jim out of the bag. In less than a minute, I was sitting behind the wheel and breaking off the cylinder lock. Hot-wiring a car was one of the first tricks the Agency taught me. I hadn't used that particular skill in a while, but your fingers don't forget. I had the Chevy rumbling up the street in another sixty ticks.

"Phil."

"Yes?" I imagined he'd been holding his breath the whole time, letting me concentrate. Good boy.

"The nearest safe house is still Benny's place?"

"Yes." Phil hesitated. "You know he hates it when you just pop in—"

"Call you when I get there."

There's no place like the Center. Situated on a sprawling forty-five-acre lot just west of Chicago's Loop and the I-90/94 Kennedy Expressway, the massive stadium plays host to our world-famous professional basketball and hockey teams during all their home games, as well as anything from rock concerts to wrestling matches. Tourists come from all around the world to get their picture taken under the giant bronze statues of the local sports gods that adorn the perimeter. When our boys are in town, playing to a capacity crowd, the roar from inside causes car alarms to go off half a mile away.

was that Schober had tried to make the collar and not Druison. Why would he stay away? What could it mean? "Maybe . . . maybe someone wants to put pressure on me; maybe they want to force someone else's hand. I don't know. But that's what I need you for, Phil."

"Me?" Phil sounded apoplectic.

"Everything started with Delgado. Keep digging there. Cross-reference everybody he's come in contact with for the last month. And track down the chain of custody on my weapon. Who had the gun from the time they took it out of the car? Who at the lab could have tampered with the report? Find me the person, and we'll find the reason."

"Kyra . . . you know the Agency won't like me snooping around government databases like this. It's not pertinent to any pending contract."

Omigod, he was such a geek. "It's pertinent to me not getting caught and thrown in jail, Phil! Or how do you think it will play out on the evening news when they start showing proof of the lady with snakes for hair? How will the Agency explain that?"

Phil made a noise deep in his throat. "You know what the Agency's motto is . . ."

Yeah. "'There is no Agency.'" I knew.

"If I tell them what I'm doing, I could get in trouble."

"So don't tell them. Just poke around a little."

"Okay . . . I'll try. I can't promise anything, though, okay? What are you going to be doing?"

"I need to get out of town for a while, let the heat die down." That made sense. The problem was . . .

The problem was I had no money. The Delgado contract had been a standard five-thousand-dollar kill fee, but half of that had already been direct-deposited to the First United Bank of Greece. Even if I could risk hitting an ATM or branch for the rest, I'd need a lot more than that to really disappear for months, if this could even be fixed in months. To really be sure, I'd need . . .

I'd need . . .

"Phil. Is that other contract still on the board?"

"The Rougnagne contract? It's still . . . whoa!"

"What?" My normally low tolerance for surprises was at an all-time ebb.

"It's up to three million, Kyra. And now it expires tonight, at midnight."

CHAPTER 4

As a general rule, Mythic tend to be a pretty superstitious lot. Seeing as how most of us are the stuff of myths, I guess this makes sense. And while I don't throw spilled salt over my shoulder or knock on wood to drive out bad-luck fairies (most of the time), the idea that this contract would come along just when I needed serious money to skip town seemed a little too fortuitous to be merely the result of good timing. But since I couldn't just ignore the chance of a lifetime, I decided I'd see what the Vegas odds were on taking it before sticking my neck out. So after I left the safe house, I made a pit stop at Magdalina's.

Magdalina kept a shop in a back alley of the Greektown neighborhood of Chicago, so close to the West Loop you could hear the rumbling of traffic through the old plastered walls. She claimed her ancestors had been in Chicago since the late 1800s, her great-great-grandmother having been the wife of a Greek sea captain who plied his trade on the Great Lakes. More importantly to me, she was a descendant of an unbroken line of witches and was one herself, with no small ability to suss out hidden things.

Magdalina and I weren't exactly gal pals, but she could usually be counted on to come up with what I needed when a job wasn't going to get done strictly through firepower. The tricky thing was meeting her price. Sometimes it was money, sometimes it was blood; but whatever it was, it was never cheap.

I just hoped she could tell me if I was sticking my neck in a noose, and if I could afford to pay for her answer.

The rusted bell over her door jangled just before I pushed on it. Damn; I could never get used to that. The smell of herbs and bitter incense washed over me at once, stinging my nose and eyes. Magdalina was behind her counter as though she'd been waiting for me for some time. Her black eyes peered out from under her bushy gray hair. Perched on her stool and bundled in an oversized purple sweater, she looked like a half-mad crow on a line.

"Maggie."

"Kyra Anastas," she said, her broad lips making every syllable smack the air. She might have been announcing the name of a dish she liked to eat, which was not a reassuring thought. "What can I do for you?"

I rested my palms gingerly on the counter between us. There were scores of old marks in it, some of which looked like they'd been made by a butcher's cleaver. Except Magdalina didn't sell meats. I swallowed deeply.

"I have . . . an opportunity," I said. "But it involves risk. I need to know if the . . . path is one I should take. If it's safe."

"Hoo-hoo," cackled Magdalina. Nobody could cackle like the old broad. Maybe she thought it was expected of a witch and threw it in for ambience. "No path is safe in life," she grinned. "All roads have their risks."

"I didn't come here for a fortune cookie telling," I snapped, venting my nervousness. I was pretty sure Magdalina knew exactly what I was, but she never flinched from my gaze. Usually it was me having a hard time meeting hers. Like, um, now. "I want the real thing. If this opportunity is a setup of some kind, I need to know it. Now."

Magdalina bobbed her bushy head. "Trouble follows you," she said. "It nips at your heels, forcing you to quicken your step. And what will you pay to know the way ahead?"

"What's the market bearing?" I said tightly, taking a mental breath. Here we go.

"Let us see," she said, and seized my wrists. Yow, I hadn't even seen the old biddy move off her stool. And now she held my arms in hands that felt like vises. I winced but held still, letting her eyes crawl all over me. Just when I was losing feeling in my fingers, she let go.

I rubbed at my wrists as she clambered back onto her stool. Man, I hated these readings. "So?"

Magdalina's head retreated into the fluffy collar of her sweater until only her eyes could be seen. "You go toward death on this path."

That was a good start. "Mine or someone else's?"

"Another's. Though beyond that death, there are more, and more—"

"I'm just interested in this contract," I said. "And if I'll get paid."

"You will receive your money," nodded the witch. "And more."

"Good enough—wait." I scowled. "Is this like a *Macbeth* kind of thing? Are you doing one of those Three Witches tricks, where your answer sounds like one thing but really means the opposite or something?"

"I am not one of the Fates, Kyra Anastas," Magdalina snapped. "The Moirai have not been seen or heard from in millennia, more's the pity. And I claim no such power as they once had to guide and shape our destinies. I cannot see further than the first turning. You will come to death, and bring death, but beyond that . . ." She shook her head. "I see only darkness and . . ."

Pregnant pauses from a prophetess were not usually a good thing. "*And . . . ?*"

Magdalina scowled, her beady eyes squinting into the unknowable. "And in that darkness," she murmured, "the smallest glimmer of light."

I hadn't known the old witch to be so poetic. "Light? What light?"

"The light of hope," she murmured in a wondering tone. "Of change."

"I don't follow."

Magdalina seemed to come back to herself. She turned her black gaze to me, once more inscrutable. Guess that was going to be all I got. "So . . ." I braced myself. "What do I have to pay for that particular pearl of wisdom?"

I couldn't see Magdalina's lips behind her collar, so I didn't quite trust that I heard her muffled reply: "Nothing."

I blinked. Here was a first. "You always want something," I mumbled, then bulled ahead. "But not this time? Why?"

"What I desire," said the witch. "You cannot give. Yet. But if you succeed . . . ? Who knows?" She waved a hand. The bell behind me jangled, making me jump. "Go, Kyra Anastas. Should you endure, we may talk of this again. But not now."

I paused at the door. "The thing you want," I said, not daring to look back at those black eyes. "Can you at least tell me what it is?"

"Order," came the witch's reply. It came to my ear like a prayer. "Order from chaos."

"Kyra, I still don't know about this . . ."

I was nearly done with my preparations, and still he was harping in my earpiece. "We've been over this a dozen times, Phil. Do it."

"Once I do, you know . . ." Phil's voice trailed off.

Yeah. I did. Once the contract was accepted, it was irrevocable. The transfer of funds into the Agency's account would trigger a spell that set a compulsion on the Mythic who had accepted the job. The Mythic would have to fulfill the terms of the contract or pay the price themselves. And, depending on the strength of the spell, that price could be your life. At that point, it would be kill or be killed.

"Do it."

"Initializing acceptance now." *Tappity, tap, tap.* "Funds transferred." He paused. "Anything yet?"

I shook my head, unsurprised. Usually it took at least a few minutes for a spell to find its way through the world to you once it was released. "No, I—"

A sudden tingling began in my feet, as though ants had started swarming up inside the soles of my boots. The spell, finding me through the stone under my feet, flowed up my legs, eager to bond with me.

Damn, it was strong; I'd never felt so much power behind an enchantment. Usually a client negotiated the contract directly with the Agency and the Agency used one of the spellcasters they had on retainer to create the *geas*. But this was something different. Whoever had called in this contract had used their own talent, and it showed. I felt the spell doing more than just coating me like a second skin, as I was used to. It seemed like it was suffusing my every cell as it surged upward.

When it reached my heart, I gasped as though a fist of fire had closed over it. I sensed the enchantment battering away at my chest, trying to permeate the organ within. I resisted, and for a moment the spell hovered there, fire against ice, the ocean waves against the obdurate rock of the cliff. Then, unable to gain purchase, it flared past, traveling through my veins and arteries, up, up, until it filled my brain and eyes, blinding me with its energy.

Having bonded, the spell ended. But I felt it as part of me now, an intangible burden, anchored in my flesh, melded with my bones. And there was no question about what was at stake now; I was committed. By midnight tonight, either Elspeth Rougnagne or I would be dead.

I opened my eyes and found myself on my knees without realizing I had fallen. Still breathing hard, I got back up and checked my watch: Outside, it was early Sunday afternoon. The good people of Chicago would be coming back from their churches and family outings or, later, getting ready to go out to dinner or parties. In a little while, I'd clear out.

"Kyra?" Phil, still tucked in my ear like a tiny djinn. "You good there?"

I turned to the full-length mirror on the wall and surveyed myself. Under the naked bulb hanging from the ceiling of my storage locker, I was a figure swathed in midnight, the high-collared black tunic fitting comfortably over my custom-made Kevlar vest, the old duster like an enveloping cloak.

I pulled my sniper gloves taut over my hands and snapped them into place. The snakes were still immature, their scores of wedge-shaped heads each no bigger than my thumbnails, but they coiled and snapped at the air as though they sensed what was coming.

"Oh, yeah," I said to my reflection. My voice sounded like flame to me, restless and eager. "I'm real good."

The Rougnagne estate was located on a range of softly rolling hills twenty miles west of the city proper, in the Burr Ridge district. After parking the loaner from Benny just out of sight off the access road, I had scouted around until I'd found a suitable position to do some surveillance.

Now, a mile from the target, I scanned the place with my binoculars for the best means of entry. I had the westering sun behind me and my hood thrown up over the serpents to keep them quiet. Except for the lack of birdcalls around me, there was nothing to mark my presence among the trees that dotted the ridge overlooking the mansion.

My respect for Elspeth Rougnagne was growing by the minute.

At first I'd thought she'd shown poor judgment, building her marble monstrosity in the lowest level of the surrounding topography. When in doubt, basic battle tactics called for choosing the higher ground. But then I fitted my binoculars with a special lens—one I'd purchased "off market" a few years back—and got my first glimpse of what I was going up against.

Phil had warned me about the ley line convergence, but it was one thing to hear about it. It was quite another to see up close what she'd done with it.

Under the ruddy light of the setting sun, the marble columns and curved facade of the three-story mansion below reflected subtle hues of red and orange against a darkening sky. But when I slipped the spellified lens over the regular binoculars, the building and grounds all but disappeared under a shimmering dome of golden light.

It wasn't a tangible thing, strictly speaking. Every now and then I caught a glimpse of a bird or squirrel passing unscathed through its borders. But I had no doubt that its magical punch was potent enough. Somehow Rougnagne had tapped into the natural currents of mystical energies that wrapped themselves around the Earth like a network of underground rivers and drawn them up into a protective caul over her home. No spell would be able to penetrate it; no sending would be able to cross it. And a Mythic like myself would feel like they had run into a brick wall. All in all, it was an effective means of creating the sorcerous equivalent of a bomb shelter.

Not that she'd neglected the possibility of attack from more prosaic quarters. A long sidewinding gravel road was the only means of reaching the premises, unless you wanted to opt for a bone-jarring ride down the descending folds of the encircling hills that would probably tear out the transaxle of a Hummer. A ten-foot-tall white stone wall enclosed the entire estate, except for the broad gate where the twin guard stations were positioned. I counted two sentries in each guardhouse. Half a dozen more were patrolling outside the wall. I caught glimpses of more from time to time within, sweeping the palatial grounds. All were armed with compact automatic weapons and dressed in what looked like riot gear.

They were expecting trouble. Great.

My own eyesight extended beyond the narrow band of the spectrum visible to normal humans. With just a little extra concentration, I could perceive wavelengths as long as the infrared and as short as the ultraviolet regions. So the skein of red security laser beams crisscrossing the grounds beyond the wall stood out for me like fissures of magma in the dark grass. Negotiating the zone between the woods and the wall would be easy enough under cover of night. But even setting aside the mystical shield, getting over the wall and into the grounds proper without being cut in half by someone's Uzi was the tricky part.

A charge down the winding road would obviate the need for stealth and might even catch the sentries off guard. But there was just too much firepower down there. If I tried a frontal assault, all I'd do is get myself killed.

Which meant I'd lugged Big Bertha out of storage for nothing. Too bad; the occasion had seemed tailor-made for me to finally try her out.

I'd given some thought to a Trojan Horse gambit, but these guys were just too on edge; any unscheduled van appearing would raise the alarm, and I doubted that I'd make it halfway down the slope before they reduced the van to confetti. So that was out too.

I needed to find a flaw in the defenses. So I waited on my belly and watched, marking the changing of the guards, the tics and manner of their routines, while the clock ticked and the night deepened and the grass grew stiff with frost around me. My shoulders ached from holding the binoculars up to my eyes, and I was considering a change of locale when I noticed something through the special lens.

Half an hour ago, the bubble of magical energy around the property had extended some twenty yards beyond the white-wall perimeter. Now the curtain of dancing lights that marked its terminus at ground level was only ten yards beyond the wall. Uncertain of myself, I fixed a few landmarks in my mind's eye and waited. After another five minutes, I was free of doubt. The dome was shrinking, slowly but steadily. In another half hour, it would no longer cover even the walls.

And there was something else too: The shield was showing signs of deterioration. I'd noticed earlier that the shield was actually a series of energy lattices, rolling down from the peak of the dome and sinking below the earth. Now, though, there were intermittent gaps in the curtains of light, and they were gradually growing more frequent.

I did some quick figuring. At this rate, in just over two hours, the shield around the mansion would have dwindled to nothing. Unfortunately, I didn't have two hours to wait. A glance at my watch told me it was already quarter to eleven. Maybe it was my imagination, but it felt like my heart was already beating slower. At midnight, it would stop entirely.

At least I knew that Elspeth Rougnagne must be human. Her defenses were nigh impregnable, all right, but the fact that they were failing showed that she needed to renew them constantly in order to maintain them. That

72

pointed to mortal limits, which was a relief; if she had been another Mythic or some sort of extraplanar creature just masquerading as human, who knew what other powers she might have. But to be casting spells to harness the ley lines' energies meant she was human, and all humans could be killed.

And now I knew where she had to be hiding too. As it contracted, the position of the dome's peak was shifting slightly, revealing that its center was somewhere near the west wing of the mansion. As the locus from which the spell was generated, Rougnagne would be there.

I crawled backward on my elbows and knees from the crest of the hill until I was sure I was out of the mansion's sight line. Then I made my way back to the thicket by the side of the road where I'd stashed my vehicle, a nondescript cargo van that Benny would report as stolen in twenty-four hours. I popped the rear doors and quickly picked my tools: two Glock 27s, each packed with magazines carrying nine .40 caliber bullets and equipped with silencers. If at all possible, I wanted to get in and out without a fuss. With that happy thought in mind, I slipped an extra pair of fixed-blade daggers into the special sheaths I'd sewn into the lining of my duster and jammed a three-and-a-half-inch-bladed boot knife into my boot. For the wall, I strapped on a pair of stainless-steel climbing claws. Then I got moving.

The night was moonless, and only the stars watched as I stole down the hills, silent as the Angel of Death, keeping to what little cover I could as I went. By the time I reached the level ground of the basin, I had picked my spot on the curved wall, where the shield stuttered and fluttered with some regularity. Stealing through the maze of thin red beams that marked the lawn, I took a last look with the special lens, then sprang as the gap opened. Rolling forward across the grass with my arms tucked in, I drew up against the wall. Stucco. Perfect.

But first I needed to make sure no one came at me while I was climbing. The guard patrolling this section of the wall had been stopping every twenty minutes to sneak a cig a few meters to the east, where he was still out of sight of his fellows. I inched along the wall until I caught the telltale whiff of sulfur on the air. Peeking around the bend, I glimpsed him standing there, blowing out a cloud of smoke. I waited till he glanced to his right. Then I closed with him.

Even though I had his blind side, some instinct warned him. And he was fast.

Just not fast enough. As he spun, raising his weapon, I chop-blocked his firing arm. You'd think that a girl who weighed 125 pounds soaking wet couldn't deliver a lot of punishment to the arm of a man wearing riot gear. But I'd fitted my forearm with a studded iron bracer from my inventory at the storage facility. Arm bracers are a holdover from medieval times when knights wore body armor to protect themselves, and when you get hit with one—trust me on this—they *hurt*. I heard the guard gasp as the blow landed, breaking his wrist with a snap. Before he could cry out, I pivoted and took him across the throat with my elbow. He went to his knees and a Shutō strike to the exposed carotid artery laid him out.

I knelt and checked his pulse. With luck, he'd be out long enough for me to get my work done and be gone from here.

I pulled his radio from his belt and stuffed it in my pocket. His cig lay in the grass where it had fallen. I took a quick drag before putting it out with the heel of my boot. Waste not, want not.

I drew back a few steps, as close to the inner edge of the shield as I dared, then took a running jump at the wall. The grips on my boots held, and I used the claws to scramble up to the top, throwing my torso over. From there, I scanned the interior grounds.

The manse still lay a hundred yards in the distance. Before me was a perfectly manicured lawn with broad cobblestone lanes that wound past a patio, a fountain, and an in-ground pool the size of my apartment complex. Two sets of curving steps led up to either side of a half-moon-shaped balcony that projected out from the second floor of the building, all tastefully lit with recessed floods. Lovely.

But I wasn't here to sightsee. One of the guards was just completing a circuit past the pool. I waited until the reflected glare from the waters would most diminish his night vision, then swung over the wall and dropped to the grass. From here, the quickest route into the mansion was straight ahead. Sprinting to the patio, I marked the locations of the sentries. Another twenty seconds and I could risk the last stretch.

I was just about to go when I noticed a flicker of movement on the second floor. The guard had moved out of sight to the right. But through the brightly lit windows, I caught a glimpse of two tails trotting in his wake.

Dogs. Seriously? Phil and I had gone over every security purchase Rougnagne had ever made online; guard dogs had not appeared on any order or invoice. Maybe she had paid for them in cash, or the security team had thrown them in gratis for her. Maybe anything.

This was bad. Dogs, like every other warm-blooded animal, were not fans of mine. And a trained guard dog would do more than just howl and carry on once it caught my scent. It would lead the sentries right to me.

But we were way past the point of no return here. My watch told me I had exactly fifty-three minutes left before midnight. I'd have to hope for the best.

I took off at a run, skirting the illuminated pool by a wide margin, and swept up the stone steps onto the balustraded balcony. The sliding doors had been left open, their filmy white curtains swaying in the evening breeze. I frowned at the oddity of the landing being open at this time of year, but there was no time to look a gift horse in the mouth.

I passed inside and found myself in a broad corridor that was sparsely adorned. I crept down the hall toward the west wing, hunting for the stairs to the third floor. I felt intuitively certain that if Rougnagne was likely to be anywhere, it would be on the top floor.

I'd known from the schematics Phil had sent me that the mansion was huge, some twenty thousand square feet in floor plan alone. But I hadn't expected it to be so empty. I glided through three chambers, each as big as a grand ballroom, which had scarcely any furniture or decoration. One held only a tangled snarl of cables and wires for electrical connections that had been disconnected—or had never been made.

The feeling of emptiness grew more intense as I made my way up the west wing stairwell, whose polished wood banister was coated in dust. The air was too still, too stale. No one had walked these halls in years. But why? Had Rougnagne spent all her vast fortune on the building and grounds, intent on showing off her wealth to the spying world, only to have none left to furnish it? Was that why she had never allowed visitors? There was something sad about the thought of so much vanity, of a pride that led to such self-inflicted wounds.

I shook the feeling off. I was here to kill the bitch, wasn't I?

I came to a T intersection. To my left, I spied a door limned with light. At last; someone was at home. I slid out my Glocks and made to head that way, only to find I'd turned completely around and was facing the other direction.

What in the Seven Hells . . . ?

I started toward the door again. And again my legs swung me around and pointed me the opposite way, toward a set of double doors that lay down the right-hand end. There was light coming from under them too, but it was dimmer, like the misty blue glow you get when your cable's been cut off and your TV shows you only idiot swirls of static.

Now, put a mule and me on the "naturally stubborn" scale, and you'll find we balance each other out pretty nicely. But if some kind of misdirection spell had been left hanging in the corridor, it could take precious time to overpower it, assuming that could even be done. And time was something I did not have. Better to go with the flow and find another way around the compulsion, I told myself.

Yeah, right.

Still, I had no better ideas up my sleeve. So I holstered one gun and put a hand on one of the double doors' ornate crystal doorknobs. It turned easily. I pushed the door open, drawing my Glock again, and swept the room as it came into view.

It was a large space, clearly intended as some sort of master bedroom. But again, the walls were bare of paintings or tapestries, the corners empty of bureaus or dressers. Only a thick Persian rug covered the center of the floor where a bed had been placed, surrounded by medical equipment. The soft blue light was coming from the monitors that faced the head of the bed, huddling against one another like silent mourners. I'd seen less-elaborate setups at hospitals; there were cardiac machines, respirators, an EKG monitor, and others whose purpose I didn't recognize. And resting in the bed, with her arms connected to drip lines from the IV poles, was my prey: Elspeth Rougnagne.

Or her corpse. Despite the steady beeping of the machines, this woman hardly resembled the images Phil had gleaned from the internet. Even granting the passing of a decade and a half, the degeneration was staggering. According to her birth certificate, Elspeth Rougnagne should have been fifty-eight last January; the woman on the bed looked at least three decades older than that. Her hair was thin and white, though it had still been carefully combed out to fall away from her brow and cheeks. Her face was nearly as white, with the cheekbones protruding against skin as translucent as onion paper. Her closed eyes were sunk so deep into their sockets that they appeared on the verge of disappearing into her skull.

This was the woman who had to die before midnight? The . . . mark that someone was willing to pay three million dollars to have removed? It seemed somebody had more money than patience. A few more hours and nature would just take its course without any help from me. Standing at the foot of the bed before this pathetic figure, I found myself wishing that it would.

I checked my watch. Only twenty-two minutes to midnight. I worried at my fingernail in indecision. Should I wait a little, just in case—?

I was so distracted by my thoughts, it took me a moment to realize the woman had opened her eyes and was glaring fixedly at me. The parchment lips parted.

"Well," she rasped in a low voice as dry as sandpaper, "you certainly took your time."

77

I stood there, transfixed by the unreality of the situation. The moment yawned.

"You shouldn't bite your nails," Elspeth Rougnagne said.

I snatched my hand from my mouth and hid it behind my back. A hissing sound issued from the woman's mouth. For a moment I had the impression she was laughing, then she broke into a series of hoarse coughs that made her emaciated frame buck and the machines beep in distress.

"Water," she gasped.

You're allowed to grant a dying person's last request, right? I spotted a pitcher and brought her a cup. She drank the water greedily. Then she coughed again.

When she had finished, she looked at me. The vitality in those eyes was amazing; it was so at odds with the body. "We need to talk," she whispered.

Quarter to twelve. "I'm afraid we don't have much time for that."

"I know." The wizened lips might have been smiling. "Midnight, correct? My instructions were brief, but specific."

I glared at her. She might have been joking, or bargaining for time. But there was no fear in those bright eyes, and no doubt. She absolutely meant what she was saying.

"You…" I fumbled for words. "You…called in the contract…on yourself?"

Elspeth Rougnagne nodded once.

"Why?"

"Isn't that part obvious?" The bony chest rose and fell with silent amusement. "To bring you here."

"You *want* me to kill you?"

"Want," she panted. She shook her head. "Not want. But I *need* you to."

This was getting way too weird for me. "Why?"

There was a strange look in Rougnagne's eyes, a mixture of sadness and resignation and triumph. "Because that is how it is to be. She has seen it, and she knows. And when she knows, she is always right."

"She? She who? What are you talking about?"

78

"My daughter," said Rougnagne. "The one who said it had to be you. The one you have to protect."

I was beginning to think I had a hearing problem. Daughter? *Protect?*

"Lady . . ." I hardly knew where to begin. Thirteen minutes left. "You've got the wrong person. I'm not a cop, or a security guard. I'm a—"

"Killer," snapped Rougnagne. "A murderer." The bright eyes glittered. "Do you think I would let you get this far without knowing exactly what you are, Miss Anastas? Don't let your eyes deceive you; until I breathe my last, I am very much in command of my faculties. Oh, yes, I know you—better, I think, than you know yourself."

Twelve minutes. "You don't know me at all," I said, but my voice was shaking.

Maybe she noticed, because she nodded slightly. "Kyra Regina Anastas, twenty-six years old. Born and raised on Anafi, in the Cyclades Islands of Greece. Immigrated illegally to the United States when she was twelve years old. Purports to be a woman of meager means, living off her software consultation business. Pretends to have an intractable illness to hide her frequent deformity." The silent laughter again. "And, of course, a gorgon, who really makes her living as a hired killer, luring her victims to their death, turning them to stone and reducing them to rubble with a mallet. Erasing her crimes as she goes through the world, answering to no one. A creature without conscience or remorse. Yes, I've watched you from afar, Miss Anastas. Watched you closely."

So *this* was my ethereal stalker in the flesh. Eleven minutes. I shook my head. I didn't need to hear this. Why was I delaying?

"I could've killed half your men getting in here tonight," I said. "I didn't."

"Does that justify you, gorgon?" Spittle flew from Rougnagne's mouth, clung to her lower lip. Her whole body shook with feeble violence. "Does it somehow make your existence anything more than a blight on the world? Is that your defense? That you withhold your hand from murder *some* of the time? Is that paltry excuse supposed to make me think you worthy to be the protector of my child?"

"I don't give a damn what you think," I flared, stung. Less than ten minutes now. I felt my heart tightening as though a vise were around it. It was the spell, closing in. It had to be. *You're not supposed to have a child, goddammit!* "I'm not here looking for your approval, you crazy old bitch! And I'm sure as hell not here to protect anyone's daughter! You hired me to kill you? Okay, you get your wish."

I shoved the machines out of the way and moved to the side of the bed. Rougnagne looked up. With both hands, I threw my hood back and let the serpents uncoil and rise around my head. She stared at them; yet there was still no fear in her eyes.

"Will you answer one question?"

Just do it and get it over with, Kyra! "What?" I ground out.

"What are you?"

A chill that had nothing to do with the compulsion spell stole over me. Delgado's question again.

"I don't—don't know what you mean," I stammered.

"No?" wheezed Rougnagne. "You're telling me you've never thought about it? Never wondered as you've made your way through the world, without friends or family, without hope or love, why you are here? What you are?"

"What good would that do?" I snapped. "You are what you are. Wishing won't change anything."

Something like sympathy gleamed in her eyes. "What if you could be something more?"

"Look . . ." I began, but my voice cracked. Rougnagne's face blurred before me. Christ, was I crying? I raked the sleeve of my duster across my eyes to clear them. Now there was a trace of worry in her features, but it was oddly impersonal, as though the question mattered more to her than her own death.

Maybe I should have lied. But I couldn't do it, not even to spare us both. "I'm not a good person," I said. "I wouldn't know how. I'm just what you see: a monster."

Instead of arguing, Rougnagne sighed and closed her eyes. "It's a start," she murmured. Just as I was trying to decide if I was going to pry her eyes open, she looked at me again.

"I was like you once," she said. "Nearly sixteen years ago, I was at the peak of my worldly success, achieved by certain . . . arrangements I had made with various practitioners of the black arts. I had all the wealth I'd dreamed of in my youth, all the power I'd ever wanted.

"But I was empty inside. My heart was ashes. I had done . . . terrible things to get where I was, things no one knew about. The memories were like thorns in my flesh. Every day I wanted to die. Then . . . I agreed to have Stephanie. And when she was born, everything changed. *I* changed."

Rougnagne's voice had sunk until it was barely audible. She seemed to have forgotten about me as her gaze wandered about the room or among her memories.

Six minutes. It was getting harder to draw a breath.

Suddenly Rougnagne seized my wrist. I gasped at the strength in that bony grip as she held me fast, drawing her head up from the pillow. "Do what you came to do," she hissed and lapsed back against the bed.

It was now or never. I leaned against the rail of the bed and looked down. She met my eyes unflinching. I had never wanted to do it less, but in that instant I aimed the power of my Gaze, felt the lethal energy snake out of me and into her.

There was a silent concussion unlike anything I had ever experienced before. Instead of releasing the power into her, I felt like I was being drawn along with it, ripped away from where I stood. A great tumult rose around me.

"What the hell is happening?" I screamed and then found I couldn't speak.

"This is what the fakirs of India call a 'soul-lock,'" said a voice that was unmistakably Rougnagne's, though the mouth of her body wasn't moving. It rolled and echoed through my head like thunder. "The binding together of two spirits. Haven't you ever wondered how it is that your Gaze works, my dear? The eyes really are the windows of the soul, and every time you loose the power of your Gaze, you let a little of that darkness inside you escape, pouring it into your victim until they become like you—dead inside, stone."

No. *No!* That's not true. I shook my head in furious denial. But I couldn't wrench my eyes away from hers.

"But the link you create runs both ways," the voice continued remorselessly. "You can't open a window to let something out without running the risk that something will come in. And that's what I've done to you: As you've invaded my soul, I've invaded yours. We are bound together now, inextricably linked by my will. As my body dies, so will yours."

I struggled with extravagant fury against what she was saying, what she was doing. But I didn't know how to fight a battle like this. And I could sense myself losing, could feel myself being drawn into her, falling into the growing black well I myself was creating.

"Why?" I shouted soundlessly into her. "Why are you doing this?"

"Because in the soul there is only truth," came the answer. "And I must have the truth from you before I die."

"What truth?" Every second, the world was growing dimmer, contracting until all I could see was that widening gyre of darkness. I wanted to backpedal away from the bed, flee for my life, but my legs wouldn't move, my hands wouldn't pull free from the rail. Trapped; I was trapped—

"My daughter is the best thing I ever did," Rougnagne went on. "The only good thing. She gave me back my reason for existing. I sacrificed everything for her, and so won everything. She gave me back my soul. But she must live, to fulfill her destiny. I have guarded her as long as I could, but my strength has failed me, as she knew it would." The voice grew rueful. "I was so close. . . . Two days more and she would have been of age, strong enough to make her own way in this world. But this is the last price I must pay, for all that I did before her.

"The forces aligned against her know she is nearly mature enough to protect herself; they are desperate, and they are close. I can feel them, pressing against my defenses. She must be protected from them, and she has chosen you as her protector. She has the gift of foresight, and sometimes sees the things that must be. But I am her mother—and I must be sure. Give me your word."

"What? My what?"

"Your word," Rougnagne repeated. "Your word of honor. Swear to me on your life that you will protect her, until she is ready. Swear that you will keep her safe until midnight, two nights hence. Give me your vow, and I will release you. Or die with me, and be damned for all time."

Was she serious? Just say the magic words and I'd be free? There had to be a catch. But I didn't care. I'd say whatever she needed to hear. Everything was dark and cold around me, and the howl of the gyre was deafening in my ears. I could feel the link to my body like a loose tether, ready to detach and plummet something—some essential part of me—into that unending blackness.

I tried to answer with my mouth, but my lips were frozen. The words wouldn't come. I started to panic, struggling like a fish on an intangible line, thrashing inwardly in mad fear. I was going to die, to fall into that bottomless void, to be lost forever . . .

In the soul there is only truth.

My heart had slowed to a weak, thudding beat. The body was dying, the threads connecting me to it unravelling faster and faster. But for a moment, the part of me that was spinning helplessly into the dark found a space of stability, the calm in the eye of the storm. And I understood what was needed.

I promise, I said into the void in a voice that I had never heard myself use before, a voice I scarcely recognized as my own. *I will protect your daughter. I will keep her safe. I swear it on my life.*

At once, there was a tremendous shock, and I felt myself being thrown backward, released from that awful, inexorable pull. I thought I'd been knocked to the floor but, as my vision of the room returned, found that I was still standing at the side of the bed, bent over Rougnagne.

The Change was almost complete, the gray tide rolling up the taut muscles of her wasted neck, eating into the flesh of her face from all sides.

Yet she wasn't entirely gone yet. And she could still see me. Tears brimmed in her sunken eyes.

"Thank you," she whispered. A slight smile twitched on her lips. "You know . . . she was right," she said, and her voice was slate sliding across stone. "You really are . . . quite . . . beautiful . . ."

Then she was gone.

CHAPTER 5

It felt like I stood there, unmoving at the foot of the bed, for a long time. Then the timer on my watch buzzed, startling me. I glanced down at it: midnight. Everything that had happened between us, the whole thing, had taken less than five minutes. It didn't seem possible.

But already the *geas* was dissipating, cracking like ice and sliding off my skin to vanish into the ether. Contract fulfilled, the compulsion was gone.

But what had taken its place?

I felt weary and shaken to the bone; all I wanted to do was smoke a cigarette and plow into as much alcohol as I could buy. And with three hundred thousand dollars in my newly-minted offshore bank account, that should be plenty. But I had business to attend to. I didn't know how to measure the magnitude of what had just happened, or the consequences of my vow. Yet one thing seemed clear enough: I had to go tell someone that I'd just killed their mother.

Not something I was looking forward to.

Still, delaying it wasn't an option. By now, the sentries had probably found the guard I'd laid out. Since they hadn't raised the alarm, it meant they were hunting for the intruder, probably with the damn dogs. Someone would be coming to tell the boss what was up soon, if they weren't already on their way. I had to get a move on.

There was no time or way to dispose of Rougnagne's body now. If there was an autopsy, I'd have to arrange that one of the Agency's plants handled it. There'd be a furor over the mess, but I could deal with that later.

The hallway was still empty. True to my prediction, the misdirection spell was gone. I had no doubt that the shield around the mansion had already evaporated too. Which meant the place had lost its primary defense. If what Rougnagne had said was right, an attack could come at any time.

I put my hand to the doorknob of the door limned with light. Then, on impulse, I knocked.

"Come in."

Swallowing my trepidation, I opened the door.

Okay. Not what I was expecting. In contrast to everything else I'd seen throughout the mansion, the room before me was beautifully appointed, from the four-poster bed with its gold satin curtains to the white marble furnishings. The walls were adorned with all manner of paintings, each a dazzling work of art worthy of a master. The floor was strewn with thick furs, an opulent mix of creams and ivory.

Next to a mirrored dresser, a girl sat on a high-backed chair, facing me. She was dressed in a high-collared red coat and black slacks. A small purse was set in her lap, and she held herself as though ready for travel.

The first thought that came unbidden to my mind was that the girl was lovely. Her hair fell in long, silken strands, catching the light of the many lamps around the room like the finely-spun gold of the old fairy tale. Her face, turned up so that she seemed to be looking toward the ceiling behind me, was a marvel of symmetry, the small, narrow nose perfectly balancing the high cheekbones and dainty chin. Her lips were pressed together with apprehension, but still hinted at the first blush of the woman she would soon become. I'd never seen smoother skin either; unlike the rough, wide-pored flesh of my own face, hers was like alabaster, flawless.

In the legends of ancient Troy, the youthful Paris was so smitten by the beauty of Helen of Sparta that he stole her away from her rightful husband, precipitating a cascade of military reprisals that ultimately drowned his home city in blood. Helen had reputedly been the most ravishing woman in the world, creating a yearning in men and gods alike so great that half the armies of the world were drawn into war because of her.

I've always kind of hated that bitch for being so damn beautiful that men would kill and die just to look upon her. And I've always felt that the men of those times must have all been half-mad or particularly hard up to let themselves go so bonkers over one girl because of her looks. But for a moment, staring at the girl before me, I caught a glimpse of the reason they had done it, how they had surrendered to that instinctive desire to be close to, to protect such a thing of surpassing loveliness.

Then I saw her eyes.

Under the long eyelashes, they were white—utterly white—as though a caul was wrapped over them. When I moved into the room, she cocked her head, following the sound. Then I was sure.

She was blind.

Fantastic. Just fantastic. I had been hoping this could be made even more difficult than I'd imagined.

"Um." Not my best beginning. I cleared my throat. "Uh . . . hi."

"Hello."

"Uh, okay, here's the thing," I said, bulling ahead. "I've, uh, I've just been to see your mother." Crone take me, this was a disaster. Just tell her! Let the screaming and cursing begin. "Right. So, you should know—"

"I know what you've done."

"You do?"

"Yes."

She was too placid, too calm about this. Was she medicated? Just in shock? I didn't know the psychology of teenagers.

87

Abruptly, she stood up, holding her purse in both hands. "Is it time to go?"

"Go?" I repeated. "Where do you think you're going?"

"Away from here," she said. "With you."

I kept checking the hallway, expecting to see guards turning the corner at any moment.

"Don't you think you should stay at home?" I said. "You've got the makings of your own small army here."

She winced, her poise faltering slightly. "Not anymore."

There was something disturbing about her conviction. Foresight, Elspeth Rougnagne had said. What my ancient forebearers had called "second sight." It was rare, but not unheard of. And it would make her valuable. Was that why the forces Rougnagne had mentioned were after her?

The Oracle of Delphi had been blind too. And never wrong.

I fished out the comm unit I'd taken off the guard outside the wall. "What's the name of your head of security?"

"Major Eddings," the girl said without hesitation. "He lets me call him John."

I toggled the transmit button. "Attention," I said. "Major Eddings, I have Rougnagne's daughter. I am willing to negotiate terms of her release in exchange for safe passage. Respond."

Static.

I checked the corridor again, then hit the broadband. "Major Eddings, I have Stephanie. If I do not hear from you in ten seconds, I will put a bullet in her brain. Respond."

Ten seconds ticked by. Twenty. Thirty.

Something was definitely wrong. No way would they just risk their charge being executed. They would have responded in some fashion: either by trying to bargain or by crashing in.

The girl stood there waiting, like she had all the time in the world.

"Come on," I said, grabbing her arm. I couldn't just leave her standing there without at least knowing what the situation was. And if they were lying in wait, I'd need her as leverage. She didn't protest or struggle as we made our way out into the hall.

The third floor was still empty, but now the stillness had an ominous feeling to it, as though the atmosphere was charged with something, some energy that was building toward eruption. Or maybe it was just my nerves.

Down the marble steps to the second floor. Should we go out the way I came in? It was a long trek up the hill to the cargo van. If I was really going to tow a hostage the whole way, I'd be too exposed.

I stopped in the middle of one of the vast bare chambers and turned to the girl.

"Your mother never took you out of this place?"

"No."

"But the guards . . . they leave when their shifts end. Where do they park their vehicles?"

The girl cocked her head. Right. I was asking a blind kid for directions. Stupid.

But then she surprised me. "Mother kept her cars in the garage," she said, "under the east wing."

"How do you know that?"

"She talked about them from time to time. She used to collect cars; they were her trophies. Before me."

Oh . . . kay. I mentally consulted my map of the place. Cutting across the front hall of the mansion would expose us to sniper fire, but it was the quickest way to the east wing. And I had an instinctive sense that I had to hurry.

Looking out through the first window that ran along the facade of the building, I couldn't make out any movement inside the wall. Where the hell were all the guards? The place should be swarming with them by now.

We'd have to risk it. I pulled the girl to my side, keeping her closer to the windows. "Don't do anything stupid," I muttered.

"I won't."

Uh-huh. Well, we'd see, wouldn't we? With one Glock in my left hand, I steered us down the long hall, sneaking a peek whenever I could. No one. I had to resist the urge to break into a run. The girl was nearly as tall as I was and could probably keep up, but I couldn't run the risk of her tripping and pulling us both down.

We were nearly halfway down the broad hallway when I saw a guard dog come through the swirling curtains from the balcony. I scanned for his handler, but the landing looked empty. The dog had turned and was trotting toward us. Damnation, he was a big sucker. Not a German shepherd but some other breed, the size of a mastiff but with bigger shoulders and chest. On his hind legs, he would probably stand as tall as me.

Not that I was planning to find out. I ground to a halt and shoved the girl in front of me. With any luck, the animals would have been trained to respond to her commands.

"Okay, kid," I gritted in her ear. "Tell the nice doggie coming our way to stand down."

"What?"

The beast was still loping along, but its stride was so huge it had closed half the distance between us. In another few seconds, I was going to have to shoot it right between the eyes.

"Your guard dog!" I hissed, squeezing her upper arm in a tender spot. "Tell it to 'sit' or I'll kill it."

The girl cocked her head at me. "We don't have a guard dog," she said in a dull tone.

Shit!

Too late, I saw the bloody paw prints behind it on the marble floor, marked the unnatural luminescence in the slitted eyes. As the beast leapt, I threw the girl to the side and loosed a shot. Then everything went crazy.

My aim was true, and the bullet should have taken the thing right in its narrow, sloped forehead. But as I fired, the dog rippled, fading like a shadow, and the bullet passed through it as though it were as insubstantial as smoke. I gaped—and then it was on me, solid again.

The beast was heavy and drove its paws into me like battering rams. I went to the floor under it and heard as much as felt the back of my skull hit the floor, hard. The air went out of my lungs and I saw stars. Awash in

90

the stench of blood and gore from the dog's hot, fetid breath, I tried to brace myself for a fatal bite.

But the creature didn't go for my throat, wheeling instead toward the girl, who had fallen to the floor. As the dog closed on her, she scrambled backward until she came up against the wall.

Double images danced before my eyes. But I ripped my other gun out and rolled onto my side, squeezing off two rounds. The dog yelped and bounded into the air, twisting and biting at the wounds in its haunch. As it landed, I fired two more shots. But these only blew off chunks from the wall over the girl's head as the dog sank through the floor like a phantom, disappearing.

Still dizzy, I levered myself up. I might have fallen again, but the girl was there, catching me under my arm and helping me to stay on my feet. I was dimly amazed at her strength.

"What was that thing?" she asked.

"Damned if I know," I gasped, scooping up my other gun. We reeled forward like a pair of drunkards. "But it's not dead. Come on; we've got to get out of here before it comes back. How much farther?"

"Two hundred and twelve steps, then fifty-three down the stairs," the girl said. "Mother made me count all the ways throughout the house so I could always find my way."

"Great—" I panted, then ground to a halt. We were just passing the billowing curtains of the landing. I glanced to my right and saw another dog hopping up onto the balcony. Its jaws were dripping with blood. In the gloom, its eyes glowed like embers.

"Go!" I shouted, propelling her forward. "I'll catch up!"

Without waiting to see if she complied, I stepped outside, drawing a bead on the beast. It sprang as I fired, but I rolled out underneath it as it became intangible in midair, flipping onto my back. In the instant its solid paws hit the surface of the landing, I emptied both magazines into it. The dog staggered and went down in a heap, dead.

I rose, slapping a fresh magazine into each Glock, and was about to hobble back inside when I caught the flicker of lights from beyond the balcony. I went to the balustrade and scanned the vicinity.

Nothing moved inside the wall, though here and there I picked out the small forms of crumpled bodies on the grassy lawn. Just on the edge of my sight to the right, one of the guardhouses was lit and I could see the red smears against the glass of the control booth for the gate. And beyond . . .

Beyond the wall, the dark hills were crawling with scores of red lights, winking in and out like bloody fireflies. As I watched, they made their way stealthily down toward the mansion.

Laelapi.

The name slithered coldly into my thoughts, nestling there like a snake. I'd never thought to see them, but in that moment, I didn't doubt my intuition. Someone had loosed the innumerable offspring of the legendary Hound of Zeus, the dog that never failed to bring down its prey, that no distance or obstacle could deter.

It wasn't hard to guess what they were seeking.

No wonder none of the sentries had responded. The creatures had probably been kept out only by Rougnagne's shield. Two of them must have slipped in through the gaps as it started to fail, just as I'd done, and from there began wreaking a silent slaughter. With their ability to phase in and out of solidity, the dogs had made short work of the mansion's defenders.

This was trouble. There was no way I could take them on en masse. We had to get out of here. But then what? The *laelapi* would just run us down, no matter where we fled. They would never tire, never stop. Sooner or later, they would get to us.

Did I just say "us"? It wasn't me they were after; the girl was their quarry. If I just stepped aside . . .

They'd tear her to pieces. These things weren't here to capture anyone; they were animals, intent only on bringing down prey. In a flash, I saw the girl surrounded by the pack as she stood next to her mother's car, waiting for me, saw them leaping on her as she flailed in blind agony and went down.

Maybe it was the smarter play. But I needed a car anyway; I'd never get past the *laelapi* on foot. One look at the bodies strewn across the lawn was proof enough of that. Cursing under my breath, I turned and headed back toward the mansion.

At the same moment, the breeze parted the curtains just enough for me to catch a glimpse of the giant form coiled there. I sprang back, raising my guns as the dog came out. It was limping slightly, and blood oozed from the wounds on its right flank. My sparring partner had made its way back.

The dog's head bobbed toward its fallen comrade, then back at me. The ruddy eyes burned like slits of fire. It didn't leap this time but padded out cautiously, favoring its injured side. The errant wind had spoiled its ambush, so now it changed tactics, circling in a wide arc, trying to come around me. I turned with it, sights on the stooped head, the massive chest. Just one bullet through the heart or brain and I'd finish it. But every time I fired, the creature faded like mist. Bullets ricocheted around the balcony, hitting nothing vital.

A sudden lunge cost me four from my magazines before I realized the move was a feint, the shots passing harmlessly through the suddenly intangible body.

Round and round we went, the dog edging closer and closer, driven back into ghost form only by the rapid fire of the guns. I was running low on ammo now. The Glocks had no more than two shots each left. And in the time it would take to reload, the dog would have my throat out. I couldn't make a break for it either; the second I turned my back, it would be on me.

Was that great, slavering mouth grinning? It knew it had me, and time was on its side. In minutes the rest of the pack would be phasing through the walls to join in the hunt. I had to act now.

I fired the last two rounds of my right gun, jumping backward as I did to gain a second's grace. Dropping the useless weapon, I reached in for my fixed-blade knife. I got my hand on the pommel and was drawing it out when the beast sprang. My last two shots zipped out, but I had no chance to see if they hit anything as the dog crashed into me, bringing me down. I got my left arm up just in time for the massive jaws to close over it.

Instead of crunching down on bone, though, the sharp teeth skittered across the iron bracer, clamping on but unable to penetrate. Confused, the dog hesitated. In that instant, I brought my knife up and in. Nearly five inches of high-carbon stainless-steel blade pierced the great muscles of the thing's neck and the dog howled, throwing its head back. The knife was wrenched out of my grip.

Snarling and slobbering, the dog bent to snap at my face. I threw my arm up again, but the angle was wrong, and my hand went straight into the creature's mouth. The jaws bit again, and this time some of the teeth found the flesh above my bracer, sinking like needles into my bicep. I screamed and the dog drove its head into me, pinning me to the ground so that its nose was on my chin and our eyes were within inches of each other.

As it did, I threw the power of my Gaze up like a javelin. I was drained from the encounter with Rougnagne, and my Gaze was weak. But the snakes weren't dead yet, and I put every ounce of desperate strength I had left into it.

The dog stiffened, trying to pull its eyes away. I held on, physically and psychically, willing the Change into those powerful muscles and ligaments. For a moment that seemed to go on forever, we were locked in an impasse, the beast trying to crush and worry me to death as I strove to transform it into stone. Then the dog felt the Change reaching for its vitals and it went mad with pain and terror. It clawed at my chest and stomach, shredding the flimsy fabric of my collared shirt. But the Kevlar vest protected me from the worst of it. A muffled wail erupted from the dog's throat. It charged forward, dragging me along the balcony under it, then pitched on top of me as if it meant to suffocate me under its bulk. Suddenly the world faded like a shadow around us, and I realized we were falling through empty space together.

I couldn't have done anything to save myself, but as we plummeted, the dog's shoulder struck something, sending us cartwheeling through the air. We landed with a crash that rattled my teeth, but the creature was now beneath me and took the brunt of the impact. When I rolled off it, I knew at once it was dead.

Dazed and sick with pain, I needed a few seconds to get my bearings. The dog must have phased through the floor of the balcony, taking me along with it. Now I was somewhere underground, in the mansion's basement. I ripped loose some of the tattered remnants of my tunic and wound them over my left arm to staunch the worst of the bleeding, then got unsteadily to my feet and took in my surroundings.

The room was vast, running nearly the length of the mansion's floor plan. The ceiling was some twenty feet over my head, testament to how far I had fallen. From floor to roof, the walls were lined with a nest of pipes and conduits, going in every direction. Power thrummed through the air, made the floor vibrate under my boots. Furnaces and tanks rose in orderly rows along the walls.

The mansion was its own physical plant. Of course; Rougnagne wouldn't have risked being dependent on outside sources for her heat and light. Struck by an idea, I limped over to the pipes, reading the tracery of letters on each until I found what I was looking for.

Natural gas. Maybe the gods were good, after all. Fishing out my other knife from my duster, I sawed through the two-inch-thick plastic main until it snapped off. Instantly the gas began hissing out. I sniffed the air but could detect nothing. Perfect. Rougnagne had chosen her fortress with care, tapping into not just the ley lines but a natural gas pocket in the earth, and there was no telltale smell of rotten eggs to betray that gas was now gushing out into its bowels at a rate of 60 psi.

I was in a bad spot to linger; any spark or flame could set the volatile stuff off. So I made for the eastern end of the chamber and went up the first flight of steps I found. A glance at my watch told me it was half past twelve. With luck, the first wave of the pack would just now be penetrating the mansion above me.

The stairwell took me to a landing. I cracked open the heavy metal door and peered out. A space with a vaulted ceiling spread out before me, lined with row after row of automobiles. "Collection," the girl had said. More like "cathedral." Under the mellow radiance of recessed lights gleamed cars of every sort: convertibles, coups, sedans, even pickup trucks. I recognized red and yellow Porsches, a ravishing black Koenigsegg, Rolls-Royces, and Lamborghinis. But my eye was drawn like a magnet to the midnight blue Bugatti Veyron in the center of the room.

It was almost enough to make you forget that a pack of hellhounds was close on your ass. Until I heard the distant echo of their baying. They'd come upon the body of their kin on the balcony. Time was running out. I headed for the Veyron, then skidded to a halt when I realized that the girl was already there, strapped into the passenger seat.

For a blind person, this kid really got around.

Shaking my head, I slid into the contoured driver's seat.

"Oh, my god . . ."

The girl shifted in her seat. "What is it?"

I laid my hands on the leather-gripped steering wheel and took a deep breath. "Assuming we're not already dead and this isn't Heaven," I murmured, "I want to be buried in this car." *And you probably will be, in about three minutes,* my mind added.

Until I shut it up with a push of the ignition button. The Bugatti's sixteen-cylinder engine roared to life, deafening in the confined space. With a spin of the wheel, we took off down the center aisle.

"The doors—" I began, casting about for the remote control, but the girl was already reaching up to press a button on the rearview mirror. The doors rolled apart as we raced through them.

If I remembered my specs right, the Bugatti Veyron pulled in just over one thousand horsepower, which gave it bragging rights as the most powerful production road-car engine in the world. Maybe too powerful, as I turned the first curve at the end of the drive a wee bit tightly and we found ourselves sliding out of control. A quick shift in gear, and I got us back on track.

"Sorry," I said. I was giddy with blood loss and adrenalin. Or maybe it was the fact that I was driving a car that was probably worth more than a million dollars.

The drive snaked around the back of the mansion, following the curve of the perimeter wall. I gunned the engine for the straightaway, letting the Veyron find her feet, gratified by the din we were making. Hopefully the pack would hear it and be drawn further in. As we came around the corner, I eased off the accelerator and crept along the side of the building until the gate came into view.

Hot damn; it was partly open, with one of the wrought-iron gates retracted back from the path. From the carnage evident inside the control booths, there had been a firefight before the guards were killed. Someone must have hit one of the opening mechanisms, maybe in a bid to escape. It looked like a tight fit, but there was no way I was getting out of the car if I could avoid it. I doubted we had more than five minutes before the dogs realized the girl wasn't in the mansion and traced her scent to the garage.

I coasted forward, scanning the grounds for any hint of movement, but nothing stirred.

"Hang on," I muttered and floored it. We roared up the path, hurtling the last hundred yards. Sparks exploded along the passenger side as the Bugatti scraped against the other arm of the gate, then we were flying up the winding road, slaloming back and forth as we slammed around the curves. Twice I nearly sent us off into a ditch, but the low-slung chassis and sure-footed wheels kept us on the road until we surged onto the crest of the hill. I brought the Bugatti to a bone-jarring stop, then hopped out and scrambled through the high grass to the cargo van. Yanking the doors open, I hauled out my other equipment bag and unzipped it.

By the time I was running back onto the road, the girl was standing by the open passenger door of the Bugatti.

"What's happening?" she called out.

"Get back in the car!" I shouted, hoisting Big Bertha's fifty-five-pound weight onto my shoulder. At the crest of the hill, I bent to one knee and lined the center of the mansion up with the launch tube's optical sight. A mile down the slope, flickering shadows were still racing past the brightly lit windows on the second floor.

I was too winded to say something pithy; too bad, really, since I was never going to get a second chance. Instead, I held my breath, wished luck from whatever gods might be out there, and squeezed the trigger. The recoil blast from the rocket-propelled grenade launcher knocked me to the dirt as the projectile streaked out. I'd aimed slightly high, trusting the ballistic arc to carry the explosive down a few degrees to target. As I pushed myself up, I saw a puff of smoke as the initial charge went off against the front of the building above the balcony. An instant later, the second, shaped charge detonated, blasting in a section of the wall.

Hell's bells, I'd have sworn the gas would've—

WHOOMP!

For a moment, the horizon seemed to turn white with the glare of the midday sun. Then a puff of warm air lifted me off my feet just as the tremendous roar of the explosion squished my ears into my skull. I had a second to think that I really should've trusted myself more before I landed against the Bugatti's rear window hard enough to splinter the glass.

It's going to be a bitch selling this thing if I keep taking it apart piece by piece, I thought dazedly, and then slid to the ground when my limbs wouldn't do anything more than flop around me like useless noodles. Somehow I kept from passing out. When I was able to force my feet under me again, the air was full of embers, drifting down around me in a fiery rain. Ahead, a massive column of black smoke blotted out the stars.

I reeled to the crest of the hill. The mansion—or, more precisely, what was left of it—was blazing like a bonfire, and the conflagration had already spread to the grounds and surrounding woods. I stood there, leaning with my hands on my knees, and counted to sixty. Nothing emerged.

Even a mile from the inferno, the atmosphere reeked of smoke. When I started coughing, the pain in my ribs made me sick to my stomach. At some point during the various times I'd been used as a living piñata tonight,

The room was plainly furnished, but the bed was where it needed to be, which was good, and the bathroom was where it needed to be, which was even better. After making good on my prediction of retching, I splashed my face in the sink and looked in the mirror.

Gods below, I was in bad shape. My face was swollen along one cheek with a mass of bruises, tender to the touch. When I was able to drag off the duster and vest with my good hand, I could see that the skin of my left arm was puffy and purple all the way up to my shoulder. The puncture marks from the dog's teeth looked black and deep, clotted with dark blood, but at least they'd stopped bleeding. It took me five more minutes to undo the clasps of my arm brace. When I did, the rush of returning circulation was agony.

I knew I needed to dress the wounds properly. I needed to do half a dozen things. But I didn't care anymore. Every breath was an effort. I tottered to the bed and fell into its embrace like it was an open grave.

When I woke, I felt warm and drowsy, and wonderfully at peace. It was so much like being pleasantly drunk, I spent a few minutes trying to remember what I'd been downing the night before so I could run out and get some more of it. The last surviving serpent still hissed and slithered around my cheeks, first one and then the other, tickling my skin as though it were trying to be everywhere at once. I took in a deep, easy breath, thrilled by the marvelous feeling of the air filling my lungs. Then the events of the evening suddenly came back to me.

What the hell —?

I bolted upright, then winced, expecting to feel the pain in my ribs and skull come rushing back. But there was nothing, no discomfort, zip. I didn't have an ache or pain throughout my entire body. My left arm was pristine. I raised my left hand and flexed it before me as though I had never seen it before. Shaking my head in disbelief, I went into the bathroom and confronted the mirror.

The angry black-and-blue mottling along my arm and shoulder was gone, replaced by a healthy pink hue. The puncture marks in my bicep were faded to pale scars. Even my cheeks matched each other again. And on my head . . .

My breath whistled out from between my teeth in shock and alarm. Not one lingering survivor but scores of snakes were piled on top of my head, twining around themselves in intricate loops, luxuriating in the warmth of my skin and each other. I'd never seen so many mature ones there before, their olive-and-emerald bands undulating with a languid grace that resembled something like an intricate ballet dance. Tiny forked tongues tasted the air, fanged jaws yawned. They actually seemed . . . happy.

But they shouldn't have been there at all. I should have been alone, goddammit, *alone*. I should have been free, even if it was only for a little while—

No healer could have done this. No healer would have dared to even try.

Benny wouldn't have told anyone else I was here. And that just left . . .

Her.

In an instant, I was out the door, storming down the hall in my bare feet, all my amazement and horror transmuted into fury. I found the girl just inside an open doorway a few rooms away, sitting at a table picking through a small red-and-gold cardboard box.

"*You—!*" I snarled.

"Kyra?" The idiot actually smiled toward me. "Benny brought me this marvelous food. It's called popcorn—"

I slapped the proffered box aside and pinioned her arms, yanking her to her feet.

"What did you do to me?" I shouted, shaking her like a rag doll. "What the hell did you *do*?"

"You were hurt," the girl said, the delight on her face collapsing. "Part of you was dying—"

"*They're not part of me!*" I howled, throwing her down to the carpet. I was trembling with anger and revulsion. If I'd had my knives, I might

104

have gutted her like a fish. But I'd lost one back at the mansion and the others were still in my duster. As it was, I had to settle for standing over her crumpled form, shaking my fist down at her. "They're foul, disgusting—" My voice cracked. I wanted to kick her and kick her until I had expelled all the vitriol inside me. "You shouldn't have done that! You had no right—!" *No right to touch me,* I wanted to say. But the words jammed in my throat.

"I don't understand . . ." The girl's blind eyes were bright with tears. "Why are you angry with me?"

The sight of her starting to cry just stung me to greater outrage. My knotted hands shook with the need for violence. Panting hugely, I swung away from her and stalked back to my room. My duster was nowhere to be found, so I yanked a white T-shirt I found in the closet down over my head and shoved my feet into my boots. As I went up the sloped hall, shrugging a hooded satin team jacket on, the giant form of Benny approached, fuzzy red mask in hand.

"Kyra," he called. "It's going to get busy soon. We have a game—"

"Not now, Benny," I said. When he heard the snakes hiss under my hood, he shrank back against the wall and let me pass.

I needed some fresh air. But when I pushed through the last door to the outside, I stopped dead in my tracks. To my astonishment, the parking lots were jammed with cars beeping and crawling about, crowds of people pouring in from all sides along the walkways and parking lanes.

What the hell? The team wasn't playing until tonight. But the setting sun's glare was nearly level with the trees over Garfield Park. I glanced at my watch and saw that it was already a quarter past six. I'd slept the whole day away.

A healing sleep. I hadn't gone through one of those since that debacle in Bahrain, over a decade ago. Not since . . .

Too many people. I avoided crowds even when I was by myself; being up to my elbows with thousands of people with a nest of snakes sprouting from my skull was a sure-fire recipe for someone coming down with a severe case of Unexpected Envenoming Syndrome. Noticing a clump of decorative bushes out of the way on the narrow strip of grass above the loading bay, I made for it and sat down away from the throng.

I was still shaking from reaction. To work that level of healing, the girl would have had to go deep, *way* deep, and that was someplace I didn't let anyone go, not after Bahrain. She had no right to do that without my permission. I had no idea what she had seen or learned forging that kind of psychic bond between us. What her mother had done was bad enough, but that had been an all-out attack, the desperate gambit of a dying woman. I could almost respect that. But what the girl had done was like waking up to find someone had invaded your home while you were asleep. That was upsetting enough on its own.

The fact that the snakes were back—and back in force, no less—was worse; though as I sat there on the cool grass, I had to admit that if the alternative had been dying, I would have at least been willing to flip a coin on the issue. And I'd surely pissed someone off last night, blowing their personal kennel back to Hell. Having the Gaze back up to full power right now might not be the worst thing in the world, at least until I'd figured out what I'd stirred up.

No, what was really twisting my guts into knots now was what the girl had said, last night and again tonight. Sure, I knew the snakes were attached to me; it had never required more than a trip to the bathroom mirror to see that I was a freak, even among freaks. But I'd always been able to deal with it by treating it like it was a condition I had, something that was separate from who I was. I used what I had to, but it wasn't me, not really.

The girl had spent hours walking in my head, poking into the nooks and crannies of my mind, my soul. The way she had said "a part of you" made me shiver. I didn't want to think about it. And I couldn't stop thinking about it.

The sun sank below the horizon, dipping the parking lot in night. It was getting too cold to sit here on the ground with the breeze picking up. I could hear the muffled roar of the crowd, felt the vibration under my crossed legs. The game was under way. It was time to get back. But I still didn't want to see her. Maybe I was still angry. Maybe I just didn't want to talk to her yet about what had gone down last night. So when a van pulled up to the loading bay and the driver lingered at the open rear doors of his vehicle to light up, I got to my feet and made my way down to him.

"Hey," I called, pulling the drawstrings of my hood a little tighter. The snakes had begun hissing in irritation, probably due to the smoke. See? Separate.

The guy started when he saw me, but I held up my palms. "I'm not here to bust your stones, man. Spare a smoke for a lady?"

He hesitated. Not a handsome guy: His eyes were dark and somehow overlarge for his head, which made me think of a peanut. And someone had forgotten to tell him that combing a tuft of ruddy hair back from a receding hairline and growing out your straggly chin hairs was not a winning combination. He probably wasn't used to being approached by a young woman with a pulse.

I worked up a winning smile, and that seemed to do the trick. "Here," he said, rummaging through his coverall's pockets until he dug out a pack. With what seemed like almost too much care, he tapped a cigarette out. He had large, awkward fingers, and his hands trembled slightly as he extended it to me.

"Thanks," I said, leaning in to the proffered Bic to light up. The flame threw a confused shadow against the van's doors behind my benefactor, which faded as he doused it. I took a moment to enjoy the sensation of dousing my heretofore pristine lungs with a heady dose. "Got a name?"

The dark eyes blinked and batted like telephoto lenses on a fashion photographer's camera. Brother, was this guy tense. "Martin," he said with a nervous grin, exposing rows of crooked, stained teeth. "Just like it says on the van."

I glanced at the crimson stenciling on the side: "MARTIN AXWAR JANITORIAL: We Leave Nothing Behind!" Under the letters there was a garishly painted logo of a snarling lion pushing a cleaning cart with its paws through a pile of garbage that vanished in his wake.

"Cute," I said.

"Most people call me Marty, though," he was saying, building on his initial theme. I'd seen more attractive smiles on hobgoblins. But he'd given to a friend in need, as the old saying went, so I nodded and said, "I'm Sally."

For some reason, this struck him as funny, and he tittered, then ducked his head as though embarrassed.

Hoo boy. I took another drag. I hadn't recognized the brand, and there was an unfamiliar aftertaste that reminded me unpleasantly of the cheap shit they sell in the stalls of Cairo. I doubted "Marty" here had ever been within five thousand miles of Egypt, though. Oh well; beggars can't be choosers, right?

"Sure smells good out tonight, don't it?" he said, sniffing the air.

Unlike my eyesight, I don't have a particularly good olfactory sense. And if this was his best pickup line, it needed work. I grimaced a general agreement, then concentrated on finishing my cigarette as fast as humanly possible.

That furtive grin was starting to get on my nerves. There was a quality like expectation in it. Maybe he was thinking he'd get lucky tonight.

"Sorry, Marty," I decided to say, but what came out of my mouth instead was "Nhlf."

Okay, that was . . . odd. I smiled to reassure my geeky friend, but the muscles of my face felt suddenly numb. And now the blazing white roof of the stadium was tilting to one side.

I didn't even feel my temple smack against the concrete. But then I was on the ground, with my limbs splayed out around me. My head was filling with mist.

"Whfuh," I mumbled and then he'd grabbed me by my feet and was dragging me into the back of his van. I heard more than felt him drop me roughly on top of a loose pile of tools and equipment.

Seriously? I mean, are you friggin' kidding me? I hit on a guy to get one lousy cigarette and he's going to turn out to be some sort of stalker type? He had to be the only one in the Chicago area who came to a game to do his dirty work. On another night, it might have been funny.

But there was nothing amusing about the efficient way he was tying my ankles and wrists together with zip ties. This guy wasn't an amateur; he'd done this before and knew what he was doing. Great; we were moving into serial killer territory here.

Hunched down like a grinning gargoyle, he sniffed me, seeming to savor some secret scent in the air.

"Ooh, I was right," he tittered, hopping up and down. "She's all over you.... Golden girl, child of light, child I've come to claim tonight! And a bonus for Marty, my very own, a Snake-Charmed one! But mind her pets ... remember. They'll need to be plucked off, one by one; yes, they will. Then we'll play ... we'll play for a long time!"

He withdrew. For a minute, I could hear him fumbling about. Then he came back into view, brandishing a long-handled pair of cable cutters. His hands were now covered by heavy leather gloves.

He was going to snip the snakes off my head, one at a time.

I could feel them whipping about under my hood, struggling to get free of their confinement. They were picking up on my panic and didn't seem to share in my paralysis. If he came close enough ...

But Marty wasn't as dumb as he looked. Careful to keep his legs away, he extended the cable cutters toward my hood, prodding the edge, trying to draw one out. I tried to focus my concentration, but my vision was swimming and I couldn't pull it together. I sensed one of the serpents wriggling its head out—

And a loud beeping sound filled the air. Scowling, Marty stepped back and consulted his wristwatch.

"Yes, yes," he muttered, annoyed. "Must stay on schedule, mustn't be late. ... Get your dinner now, play with it later." Tossing the cutters aside, he popped open the van doors again, hopped out, then dragged his cart to the ground. Out of the corner of my eye, I saw him affix it with an industrial-size blue canvas bag. "We'll have a golden surprise inside when we come back," he chortled, patting it. Then the doors slammed shut.

Well, I thought in disgust, this was a fine kettle of fish. If I could just get some feeling back in my hands, my nails would make short work of the zip ties. But I didn't know what he'd laced the cig with, so I couldn't even guess how long it would take to metabolize it. If it was PCP or some other dissociative anesthetic, it could take hours.

Who the hell was this guy? He obviously knew I was a gorgon; it seemed he'd known from the moment he saw me. And the snakes had cued on the fact that there was something wrong about him from the start too. I'd thought it was the smoke they were reacting to with such sullen hostility, but now I wasn't so sure.

I'd picked a helluva time to ignore them.

And the "golden girl" thing...

Oh, crap. Stephanie.

Marty wasn't just here looking for opportunity. He'd been sent, probably by whoever had sent the damn dogs to the mansion last night. He must be hunting for the girl right now.

But this was a safe house, goddammit; neutral territory. No Mythic in its right mind would break that sacred trust by going on a job here. Marty would have to be out of his...

Yup.

At least he wouldn't get far. Unless he was recognized by the spell that warded the door, he could scratch and sniff all day, but the girl would be safe so long as she stayed inside the sanctum. If I could just get loose before he realized that, I'd pin him in a dead end and make the world's ugliest statue out of him.

Which made snapping out of this drug-induced haze Job Number One. Only it was all I could do to even focus my eyes on one spot inside the dim van. My arms and legs remained stubbornly unresponsive. Only the snakes were mobile, coiling around each other in restless agitation. Too bad my "pets" couldn't do more than just flop there, irritating the bejeezus out of me. I mean, Lassie or a Saint Bernard could've at least barked for help or sucked the poison out of me or something...

Poison.

My breath shuddered out of my lungs. I didn't know if that could work. Part of me didn't know if I *wanted* it to work. I'd never consciously willed them to do anything. I'd spent as much time as possible every day of my life not thinking about them.

But if . . . if she was right . . .

Uh, hey, I said uncertainly. You . . . guys. If you can hear me, how about a little help here?

There was no response. That was almost a relief. I wasn't sure what would have been worse: finding out the snakes could actually hear me or realizing I was talking to myself—

A small wedge-shaped head slid past my right eye, over my cheek. Another came down past my left eye. What were they doing—?

I felt the coils tense and had an instant to realize what it meant. Then the snakes struck, sinking their fangs into my neck just above the breast bone. I couldn't feel the strikes through the numbness wrapped over me, but I felt the pressure of their heads against me as they writhed and pulsated.

A burning warmth began in the base of my throat. It quickly spread, sending tendrils into my face, my head. At the same time, I felt a tingling in my toes and fingers. Then pain slammed into me with the force of a freight train.

For half a minute, my heart pounded so hard I thought I was going into cardiac arrest. Then, like a bubble popping, the pain vanished. Gasping, I realized I could feel everything again. My head was clear.

Hissing contentedly, the snakes withdrew back into my hood.

I wasn't exactly sure what they'd done, but I didn't waste time wondering about it. Marty hadn't bothered to tie my hands behind my back. All I had to do was use the razor-like sharpness of my nails to—

Oh, for Hecate's sake. I couldn't find one finger that I hadn't chewed down to the quick. Why did all my bad habits always come back to kick me in the ass?

I cast around the gloom of the van for something I could use, and my gaze fell upon the discarded cable cutters. A few tries to get the angle right, and I was free.

I wasn't sure how long I'd been in the van. But as I ran back down the halls toward the lower level of the sanctum, I could hear the muffled roar of the crowd and the blare of the buzzer. The game was still going on overhead.

And there was Benny, coming down an adjoining flight of steps. I was never so glad to see the big dummy in my life.

"Benny!" I said. "We've got trouble—"

"Kyra!" he called. "I ducked out for a minute to see if I could find you. You can still catch the fourth period if you get up there. You should've seen me at the halftime show! I'll bet your cousin loved it—"

What the hell was he talking about? Couldn't he shut up for one second? "Benny, listen," I said. "There's some lunatic here, hunting—" I stopped. "What do you mean, 'my cousin?'"

"Stephanie," Benny answered. He waved a fuzzy red paw over his head. "You told me to show her the sights, so I put her in one of the theater boxes on the Club Suite level. A full buffet spread, though all she keeps asking for is popcorn. You can join her—"

I reached up and seized him by the horns. "What are you saying?" I asked, horrified. "She's not in the sanctum?"

Benny recoiled. "No. . . . Why should she be? You said—"

Gods! And the Agency wondered why I would never agree to take a partner on assignments. "Someone's hunting her, Benny!" I shouted at the big dumb fake cow eyes. "Some—some *thing* that can smell her out! She's only safe if he can't get to her!"

"But no one would do that here—"

"This guy would. He *is*! He's some sort of psycho." I forced myself to take a deep breath. "Where is she? Where did you put her?"

"Penthouse level, west side. Suite 68."

I took off at a dead run. The Penthouse level was several floors up. I found an elevator and stabbed the button for the top floor, marked in red. My hands fell to check that my clips were full—

Guns. I had no guns. Nothing.

Great! The door chimed. I came out of the car and found myself on a busy concourse, with knots of people moving to and fro among the concession stands. Neon signs blinked and flashed all around, and the subdued tumult of the crowd poured in from the inner stadium entrances. I hugged my hood tighter and followed the numbers until I came to an executive suite with the number 68 in gilt tracing on the door.

There was no time for subtlety. But I couldn't just blunder in; my best weapon right now was still my Gaze, and to use that, I couldn't have spectators. So I turned the doorknob carefully and slipped inside without a sound.

Geez. A cozy room spread out before me, furnished with black leather armchairs and a sofa around a center table laden with fruits and snacks. Granite countertops for the wet bar and liquor cabinets. Benny had never set *me* up in one of these—

Sudden movement on the other side of the food and drinks rail where a row of black padded seats looked down on the arena. I had just a glimpse of two bare feet sliding upside down out of sight into an enormous blue canvas bag.

"Stephanie!"

"Kyra!" cried the girl's muffled voice, and it was scary how the word cut into me like a blade.

Marty reared up from the other side of the rail. If I'd had one of my Glocks, I could have put a bullet in the center of that grinning face and ended the matter right there. As it was, I needed to close with him to hit him with my Gaze. I rushed forward then skidded to a stop as something rose from behind Marty's head: a long, segmented tail that bristled with curved quills.

What in the name of—

113

The tail quivered, like a dog shaking its head, and suddenly the air was filled with spikes flying at my face. I dove to the carpet and they streaked over my head, shattering the bottles of booze on the wet bar and showering me with glass and Scotch whiskey.

Manticore!

Damn it, how could I have been so dense? If I'd picked up earlier on the fact that he was a Mythic, I wouldn't be in this mess. But I'd been distracted by the business with Stephanie, and by my need for a quick cigarette to calm my nerves. I guess smoking really was hazardous to your health.

I was in for a fight here. Unless . . .

"Marty!" I shouted from the cover of the onyx table. "Truce! We don't have to do this! Come on, man; let's make a deal!" All I'd need was to get closer . . .

"Not listening to her," said the manticore in a singsong voice. "Don't talk to your dinner, never talk . . ."

I really hated this guy. But unless he was allergic to elegant fruit displays, I was short on weapons to use. I peeked out from my shield and saw that he was busy loading the canvas bag into his cart. The tail had dipped out of sight.

This might be my only shot. I gripped two of the table's legs and brought it up with me, surging forward, hoping to pin him against the side wall for just an instant.

But the corner of the heavy table caught the edge of one of the spectator seats, sending me off balance and spoiling my charge. The manticore seized the table in his overlarge hands and lifted it over the rail, scooping me up with it like a sack of potatoes. I had a confused impression of the crowd far below me, and then I was plummeting headfirst out into open space.

CHAPTER 7

I threw one leg back and caught the edge of the glass safety rail with my trailing boot, hooking onto it as I fell. The jolt sent my body in a tight arc back to the balcony. I saw the bowed wall rushing up and crossed my arms over my face.

Ow! Not entirely successful.

And now my boot was slipping off the rail. My fingers scrabbled up past my swaying body and found tiny purchases in the lip at the base of the glass partition. I'd bought myself a few seconds, but there was no way I could haul myself up while hanging upside down.

That's when the screaming started. It took a second to realize it wasn't coming from me. I twisted my head down. Some thirty feet below me, a woman had been spattered with food debris from the flipped-over table. She didn't look hurt, so why the hell was she shrieking like her hair was on fire? She was even saying the word "hair" as she looked up—

Oh dear.

My hood had come partly off my head as I fell. Half a dozen of the serpents were lolling out over my right temple, writhing angrily at the sea of light and noise washing over them. As I twisted, I saw hundreds of cell phone flashes going off all around in the throng below.

If I was lucky, I thought, Marty the manticore would take this moment to finish me off with a deft push. Then I felt fingers seizing me around the ankle.

"I didn't mean it—!" I shouted to the stupid gods, then felt myself plucked off the rail and lifted bodily back into the executive suite.

"Cover yourself up!" said Benny, righting me with his other hand. "People can see you!"

"I know, I KNOW!" I snapped, throwing my hood on and scrambling up the steps to get out of sight. Benny stayed where he was, waving back to the crowd. He made an exaggerated kick after me, then clasped his hands together and pumped them in mock triumph. There was a spattering of uncertain clapping. Benny bowed and retreated to where I stood by the doorway.

"I'm sorry," I said, and meant it. "It was an accident—"

"I'll deal with it," he said. "Lucky we're playing Orlando tonight. What happened here? Where's Stephanie?"

Stephanie. Damn it, damn it, damn it. I threw open the door and dashed onto the concourse. People clotted the curved hallway in both directions. I stood on my tiptoes, searching for that crown of ruddy hair but couldn't find it.

Benny was at my elbow.

"He took her," I panted. "A manticore. He has her in a blue bag in his cleaning cart."

"Cleaning cart?"

"He's dressed like a janitor." I stopped, seizing Benny's arm. For the first time in our history together, he was too distracted to flinch. "He *is* a janitor. Martin Axwar Janitorial. His van's backed up to the loading bay. Get Security down there and we can cut him off. Hurry!"

116

Benny nodded and trotted over to a security guard. After a few seconds, the man started talking rapidly into his walkie-talkie. I started to run for the elevator, but Benny caught me by the arm.

"Stop," I said, struggling against his grip. "What the hell are you doing?"

"Kyra." Benny's voice was low but deep enough to cut through the din. "You've got to get out of sight. Too many people saw you back there. And Security will report the alert to the Chicago PD. They'll be here in minutes."

"But—"

Benny shook my arm, hard. Sometime you forget a minotaur's strength. "You're a wanted fugitive, remember? You can't be caught here. Come on. We'll find the manticore. He won't get away."

"Got away?" I shouted nearly two hours later. "What do you mean he got away?"

Benny put his paw over the phone, frowning at me until I threw up my hands in disgust and stormed away from his desk. "Thank you, Sergeant. Please keep us informed. Yes, we'll call you if we find anything on our end. Thank you again." He hung up.

"Kyra. . . . They'll keep looking. But they had all the exits watched within half a minute of my alert. Nobody matching your description came through, certainly no one with a cleaning cart or a blue body bag."

"Then he's still here," I snapped. "We have to keep searching."

"We will. Center security and the Chicago Police units have been checking the place from top to bottom. I've had my own staff check the lower level and the safe-house chambers, in case he somehow got access there. So far, there's no sign of him."

"This is insane!" I said. "What about the truck?"

"It's still there," said Benny. Sitting at his desk in an administrative office secreted away on the penthouse level, he had resumed scrolling through the security camera feeds, watching three monitor screens at once. "He hasn't gone back to it. See?"

I came over. The black-and-white video showed a side view of the vehicle, still stationary by the loading dock. Figures in stadium security jackets were moving around it while uniformed officers walked back and forth.

"He'll never go for it with all that traffic," I muttered. "They should pull back."

"Maybe." Benny scrubbed at his tufted chin and squinted at the lettering on the van. "Huh. 'Martin Axwar.'"

"Yeah? So what?"

Benny shrugged. "'*Martyaxwar*' is the Middle Persian name for a manticore. It means 'Eater of Man.' Kind of obvious, really."

"Well, forgive me for not being up on my dead languages!" I flared. "Are you saying this is my fault?"

Benny blinked at me. "What are you talking about? How could this be your fault?"

"Never mind." I stalked back to the tinted plexiglass windows that overlooked one side of the vast parking lot. Delayed by the additional security measures, people were still leaving the Center. I stared down at the shifting sea of moving figures. Any one of them could be him, bobbing away with her on the human tide.

I didn't like feeling helpless like this. I was angry and scared at the same time. And it was her fault. If Rougnagne hadn't forced me to make that damn promise, I'd already be out of this burg, with three hundred thousand dollars to drink my cares away. Instead I was here, hiding from the cops, and worried about a kid I should have never even met. It wasn't fair.

"Benny . . . ever hear of something called a 'soul-lock'?"

Benny's ghost reflection in the glass shook its horned head. "No. What is it?"

"Forget it." I needed to get free of this deal, preferably before it got me killed. But I'd have to keep the girl from being manticore chow first.

Think, Kyra. Manticores. . . . "What do you know about manticores?" I said, changing tacks.

"Not much," Benny admitted. "They're relatively rare. Pretty scuzzy types. I never thought to see one, really. I can't believe it would hunt here." He cocked his head. "Why would it be after your cousin?"

I blew out my breath. "She's not my cousin, okay? I just said that to shut you up."

Maybe I'd hoped he'd take offense and go back to his search. But Benny was bullish on the subject. "She's not of your blood?"

"Does she look anything like me?" I drawled, waving my hand at my hooded head. "She's blonde and beautiful and I'm—whatever."

"Then why was she with you?" Benny persisted.

Because I don't want my head to explode or my blood to boil or whatever else happens when you break a promise you made during a soul-lock, I thought. But outwardly I just shrugged. "It's . . . complicated."

"Do you—?"

"Hello!" I said, coming over. "'It's complicated' is girl-speak for 'drop it,' okay? Now why don't you spend a little more time looking at those screens and a little less time hassling me? I can't believe you still can't find any footage showing where he went."

Now it was Benny's turn to become defensive. "Ninety-nine percent of the Center is under constant security surveillance," he huffed. "This manticore of yours couldn't have stumbled into a better-protected sports arena."

He didn't stumble, I wanted to say. *He came here on purpose.* But that was more sharing than I was in the mood for. And though he had been caught off guard by my approach, "Marty" hadn't seemed truly surprised about my being with the girl. I mulled that over for a minute, not liking the implications. At the mansion, the *laelapi* had come for the girl. But they hadn't been expecting me. That had given me a tactical advantage. But not only had they recovered from that loss, they had tracked her here in less than a day, and anticipated or figured out who was with her.

How?

And why? What made her so damned important? She sensed things, maybe even future things. So there was value there. But there were many avenues to go down if you wanted oracular help, even in the Windy City. Magdalina wasn't the only witch for hire. Probably half the fortune tellers and palm readers in Chicago had at least some smattering of real psychic ability if you dug deep enough. The girl also had prodigious healing power, if what she'd done to me was any evidence. Value there too.

But not enough to warrant this level of interest. And these were abilities that made you worth catching and keeping, not exterminating. But instead of trying to preserve her, someone had issued a death notice for this kid and was pulling out all the stops to see that it was served.

Why?

Too many questions. I needed some answers. If the girl bit it before I could find her . . .

Scratching at the back of my hand in restless agitation, I went over to Benny, who was still dutifully following the carrot at the end of the plow. I tapped on his skull to signal I wanted his attention.

"Ninety-nine percent," I said to him. "Why did you say that? Why not a hundred percent?"

Benny shrugged. "You're not going to cover everything. You know, areas where no one has access."

"Such as?"

"Ventilation shafts, ductwork, stuff like that. The roof."

"You can get on the roof?"

"No," said Benny with a trace of asperity. "That's what I'm saying. You can't. Not without an access code or a sledgehammer to break down the door. And you'd have to be crazy to try; it's slippery even on a night without wind. Tonight . . ."

"This guy's strong enough and crazy enough to try," I said. "Send someone up to check it out."

Half an hour later, I was pulled out of my mordant reflections by a knock on the door. Benny donned his mask and went to answer it. A moment later, he summoned me out of hiding.

"This is Diego," he said, gesturing to a wiry fellow wearing a Security jacket. "He's one of my people."

When he saw me, Diego blanched and crossed himself. But I was more interested in the cleaning cart he'd brought with him. It was definitely the same one, but now—

"The bag," I said. "Where's the blue bag?"

"No bag," said the man. "We only found this, on the other side of the door, up on the roof." He hesitated, trying to look at me without meeting my eyes. "A little farther, we found this." He held up a small trash bag. Heart pounding, I grabbed it and spilled the contents onto the carpet.

At first I thought it was just a jumble of tattered plastic shreds. Then I bent for a closer look.

Skin. *Ew.*

"Is that—?" began Benny.

"Yup." I couldn't afford to be squeamish. Pulling the pile apart, I found a familiar, ugly face staring back at me, slack-jawed and hollow-eyed. An improvement, really. I breathed a small sigh of relief; at least it wasn't her. I was still in the running.

Marty had gone straight to the roof and then stopped to shed his skin. Why? To pass himself off as someone else? But unless he could do the same thing for Stephanie, he would still have been stuck with carting around a conspicuous blue bag. So what had he gained by transforming . . . ?

The answer took another few minutes of taffy-pulling to produce. Two ragged, vertical rips in what must formerly have been the skin of the upper back. I straightened up, wiping my hands on the sides of my pants. "He molted," I said in clenched dismay. "Grew himself a pair of wings and flew off with her. No wonder you didn't catch him." It was the best apology I could muster.

I went to the window and pressed my forehead against the cool glass. Screwed; I was royally screwed here. The tittering maniac could be anywhere by now.

"Kyra . . ." Benny had come up quietly to stand behind me. One hand rested lightly, tentatively, on my shoulder. "I'm so sorry."

I have this habit of taking a tender moment and turning it into something bad with a snide remark. Maybe you've noticed. But this time I didn't have the heart for it. So I just patted the fuzzy red paw. "Thanks, Benny."

So that was that. Game over. I wondered what it would feel like, when the girl's death triggered my own. In my time, I'd been beaten, shot, stabbed, bitten, and burned. I'd nearly died five or six times. It was something I had learned to accept. But somehow, having to just sit and wait for it, not knowing how or when it was going to happen, made it more terrible to contemplate. Maybe my heart would just seize up. I'd feel that moment of intense, squeezing pressure, an icy chill, then nothing. Maybe I'd get no warning at all, no chance for a last word, or curse, or regret. Just . . . nothing.

And Benny would be the only witness I got. Not even a mourner, really; more like the guy who had to clean up after the funeral, moving decorously if disinterestedly through the debris, gathering up the mess. After, would anyone even notice? If they did, would there be anything besides relief? Ding dong, the bitch is dead . . .

I cleared my throat. "Hey, uh, Benny," I said, "that thing we were talking about before. About . . . how it works when I, you know,"—I did his little freezing gesture—"zap someone. Is that what . . . what the other Mythic think? That it could just happen? Is that why they've always . . . you know." *Hated my guts. Treated me like a leper. Whatever.*

Benny's dim reflection moved to stand next to mine.

"You make them afraid," he murmured. "To them, you're not just *like* one of the old legends. You *are* the legend. They don't know what you might do. And, well . . . you haven't exactly been . . . warm to most of them." He scrubbed at the hair on the back of his tree trunk–sized neck, scuffed a hoof on the carpet. "Any of them, really."

Present company included. He didn't need to say it; it just hung there between us.

I tried to clear my throat again. Damn sinuses. "Well…do me a favor, okay?"

"What?"

"Just—" I hesitated, then forced the words out. "If anyone asks…later, tell them…what I told you. That I wouldn't have just done that. Not for no reason."

Benny turned toward me, arms folded across his massive breast. "Why don't you tell them yourself?" he said.

Because that's likely to require a Ouija board and the willingness to summon a gorgon out of her grave, I thought. But there was no point in saying that. As a motivational speaker, Benny could use some work on his delivery. Still, what he'd said had struck a spark in the cooling embers of my spirit. It had reminded me of the basic truth of my existence: I was a predator, not prey. I didn't do helpless.

And I owed Marty. Big time. While there was still a chance—any kind of chance—I could get in a little payback, I was sure as hell going to take it.

Below, the lot was emptying out. Soon the Center would be as quiet as it got. I needed to get out of here, do something, anything.

I turned away from the window. "Call off the search," I said. "Tell them we found the girl, that it was just a misunderstanding. Whatever you need to. Just clear me a path." God help anyone that got in my way tonight.

"Where are you going?"

"To go make someone else afraid."

It was a good speech. But if I was going to give it teeth, I'd need help.

Enter my electronic genie. "Phil."

123

Phil's tone in my earpiece was characteristically anxious. "Kyra! Where have you been? What happened last night? It's all over the news!"

"What is?"

"The fire! The explosion! I thought you'd been killed! Are you okay? They didn't get the fire under control until late this morning. Forty acres burned, Rougnagne's mansion gutted down to the foundations. Everything lost."

Not everything, I thought with grim satisfaction, patting the Veyron's wheel as we sped along Edens Expressway West. Benny had been kind enough to fit me with diplomatic plates. He'd even had the blood scoured out of my duster and dry-cleaned it for me. I shook my head mentally. It had been a real night of firsts for Benny and me.

"I'm fine," I said. "I've just had my phone off. Listen, Phil. Rougnagne's dead, but I've, uh, developed a small complication."

"What do you mean? What kind of complication?"

The fatal kind, I thought, if I couldn't catch a break soon.

"Well, before I removed the mark, I . . . kind of agreed to look after her daughter for a bit."

"You *what?*" squeaked Phil like an enraged mouse. "What daughter?"

That's what I said, I nearly retorted. But Phil couldn't have known of this one. Rougnagne had been too careful for that.

"Her daughter. She'd been hiding her for fifteen years." Fifteen minus two days, technically. And if she could make it one more, I'd be in the clear. But I had a bad feeling Marty was going to start feeling peckish soon, if he wasn't already. "Anyway, the daughter's sort of in trouble. Last night, a pack of *laelapi* came for her at the mansion, and I had to blow the place up to get rid of them. I took her with me to the safe house, but she's been kidnapped by a manticore. So I need your help to find her. Him. Them."

Normally I could have enjoyed the sound of Phil's sputtering for a whole minute before interrupting. But I was on the clock tonight. "Time's a factor here, Phil. You gonna help me or what?"

"Why—why did you . . . why would you . . ."

"We'll go into that later, okay? Right now, I need you to run down everything you can on Martin Axwar, of Martin Axwar Janitorial, out of Chicago."

"*Martyaxwar*? Hey, that's actually Middle Persian for—"

"Yeah, yeah, I know," I snapped. Geez, was everybody up on ancient Middle Eastern nomenclature but me? "Save the history. Where can I find this guy?"

"Okay, hold on. . . ." The blessed sound of soft, rapid tapping began. My exit for the storage facility I kept outside the city was coming up. I switched to the right lane without signaling, ignoring the honking umbrage of a slowpoke. Yeah, I could get used to having diplo plates.

"All right," said Phil. "Martin Axwar Janitorial. They have a business listing off Fullerton Avenue, in Bucktown. Twelve miles east of your current position."

I knew that area. I could hit my storage locker and be there in twenty minutes. Still . . .

"Run that address," I said. "Any other listings for it?"

"Checking. Hmm. Yes, there's at least four businesses that also have that same address."

Damn! "It's a front," I fumed. "Marty just uses that address to look like a legit business. There's nothing there."

Tappity tap tap. "Correct. Phone tracking data indicates an interplex router is being used to transfer calls from his business number to other locations. And there's no record of any power or utilities bills going to that address."

So . . . crazy but not stupid. I eased the Veyron onto Oakton Street. "What about Axwar himself? Any residential or commercial addresses for him?"

"N-n-n-nope. Nada. Guy covers his tracks."

No shit. I slapped the steering wheel in frustration. I was so going to kill this guy. "What do you know about manticores?"

"Aside from their Persian name? Lots. Ask away."

I pulled down the side street to the facility and keyed in my passcode at the automated gate. Over at the booth, the guard barely glanced up from the television he was watching. I still tugged the black beret I'd borrowed down lower on my forehead. It was lined with warm, fuzzy felt, so the snakes were comfy and quiet. I needed them to stay that way for now. "I don't know! Tell me everything."

"Well, let's see: manticore basics. Head of a man, body of a lion. Tail equipped with poisonous spikes, which can be fired at prey from both an erect and a four-legged stance. Called 'Man Eater' by the Persians; they like to trick their prey into coming close and then devour them whole, flesh and bones and clothes, leaving nothing behind. Variations exist, with some having horns or even wings—"

"That's this one," I interrupted. I parked in front of my locker and jumped out. "What do they do once they capture a victim?"

"Hmmm . . . manticores will sometimes take prey back to their lairs, to tease and torment them before eating them. Kind of like cats and mice, you know . . ."

"Or gorgons and their case managers," I growled, dialing the numbers on the combination lock. "Give me something I don't know, Phil! Something I can use."

"Okay, okay . . . well, the winged manticore, once mature enough to fly, will often make its lair in cliffs or mountains, choosing caves or warrens with multiple exits. When defending their lair, they draw the intruder in and use the other tunnel exits to attack from the rear. Out in the open, they attack from above."

"We're a little short on cliffs or mountains in Chicago," I said, clicking on the light and rummaging through the nearest box. Flares, flash grenades, concussion grenades . . . what was a girl to wear?

"Right. Unfortunately, there's not much on record for them choosing urban locales. They prefer grassy plains and deserts mostly, with the winged ones going for the higher ground. But if one lived in Chicago, maybe . . . maybe he'd choose an empty or abandoned high rise?"

126

"Phil, that's—" Actually pretty good thinking. But it left too many options. There were some fifteen thousand foreclosed and empty properties in the city alone; I periodically checked the list to update my own hidey holes. I couldn't begin to search all the possible candidates in the time I likely had left. "What are a manticore's vulnerabilities? Any weak spots?"

"Not that I see. Though there's a line in the *Bestiary*: 'The Manticore makes up for the Softness of its Face with the Sting of its Tail.' Dunno if that helps."

I threw the lid of a crate to the floor. "Kyra! You okay? What was that?"

"Nothing. Phil, I need more. This girl could be dead before sunrise."

There was a long pause.

"Kyra . . . I'm sorry. I've got nothing else here. The database only gives me what's there. I don't have . . . you know, a wand or magic beans or whatnot to just conjure up the answers—"

"What?" I stopped dead.

"I said I don't have magic—"

"Beans," I breathed. I stuffed the last of my gear into my bag. "Phil, you're a genius."

"Wait, what did I say?"

"Call you later. If I'm not dead." I toggled off and headed for the car. My watch said it was nearly midnight. Maybe there was someone who could help me after all.

It was time to pay a call on the magic Bean.

To most folks, the world around them seems like a pretty solid place. They take for granted that when they put their foot out the front door, the ground will be there to catch them, the highway they take to work won't open into an abyss. Without even thinking about it, they assume that they won't wake up in the morning to find they've transformed into a giant cockroach or that their children have been taken in the night by faeries and replaced with changelings.

But there are cracks in the great machinery of the universe, fracture points where things break down and weird shit can happen. There are soft points in time when the spaces between the world we know and those that exist beyond will warp enough to touch, to overlap. Some of those convergences in time are predictable and minor, like the stroke of midnight. Others are occasional and major, like the winter solstice or All Hallows' Eve.

Just as with time, there are locations where the soft spots fold and meet, where the lines blur and the rules bend. And when you're at one of those places at the right time, all sorts of things are possible.

Millennium Park was one of those places. It had been built over the old railroad lines of Grant Park in the city's Loop community area as part of a massive public works project, intended to be unveiled in time for the millennial celebrations in 2000. That level of awareness and effort and anticipation had infused the area with a massive amount of psychic energy, warping the folds of space and time and drawing the etheric planes closer. Even though the park hadn't officially opened until four years later, the imprint of those energies had remained, soaked into the soil, the land, the air itself, awaiting a lens to focus it.

Enter *Cloud Gate*, or—as most Chicagoans had taken to calling it—The Bean. The Bean was a public sculpture set atop an underground garage on the west side of the sprawling twenty-five-acre park, fronting on Michigan Avenue. Inspired by the shape of a drop of liquid mercury—the only metal on the planet to exist in liquid form in its natural state—The Bean was an imposing elliptical structure, extending some thirty by sixty feet, with the apex of its curve reaching over forty feet in height. Because the public was immediately struck by its resemblance to a kidney bean, they nicknamed it "The Bean."

I've heard the sculptor was not amused.

The surface of The Bean was a series of stainless-steel plates, so highly polished that the seams between them were invisible and the entire sculpture resembled something like a gigantic funhouse mirror, reflecting and distorting the Chicago skyline and the skies above it, as well as the thousands of residents and tourists who came there to be photographed with it.

Underneath The Bean's center was a concave chamber called the omphalos, the Greek word for "navel." According to legend, Zeus once sent two eagles to fly across the world and meet at its center, its "navel." Long ago, omphalos stones were set up by the ancient Greeks to denote the location where the eagles were supposed to have met, with the most famous of these stones erected at the oracle temple at Delphi; they were thought to be propitious, facilitating direct communication with the gods.

I wasn't aiming that high. But I knew that the omphalos was the best place to be if you wanted to talk to the spirits inhabiting the realms closest to ours. By its very design, The Bean deformed light, bent the laws of perspective, making it a lodestone for dimensional turbulence. Putting it near the center of Millennium Park was just the icing on the etheric cake.

The park closed at eleven o'clock every night, so by the time I jogged up from the parking garage onto the plaza, there was no one about. That was a good thing; this close to midnight, I didn't have time to clear the area of bystanders. Opening the door to the intangible worlds could be a risky business, and I didn't need some idiot blundering in while I was doing it and getting us both killed.

The Bean gleamed mellowly in the reflected lights of Michigan Avenue—a disembodied, luminous shape that seemed to float just above the surface of the plaza. The buildings behind me rose up the bulging surface of the sculpture as I approached, their black cylindrical shapes bending like the distortions of a fever dream. I didn't look at myself as I passed under the twelve-foot-high arch and entered the omphalos. Nature had already played enough carnival tricks on me.

I sat down cross-legged in the center of the chamber and quickly unpacked my goodies: five votive candles and a trio of shallow serving bowls. Then I took out the blood.

Homer got his fair share of things wrong, but his description of Odysseus's trip to the realm of the dead was spot on: If you wanted the spirits to talk turkey with you, you had to give them what they wanted. And what they craved most was the taste of blood, the essence of the living. Odysseus sacrificed a black sheep to get the shade of Tiresias to prophesize his way home. I'd have to make do with what I had gotten from the all-night butcher's shop I'd hit on the way here: a bag of blood from some of the hogs they had slaughtered in the last hour. I poured out a little blood into each bowl and lit the candles. A thousand tiny flames appeared all around me as the polished underside of The Bean reflected the lights.

Midnight.

I said nothing, sitting with my palms resting on my knees, willing myself to remain still. A minute crept by. I tried to stop imagining the sound of the girl's screams as the manticore tore into her. If she was already dead or dying, surely I'd know it, somehow.

Two minutes past.

Despite the chill, I felt the first beads of perspiration start to trickle down my temples. Come on, you bastards . . .

Three minutes.

The candles flickered. I stared hard at the bowls. Not a ripple.

"*Hello—!*" I cried, losing patience. I got to my feet, glaring up at my own warped image, multiplied many times over. "I brought the damn offering! Let's get on the stick, people!"

No reply. Then I felt something, a sudden chill in the omphalos that was deeper than the bite of midnight, a cold that went past the skin and sank right into the bones, as though a door to a dank crypt had just opened all around me. The frigid stillness of space. Or the grave.

The candles guttered, responding to a disturbance in the ether. There was the faintest sound at my feet. I looked down and saw that the bowls were draining, slowly but steadily.

The dead had come to drink.

130

I stayed where I was as the bowls emptied. The blood served as both offering and lure, temporarily anchoring the spirits who partook of it to this material plane. But I was no spell caster to hold them longer; any disturbance of the tenuous connection could tear it. If that happened, I'd be back to square one, with little hope of gathering them together again.

I had a foothold in the other realm. I had to make use of it while it lasted.

"I seek one who was Elspeth Rougnagne," I called out. Mustn't forget your Dickens at a moment like this. The dead demanded a certain etiquette of address, even in this age. "Is she among you?"

A susurrus of whispers echoed through the chamber, though the air had grown still, as if the breeze itself had been struck dumb.

"I say again: I seek she who was Elspeth Rougnagne while she was among the living. Is she present?"

I turned my head back and forth, hunting for a face, a shape, anything. The dead were close; I felt them crowding about me, brushing against my skin like cobwebs. But no one answered me.

Then the candles fluttered again. The feeling of being hemmed in frayed away. The whispering receded. I heard the sound of crumpling plastic and looked down. The bag of blood I'd left on the ground was draining, fast. In seconds, it was completely empty.

A vague phosphorescence glimmered before me, as though moonlight were coalescing. It was hard to discern whether it was in the air or the mirrored surface of the omphalos, but it took on a vaguely familiar shape, like a crude sketch of the woman I had so briefly met the night before.

Elspeth Rougnagne was in the house.

The faint impression of the head seemed to dip down.

"No circle of protection," soughed a soft voice. "Not even salt. You are sloppy, Kyra Regina Anastas."

I was going to be lectured now? I didn't think so.

"You did this . . . thing to me," I said. "The soul-lock. You made me promise to protect her. I want out."

The ghost wagged its head. "Did you honestly think I could—or would—release you from your oath? Is that why you have risked her ruin like this? You should not have summoned me."

"Tell me how to get free," I gritted. "Tell me now, or I won't even try to save her."

There was an echo of fire in the silver eyes. "You will. You must."

What if I can't? I wanted to shout. Did you ever think of that, lady? That I—that no one—can save her? That you're risking my life for no good reason? "And if I don't?"

"Breaking the soul's vow tears it beyond hope of restoration. You would become a damned creature, a thing accursed."

I almost laughed. "I guess you hadn't noticed. I'm that already."

"Are you?" The rippling mist seemed to shrug. "Are you?" it said, more softly. "Well, it is your choice."

How was this woman still managing to make me feel bad? She was reminding me uncomfortably of my mother.

"Why is she so important?" I demanded. "Half the Mythic in the city are after her. Why does someone want her dead so bad?"

The face sharpened for a moment, then blurred. "I cannot tell you that. Even speaking of her is dangerous, dangerous for her, for you—"

"Why? Who would want—" I stopped, chasing after a sudden intuition. "Elspeth . . . who was Stephanie's father?"

The silver mist fluttered and wavered.

"You made a deal," I said, comprehension dawning. "Didn't you? You made a deal with one of the Powers, to have its baby, to bring something into this world." I shook my head. "Geez, lady, you're even crazier than I thought. You thought you'd get out of your pact with dark magic by just making another one?"

Rougnagne's face drew closer, the features becoming clearer. I could make out the fear there. "You don't understand. And you should not have summoned me. Release me, before it's too late."

"What are you talking about?"

132

"Think, child. Why do you think I made you petrify me? So that they could not use my blood to call upon me, to seek to use my shade against her."

I was officially nonplused. "Then how did I call you? I'm no mage."

"You are bound to her, she who was of my blood. And I am bound to answer her blood."

"I'm bound to her . . . how exactly?"

"You made your vow to protect her, and she holds it now, in her blood."

Great. We were one big bound family. I ground my teeth.

"She's in danger," I said. "A manticore has her. How do I find her?"

"Don't you know? Think, Kyra Anastas. She holds the promise you made. That link is all you need."

"I don't understand."

"Look," said the shade, pointing a pale finger at my chest.

I plucked the collar of my duster open. Nothing but cotton, Kevlar, and me. "I don't see anything."

"Look with your heart," sighed the ghost. "Look with your soul."

This was ridiculous. This was just another cosmic joke, and I was the butt of it. Again.

But Rougnagne was already dead. She'd gain nothing by a charade. And it wouldn't help her daughter. She had to be serious.

I closed my eyes and thought back, remembering that strange sensation I'd had during the soul-lock, that feeling of finding the calm amidst the chaos. It had been like stepping out of a thunderstorm or sinking into a clear, tranquil pool. I let my breathing slow and tried to visualize it. For a time, all I saw was the darkness behind my own eyelids.

Then a pinpoint of light glimmered in the blackness. As I focused on the sight, it grew larger, or maybe I drew closer. It flared with a soft, diffuse radiance, driving away the dark.

It was Stephanie; I knew it at once, and the realization astounded me. I was looking at Stephanie's soul.

And it was *beautiful*.

I opened my eyes and gasped. Hovering in the air before me was a gently swaying tendril of that same radiance, pouring into my chest. It stretched away, looping under the omphalos and out into the night sky.

"Geez," I breathed in amazement. "I see it. I see it!" I turned back to Rougnagne. "And I can follow this—?"

The ghost was no longer facing me. Her head was turned as though looking at something over her shoulder. When she turned back, her silver features had become contorted with horror.

"Release me!" she cried. "It has found us! It's coming—!"

The effect of seeing such intense terror on the face of something that was already dead galvanized me. Without thinking, I said: "I release you!" At once, a gyre seemed to take hold of the ghost. Her silver form began to disappear.

"*You should not have summoned me!*" she cried. She had dwindled to a glimmering smear of light. I heard a last, faint call: "Save my daughter!" With that, she was gone.

In the same instant, the candles were suddenly snuffed out, plunging the omphalos into darkness.

Something entered the chamber. It felt like an invisible pressure wave clogging the atmosphere and squeezing my eardrums into my skull. The weight of it nearly drove me to my knees.

"*KYRA . . .*" The voice filled the chamber, springing from everywhere and nowhere. "*KYRA SPELLBORN, KISSED OF SERPENTS . . . THE ONE WHO STANDS APART . . . WE SEE YOU . . .*"

"Good for you," I rasped, though my heart was pounding like a trip-hammer. I couldn't seem to get enough air in my lungs. "What . . . what do you want?"

"*THE CHILD . . .*" The voice continued. Was it one throat or hundreds answering? I couldn't tell. "*LEAVE HER TO US . . .*"

"Gee whiz, I'd love to," I panted. Whatever was trying to press through from the other side was immensely powerful; I sensed without seeing the concave walls of the chamber rippling and distorting, closing in on me. The

134

exits on either side shrank to dim shafts of light. "But I'm kinda committed to breathing, so—"

"*FOOL—!*" The vehemence in that voice nearly left me flattened on the stone. I'd never felt such sheer malevolence. It was like a storm of bees swarming over my skin. "*SHE WILL DESTROY YOU . . .*"

I had to get out of here. Now. I fixed one of the exits in my sights. It looked miles away.

"Yeah, well, you know how it is: Damned if you do—"

I jumped. The muscles of my legs felt filled with sand. But I tucked my head in and rolled, praying I could push through the overburdened atmosphere before the omphalos closed entirely. For a moment, it seemed I was straining against a barrier that would refuse to yield. Then, like a bubble bursting, I fell through and found myself flat on my back under the cloud-locked skies, the curved edge of The Bean looming over me.

Crone's blood. I levered myself up to a sitting position, shaking in every limb. What the Hell was that thing? And what it had said—

"Well, well," chuckled a voice that was at once both familiar and difficult to place. I turned my head and found myself staring down the barrel of a SIG Sauer P226.

"Kyra Anastas," said Detective Druison, fishing out his cuffs with his free hand. "I've been looking all over for you."

CHAPTER 8

Seriously?

Druison? Here? Now? I was so flabbergasted by the sight of him bending over me, I didn't resist as he slipped the manacle over my wrist and drew me up. Turning me around, he did the other arm.

"Little late for sightseeing, isn't it?" he murmured into my ear.

I was too surprised to respond. The omphalos had resumed its normal shape; The Bean still cast the gleaming cityscape's warped reflection back at it. Even the candles and bowls were gone.

There was nothing to show I'd just nearly triggered a major extraplanar incursion into our universe.

Which was . . . good. Except—

My brain kicked back into gear.

"Wait, wait!" I said, just before he started to pat me down. "Listen to me. I wasn't sightseeing. I was meeting someone with information. Hear me out; a girl's life is hanging in the balance."

"A girl," Druison repeated dully. "Who?"

Oh . . . what the hell.

"Her name's Stephanie," I said. In for a penny . . . "Stephanie Rougnagne. She's the daughter of Elspeth Rougnagne, the millionaire."

"Rougnagne, whose house just blew up in that gas leak last night out in Burr Ridge? I heard about that." He smiled grimly. "Only she didn't have any family."

"That's what she wanted people to think. She was always afraid of blackmail. So she sent her daughter away to Europe when she was little and hid the fact that the girl even existed. But Stephanie wanted to come home. So Elspeth hired me to be her bodyguard, to make sure she got here in one piece. But something went wrong last night. Now Elspeth's dead and Stephanie's been kidnapped." Damn, I'd half-convinced myself. "I was meeting an informant tonight who said he knew where the kidnappers had taken her."

Druison looked at me dubiously. "You," he said. "You're her bodyguard. You expect me to believe that?"

"If I convince you of that, will you hear me out on the rest? Give me five minutes."

"Sure," grinned Druison. "How exactly do you plan to prove it?"

"Open my coat."

"Excuse me?"

"I'm cuffed, right? Take a look. You were just about to frisk me anyway, weren't you?"

Druison frowned, then tugged my duster open.

"Whoa—" It would have been nice to think he was just taken aback by my dynamite figure. Except he was more likely ogling the Glocks I had tucked into my twin shoulder holsters. Unless it was the Ruger LCR .38 I'd strapped to my thigh he was noticing. Or the dagger blades in their sheaths.

He took a step back, all shock in those puppy dog eyes. I almost felt bad for him.

138

"I'm not a sculptor," I said, stating what had to be obvious by now. "I'm . . . insurance for people with very bad enemies. Now, do I get those five minutes?"

Druison was getting over his surprise pretty quick. But the doubt on his face was difficult to read. For a moment, I didn't know which way the coin was going to land.

"There's a diner across the street," he said, nodding toward South Michigan Avenue. "Five minutes. And I'll want to hear about Delgado too. The truth this time."

It took us fifteen minutes to get to the diner, a cozy little Greek place set in the first floor of a dorm building. We'd have been there in four, but Druison needed the extra time to confiscate my weapons and toss them into a satchel. He was thorough. Found almost all of them.

Before we went in, he tugged off his scarf and wound it over my manacled wrists. Then he pulled the door open for me.

"Thanks," I said. He raised an eyebrow but said nothing.

"Kevin!" called an older woman from behind the main counter. "Coffee, hon?"

"Just a booth, Aurelia."

Her eyes darted to me, narrowing slightly.

"I'd love some coffee," I called loudly. "Black, two sugars."

"No coffee," said Druison firmly, steering us to the booth furthest from the front. He tossed his satchel on the seat across from me and scooted in next to it. The booth was so tiny, our knees were practically touching.

"C'mon, it's late. I could use some caffeine."

"And have you toss it in my face and make a run for it? I don't think so."

"I wouldn't run," I said, truly hurt at the assumption. Incapacitating him and calling for an ambulance would buy me twice as much time. It wouldn't be hard to slip out in all the confusion.

"Five minutes," he said. "Talk."

"I didn't shoot Delgado," I said, choosing my words with care. "The ballistics evidence has been tampered with."

"How do you know about the ballistics report?" he demanded.

That wasn't going to be a productive line of conversation. "A little birdie told me." When his scowl only deepened, I leaned forward. "Look, I'm being framed here."

"Uh-huh. Keep your hands where I can see them."

He'd noticed that little trick. Cute *and* smart.

I put my hands back on the table, my wrists still wrapped in his scarf.

"Why would someone want to frame you for Delgado's murder?"

"I don't know," I admitted. Lies should be the skin on the bones of the truth, an Agency mentor had once told me. "You said I was the last person seen with Delgado, right? Maybe somebody wants to keep the focus on me and not on themselves."

"Who?"

"Someone in the Department."

He bristled at once, but I could tell his ire was mixed with something else, some emotion I couldn't read. "How do you figure?"

"Isn't it obvious? Who else would have had access to the gun? Or the lab?"

"The report could have been electronically falsified," Druison pointed out. "An outside hacker could do that."

Was he trying to help me or draw me into a trap? Either way, I was vaguely gratified he wasn't simply dismissing the theory out of hand. "Maybe, but an inside job is the simpler answer. Who had access to my gun?"

"Anyone in the forensics lab," Druison answered. "Or at the impound lot, for that matter. Doesn't exactly narrow it down." Now it was his turn to lean forward. "And it doesn't explain what you were doing with Delgado in the first place."

Ah, no; it didn't. This felt like speed dating with a gun to your head. One wrong move, and the fun was over.

"Delgado was on my short list of people who might know who was after the Rougnagne girl," I said. That was my boy Marco, doing good from beyond the grave. You gotta love karma. "He gave me a lead after a little . . . persuasion. But it turned out to be a dud." I let frustration leak into my face. "If I hadn't wasted time with that, I might have been at the mansion when they came for Stephanie."

And there was that expression again, the gleam in his gray eyes that I'd seen back at my place. If I hadn't known better, I'd have said it was admiration. It made my cheeks feel strangely warm.

"You got better information tonight?"

I nodded.

"So who has her?"

"The Obshina." When in doubt, go with the Chechen Mafia. They had cells across most of Europe and had been making inroads into the States for a while now. And they were well-known for kidnapping and murder. Invoking them gave the lie plausibility without risking verifiability.

"Why would the Russian mob be interested in this girl?"

I shrugged. "Ransom, most likely."

"But if her mother's dead—"

"The estate will need her back. And she's heir to millions. Lots of European banks would just open their vaults at her say-so." There was my hook. "That's why I have to get to her, tonight. They're moving her within the hour. Once they get her out of the country . . ."

"Where is she?"

I wish I knew. But I hadn't had a chance to see where the soul tendril led before all hell had broken loose in the omphalos. I shook my head. "No way. I tell you that, you'll call in the stormtroopers. Stephanie might get killed. I need to handle this myself."

"You're not really in a position to give orders, Ms. Anastas, in case you hadn't noticed."

Maybe not, but I was in the perfect position to stun Druison with the merest flick of my Gaze. That had been the plan, but now I hesitated.

Ever since Stephanie had healed me, the serpents had felt different, more *real* somehow. If I accidentally used too much of their power, I could put Druison in a coma, or kill him.

He was delaying my going after the girl. Why was getting him out of the way suddenly a problem?

"I can't just let you stroll out of here," Druison said. "You're a suspect in a murder investigation."

"Based on what? Has there been any evidence that the blood on my gun is Delgado's? 'Cause I can guarantee you it's not. For all you know, he could still be alive. There's no body, is there? If you take me in, you'll still have to release me within twenty-four hours. You'll have accomplished nothing. And by then, a fourteen-year-old girl will be long gone."

"You really care what happens to this kid?"

Gods, I didn't know. I barely knew her. She'd violated my privacy. And the sight of Stephanie's soul had shaken me almost as much as the Thing that had intruded into the omphalos. I could only imagine what my own looked like. Or maybe I didn't even have to imagine it. The soul-lock with Elspeth Rougnagne had told me more than I had ever wanted to know about what lay within me.

"She's my client," I said finally, choosing what honesty I could. "I take my contractual obligations seriously." And there was a question I wanted to put to her.

Druison's eyes narrowed. "I'll bet you do." He shrugged. "Still, it's not enough. I take my obligations pretty seriously too. So far you haven't even proven this girl exists, much less that anyone's kidnapped her. And your five minutes are up."

Speaking of time, I'd given this about as much as I could afford. I sighed with something like real regret. He had forced my hand.

"Don't take this personally . . ." I began and locked my eyes on his, willing only the slightest whisper of power to escape. Hopefully it'd be enough.

He grinned. "Don't take what personally?"

Okay . . . I'd overestimated the new and improved Medusa's Gaze. I focused my will, let more of the power loose. "This."

He shook his head, eyes still on mine. "This being . . . ?"

What?

Nothing was happening. Druison was sitting across from me, at point-blank range, and nothing was happening. I pushed harder. He returned a quizzical smile.

I sat back, stunned. "Sorry," I mumbled dazedly. "This has never happened to me before."

Druison said something but I wasn't listening. Was I that rattled by the encounter in the omphalos? Or was it worse than that? Had Stephanie . . . had she *neutered* my snakes?

"I'll kill her," I muttered under my breath. "I will effing kill her."

"What?" said Druison. "What did you say?"

I should just let the manticore grind her into hamburger meat, I thought with gathering fury. Elspeth Rougnagne be damned. Had the voice been telling the truth after all? Is that what it meant when it said she would "destroy" me?

Except . . . except the Thing in the omphalos had been several orders of magnitude above just creepy. I couldn't shake the conviction that anything it wanted was bad for the greater Chicago metropolitan area. And I'd seen the girl's *soul*, for God's sake. There was no questioning its purity, its . . . goodness. It hurt to look at it. And I wanted to see it again.

Then there was the little practical matter of my head being on the chopping block right alongside hers. Best not to forget that.

"We done here?" asked Druison, making as if to rise.

"Wait," I blurted out. "I can prove it, all of it. Come with me. Help me save her."

Druison stared at me as though I'd gone mad. Who knows; maybe I had.

"Why should I trust you?" he demanded. "You've already lied to me twice."

Twice was being generous.

"Come on," I grinned. If the Gaze really was off-line, some additional firepower could come in handy. Not that I wanted anyone but me to have the pleasure of blowing the smirk off my buddy Marty's face, along with the rest of his head. "It'll be like a date. Just with more bullets."

Druison's jaw worked in indecision. I gave him my sweetest smile, the one I usually reserved for a mark just before I killed him.

"I should have my head examined for this," he muttered, shaking his head. "Okay. I'll go along with this, for now." He gestured for my hands. "Let me unlock those."

"Oh." I winced, drawing the cuffs out from under the folds of the scarf and pushing them across to him. "Sorry; I got out of those five minutes ago. Forgot."

He stared at the metal rings on the table as I slid out of the booth.

"You ready?" I asked, winding the scarf around my shoulders. It had a nice, soft puppy dog feel against the skin of my neck. "Time's a-wasting."

෴෴෴

"So, what's the deal with Delgado?" I asked. "Why do the police want to find him so bad?"

Druison glanced at me, then turned his gaze back to the road. I'd insisted he drive while I navigated. It helped me keep my focus on the soul tendril, which kept threatening to loop out of sight over the building tops of downtown Chicago. It had taken ten minutes of silent concentration to find the damn thing again, made harder by the way Druison kept drumming his fingers on the hood of his car, coughing at regular intervals, and just in general breathing too loudly while he waited.

"I told you before," he said. "It's an internal matter."

"IA, huh?" I said, and was rewarded with a brief flicker of disquiet on his face. So . . . Delgado *was* a witness in an Internal Affairs investigation. The big lug knew something about a cop who was under suspicion, and now he'd disappeared. No wonder the anthill on 35th and Michigan was so stirred up.

"When did Marco become your CI?" No way a psychopath like him was an undercover cop; that left confidential informant.

"I told you," he said trenchantly, "we're not talking about this."

It was cute watching the puppy get angry. But, as I'd pointed out myself earlier tonight, I wasn't here to sightsee.

"Left," I said, gesturing. "Make a left ahead." If Druison was wondering why I kept craning my head up to look out the windows, he had the sense to keep his mouth shut about it. I found I liked that feature in a driving companion.

Which made that probably the only thing about my current situation I *did* like. On top of everything else I had to worry about, the failure of the Gaze was freaking me out. What the hell did it mean? The snakes had never felt more potent, yet when I had called upon them, they'd done exactly bubkes. The only person I could even think to call to ask about it was my mother. But even if she did talk to me—which was stratospherically unlikely—I could only imagine the can of worms that would open. *What do you mean, you've been using them? Why does a schoolteacher need to petrify people? Oh, so you're an assassin for hire? So you're a freak and a murderer?*

Yeah; no thanks.

Part of me thought I should be glad the snakes were . . . inert or whatever; it meant I couldn't hurt anyone with them, right? Wasn't that why I'd always hated them? I felt . . . weird, like I'd just been betrayed by someone I hadn't trusted or even liked in the first place. It didn't make any sense to be mad at them; it's not like they were . . . people.

Yet I *was* mad. Almost as much as I was scared.

Of course, that could just be because right before going into battle against a manticore probably wasn't the best time in the world to find your primary weapon was malfunctioning.

And it wasn't helping that the clock was ticking, the sands in the hourglass slipping away by the minute. It was nearly one o'clock in the morning, and there was as yet no way to tell how close we were. The filament of lambent light that still poured into me had grown no stronger or brighter in the last twenty minutes. Worse, I was pretty sure we were driving in circles. If the tendril was really a link to Stephanie Rougnagne, it certainly wasn't using GPS. I ground my teeth. Ghosts can never just give you the damn address.

Screw this noise. Maybe I could force a reaction from the link. "Left!" I snapped. "Left!" The Hyundai rattled on without turning. "I said make a left!"

"You can't turn left on Lake Street," Druison said. "I thought you lived here. Why don't you just tell me where we're going now? We've been driving around in circles for nearly half an hour."

Twenty minutes, smartass. "We're close," I said, hoping I could will it to be true. Druison grunted then swerved left through a break in the median, ducking into a side street bordered by looming high-rises. I glared at him in surprise.

"Hey," he shrugged, wagging his eyebrows. "Police prerogative."

I covered my mouth to hide an answering grin. It wouldn't do to send the wrong signals. Unless I got the drop on Marty before he could use his quills, I hadn't quite figured out how to neutralize his distance weapon yet. Odds were, I might be using my companion as a human shield before the night was over.

The soul tendril had arced up and to the left almost the moment we got onto MacChesney Court. I strained for a better view and made out that it was streaming down from a gray, drab building that backed into the empty side street. Only seventeen stories, the structure huddled in the shadow of its taller brethren on either side. "That's it!" I shouted, pointing. "There!"

"Wacker Tower?" asked Druison, bringing the car to a stop behind the cover of a dumpster. "Huh."

"What?"

"I'd have expected the Chechans to pick a place a little more out of the way."

Oh, right: the Chechan thing. Now would be an inopportune moment to explain how I'd bent the truth a wee bit getting us here. On the other

146

hand, if Druison was really going to go in on this with me, he had to know something of what to expect. Otherwise, he might get us both killed.

"Listen," I said, slipping off my seat belt and reaching in the back for his satchel. "You've got to be ready for anything with this group. My informant told me they may be using feral guard dogs." I couldn't very well say lions now, could I? "If you see—or even think you see—anything like an animal coming at you in there, shoot first, think about it later. Got it?"

"Sure," he said, turning off the engine. "But until I see these guys for myself, I'll hold onto the weapons."

Oh, well; it had been fun while it lasted.

"Good idea," I said, and coldcocked him with his own bag.

⌇⌇⌇

Wacker Tower. The former home of the Chicago Motor Club, it had been built back in the '20s in the Art Deco style of the time as a sort of homage to the rise of the automobile culture in the United States. There was even supposed to be an enormous fresco or something in the lobby depicting popular driving destinations around the country back then. But I'd read somewhere that it had been empty for a long time, ever since the club had moved on and a developer's plan to turn it into condos had fallen through back in the '90s.

This was where the manticore had made its lair. A ninety-year-old building just chock-full of lots and lots of halls and doorways to pop in and out of. It was probably black as pitch inside too.

Great.

I'd rummaged through the piles of junk in Druison's satchel and gotten most of my gear back, though I was damned if I could find one of the spare clips for my Glock. Too impatient to hunt further, I popped open the door and slipped down the alley to the rear of the building.

The back door was chained and padlocked. So that was easy enough. I stepped inside to find myself in a dark service way, with steps leading up and down. Phil had said the winged versions liked the heights. So up I went.

I came out to a two-story lobby area, flanked at either end by tall windows that rose from balconies on the mezzanine level. Through their plastic tarps, the lobby flared with the occasional passing lights of traffic going by on Wacker Place. There was the mural of the country, faded to a pale green by decades of sun damage and disrepair. The diamond-patterned tile floor kicked up clouds of dust as I went to the foot of the spiral staircase.

Seventeen stories on foot. Again, I asked myself if I was doing this to save the kid or so I could kill her myself. I shook my head; I guess we'd just have to wait and see.

The stairs wound up and up around a central shaft in curvilinear fashion, making it a dizzying experience to stare up or down too long. I'd made it to the tenth floor and was really beginning to feel it in my quads when I picked up on the smell.

It was a noisome stink, seeming to come from everywhere and nowhere. But before I could decide to follow it, a glint of light from down the hall caught my attention, the first hint of movement I'd seen in the oppressive stillness of the place. I crept down the hall and came into a wide, hard-wood-floored chamber whose far wall was lined with a huge mirror. Various pieces of furniture had been piled up and left under sheets in one corner, including a vague shape that was probably a piano. A dance studio, then, one that had probably lain unused for half a century or more. Kind of sad, I thought, hovering at the door and catching my dim form reflected back to me half a dozen ways from the cracked glass surface. Once this might have been a place for little ballerinas and aspiring dancers. Now only monsters walked its floors.

A flash again, but now I perceived that it was just light reflecting on the myriad glass facets from outside. I stepped over to the window. Below, the faraway headlamps of cars rolled over the bridges that spanned the Chicago

River as it followed its final curve before emptying into Lake Michigan—the ghost gleams of motorists, sending their silent regards to a vanished era.

The lobby's fixtures had all been removed. But a large, gilt Deco-style chandelier still presided over the old studio, its facets dull and dumb without electricity. I flicked the ornate light switch on impulse—

And the entire room lit up as the chandelier flared into brilliant life.

Shit!

I slapped the switch off, but even as the room plunged back into gloom, I heard a creaking noise of something moving fast on the spiral staircase.

Goddamn it; this was what happened when you let yourself get all distracted by maudlin thoughts. In an instant, my hands were filled with Glocks again. I made for the staircase, aiming at head and chest levels. I'd made a stupid mistake, but maybe it could be worked to my advantage; let Marty show his ugly mug for even a split second and I'd send him grinning straight down to Hell.

A shadow moved up the stairwell. Even with my preternatural eyesight, it took me a second to recognize it wasn't the manticore, but—

"Druison!" I hissed. The detective started, whipping his pistol in my direction. I had no choice but to hold my hands up or shoot him. Forbearance won out. Barely.

"You're under arrest," he said, his SIG Sauer in both gloved hands. "Put down your weapons and—"

"Will you *shut up*?" I whispered in horror. "You're going to get us killed!"

Druison came off the stairs, his weapon still targeting my heart, which—unfortunately for me—was *not* my least vulnerable spot.

"I said, put down your . . ." His voice trailed off. His eyes widened. For a moment, I thought my beret had come loose. Then a fleck of foam appeared on his lips. With a groan, he fell face-first onto the carpet.

Three long quills projected from his upper back.

I didn't think. I just moved, throwing myself backward and firing wildly with both Glocks as I fell. I heard a thin, whistling sound as something parted the air just above my head, zipping past. I landed hard on my back and kept firing, blowing chunks out of the ceiling and stairwell.

No tail, no body. Nothing visible. But I kept up the fusillade until I'd scrambled over to the relative cover of an old statue perched atop a marble column along the wall. As I scanned the area, my hands fell to reloading.

Marty must have seen my light or heard Druison's big mouth and come creeping down the stairwell. He'd been able to shoot his spikes from out of view by whipping his tail around the corner. Crone kiss me, I hadn't thought about his ability to do something like that. It took the matter from a shoot-out—a straight-out contest of reflexes, which I thought I could win—to guerrilla warfare, which I probably couldn't. Not unless I found a gun that could shoot around corners.

I paused, straining to pick up the least sound of movement. But the stairwell was empty; I'd bet my life on it. I grimaced; I *was* betting my life on it. But I trusted my instincts and my senses. Marty had withdrawn to the heights after his attack. He'd make me take the fight to him, seeking to draw me out of cover. It was what I'd do in his place.

I carefully plucked the quills out with my gloves and rolled Druison over. His breath was coming in short, shallow gasps. I pried open an eye and saw the pupil was strongly dilated despite the surrounding darkness. Some sort of neurotoxin. Given the manticore's propensity to play with its food, this might or might not be a lethal dose.

But I had no antitoxin to give him. And what the snakes had done for me, flushing poison out of my system with their venom, would be fatal for a human. He needed medical attention and fast. But even if I got him down the stairs without earning myself a back full of matching quills, leaving here meant abandoning Stephanie. And I had a feeling that playtime was over for Marty; he knew I was here for the girl and that he needed to finish the job, fast.

Sorry, Detective.

I dragged him out of the hall into a side room and closed the door behind me as I came out. If I was quick enough, maybe—

150

A scream pierced the air from somewhere above.

Stephanie!

Two, three stories up, max. I hit the stairs, trusting to speed, raking the upper levels with my gunsights for a target. One flight, two—the reek was getting worse—and then I glimpsed a movement two floors above, like the flick of a whip.

Quills struck the rail and stuck there, quivering, as I bounded back. One missed my boot by inches. I fired back, my silencers reducing the shots to a series of *phut-phut-phuts* that caused a rain of plaster to shower down while I stole up to the next landing.

Would the manticore run out of quills before I ran out of bullets? I wasn't loving the odds. And if it came to close quarters, Marty could probably rend me limb from limb. Wrestling with a hellhound had nearly killed me; a lionlike creature would probably have three times that kind of strength.

A brace of darts came arcing over the rail from the floor just above, too close to dodge. I fell back against the wall as they peppered a line across my chest. Gasping, I slid to the floor of the landing. My chin sunk to my breast where the quills were sticking out, still vibrating from the force of their impacts.

A soft growl of satisfaction from overhead. Then the light pad of footfalls, coming closer.

The manticore hesitated on the steps, sniffing the air. I could just make out the thing's figure, hunched apelike, with its folded wings jutting up from behind its shaggy shoulders. It took a step closer—

And I snatched my Glocks up, firing. The manticore roared and leapt high into the air. The brush of a sweeping wing sent me sprawling. By the time I got back to my feet, the tail was hurtling out of sight over the rail three stories up.

Damnation, I'd almost had him. Then I spotted the blood on the steps. From the splatter marks, I judged I'd scored two solid hits. *Yes.*

"*Kevlar's a bitch, ain't it, Marty!*" I shouted after him. I yanked the quills from my vest and raced up the steps, eager to deal a killing blow. The landing was empty. But there—the blood stains on the carpet marked where he'd alighted. The trail led down a short hall that branched off to either side. I followed the track until it abruptly became indistinguishable from the rest of the carpet. Startled, I jerked to a halt—and that's when the stench finally penetrated. I'd been so consumed by adrenalin and blood lust, I'd blocked it out, but now it was overpowering. I drew my collar up over my nose, nearly gagging.

A quick scan of the chamber at the end of the hall confirmed what my nose was already telling me: The place was an abattoir. Despite what Phil had said, a manticore was not a tidy eater. The large room was stacked floor to ceiling with mounds of bones and a generous helping of assorted viscera, the floor tacky with old blood. Marty must have been squatting in this building for a long time to build up such a mass of grisly leftovers. I wrinkled my nose in disgust and dismay. How many people had found their lives abruptly snuffed out by that psychopath?

And how was I any different?

Shaken, I backed out and tried the other end of the hall. It opened into a secondary stairway, probably once used for service runs. The concrete landing was spattered with drops of fresh blood.

I slapped my thigh with my fist. I had to stop underestimating this guy; he'd laid a false trail, and doubled back just that quick, to give himself time to regroup. And there was less blood going down the steps than I'd have liked to see. It could mean he was dying . . . or he could be healing fast. I hadn't thought to ask Phil about that, and now there was no time.

I started down, then reconsidered. He'd expect me to follow the trail. Which meant . . .

The sound of a drop of blood landing on a leather shoulder pad is a small thing, really. But when all your senses have been dialed up to the max, it sounds like a shotgun going off. I whipped my Glocks up, firing even before I sighted the dark figure soaring down at me.

The collision of our bodies knocked me down the steps. But I heard the manticore yelp, and then he was bounding over me and disappearing around a corner. I staggered to my feet and went after him. Man, how many rounds was I going to have to put in this guy? I was going to have to start buying my ammo in bulk.

My ankle was throbbing; I must have twisted it as I fell. But the blood trail was heavier ahead, which meant Marty was hurting too, and worse. If I could just get a clean shot . . .

The narrow corridor ended in another flight of steps, plunging down into a darkness even I couldn't penetrate. My eyes' sensitivity to ultraviolet light made a starry night as bright as day for me, but without even that faint source of electromagnetic radiation, there was nothing from the spectrum to pick up. If I went down there, I'd be blind.

I checked the wall on either side for a light switch. Maybe I'd get lucky again.

Or not. Still, there was more than one way to skin a manticore. I patted my duster for my packet of flares, lit one, and tossed it down the steps. It bounced into a chamber that had some sort of radiating pattern set in its terrazzo floor. The angle prevented me from making out any other details.

Well, what choice did I have, really? I couldn't search for Stephanie while Marty was creeping about the place. Slapping a fresh clip into each Glock, I went down the steps.

The chamber was octagonal in shape and bigger than I'd expected, the pattern radiating out from a central point. Four narrow exits gaped blackly at each compass point like mouths, raw and hungry. On either side of each exit, the walls were lined with floor-to-ceiling mirrors.

The blood smears went to the center of the room. And stopped.

Abruptly, the snakes started hissing, moving restlessly under my beret.

Trap.

I wheeled for the stairs and a soft tittering floated through the air, close by. I turned round and round, searching for the source.

"Look at the little snake-charmed girl," it echoed, "All lost and alone . . ."

"Oh, I'm not alone!" I shouted back, waving my Glocks. "Come on out and I'll introduce you to my two friends!"

153

"Don't listen to it," Marty muttered. The voice was rougher now, as though the words were being forced through a throat no longer designed for human speech. "Mustn't listen . . ."

A soft, swift padding sound of movement down one exit. I went to one knee, firing off four rounds. Damn, I couldn't tell if I hit anything. Setting one gun down, I fished out the rest of my flares, lighting each and tossing them toward the exits. With the mirrors everywhere, the ruddy glare made the chamber glow like the inside of a fireplace.

"Hey, Marty?" I called. "Got a question for you. Why the girl, huh? Who paid you to grab her?"

I had only half hoped he'd be dumb enough to answer, give me another chance to lock in on him. But the lunatic's voice drifted back. "Wasn't supposed to play with her . . . but how could we resist? Such a beautiful thing, golden girl, child of light . . . so sweet and soft. . . . We could play with her and never tire . . ."

The vents—they were throwing me off, making the sound come from everywhere.

"Yeah, she's a real sweetie," I said. "Guess you'll go back to playing with her when you and I are done, huh?" C'mon, you psycho; tell me she's alive . . .

"No more playing . . . ," muttered the manticore. Now he sounded resentful. "Time to eat now. . . . Eat before sun comes up. . . . Chew the flesh and devour the light. . . . Stop the voices from being so cross."

"What voices?" I called. "Who wants her dead?"

There was a silent pause. I tried to watch every exit at once.

"Eat now," growled the voice.

I felt a sudden sting in the back of my left hand. I glanced at it in surprise and annoyance—and saw a quill sticking out just behind the middle knuckles on my glove.

Oh, no . . .

The Glock dropped out of my suddenly nerveless fingers. I stumbled back and hit the mirrored wall, losing my footing. I tried to raise the other arm, but it was already beginning to shake uncontrollably. The gun clattered to the floor at my side.

I pulled my head up on neck muscles that felt like heavy cables. Down the exit on the opposite end of the chamber, a shape was translating out of the dark beyond the glow of the flares.

Marty the manlike simulacrum was gone, and what he had molted into was pure manticore. The face still held the wide, staring, light blue eyes and the shaggy tufts of red hair, but it had lost all other human aspect. The lower jaw was distended, revealing three rows of sharp teeth in the slavering mouth. And the upright body of the man I'd met had enlarged and lengthened into the tawny shape of a leonine predator with wings folded on the great shoulders. Over the stealthy, powerful form, the arched scorpion's tail swayed back and forth.

No. No way was I going out like this. Eaten by a *geek*? No freakin' way.

As it stepped over the flare, the manticore began picking up speed, loping toward me with longer strides.

My vision was starting to blur. I squeezed my eyes shut and appealed to the only source of aid I had left.

Help, I begged, throwing my heart and soul into the thought; *please help me*—

Under my beret, the snakes grew instantly still. I felt the power suddenly quickening behind my eyelids, sharpening to a laser-like focus. I opened my eyes again just as Marty reached the center of the chamber and leapt.

The Gaze loosed as he went into the air, blasting free from me with the shock of a cannon going off. The manticore turned its head, as though sensing the lethal energy springing up to meet it. But the power seemed to chase after it, careening off the mirrored walls and ceiling, infusing it from every side.

When the manticore crashed to the terrazzo floor at my feet, the force of the impact shattered its body into a thousand stone fragments.

And that's how Kyra got her groove back, I thought deliriously just before passing out.

155

CHAPTER 9

When I came to, the first thing I became aware of was that I ached like hell. I touched my neck and felt the tender area at the base of my throat. Raising my hand, I made out a dab of blood on my fingertips.

That was twice, then. Two times in as many days, the snakes had saved my ass. And this time I hadn't even asked them to counter the manticore's poison; they'd done it on their own while I was unconscious.

And the Medusa's Gaze . . . it had *never* worked like that before. The speed and furious power of it left me aghast; it had completely petrified the manticore in the space of a heartbeat, something I—it—had never been capable of doing before. And the way it had chased after the manticore's eyes as though it were alive and hungry. . . . I repressed a shudder.

What in God's name was happening to me?

The first flare I'd thrown was starting to sputter. That meant I'd been out no more than fifteen minutes. I brushed off the pebbles that had been scattered all over my legs and lap and pushed myself to my feet. My twisted ankle felt like it was the size of a honeydew in my boot and hurt when I put my full weight on it. I had a suspicion I could thank the snakes' venom for that little side effect. And speaking of which . . .

I reached up and patted the top of the beret. "Um . . . thanks," I mumbled uncertainly.

There was a muffled hissing and then silence. Maybe they felt the awkwardness of the moment too.

Time to deal with that later. The flare in the center of the chamber had guttered and fizzled out. The others would follow in a minute or two. I hobbled to the steps and made my way back to the sixteenth floor. The trek up the spiral stairwell to the penthouse level took way longer than it should have, but every step was becoming a misery for my ankle. I was nearly hopping by the time I reached the suite's double doors.

I wasn't expecting trouble, but the habits of a lifetime aren't easily set aside. Even so, when I shoved open the doors with my shoulder, razing the room with my gunsights, I wasn't surprised to find the master suite empty except for the girl.

She was slumped on the floor next to an enormous four-poster canopy bed, her wrist chained to the headboard. Her golden hair was splayed over her face so that I couldn't tell for a moment if she was awake or asleep, living or dead. But the noise of my entrance stirred her and she raised her head.

"Kyra . . . ?"

How the hell did she know that? And why was it so painful to hear the anguish in her voice? I holstered my guns and went over to her.

"Yeah," I said, bending to one knee in order to work on the manacle's lock. "Yeah, kid; it's me." It was a simple enough latch mechanism to pick—

"Oh, Kyra!" the girl sobbed and threw her arms around my neck.

"Kid, let me just—" Great; now I couldn't reach the damn lock. "I'm trying to . . . fine." I sat back and let her hug me while her body shook with spasms. I didn't know what to do with my hands. After a minute of leaving them in the air like I expected to be cuffed myself, I felt ridiculous enough to drop them onto her upper back. Now I guess I was supposed to comfort her. I blew out my breath: First Benny, now her; I was just going to pat everybody today, was I? I slapped her back a few times and was rewarded by her sobbing even harder. Terrific.

Was there a time limit on this? I guess it'd be rude to ask. Let's say three minutes.

Actually, it wasn't all bad. Her hair felt like warm silk under my fingers. It was even a little nice to be touching someone for a reason that probably didn't have anything to do with killing them later. And my ankle . . . I reached down and gave my foot an experimental squeeze. No pain. Wow; she was so potent that just touching her triggered the healing effect? I'd never heard of anyone who could do that.

All right, that had to be three minutes. It seemed the worst of the crying had subsided. At least I was willing to assume so. I unwrapped her arms as gently as I knew how.

"Hold still," I said, more harshly than I intended, and got out my lock-pins. Standard A7 slide should do the trick. A few seconds later, I tossed the manacle aside and drew the girl up. Somehow, over the course of the last twenty-four hours, I'd forgotten she was only a few inches shorter than me. She'd be tall when she was full-grown, and probably even more lovely than she was today. Some girls have all the luck.

Her long-sleeved blouse and slacks had been torn, exposing her pale, slim limbs. There was a wide, ragged tear across the waist of her shirt. Sharks can detect a drop of blood in a million drops of water, or so I've read. But I didn't need a supersensitive nose to see that the fabric edges were rimmed with dark stains.

"Are you hurt?"

She shook her head, sniffling. "Not . . . now."

Frowning, I checked her extremities. There were a number of fine white scars set in the alabaster skin. I tugged up the shirt to expose her abdomen. A mottled pattern of scar tissue covered her right side, as though—

"He tortured you."

159

Her grimace was answer enough. "I told him I could . . . heal him," she said. "He . . . wanted to see how far I could heal myself."

Slashing at her arms and legs hadn't been enough to satisfy the sick bastard. So he'd had her play Prometheus for him, making a chew toy out of her. And she just stood there and took it, the same way she silently endured my poking and prodding now. I didn't know what appalled me more: her helplessness or her toughness.

Marty . . . I ground my teeth. A quick death had been too good for you; you should be writhing in agony with your own quills sticking in your—

Druison.

I'd forgotten—! I checked my watch. It had to have been half an hour since—

"Stephanie," I said, drawing her hands together. "I need your help. There's a detective downstairs. He was hit by the manticore's spikes. They're poison—"

"Take me to him," she said at once, turning her face toward the doors. I led her back to the spiral stairwell and held her hand as we went down.

There was no way; thirty minutes was far too long. One of the manticore's quills had carried enough neurotoxin to nearly paralyze me within seconds. Three would probably have sent Druison into cardiac arrest or respiratory failure by now. It was stupid, futile to even hope—

But when I guided Stephanie off the steps onto the tenth floor, I heard the sound of Druison's labored breathing coming from the side room I'd tucked him into. As I shoved the door open, Stephanie brushed past me and fell to her knees by his side.

This was one tough cop. "Can you—?"

"Shh." She placed her palms over his chest and head. I stepped back when a soft radiance bloomed under her hands, writhing like a living thing as it spread over his body. Curlicues of light reached up over her bent head, rising in a mist.

"His spirit is leaving," she said in a dull tone. "Should I restrain it?"

"Yes!" I snapped and was surprised a little by my own vehemence. But what kind of question was that? And why ask me? I wasn't his mother, or keeper, or . . . or anything.

"Why?" Stephanie was looking up at me; her face trembled with strain. Fresh beads of sweat had sprung up on her brow.

"What?"

"Why life . . . for him?" Stephanie panted. "You hold death close . . . like a newborn child. It permeates your aura. His . . . would be a natural end. Why should I halt it?"

"Because . . ." My hands fumbled uselessly at the air. "Because there's nothing natural about this. He was poisoned by a *manticore*, for Crissakes. He wouldn't even be here if he hadn't—" Listened to me. Trusted me. "—if he wasn't a cop." I seized on that; it was sensible, safe. "And if he dies here, we're going to be chased by more cops than you can imagine even exist. We need him to live."

Stephanie bowed her head. "Give me your hand."

Ooh, I did not like the sound of that. Gingerly, I put my hand forward. As though she could see, Stephanie took ahold of it, then clenched her free hand in the folds of the detective's shirt, as though trapping something under the fabric.

"What are you—?"

"Sshh," she hissed, her face hidden by the spill of her silken hair.

The brain goes to some strange places at a moment like this. As I stood there fidgeting with my hand held captive, I found myself suddenly remembering the fish I'd tried to keep as a pet when I was six. I'd come upon it in a tiny tide pool among the rocks one afternoon, thrown out of the ocean by the spray, gasping as the sun dried up its tiny refuge. I'd brought it home in a bowl, so pleased to have preserved it during the long trek. I'd been so proud of myself, showing it off to my mother, the little thing I'd saved. I remember my mother being unimpressed; she said something about fish belonging in the sea, not in a house. But I'd argued passionately for keeping it, swearing with the fervor only a little girl can have that I would feed and care for it. I gave it a place of honor on the old, gnarled wooden dresser in my room. For two days I doted over it, marveling at how bright the colors were on its small scales and fins, making up a story of how drops of light had fallen from a rainbow into the sea to coat it. In all the world, it was mine alone and I was its Momma. Then, on the third day, I came home from chasing rats out of the chicken coops and found it on the woven mat next to my bed. My mother said it had probably tried to go home, where it belonged. I cried for a day and a night, and, while my tears still fell, my mother fed it to the cat.

Two days later, the cat fell off a stone wall it had previously negotiated every day for six years without difficulty. My mother had seen us playing together earlier that day and demanded an explanation.

There's no literal translation for my reply. But the closest phrase in English would be "Lady, shit happens."

We didn't keep a lot of pets after that.

Abruptly, I became aware I could feel my heartbeat pounding in my ears. Only, for a few moments, it sounded like two thudding pulses, one overlaid on the other, as though . . .

The sensation faded.

Druison twitched and groaned. The light collapsed back into his chest like a bubbling fountain returning to its source. Stephanie sank against me in the darkness.

"Is he—?"

"He is like you," Stephanie nodded. She sounded weary. "Kindred. He has strength beneath what can be seen." She turned her wide, blind eyes up toward me. "There is a thread between you, something that has happened or will happen. I saw it, glowing red."

Red for Valentine's roses or red for blood? I wanted to ask. But just then Druison groaned and opened his eyes. I eased Stephanie into an upright sitting position and knelt next to his head. "Hey, cop. You okay?"

He blinked slowly, uncomprehending. Then recognition kindled in his face.

"Kyra Anastas," he murmured, smiling like a happy drunk. "You hit me."

"Not this time," I said and couldn't help but grin at his goofy expression.

"Wait. . . . You're under arrest," he mumbled and tried to sit up.

"Let's not start with that again," I said, pushing him back, which wasn't hard. "You've had a busy night. I'll be running along in a moment." I shouldn't be feeling so much relief right now. This detective was a complication I simply did not need. "I just thought you should meet my client." I hauled Stephanie into view. "Detective Druison, meet Stephanie Rougnagne, the girl who doesn't exist."

"Pleased to meet you," said Stephanie. "You rest, Detective. We'll meet again one day, I think. At least I hope so."

Druison mumbled something, but his eyes were already closing. I frowned and patted his cheek with the back of my hand. "Cop?"

"He can't hear you," Stephanie said. "He's still healing. It was a near thing, but his resistance to the poison was strong, and helped by the strength you shared. He'll sleep now till the healing's complete."

"Oh. Okay. Sure. That's probably good for us." Seeing as how I didn't relish trying to explain a room decorated with thousands of bones, blood spattered across half a dozen floors, and a shattered statue of a manticore, not to mention the absence of a team of Chechan kidnappers.

"Is he safe to leave here?" Stephanie asked as I helped her to her feet.

It's safer than hanging with us, if the last twenty-four hours was any indication. "Yeah, he's good," I said. "All the monsters have left the building." I shrugged. "Or will have. C'mon."

I steered Stephanie toward the doorway, then stopped. On impulse, I went back and pulled an old seat cushion off a nearby chair. Slapping the worst of the dust from it, I wedged the cushion under the detective's head.

"What are you doing?" asked Stephanie. Was that an amused expression on her face? It had better not be.

"Nothing," I said, embarrassed, and took her by the wrist. "Let's go. I want to be out of here before it gets light outside."

We went down the stairs. I was still jumpy enough to keep one hand on the pommel of my Glock. The fight with Marty had been too close for comfort. The conviction suddenly struck me that years of preying only on humans had made me soft. I had forgotten how close to death life was among the Mythic, how the struggle to survive was what dominated every waking moment. How good it felt just to be alive to greet the dawning of the new day.

Not that I wanted to greet it within the city limits on this particular morning. Things had gotten way too hot around here lately. Between the cops and the hunters, the Windy City was turning into a shooting gallery, with the bull's-eye painted squarely on my butt.

Out in the alley, Mother Night still covered all, the lowering clouds reflecting back the lights the Chicago cityscape defiantly threw at the uncaring heavens. I fished out the keys the Chicago PD had so kindly furnished to provide us with transportation.

"Where are we going?" asked Stephanie as I slid her into the front passenger seat.

"Somewhere I can get a few answers," I said. "Starting with you."

I settled in behind the wheel and turned the ignition.

"What do you want to know?"

Boy, was that a long list. Instead of answering, I backed up until I could bring the car around, then took her out to Michigan Avenue. From here we could get onto Lake Shore Drive and follow it out of the city. I felt a real pang leaving the Veyron back at the parking garage under Millennium Park, but it was too risky going back for it now. *I'll see you again, Baby,* I thought.

Stephanie still had her head cocked toward me in expectation.

"Sure," I said, easing out onto the main road. "There's one question you can answer right now." I kept my gaze on the light up ahead. "Did—did you really tell your mother I was . . . beautiful?"

I sensed more than saw the smile on the girl's face. "Yes."

The light turned green. I shook my head.

"You really are blind," I muttered, and stamped on the accelerator.

164

෪෪෪

Chicago boasts one of the most gorgeous highways in North America—the famous stretch of four-lane magic known as Lake Shore Drive. If you want to start an argument with a native Chicagoan, tell them the Drive—or LSD, as many call it—is nice but not the equal of the West Side Drive in New York City or the Pacific Coast Highway in California. Sparks will surely fly.

Running north and south for nearly fifteen miles, the Drive wraps itself like a lover around the gleaming heart of the city even as it hugs the western shore of Lake Michigan. Starting down on the South Side, it wends itself past many of the Windy City's signature landmarks—Soldier Field, the Shedd Aquarium, the Field Museum, Navy Pier, the Gold Coast District—and continues past a variety of parks and beaches until it terminates at Hollywood Avenue. Plans to extend it further north have been repeatedly opposed and scuttled by residents of the suburbs fearful of being overrun by traffic and cut off from the lake.

During the day, the corporate headquarters and exclusive high-rise apartments, condominiums, and co-op buildings that crowd the eastern border of the city look like glittering stacks of coins piercing the blue skies, a tangible reminder of the economic power that has enabled Chicago to be consistently ranked among the ten greatest cities in the world. But at night—especially now, with dawn still many hours away and the beacons of downtown receding in the rearview mirror—the complexion of the Drive changed. The gleaming buildings that thrust up from the granite bedrock like monuments to the restless, unappeasable anti-gods of progress and technology fell behind, and all you were left with was the black, primordial mass of the lake on your right. The sinuous winding of the road became hypnotic under the overhanging streetlamps, their watchful lights like the lures of angler fish, inviting you to chase them into the dark that surrounded the city and, beyond that, the planet itself.

The Great Lakes were older than civilization, formed by unimaginable amounts of meltwater left behind when the frozen sheets from the last ice age had withdrawn ten thousand years ago, back in the days when the old gods supposedly walked the Earth. Of the five bodies of water that made up the Great Lakes, Lake Michigan was the only one entirely within the borders of the United States. Its sandy shores were seductively soft, sometimes called the "singing sands" because of the way they squeaked under your feet when you walked across them.

It would be nice to walk on a beach again, to feel the sand beneath my toes, to listen to the singing . . .

I shook my head to clear it, squeezing the wheel under my palms until they ached. I'd been running on an adrenalin high for most of the night, and now that it was wearing off, I was dog tired. We needed to go to ground, and soon. But first we had to get clear of Chicago.

One more day, I thought. Less, really. All we had to do was make it to midnight tonight. And then . . . what? I glanced over at Stephanie and realized she had nodded off, her magnificent golden hair slipping down to cover most of her face.

What was supposed to happen at midnight? What would this sheltered kid suddenly be capable of? Would it really be over then, or had Elspeth Rougnagne tricked me into a lifetime of battling her enemies for her? *In the soul there is only truth*, she had said. But maybe even that was a lie.

And who were her enemies anyway? What were they doing right now? They'd tracked us to the stadium. Could they track us again?

They are desperate, Elspeth Rougnagne had warned, *and they are close.*

I had planned to stay on the Drive until near the end and then cut through Edgewater until I picked up the Skokie Highway and could go north again. There was a little safe house tucked away in Waukegan, about an hour away. But one of the Agency's safe houses had already proven no haven.

On impulse, I turned off at Foster Avenue and headed west, turning my back on the lake and all my familiar environs. From here I could pick up Route 90, which would take me halfway across the state. I'd drive straight to Iowa, if that's what it took to get clear of this mess.

A soft noise made me look over at the passenger seat. Then I had to cover a smile. No one was looking, of course; it was more reflex than anything. Stephanie Rougnagne—child of light, golden girl, mystery kid with the big destiny—was snoring.

The gentle patter of raindrops on the windshield began. I put on the wipers. I felt a little more alert since making a decision about which way to head. But we were still a ways off from where I wanted to be before sunrise. I turned the radio on for company then grimaced. Druison had left the channel on some country station. I shook my head; as if I needed more evidence that that relationship had been doomed from the start. I pressed the scan button until I found WRXQ, Chicagoland's hard rock station, and dialed down the volume. Someone was singing about whether she should listen to her heart or her head, wishing she could turn back time and start all over again. Don't we all, sweetheart.

I've heard it said that the universe sends you messages at times, to guide you on your way. All you had to do was listen. If that was really true, I was overdue for a broadcast showing me the path I needed to tread today. Instead, all I was getting was the plaintive cries of a songstress, cut off at the end by an annoying jovial deejay.

"Hope you enjoyed that as much as I did," he chirped. "That was 'Sleeping With Si—'"

I stabbed the scan button, irritated. So much for my cosmic connection. A few more tries garnered the opening piano chords of Queen's "We Are the Champions." I listened as a man who'd died while I was still in diapers sang about loss and triumph.

I let the bittersweet melody lead me through the rain and dark.

Two hours later, the brightly lit sign for a rest stop proved too much of a temptation. I pulled off Route 90 and found us a parking spot away from the half dozen or so other vehicles that occupied the lot. The rain had kept pace with us, gradually increasing as we made our way west. The lot was filled with small puddles, reflecting the red and yellow neon lights.

Considering the circumstances, we'd made pretty good time getting this far. I'd made two stops on the way: the first at a long-term parking garage to switch cars so we'd be less easy to track; the second at an ATM to cash out some of the Rougnagne contract. The Agency issued special black cards with an embedded chip to "contractors" like myself. I could put one in any bank's machine on the planet and use it to withdraw my fee. Phil had once tried to explain to me that the chip scrambled the data so that it looked to the bank like an ordinary transaction was happening among its own accounts, while in reality the card was facilitating a transfer of Agency funds to legitimate accounts, depositing it and withdrawing it at the same time, and then erasing the transaction from the bank's electronic records. I'd zoned out after the technobabble got into high gear, but there was no arguing with the process. In less than five minutes, I was all set. I'd felt a sense of real relief when I slipped back into the car and found Stephanie still soundly asleep; I hadn't wanted to answer any questions about what I was doing.

Now I had nearly one hundred thousand dollars in small denominations stuffed into the satchel I'd borrowed from the detective. That should be plenty to work with, for the time being.

I turned off the engine and shook Stephanie's shoulder.

"Kid," I said. "Hey, kid. Wake up."

Stephanie brushed her hair back and blinked her milky white eyes. We were going to have to do something about those. While she stretched and yawned her way back from sleep, I fished through the dashboard compartments until I found a pair of banged-up sunglasses.

"Here; put these on."

"Why?"

"Because I don't need people ogling you more than they're going to already," I said. "We're trying to fly under the radar here. Speaking of which

. . ." I dug in the back seat for a sweatshirt I'd stolen earlier from the good detective's trunk. Even though it smelled like Druison's last visit to the gym had been fairly recent, I was still oddly reluctant to put it on her. The slight musky odor made me wonder where he worked out, and what he looked like while he was doing it. Pulling it down over Stephanie's head felt like I was giving something up. But we couldn't have the girl traipsing around with torn clothes in front of the whole world, or at least whatever part of it had had the misfortune to find themselves in central Illinois in the dead of night.

Next, the sweatpants. I tucked her hair into the back of her collar and finished the job off by putting a baseball cap on her head. Then I surveyed my work.

Well. There was nothing that was going to make that perfect face plain enough to not turn heads. But we'd just have to deal.

"All right," I said, making sure of my beret. "We're not staying here long. Just a bite and a bathroom break, and we'll be on the move again. With luck, we can find a motor lodge nearby and crash."

Stephanie had endured my tender ministrations without complaint. But now she looked up with an expression of concern. "Where are we?"

I rubbed at the corner of my eye, which was developing a tired tic. What had the last road sign said? "Um . . . Belvidere, I think. Or Garden Prairie. Something like that."

The look of shock and alarm that swept across the girl's face was jarring. "We're outside the city?"

"Yeah," I said. "Look, it's okay. I don't know what you've heard about these rural areas, but they're not so bad; I mean, they're not totally bad—"

"No, no," she said, whipping her head back and forth. "We have to stay in the city! You have to take me back!"

Maybe it was just a measure of how beat I was, but I felt like sparks were suddenly showering down on the tinder pile of my mood. I made an effort to control my temper. "What are you talking about?"

"We have to go back!" she whined again.

169

"I heard you the first time!" I snarled. "Why?"

"Because—" She shook her head. "This isn't the way it happens! There's no threads out here, nothing that shows the way! I'm *blind* here!"

And she looked it. The calm self-possession she'd shown since the moment we'd met was gone, replaced by naked fear. Even when she'd been crying in my arms, she hadn't been this miserable.

I caught her shoulders, torn between anger and empathy. Part of me wanted to comfort her; part of me wanted to shake her until her teeth rattled. How much more of this was I going to have to put up with? Did she have any idea what she'd put me through already? "Listen. Listen to me! I understand: You're scared. I get it. But we can't be in the city right now. I have the whole Chicago Police Department looking for me. And you—God knows what else may come looking for you. We needed to get out of there. So we're going to keep moving. Do you understand?"

She ducked her head, breathing heavily. "*You* don't understand," she muttered.

I pressed my lips together. "Maybe," I said. "There's a lot of things I don't understand. Like why you had to drag me into all this. But needing to pee and eat and sleep? That I *do* understand. So let's go."

I threw my collar up against the rain and pushed open the car door. Getting Stephanie out the other side and across the parking lot was a minor feat, and by the time we trudged into the diner, we were both soaking wet. That improved my mood considerably. I steered Stephanie straight to the ladies' and took a few minutes afterward to dry off the worst of the wet with some paper towels. She endured my efforts in stony silence, shivering with her eyes shut.

The next time I'm trapped in a stroller park with one of the Natalies of this world, I thought dourly, I'll tell them about the surly teenager I had and how I sent her off to boarding school. That would be enough to shut someone up.

We found a booth where I could sit with my back to the wall. The waitress, a beefy woman with a face like a friendly bulldog, came over right away.

170

"Coffee, hon?"

"Yes, please."

"How about your little sister?"

"She's not—"

"Do you have popcorn?" Stephanie interrupted, perking up.

The waitress laughed. "No, sweetie, I do not. I do, however, have some excellent apple pie, fresh from the oven. What's with the shades? You famous or somethin'?"

"She's blind," I said, to forestall further friendliness. People were always willing to shy away if they thought there was something wrong with you. "And the pie sounds great. She'll have a slice." The air was heavy with the salty smells from the kitchen, making my stomach rumble. Small surprise; I hadn't had anything to eat for a day. "I'll take the, uh, eggs and sausage plate."

"Something to drink, hon?"

"Just the—oh, for her. Milk." Teenagers were supposed to drink seven glasses a day, I'd heard. It was good for their bones or something.

"Okay. I'm Marge, if you need anything else."

"Doubt it."

The waitress withdrew. I turned my attention to the three people sitting at the counter. They were watching the rebroadcast of the evening news. The stock market was down. Everything was going to hell. It hardly seemed worthwhile to call it news.

"Why do you do that?"

I turned my head away from the TV screen. "Do what?"

"Talk to someone like you hate them when you don't."

I shrugged. "Maybe I do."

"You talked to the detective that way too. But you saved him."

I laughed. "That was all you, kid. I was just along for the ride."

"No." Stephanie straightened in her seat, managing somehow to look regal even in her rags. Her solemn expression gave her an older appearance, hinting at the woman she would one day become. "You anchored his spirit with your own. I could not have held him without your strength."

171

I felt an answering warmth in my cheeks. I was suddenly glad the girl was blind. People didn't usually have complimentary things to say about me, truth be told. Of course I could probably count on even this good deed coming back to bite me in the ass.

"Is that why your aura is so confused?" Stephanie asked.

"My what?"

"Your aura," said Stephanie. "It's so turbulent, conflicted, like you're trying to go forward and backward at the same time. Like you're a trapped animal."

And this is why I don't do small talk. Because sooner or later, it always comes back around to what's wrong with me.

"Yeah? Well, saving that cop was just good business sense, kid. I try to leave as little mess behind me as possible. In my profession, bodies have a bad habit of coming back to haunt you."

Above the sunglasses, Stephanie's brow pinched. Even that looked pretty on her. Shaking my head, I surveilled the room for the tenth time. Just yokels being yokelly.

"Do you like it?"

I pulled my eyes off the surroundings. "Hm? Do I like what?"

"What you do. The hunting. The killing."

I scowled. "What's your interest?"

The girl cocked her head at me, uncomprehendingly.

"Why do you care?" I said, a little too loudly. Marge the Waitress took that opportune moment to arrive. Great. I took my coffee with a forced smile and pushed the pie and milk toward Stephanie.

"Special be out in a minute."

"Thanks." After Marge walked off, I leaned forward. "Your food's here. Eat. I don't know when we'll get another chance before—" *I'm through with you.* "Before tomorrow."

The waitress glanced over at us, her gaze lingering before she turned back to wiping down her countertop. On the overhead TV, the weather girl was explaining to everyone how spring had finally arrived. It was nothing but clear skies and warm weather out there. I glanced at the parking lot surface, dancing with the gusting rain. Maybe they didn't have the boonies on their fancy radar.

"I just want to know."

She was still on about this. "It's just a temp job until my modeling career takes off," I drawled. "I'm sure Victoria's Secret will call any day now to say that snake hair is in again and they need me for their cover shoot."

"You're not being serious."

"Yeah? Well, maybe that's 'cause it's none of your damn business, kid."

"I'm sorry. I didn't mean to hurt your feelings."

The eggs and sausage plate arrived. I mumbled some thanks but found I couldn't meet Marge's eyes. I stirred my coffee with a great deal of concentration.

"No," I finally said. "I don't like it."

How many times had I thought that? As many times as I'd done it, I suppose. But somehow saying it to another person made it feel different, like a confession.

"Why do you do it?"

The girl was relentless.

"Because it's what I do," I snapped. "It's what I'm trained to do."

"Couldn't you . . . train to do something else?"

More like her mother than she probably knew. But it was the same impossible question, with the same unavoidable answer.

"I'm not good for anything else," I hissed. "Okay? Is that the answer you wanted from me? Are you happy now?"

"No."

"Well, that makes two of us then. Great." I tapped her plate with the edge of my sugar spoon. "Now eat your damn pie. It's getting cold."

"Okay."

Frowning at everything and nothing, I sipped at my coffee. I needn't have worried about singeing my lips, though; it was barely warm. I sloshed the stuff around in my mouth, hunting for some vestige of heat without success.

I was casting about for Marge when my attention was drawn back to the television screen. The sportscaster was chuckling at some lead-in comment made by his equally brainless puppet co-worker.

"That's right, Charlie: a truly epic fail from our very own beloved home team. Folks, check out this video of a prank that almost went horribly wrong at last night's basketball game."

As the words were penetrating my skull, the picture switched to a jittery image of a woman hanging upside down from a balcony, her arms flailing. The camera zoomed in on her just as two green shapes appeared to slither out from around the hood of her white jacket.

OH.

MY.

GOD.

The camera zoomed back out in time to show the woman plucked up by Benny like a toy. She flattened her hood to her head and raced up the stairs, out of sight.

"—of their entertainment office says a janitor's cleaning cart banged into a makeshift platform that had been set up in one of the premium boxes. The stunt woman seen in the video was unharmed, but I mean, what were they thinking?"

"—and that getup! What was that? It looked like snakes or something—"

"Yes, and as you'd expect, the video's gone viral. Half a million people since last night have—"

From an Agency chemist, I had once learned seven different ways of inducing cerebrovascular accidents via various toxins present in ordinary household items. I knew how to cut off the flow of blood to the brain with five different choke holds and thumb jabs. But until tonight, I had never known what it felt like to actually *have* a stroke.

My stomach felt like it had just been put in a bag and slung over my shoulder. I was going to throw up. I was seriously going to throw up . . .

"What just happened?" asked Stephanie.

174

I tore my eyes away from the video. Coffee was dripping from Stephanie's sunglasses and cheeks. A spray of it covered both our dinner plates.

A giggle bubbled up in my throat. In a moment, I was going to become hysterical.

"You spilled your milk," I said, standing. "Finish your pie. Please wait here." Then I ran for the bathroom. There was Marge, washing her beefy hands in the sink. I ignored her and threw myself into a stall.

Oh my god. Omigodomigod. I dry heaved for a full minute before I could get my breathing under control. This was a disaster ... an unmitigated, full-blown, freakin' disaster. I'd seen the flashes go off while I was hanging there, but with everything else going on, I'd put the implications out of my mind. And in my worst nightmares, I'd never imagined somebody would have had the time to video it.

And it had already gone viral? Half a million people had seen it? How many more would before the end of the week? What if ... Gods below; what if my *mother* saw it? How many times had she warned me not to let the snakes grow out? She would kill me. She would absolutely and completely kill me. But no ... I'd tried to get her a computer once, but it had been too much hassle; she was too far from the town and thought the internet was just a trap set by pornographers anyway. She'd never hear or see this. But the rest of the planet could ... and would, including ...

The Agency. I caught my breath. The Agency was going to see it. And once they did, they really *were* going to kill me, and not by lecturing me to death. I had warned Phil about the danger to the Agency if I fell into the hands of the authorities, but the real danger was to me. Exposure of one their operatives risked exposure of the Agency. They'd never tolerate that. Better and easier to erase the operative. Nothing personal; it was just business.

This was all Rougnagne's fault. If she hadn't taken a contract out on herself, I'd have never gotten involved in this fiasco. Even if I avoided the cops and any more attempts on the girl's life for the next twenty hours, I was still screwed. The Agency would hunt for me without letup and, once they found me, would put me down like a rabid dog.

By the time I shoved open the stall door, my fear had transmuted into sweet fury. I was going to drag Stephanie out into the storm and leave her on the side of the highway for the next assassin that came along. I'd find a witch, or a spell, or . . . or something, and break free of this punishment. I didn't care if I was being sensible, or rational; I was through being everybody's patsy.

Marge the Waitress was still standing over the sink. The tap had continued to flow, and now the water had backed up to the top and spilled over the sides, spreading across the gritty tiles under her shoes. She didn't seem to notice, staring down at the rippling waters.

Maybe she'd caught the stroke meant for me. I almost brushed past her anyway, but some preterite instinct for empathy was apparently still left in me. I peered around her shoulder and said, "Hey, Marge, you in there?"

Her eyes were glazed, unfocused. I thought I caught a glint of lights dancing in them, reflected up from the sink. Then her big hand swept up behind me and seized the back of my neck. Before I could think to react, my head was thrust down into the water hard enough to slam my nose into the bottom of the sink.

I saw red and gasped, sucking in cold water. Big mistake. No matter how many times you've been trained and prepared for being in an underwater situation, all it takes is that first mouthful getting in your windpipe to trigger a panic reaction. I flailed and thrashed blindly, my feet skittering and slipping on the wet floor. The woman had her full weight on my neck, pinning me to the porcelain, and I couldn't get purchase to wriggle free.

The snakes were thrashing madly, trapped under the beret. I could hear them screaming in my head. Somehow their terror opened a clear space in my mind. I located the woman's abdomen and threw my elbow into it. I felt her yield slightly, but the pressure on my neck didn't ease up. She was too big and heavy to drive backward with the leverage she had, bent over me like that.

I tried stamping on her foot with my heel but kept missing a clean hit. Starbursts were going off before my eyes. I was drowning. In desperation,

176

I hooked my boot around her ankle and braced my hands against the sink, pushing backward with all my fading strength.

The wet tiles must have saved me, causing her shoes to slide under the force of my thrust. I clipped my jaw against the edge of the sink as we tumbled to the floor together. I rolled away, coughing and gagging, trying to get air back into my starving lungs.

Marge was getting ponderously to her feet. I rose as she charged at me with her head down like a bull. She slammed me against the wall before I could brace myself. I felt the tampon dispenser grinding against the small of my back as her hands fumbled for my throat.

But I'd had a second to get my wind back, and that was all it took. I blocked her hand with one forearm and then brought the heel of my palm up against her nose. She staggered back and, with the space that opened between us, I was able to deliver a kick that drove my heel deep into her solar plexus.

Despite her girth, the woman was no fighter. She dropped to her knees with a groan and didn't get up. That was lucky for her, as my next move would have been to put a .40 caliber slug in her brain.

"What the hell are you doing?" She was looking up, blood streaming from her nose. "Are you crazy?"

"*Me?*" I exploded. "You attacked *me*, lady!"

"I'm calling the cops," she said, climbing to her feet. She glared at the water everywhere. "My sink!"

"Let's not be hasty," I said, holding up a hand. "Here." I pulled out a wad of bills from my duster's pocket. "I think you may have had a seizure or something." I grabbed her wet palm and slapped five one-hundred-dollar bills into it. "Go see a doctor."

The woman gaped, her bloody nose forgotten. "I . . ."

"Great place you got here," I said and pushed my way out, leaving her standing there.

Stephanie was sitting in the booth unmolested. She seemed to sense my approach, looking up with a line of worry furrowing her flawless brow. "What is it?"

"We're leaving," I said, catching her wrist. There was no telling how long confusion would keep Marge rooted to the spot. We had to get out of here fast.

The rain pelted our backs as we fled to the car. I stuffed Stephanie into her seat and got behind the wheel. No one came out to chase us, but there could be flashing lights and sirens appearing at any moment. I peeled out of the lot and headed for the access ramp. From here, Route 90 West would take us . . . where? I couldn't think straight. If we got back on the highway and they put out an APB, we'd be sitting ducks out there.

Okay, then; change of plan. Instead of turning left onto the ramp, I made a right and hunted for a road to take us east.

My brain was spinning. That attack had made no sense. I wasn't *that* lousy a tipper. In fact, we hadn't even gotten to the tipping stage. And during the fight, Marge the Mad Waitress hadn't seemed so much pissed off as lobotomized, almost like she'd been . . . possessed.

Ah, gods; here we go again.

"Where are we going?" asked Stephanie.

I wished to hell I knew. Somehow, something had caught up with us. Until I knew what it was, running from it was the only option. But I stood as good a chance of blundering into it, or another assassin, by heading in any one direction. "You'll know when we get there," I rasped, stopping a conversation that could only have ended in blood. Speaking of which, I had the bitter copper taste of the stuff in my mouth from when I'd banged my jaw on the sink. My nose felt like it might have been broken.

"Kid," I muttered under my breath, "you'd better have the winning lottery number for tomorrow night in your head. Otherwise, I don't know why you could possibly be worth all this trouble."

Stephanie said nothing. Smart girl. Way to keep those perfect teeth.

178

Route 20 looked promising. I seemed to recall that it extended far enough that we might connect with Route 355 further south, but I didn't dare access the car's or my cell's GPS to check. We'd just have to take our chances. Maybe we'd drive to Indiana. Maybe we'd drive forever, or until we fell off the face of the Earth . . .

I started to chuckle. It was kind of funny, really. I hadn't gotten even a bite to eat back at the rest stop diner. I'd probably put more enemies on my trail.

And I'd completely forgotten to leave Stephanie by the side of the road.

CHAPTER 10

The gaunt, grizzled fellow behind the register looked dumb enough to lose a counting contest with a sheep. You'd have thought he'd never heard a woman ask for a room before. Odd—considering he was running a motor lodge, or at least the remains of one. Tucked away in a heavily wooded belt off the highway with its facade scored by peeling paint and moss, it had clearly seen better days.

"Two beds?" he repeated. This was really baffling him. Maybe I shouldn't have left Stephanie in the car. But I was trying to avoid being too easy to match up with any highway police bulletins that might have been issued. "Only got the one room. One room. With one bed."

This fascinating exploration of how far hominids could devolve and still be capable of speech was eating into valuable sleeping time. I weighed how long it would probably take to shoot the guy and find the right key on my own against the likelihood of actually piercing the haze that surrounded his brain.

I'd started reaching toward my shoulder holster when the proprietor had an epiphany. "Got a cot," he said, brightening. "It's in the closet."

"That'll do," I said. "How much?"

"How much?"

I'd be doing the gene pool a huge favor here. But I forced a smile, the last one I had left in my bag of tricks. "How much for the room?"

"Oh." He nodded as though we'd reached a deep accord. "Forty-nine ninety-nine." He licked his lips. "Plus tax."

I handed him a hundred-dollar bill.

"Can't give change for nothing bigger than a fifty," he said. "Wife's rule."

"I really could care less," I said, yawning earsplittingly. "Keep it. Get your wife something nice. Like a new husband. My key?"

"Key?"

I'd have stamped my little foot if I'd thought it would make a difference . . . or could have lifted my leg that far. "To the room!"

"Oh." He reached under the counter and fished out a small key with a red plastic tag attached to it. "It's for room—"

"Thirty-two," I said, displaying the number. "Got it."

"You just go out the door and turn left—"

"I'll find it!" I called over my shoulder.

Stephanie was sitting in the front seat. Somehow this kept surprising me. Every time I let her out of my sight, I was half expecting to come back and find her being dragged into the sky by a griffon or dragon or something. I snagged the satchel and her and walked past the row of plain doors until I found our number. Why on Earth did a motor lodge that had less than twenty rooms total in its single-story matching structures number them up to 32 anyway? The whole thing was stupid.

Inside, the room was a marvel of economy, meaning it had a bed, a nightstand, a window with faded curtains—orange ones, mind you—and a bathroom. I pushed open the bathroom door, expecting to find a closet with a hole in the floor. But what to my wondering eyes should appear but an actual tub, raised off the floor on ornate curved legs.

A bath. Sweet Hecate, I might take that over food, or even sleep.

I found the cot and set it up, dumping Stephanie onto the canvas.

"Go to sleep," I ordered. I checked my watch. "It'll be dawn soon. We'll hole up here till dark."

"And then?"

If she thought we were going to argue this point again, she was much mistaken.

"Then we'll see."

Stephanie put her head down. Within minutes, she was fast asleep—and snoring like a buzz saw. Terrif.

I sat down on the bed. The springs sagged under my weight until I was almost sitting on the floor. The whole place reeked of old cigarettes, its faux wood panels covered with years of film from accumulated smoke. As I wriggled off my high boots, it abruptly occurred to me that I hadn't lit up since Stephanie had healed me, not counting the laced cig Marty had given me. I laughed softly; maybe I'd really quit this time. Sure, why not?

The snakes were still quietly moving around under my beret. I sensed without looking that while they shared my tiredness, none of them were actually dead or dying. What the hell did that mean? They always died after I used them, and I'd used them with a vengeance to destroy the manticore. The cannibal festival should be in full swing by now, but instead I could feel them, all of them, their weight and heat, the muted potency of their collective presence like a powerful engine thrumming on idle. Was that because of Stephanie too?

Too many questions, always too many questions. But Answer Girl was snoring her golden head off, and I was in no shape for answers anyway, not unless she was going to use sock puppets to spell them out for me. I'd have to suffer their presence another night at least. Still, I left the beret covering them; it gave me at least the bare illusion of being alone with my thoughts.

I tossed my duster to the base of the bed and turned off the lamp. Lights strung on the trees outside danced in the wind, throwing capering shadows against the curtains. Raindrops tattooed against the glass. I sank into the bed with one hand on the pommel of my Glock.

I thought I'd be out in seconds. God knew I needed the rest. But my thoughts were still churning, keeping sleep at bay.

The hunters, the cops, the Agency—how many were out there right now, looking for me? If the Agency really was on my trail, I couldn't risk accessing any more of my fee monies. Odds were the little black magic card would give them my location within seconds. So I was stuck with the cash I had taken before leaving the city.

Where to go? That was the problem, but I really had no idea how to solve it. As never before, I realized how cut off I'd allowed myself to become over the years since being assigned by the Agency to Chicagoland, since before even that. Elspeth Rougnagne had cut closer to the bone than I'd wanted to admit when she'd said I was without friends or family, love or hope. I felt like I'd been bleeding ever since.

She will destroy you, the Voice had warned. Maybe she'd done that already. It seemed as though the mold of my life had been broken into pieces by the girl on the cot across from me, with the same swiftness and ease a child might scatter a carefully constructed anthill. Now death was closing in from every side. What was I supposed to do?

What are you?

Delgado hadn't known what was killing him. But Rougnagne had. Yet she'd asked me the same question. Why? Wasn't the answer obvious?

No, I'd told the daughter of the woman I'd killed. *I don't like it. But it's all I'm good for.*

Did I really believe that? Or was it just easier to say that than to try?

What if you could be something more?

"I guess we'll never know, Elspeth," I murmured to the shifting shadows on the ceiling.

Finally, sleep came for me.

184

I woke with a start, my fist closing on the grip of my gun. For a moment I had no idea where I was. Then I saw Stephanie sitting across from me, her long legs folded under her on the cot. I checked my watch; it was a quarter past twelve. For a moment the dimness outside the window had me confused. Had I slept the whole day away? Was it after midnight? But if the *geas* of my soul promise had lifted, I felt no different. If I was free—

Then I saw the little "p.m." on the digital face. It was just past noon. Which meant I'd slept about eight hours. I felt a sense of disappointment about that and yet also an odd sort of elation, as though I'd been given another chance.

To do what?

Stephanie was staring at me. Well, facing me, anyway.

"You snore," she said.

"So do you," I shot back.

She laughed. I sniggered, then scowled. I was still mad at her, at her mother, at the way they'd conspired to turn my life upside down. I'd be damned if we were doing a bonding thing here.

"You should have waked me," I said.

"You needed rest."

"How would you know that?" I challenged. "You're blind. How can you tell when someone needs rest?"

She shrugged. "When they're snoring."

I laughed. I couldn't help it. And it was a good laugh too, easing some of the tension in my chest.

But we were deep in the woods here—literally and figuratively. It was time for some answers.

"We need to talk," I said.

"I know." Stephanie cocked her head. "I heard someone outside their room a little while ago, saying there's a . . . vending machine? It's around the corner of the building. You can get food from those, right? Maybe it would be better if we talked on a full stomach."

❧❧❧

Fifteen minutes later, I marched back in from the rain and poured the goodies onto the mattress. Stephanie waited patiently.

"Okay," I said, sorting things. "No popcorn, as predicted. But I scrounged up four packs of peanut butter crackers, a Danish that looks like it's from the Middle Ages, a bag of pretzels, and some licorice. To drink we have a bottle of lemonade for you and two sodas for me." At least they had caffeine. I felt loads better after sleeping, but I wasn't about to neglect all my addictions at once. "What do you want first?"

"Licorice, please. I would like to try that."

"Here you go." She bit off a piece and chewed. I watched her face warm with delight. "You really never had any of this stuff before?"

She shook her head. "Mother was very strict. She wanted me to avoid impure influences. And cavities."

If she'd wanted you to steer clear of impure influences, she shouldn't have left you with me. I tore open a bag of crackers and fell on them. "You miss her?"

She nodded.

"I'm . . . sorry."

She cocked her head. "Sorry that I miss her, or sorry that you killed her?"

The soda bottle paused at my lips. Okay, I guess the kid gloves were coming off. I took a long swig, thinking, then wiped my lips with my sleeve. "Both, I guess."

"Why?" She seemed honestly puzzled.

"Why what?"

"Why would you regret killing her? She asked you to. She knew what she was doing."

I shook my head. "That's not what we have to talk about."

"But it is." She leaned forward on the cot, a trio of red Twizzlers sticking out of her mouth. She was halfway through the licorice already. "It's as important as anything else, maybe more so."

That was news to me. "Why?"

"Because it is."

I frowned. "This is the problem with oracles," I snapped. "They act like they're telling you something when, in reality, they're not."

"This is the problem with people who talk to oracles," Stephanie said evenly. "You try to tell them the truth, but they never want to hear it."

"Yeah? What truth?"

"That the only way for you to end this is to let yourself be destroyed. But I think you already knew that."

I sucked in my breath through my teeth. Nothing like a good jolt of adrenalin to go with your breakfast. Really helps the food stay down.

"What are you talking about?"

Stephanie swallowed then drank from her lemonade bottle. "It's kind of sour."

"It would be after licorice. Answer the question."

"But it's not the one you want the answer to."

"What makes you say that? Why would I ask a question if I didn't want an answer?"

"Because you're hiding," Stephanie said. "You've been hiding all your life."

I bristled. "What do you know about my life? I thought your specialty was the future."

"The future . . . the past . . . everything is part of the great, shifting tapestry. I see the threads, where they come from, where they go . . ."

"Ooh, spooky," I said. "Still not an answer."

Stephanie shrugged.

"Okay," I said. "Answer this, then: What are you?" Everyone liked posing that question to me; let's see how much she enjoyed having to answer it.

"What am I?" She brushed her fingers together, her unseeing gaze wandering about the little room. "I don't know."

"You don't know?" I rasped. "How can that be? Your mother said you had this great destiny. Marty—the manticore—called you the 'Child of Light.' You saying you have no idea what all that means?" Why I've been put through all this?

She shook her head, plainly unhappy. "My mother told me that I'd know when it was time. I would ask her sometimes, when I worked up the courage, but she would just give me hints: 'Something old,' she would say. 'Something new.' She said I had to wait, that a flower couldn't be pulled open; it bloomed when it was ready."

"That sounds like her," I agreed ruefully. "Even her ghost gave me the same rigamarole."

"You saw her?" Stephanie leaned forward eagerly. "How is she? Oh." Her face fell. "Of course. Dead."

I couldn't just leave it at that. "She, um, looked good. Happy." When she wasn't screaming how I'd loused everything up.

"You are a bad liar, Kyra. But thank you."

Despite everything, it was hard to stay mad at this girl. She was just so damned innocent.

"The *laelapi* . . . the manticore . . . who's sending them? Why are they after you?"

She shook her head. "I'm sorry; I don't know."

"You're only half human. You must get your abilities from your father. Do you know who he was?"

She smiled, but it was a smile of memory. "Mother wouldn't tell me his name, or his nature. Though one time . . . she said their union came down to a case of simple mathematics. She seemed to be making a joke."

Mathematics? What the hell could that mean? One plus one equals three? The square root of sixty-nine is eight something? Two negatives equal . . .

A positive.

Is that what Elspeth Rougnagne had been trying to do? Create something good out of two evils? Could that really work? I chewed my pretzels, thinking.

"How'd you lose your eyesight?"

"I was born this way. Mother said it was because I needed to see the important things first—the threads that bind us together—before the rest. She said the world would distract me."

"You put a lot of faith in what your mother told you."

"What is life without faith?"

Safe. Well, safer. "Don't you ever wish she hadn't, you know, put you through all this? That you could have had a normal life?"

"No. My mother loved me. She knew what was best for me. She was my life."

"I'm sorry."

"You keep saying that. You don't have to apologize for what you did."

"I killed your mother!" I cried, lurching to my feet, sending pretzels everywhere. "Christ, kid, how can you be okay with that?"

"You keep wanting me to punish you, to hate you. But I chose you to help her end her life when it was time. I knew you would agree to help, to protect me. And you did."

I froze. She didn't . . . "What do you think happened between me and your mother?"

"I know that she asked you to help, that she offered you a chance to walk a new path, to do more than be a killer. And that you said yes."

"You . . . saw this?"

"No. I wasn't there, of course. Mother said I had to wait in my room while she talked to you. I had told her about you, about how I wanted you to come and take me when it was time. I knew she had her doubts, but I was sure of you. I knew you would say yes."

Unable to stand, I sat down on the bed. The ancient springs groaned and sagged, carrying me to the floor. I wished they could carry me further, to the depths of the Earth, to the bottom of the abyss that had just opened in my heart.

It was true, then. Stephanie didn't know about the soul-lock. Her mother had offered me a choice, all right, but when I didn't take it, she'd extorted the promise from me, on pain of death if I refused. Only Stephanie thought I had chosen it of my own free will, that I was some sort of knight in shining armor, the hero who had shed the skin of her old life to become something new.

I felt sick. I felt dirty.

Well, what the hell had I expected? That I really was the good guy in this story? That everything I'd ever done could just be whitewashed away like it had never happened? There were no fairy tales of princesses kissing snakes and turning them into princes, were there? And in the legend of Medusa, only her dead, severed head had done anyone any good.

Why did you choose me? That had been the question I had wanted to ask her, only I had lacked the guts to come out and say the words. Instead, I'd tried to sneak up on the question, to get to it without exposing myself to being hurt.

So much for that plan.

And now I had my answer. Only it was an answer based on a lie.

"Stephanie, I—" I raised my head, but her expression jammed the words in my throat. She sat there, this pure thing, with all the trust of a child in her face, a creature of blind, misguided faith.

"I need a bath," I said, and fled the room.

Twenty minutes later, I lay soaking with my eyes closed in a tubful of water so hot it would have scalded a normal human's skin. But I was grateful for the heat and even the discomfort. I needed to feel something else besides the hollow ache in my chest.

Why hadn't I just told her the truth? Was some part of me so stupid that I was still clinging to this ridiculous notion that I was her protector because I had *chosen* the job?

That was nuts. Up to half an hour ago, I hadn't even known she had this crazy idea. But now that I did know . . . I didn't want to give it up.

Except there was nothing to give up, was there? Just a lie.

A lie that made this good, sweet, pure girl look at me with trust in her blind eyes. That made me feel like . . .

Like I wasn't just a monster.

I felt myself drifting, my arms outstretched, resting on either side of the tub, the snakes nestled in languid torpor atop my head as they enjoyed the gently curling steam. Was Stephanie singing in the next room? I heard snatches of melody through the wall, then my thoughts wandered.

In my mind's eye, I was twelve years old again, standing at the port of Anafi before dawn, with the trawler captain waiting impatiently at the end of the dock and my mother standing behind me. She'd dug her nails into my scrawny, sun-bronzed shoulders hard enough to leave marks that stayed on my skin for days. Careful to avoid my cursed eyes, she'd whispered in my ear: "Never let them grow. Do you hear me, child? You must do as I've done for you, every day of your life. Shave them off without fail. Promise this."

And I'd promised, with my sight half blinded by tears and my heart breaking that my mother was sending me away, banishing me for killing that innocent boy, my sweet Pietro.

"Now go," she'd said. No hug. No last kiss. Just a push hard enough to send me stumbling forward, down the long, awful pier, where the captain had taken the packet of one-hundred-drachma bills I'd been holding—the price for quick and quiet passage from my home—and ushered me below-decks without meeting my eyes.

I'd sneaked a peek out a porthole as the trawler had made its way clear of the harbor, fighting a heavy current. But my mother was already gone. I wouldn't even hear her voice again for four years, till I found a way to contact her by satellite phone. I hadn't seen her since. I guess I never would.

And if you could? asked a small voice in my head.

If I could . . . if she would welcome me back, open her arms to me. . . . Oh, if she'd only forgive me . . .

I seemed to see her face then, rising up out of the mists around me.

"Daughter," she said, folding her arms around my neck. "I forgive you..."

Part of me realized I was dozing, that this was a dream. But I didn't care; it was too sweet to care. I felt the tears leaking from the corners of my closed eyes, felt my arms slipping into the tub, and it didn't matter. That was happening far away, to someone else, long ago.

"I forgive you too," said a gentle voice, and there was my darling boy, my beautiful Pietro, his sky-blue eyes alive with light and humor and love again, joining us, wrapping his arms around us both. I wept with joy at the sight of his smile, the feel of his warm skin on mine. The air was filled with the sweet scent of flowers, the singing of the birds in the stone pines around us. It was too much; I could hardly breathe...

"And I forgive you," said a third voice. Stephanie, coming forward, walking across the beach to me, her arms outstretched, the wind sending her golden hair billowing around her head, whipping across the sunglasses I'd given her. The rush of the waves was in my ears, the song of the ocean...

"You forgive me?" I said, choking back the tears. "For killing your mother?"

"I do," she said, smiling. Her slim hand stole to the shades she wore, drawing them off. "And for letting me die."

"'Let—?'" I gasped, and then I saw that behind her sunglasses were two empty sockets, black holes that fell into an endless abyss.

My eyes flew open. I was lying on the bottom of the tub, the waters shimmering over my head. Phosphorescent eyes gazed down at me.

With a wrench, I clawed my way back to the surface and fell onto the mat, coughing and retching water out of my lungs. From the other room, I heard Stephanie call out if I was all right.

No, I was definitely *not* all right. I reeled up, still whooping for air, and ripped one of my guns out of its holster.

A dim face wavered on the surface of the roiling waters, like a projection. It grinned wickedly and winked up at me.

A Siren. A goddamn Siren. And she'd nearly drowned me in the friggin' bathtub.

192

"Guess adding the girl was too much, huh?" The sharp slash of a mouth pressed its lips together in mock chagrin. "Couldn't quite get her eyes—"

I answered with a hail of bullets that shattered the porcelain sides of the tub, sending water gushing all over the floor.

"My, my," the voice bubbled with mirth. "Temper, temper . . ."

I plunged my hand into the midst of the face, but my scrabbling nails found only the bottom of the broken tub. Snarling, I yanked the plug out.

"Oh, well," said the face, glancing back at the drain below it. "I tried to do this the easy way. Better for everybody, really. But if you're going to make it hard . . ."

"You bitch!" I yelled. "Come out of there so I can blow your head off!"

The Siren gave me a disdainful look. "I'm not in the water, dearie. I thought you'd have been smart enough to know that. But I'm nearby, near enough to use the water here to amplify my song, to make it irresistible. Sure you want to throw down? You could just send the girl out, let me do what I came here for—"

"Screw you," I panted. "Screw you and the wave you rolled in on, you watery tart."

The face flickered and broke apart into glints of light. "Your funeral . . ." The water drained out of the tub.

Stephanie was battering at the door. "Kyra!" I heard her muffled voice calling. "Kyra, are you okay?"

I was far from okay. But there was no time to explain. I threw open the door, only then realizing I was still dripping wet and naked. What the hell did it matter? The kid was blind.

"Get your shoes on," I barked. "We're getting out of here."

"Oh—okay." Stephanie did as she was told.

I toweled off and dressed quickly, checking my weapons as I went. If we'd been out at sea, a Siren would have presented a real problem. With enough water to act as a resonating board, songs from one of these creatures could be lethal. And they had weather-working spells, able to raise up storms to batter hulls and sink ships. It was just sheer luck that I'd turned from

193

my original route—away from Lake Michigan—when I did. Backed by the fifth-largest lake in the world, the power of her song would have been tremendous. But here, almost seventy miles from the water, she'd have to take what she could get.

Which made her cockiness unnerving. The Siren had taken a stab at me last night at the diner, putting the waitress under her spell, probably when she'd looked too long at the pretty lights that had appeared out of nowhere in the waters of the sink. After that, she'd lain in wait, looking for another opportunity to strike. My dozing off in the bath had given her an opening, which I'd foiled by waking up when the illusion betrayed itself.

None of which explained how she'd kept up with us, or her threats just now. Was it only bravado, now that she'd been flushed out of hiding? I wasn't prepared to trust our lives to it.

Stephanie was standing by the door. I threw my hood up and shrugged my duster on.

"Were you attacked?" Stephanie asked.

"Yeah," I said, slinging Druison's satchel strap over my shoulder and taking her hand. "A Siren. Tried to catch me napping." I tugged the door open. "I don't know if she'll come back, but I think it's best if we got a move on."

I stopped as the parking lot came into view. Last night, I'd counted maybe half a dozen cars at this flea-bitten hovel. Now the parking lot was full of people, standing in a dense cordon, every one of them turned toward us. Their faces were drained of expression, and they didn't seem to even be aware of the rain streaming down their cheeks, dripping from their chins, soaking their shirts and pants. One man was in his pajamas and socks. They stood like an honor guard—or a lynch mob—with the raindrops leaping and dancing in a frenzy at their feet.

The rain.

Stheno's Spit. That's how she was doing it, how she followed us, how she was controlling them—

Lambent light flickered in the throng's eyes. Forty or more mouths split into grins. "Where's your big talk now . . . *bee-yotch*?" said a voice from half a hundred throats. As one, they moved forward.

I slammed the door shut. There was only a rickety door chain to lock it. Great.

"Please tell me what's happening," Stephanie begged.

I pushed her behind me and pulled out my Glocks. They'd have to come through there, no more than two at a time.

"The Siren's taken control of all the people here. She's sending them in to get us. Stay down; I don't want you to get hit by any ricochets."

"You're going to *shoot* them?" cried Stephanie, aghast. She grabbed my arm. "Kyra, you can't!"

"Get off me!" I shouted, yanking loose. "Do you want to die? I'm not playing around here, kid!"

"Neither am I," she said. "Let them in. I'd rather die than have you hurt innocent people for me."

The first collision shook the door, but the lock held. I glanced over my shoulder, saw that she'd slumped to her knees. "Are you crazy? This is kill or be killed, Stephanie! We don't have a choice here!"

"You're wrong," she said in a small, hurt voice. "There's always a choice."

Another thump as more bodies hit the flimsy barrier. Something cracked in the wooden doorframe.

"Please."

I stood rooted to the spot for another moment as the hammering and splintering grew worse. She was out of her skull. There was no time for this . . .

Except she meant it, really meant it; I could see it in her face.

"You'd let them kill you," I panted, "all for the sake of . . . of . . . ?"

Stephanie raised her head. "Yes. If there's no other way."

There was something unnerving about her calmness, her certitude. She was scared, sure, but she should have been *terrified*. Instead, in that moment, she just looked . . . strong.

Strong in a way I didn't understand, in a way I . . . wasn't.

195

"Oh, fine!" I snapped, smothering my own fear with anger. I shoved my guns into their holsters and dragged her up off the carpet. "When this gets us both killed, I hope you'll be happy!"

The bathroom window was barely more than a skylight. But the back window by the bed was big enough. I tried tugging it open, but the frame wouldn't budge off the sill. It had probably been gummed shut by a repaint job and disuse. Well, I'd already blown the security deposit by shooting up the tub . . .

"Stand back," I said, and lifted the tiny side table, sending it crashing through the glass. I slashed the remaining shards away with the satchel and hopped through, then turned to help Stephanie. As she joined me outside, I heard the door inside collapse.

We were in a tiny courtyard, overgrown with bushes and weeping willows that thrashed and swayed with the wind. The storm made it difficult to pick out the terrain of the surrounding woods. But any place had to be better than here.

I picked a point of entry and plunged in, one hand locked in Stephanie's. The ground was uneven, broken by a maze of protruding tree roots. Even with my preternatural eyesight to guide us, it was slow going; we slipped and tripped as we went along. Before long, my pants were soaked and stained with mud. I kept glancing over Stephanie's head for signs of pursuit and, soon enough, caught glimpses of movement among the trees.

They were coming after us, advancing slowly but steadily, like an infantry unit. Judging by the faint glow of their eyes, I estimated no more than a few yards between each of them. It would be easy to take down one or two at a time, but while I did, the rest of the line would collapse in on us. Then a rock or tree limb would be all the Siren needed to bash in Stephanie's head. And that would be all she wrote.

We had to keep moving, but now I took us forward at an angle. If I could find the edge of their line, we could outflank them.

But we were already out of time. One moment, we were stumbling through the dense undergrowth, shoving the clinging branches out of our way. The next, we came out from the trees and found ourselves at the bank of a river.

It was barely more than a glorified creek, stretching some twenty to twenty-five feet across. Maybe on another day, it would have been fordable: The clay sides sloped down in gradual fashion, suggesting a maximum depth of no more than five feet. But it had been raining steadily for almost a day now, and the river had grown swollen with runoff water. I watched as broken branches and debris swept by on the churning brown flood, vanishing around a bend.

My hands itched for my Glocks. Trapped. The smug bitch had herded us here, cutting off our escape. Swiping the rain and sweat from my eyes, I turned to Stephanie.

"No killing supposedly innocent people, right? What's your position on kneecapping?"

"Knee-whatting?"

A melodious giggle rolled over the waters. I spun around, sweeping the river with my gunsights. "Why, Kyra," called an admonishing voice. "You wonderfully wicked creature! You almost make me sad to kill you!"

"I thought you just wanted the girl," I said, trying to hone in on the sound.

"Oh, that's sooo yesterday," trilled the Siren happily. "Now it's a double billing. Mind you, the fee for you is a fraction of what I'm going to get for *her*. I'd have cut you in, if you'd shown some respect. But you shouldn't feel too bad. Look, tell you what: I'll take you first. Consider it a courtesy to a distant cousin." The voice dropped to a soft purr, almost a growl. "That way, you won't have to see me feast on her heart."

Fee? For *me*?

She was trying to distract me. Worse, she was succeeding.

"The only thing you're going to eat tonight," I shouted, "is a bullet. Come on out and face me, you coward!"

"That's rich," bubbled the voice. "One seductress calling another 'coward'! What do you do, Kyra, before sending one of your victims to Hypnos's twin? Do you give them a chance to fight back? To repent, perhaps?"

Stop listening, Kyra. She just wants you to focus on what she's saying, instead of—

Instead of the dozen people who now came boiling out of the greenery, hands grabbing for me. I sidestepped the first clumsy charge by a man in a red lumberjack shirt, bringing my elbow down on the back of the man's thick neck. Then I spun and dropped the next person with a roundhouse that took her across the jaw.

Stephanie shrieked. I drove my knee into a third person's breadbasket, and turned to see two men trying to hoist her into the air.

Sorry, kid. I put a single round in both men, one in the meat of the first's shoulder and the other behind the second's knee. They grunted, barely seeming to register the pain, but I'd been aiming for support points, and the shots had the intended effect: Stephanie dropped to the mud. She bounced and rolled toward the river bank.

I started toward her, then had to dodge as a woman came at me with a broken bottle. Christ, where had she gotten that? Can't people go camping without throwing their shit all over the woods? I tried to kick her in the wrist to disarm her, but the sucking mud caught my boot and I brought my foot up an instant too late. Her bottle raked along my side, skittering harmlessly off the Kevlar vest as I twisted around her charge. I gave her a shove with the butt of my gun, trying to drive her into the mud. But she kept her footing for another second, staggering forward, and a second later had pitched over the bank. I barely saw her splash before she disappeared.

Shit! "Owe you one, Steph!" I panted, coldcocking the guy in the red lumberjack shirt I'd hit before, who had already been getting back up. More people were coming out of the woods.

This wasn't working. I couldn't keep this many people off us without using a distance weapon. And unless I shot all of them—and soon—we were dead meat. The Siren's control over them was too good, her song too strong; they had lost any fear or weakness, she had inhabited each so completely—

Helloo . . .

I spun one idiot around by the arm and sent him careening into two of his comrades, spilling them all to the ground. Then I leapt onto the chest of a teenage boy, slamming him into the mud with me on top. Seizing his chin, I forced his face up to mine. The glowing eyes glared at me.

"Knock, knock," I said, grinning savagely. "Aunty Gorgon's here with a present for you!"

"You can't touch me," the false voice of the boy grated.

"Let's test that theory, shall we?" I said, staring into her eyes. "You're linked to these people, right? I'm betting whatever they see, *you* see too." I focused, sending the first whisper of power out. "So take a good look at what I've got for you!"

"You—" croaked the voice, and suddenly the light in those eyes went out like a snuffed candle flame and it was only the confused, wet face of a teenage kid squinting up at me. "Whu—what?"

I rolled off the boy. "Chickenshit," I muttered, spitting out grit and water. Just like that, the rain had stopped, as though slapped out of the air. Around me, people were looking around with various expressions of befuddlement, clearly at a loss for how they'd suddenly come to find themselves standing in the middle of the woods. Stephanie lay where she'd fallen, propped on her elbows, her lovely hair covered in leaves and slime. I hunched down next to her and helped her up.

"You okay?"

She nodded. "I've lost my glasses."

"Here." I shook the worst of the mud off and slipped them onto her nose, where they hung at an awkward angle. "Here's looking at you, kid."

"What happened?" she asked as I guided her away from the bank. "Where's the Siren?"

"We played a little game of chicken," I said, dropping my voice to a whisper. Might as well act as confused as the rest of this bunch until we got clear; no need to make ourselves the subject of attention. And the lowering clouds still huddled over the treetops on either bank, as though listening. I wasn't sure if the whole storm had been the result of the witch's weather-working or not, but it didn't pay to take stupid chances. "I told her I was going to use the Medusa's Gaze on one of the people here, get to her through them. She didn't wait to see if I was bluffing."

Stephanie put her hand on my arm. "Were you?"

"I—" I stopped at the edge of the tree line. "Listen, kid—"

They say you smell ozone right before lightning hits. Not so much. I didn't hear a thing either. But a blue flash went off in the corner of my eye and, for an instant, every leaf and twig and branch along the river was etched in vivid light, cutting through the midday gloom. Then I tasted battery acid under my tongue and realized my legs were giving out under me.

After-images of orange and purple sparks filled my sight. I tried to get up and couldn't. My arms and legs felt numb. When my vision cleared enough, I saw that the sward was littered with bodies. I flopped over onto my side and found Stephanie in a heap next to me, her mouth open.

She lay as still as death.

I forced my arms forward, began crawling on my forearms through the mud. Her chest wasn't moving. I fell against her, pressed my ear to her breast, listening for a heartbeat. Nothing.

She must have taken the brunt of the lightning strike. I had to shock her heart into starting again. But I could barely get my limbs under me. Squeezing my dead fingers into a fist, I hammered at her chest.

TV and the movies have given people an unrealistic portrayal of how effective CPR really is. Without medical intervention, a typical person has a less than 10 percent chance of survival after their heart stops beating. But Stephanie had healed herself several times over from grievous organ wounds. She had healed me twice, once without even trying. If I could just give her enough time . . .

I began rhythmically pumping her chest with my palms. *Come on, Steph, come on . . .*

Something was happening out on the river. I craned my head around and saw a fountain of luminous water gushing up from the muddy torrent. In its center, a lithe figure rose. Her hair shimmered and rippled like the waves as it poured down over her face and shoulders. She was as pale as a corpse, but a feral light animated her eyes as they fell upon me. Her full lips, red as blood, parted.

"If we're all done with amateur hour here," the Siren said, "it's time for the main event."

CHAPTER 11

This situation had major suckage written all over it.

I had strobes going off before my eyes. I could barely control my quivering limbs. Stephanie still wasn't breathing. And now Queen Bitch of the Month was coming in for a landing.

I needed to stall.

"You must be dumber than you look," I panted. My tongue felt like it was too big for my mouth, another happy by-product of having nearly been electrocuted. "I can't believe you're still going through with this."

The bubbling geyser fell back into the river as she alighted. She looked as dry and pristine as if she had just stepped out of a salon. If she got close enough to lock my Gaze on her . . .

But the Siren stopped when we were still some twenty feet apart. Crap; I could throw my Gaze at someone, sure, but I couldn't *catapult* it.

"Why is that?" she asked with a grin as sharp as a knife.

Hell, I don't know. I was just making this stuff up.

203

"Because . . . my Agency will stamp you out of existence for this." I sneered. All in, Anastas. Time to find out who really *was* bluffing. "I'm their top agent."

"Really?" The Siren's laughter was sweet and searing. "Maybe you *were*, Kyra. But you went off the reservation this time. Now you're just another kill fee."

My fingertips were starting to tingle with the fire of renewed circulation. In another minute, I knew I could draw fast enough to give her two new eyeholes. Just keep her yapping . . .

"Who?" I rasped. "Who called in the contract? On her? On . . . on me?"

"Her?" The Siren glanced at the prone form next to me. "Who cares? Long as the money's good. You? Maybe you could ask your handler that one."

Phil? She was talking about my Phil? No way—

"Doesn't matter," the Siren said. "'Cause, sweetie . . . you dead."

Now. Now or never. As her mouth opened, my right hand went for my Glock—

And the Siren sang.

The sound sank into my ears, sweeter than honey. At the first note, my body froze in place, every muscle locking. My reaching fingers had just grazed the pommel of my gun. Now they hovered there, waiting her direction.

Kyra, Kyra . . . I could hear her voice in my head, even as her mouth poured her song into my ears. *Before I kill you, I am going to peel you apart, layer by layer. Won't that be fun?*

I sensed her insinuating herself in my mind, tangling and confusing my thoughts. With dawning horror, I realized this was unlike Elspeth Rougnagne's soul-lock. That had felt like being dragged wholesale into the depths of a void. This was an invasion, watching helplessly as she infiltrated the corners of my brain. It was worse, far worse, than the soul-lock. It was . . . it was like what I did with the Gaze, the way I invaded every living cell of my victims, consuming them like a cancer. It felt, it was . . .

Evil.

So much pain, the Siren gloated inside me. *Kyra, you are a perfect feast of need. Show me . . .*

I tried to resist. But I could no longer tell where I ended and she began. She was breaking down the walls of my thoughts, entering my memories.

I saw a cascade of images, blurred and indistinct, overlapping: my apartment in varying states of disarray; my face in the mirror, haggard, eyelids heavy with drink; my cell phone in fumbling hands—the scene played out over and over from different vantage points. What—?

Oh, look, laughed the Siren, from everywhere and nowhere, her scorn acid in my veins. *This is too delicious! The big, bad gorgon everyone is so afraid of, reaching out in her drunken stupors for companionship to the only people who will talk to her! Poor, lonely thing, just wanting someone to love her. How precious.* Derision washed over me, permeating every fiber of my being. *How pathetic.*

I wriggled in impotent fury, then gasped as another door was wrenched open.

Pietro. The first time he kissed me, in the sun-drenched field behind the chicken coop, out of sight of my mother for those few blessed minutes. The brush of his lips, gentle, unsure of himself but insistent, needing me. The sweet shock of discovery as his tongue found mine . . .

Good, Kyra, purred the Siren in an encouraging tone that left me nauseous. *That's good. Thank you sooo much. But let's dig deeper, shall we? Let's really turn up some worms!*

The Siren's song wound itself around me, carrying me out of myself, covering me with gossamer threads, lighter than silk, a gentle rain of phantom kisses, infinitely warm and comforting. I felt the music turning me round and round until I lost my bearings, lost everything, and I was falling, falling into an endless mist.

Then the notes of the song sharpened and all my grief rose up from me, piercing me as it left, all the pain of my life erupting out of my pores, soaring up into the mist around me and becoming visible in the air itself.

As though at a great height above me, a stranger's face appeared, grim and bereft, then faded into shadow as it pulled away for the first and last time.

Father—?

Pietro, as the light and life left his beautiful, innocent, sky-blue eyes . . .

My mother, the habitual dark circles under her eyes rimmed with an uncharacteristic redness as she bent my head over the bowl for the first time, the blade in her fist . . .

Brienne, her dead mouth stretched open in her final anguish, her head lolling backward with the caprice of the wind . . .

And then a parade of faces, each staring at me with horror as they realized that a creature from their childhood nightmares—this thing that should not be—had come for them, to end their lives.

So *many*. I'd lost count over the years as they'd blurred together over the long and lonely stretches of time. But now my victims thronged before me like some great host, shambling forth from the land of the dead, and I watched as each one in turn became stone. Some of them had begged for their lives, others had fought and cursed me, but in the end I had destroyed them all, stolen their vitality, their future, their humanity. And I couldn't turn away; the images from my memory were remorseless, irrefutable.

On they came. On and on and on. As though a map had been drawn on my eyes, I saw the deaths that marked the path of my life, saw the endless, solitary road that lay behind and before me until my tears burned and blinded me.

Come to me, sang the Siren's song through my anguish, twisting and transforming it into desire, sharp as razors. *Come to me and all your pain will end, all your tears wash away. Hear me and come, come* . . .

And I came. Helpless, hopeless, yearning for release; my sight of the world returned and my boots began marching forward. I went to her, to the heart of the swirling maelstrom, to where she stood with her arms outstretched at the river's edge.

Was there love there in her eyes, those eyes that glowed like will-o'-the-wisps, filling my sight? No; it was only hunger, insatiable hunger, a consuming need as deep as the abyss of my heart. And I didn't care. I ached for her to kiss me, to embrace me, to destroy me. To end it all.

I will, the Siren promised. *Your ears have heard my song, and you are mine. Listen, listen, and come into my arms.*

Drawn forward on nerveless legs, I staggered the last few yards until I stood before her, reeling, wanting to give her everything, to watch her rip my beating heart from my breast and feast on it while I cheered her on with my last sucking gasp of life. Her song was the sweetest, most exquisite thing I had ever heard, and I had no resistance left in me, nothing.

"I know," she gloated aloud, and the teeth behind her full, ruby-red lips were as long and sharp as needles. I couldn't wait for her to chew on my skin with them. The song still swirled around me, like a chorus of echoes. The Siren rested her hands on my shoulders, and I shivered in ecstasy at the touch.

"Please . . ." I was crying like a baby, so happy was I at the thought of being eaten by her.

"Yes . . . ?" The Siren caressed my chin with one long, ragged and curled nail, slicing the skin open. Exquisite.

"You have to know . . ." Oh, I wanted her to know everything, to bare it all to her merciless gaze. "I have . . . to tell you something . . ."

"Yes? And what is that?"

"Snakes," I said huskily.

The fathomless eyes blinked. "Snakes?"

I swallowed my disappointment and regret. "They don't have ears."

It took her a moment before she got it. Then her eyes flared wide and she started to yank her hands back. The song faltered around us. And the serpents came boiling out from under my hood like an explosion.

Three of them caught her retreating arms in their curved fangs. The Siren shrieked and reeled back, jerking my head forward and causing me to crash on top of her.

That's when the rest of them got into the action, stooping and stabbing at her face, her throat, her exposed breast and shoulders. The song became one long wail of pain, shattering the spell into a million brilliant fragments. And suddenly my limbs and thoughts were back under my control.

The snakes were in a mad fury, but I swept them back and got my hands around the Siren's neck. It was already puffing up with venom. But I wasn't waiting to see if that would kill her, not when I could finish the job myself. I raised her head up, then slammed it down into the mud. Again. And again.

"*You . . . !*" I couldn't find words or breath for my outrage. "You—incredible—bitch! Succubus! Goddamn you! You—you dug up things I've kept buried my whole life!" My hand fell to my holster and I tore my Glock out and jammed it against the center of her forehead. "You want to see what's at the bottom of a hole so bad? I'll put you in one forever!"

"Kyra." I didn't know where Stephanie had come from, but suddenly I felt the warmth of her hand on my shoulder from behind. "Enough. You're killing her."

I didn't see any reason for pausing in my exertions long enough to look up. "AND?!?"

"And I'm asking you to stop."

Now I did look up. "Why the hell should I?" I screamed.

Tears were streaming from Stephanie's blind eyes. In a flash, I realized that somehow she'd seen it, been there for all of it, everything.

"Because you can," she said softly. "If you choose to."

"She deserves it." I was shaking from shame and revulsion. "She deserves to die."

Stephanie nodded, once. "Even if she deserves to die."

There was no compulsion in her voice, no promise of pain or pleasure; whatever Steph was, she was no Siren. There was just the truth, whether I wanted to admit it or not. I could kill her . . . or not.

The Siren deserved to eat a bullet. Every instinct told me to do it. And I wanted to; oh, God, I wanted to. I wanted to see the light go out of her eyes, feel her body go limp under me. I was hungry for it. Yet still I hesitated. Why?

Because of the girl waiting behind me. Because somehow I knew that doing it would hurt her. And I suddenly found that fact weighing heavy in a calculus I had never even known existed in me. I wavered for a long moment, torn, pulled between two poles: the familiar, feral innate reaction of the predator that wanted blood, death, vengeance . . . and something else, something newborn and raw in me that was struggling to find the surface. Finally, I lifted my gun from the Siren's forehead.

My hand was shaking. It took another few minutes to stop my chest from heaving. Then I addressed the bloodied, beaten thing under me.

"Your ears still work, right, bitch?" I took the groan and shudder at my feet as affirmation. See? I'm flexible that way. "Good, 'cause I'm only saying this once. If I ever hear so much as a note from one of your little ditties again, I'll show you just what a gorgon can teach you about agony. You'll spend a month dying. Got it?"

I didn't wait for an answer. Just gave her a final cuff with the muzzle of my gun and pushed myself to my feet.

I found the nerve to look at Stephanie. She'd lost her shades again. I hunted about until I spotted them on the ground a few feet away. Then I collected Druison's satchel and wiped the mud off it; it gave me something to do while I tried to get my emotions under control.

The clouds above were fraying apart, letting through snatches of blue sky. It was over. I made that my mantra while my fingers flexed and itched for violence. I waited, simmering, as Stephanie moved about the sward, following some sense beyond sight, and ministered to the people scattered about. Only when she headed toward the twitching figure of the Siren did I intervene, catching her arm.

"She's hurt," Stephanie protested.

"I know," I said. Not as hurt as she should be. "And she stays that way. I won't have her at our backs. If she lives, she lives. If not . . ." I'd say a prayer of thanks later.

"All right," said Stephanie with a grimace. In the better light, I made out a bridge in the distance. Setting my face like stone to the bewildered crowd, I took Stephanie's hand in mine and led us away.

It took us nearly half an hour to find our way back to the motor lodge and get in the car. By then, I was trembling from reaction. I tried to get a light going, but my pack had gotten soaked through and none of the cigarettes were salvageable. I threw them out the window in disgust and rummaged through the satchel to see if Druison had tossed my spare pack in there when he'd frisked me. But all I came up with among my weapons was my missing beret, a bag of candles, and a plastic cereal bowl designed to look like half a soccer ball. Giving up, I tossed the bag in the back seat and swung the car onto Route 20.

The snakes were upset, but the confined warmth and darkness of the beret's interior gradually settled them down. I wished the same could have been said of me. I felt like I was primed to explode. That had been close, too close; it was just starting to sink in how narrow an escape we'd had. But that wasn't why my hands were shaking as they held the wheel, why I could barely see the road ahead—

"You didn't kill," Stephanie said. "I'm proud of you."

Hoo boy, had that been the wrong thing to say.

I hit the brakes hard enough to bring the car to a screeching halt, half on the shoulder. Then I rounded on Stephanie.

"Proud of me," I spat. "You're *proud* of me! Well, you shouldn't be, okay? Because all I can think about right now is turning this car around, finding that Siren, and sticking my gun down her throat! You should have let me kill her, Stephanie! She's not human! She's a . . . a monster! She—do you have any idea what she *did* to me?" Christ, I couldn't breathe. It felt like an elephant was sitting on my chest. I threw open the car door and stumbled to the grass under the trees. I fell on my knees, wishing I could vomit, get this awful feeling out of me, but nothing came; I could only kneel there with my arms wrapped uselessly around my ribs.

Stephanie knelt down next to me, putting her arm over my shoulders. "Tell me."

210

"You suh—saw." I couldn't lose it; if I did, I'd never pull myself together again.

"No. Not like you think. Tell me."

And then it all came gushing out.

"*She hurt me!*" I howled, and the words felt like they were ripping me apart. Tears burned my eyes, blinding me. "She muh—made me see it, every horrible thing I've ever done, everyone I've—kuh—killed! All the fear and pain I've caused!" Pietro—! "My whole life! It's not the snakes—it's *me!* I'm ugly . . . disgusting—" Evil. My mother should have slit my throat the first time she bent my neck over that bowl. She'd have done us both a favor. "*I* deserve to die. I shouldn't have been born. *I shouldn't even exist—!*"

"No." Stephanie's voice was quiet, sharp with shared grief. But somehow it cut through the sobs that racked my body. "You're wrong."

I wanted to scream. "It's true," I wailed. "It is—"

"It's not the whole truth." Stephanie pressed herself closer against me. "It doesn't have to be. You're in pain right now, Kyra, because you're feeling the misery you've caused others. That's the first step: letting that pain in. Not hiding from it."

"First step," I groaned. "To what?"

"Change."

I ground my tears away with the back of my fist, tried to find her. Stephanie was sitting on her knees in the wet grass, her hands open on her lap, the wind blowing her golden hair like a pennant. The sunlight was only a few feet away, but it felt like it only fell on her.

"I don't understand," I said, sniffling.

"This is how you begin. By facing your pain, your fear. It is the hardest thing you will ever do. But it's the only way to heal, to come back."

I swallowed the acid in my throat. "To what?"

"To the world. You've stood apart from it for so long."

I shook my head. "The world doesn't want me. There's no place for . . . for something like me."

"Make your place." She pulled up a handful of green growth, held it out in her palm. "You are as much a part of this world as these blades of grass, as the wind in the sky, as the waves of the ocean. You knew this once, felt this once. But you've been at war with yourself for so long, you've forgotten. Now, you could begin again."

I passed one hand over my eyes, trying to shut out the light. It was all too much. "I wouldn't know how to start."

"You've already started. By not killing that Siren, you spared a life you thought wasn't worth saving. By not killing those people when she controlled them, you saved all of them."

"Not everyone." Some part of me was desperate to find the flaw in her argument, the way out. "You didn't see—a woman died back there. Drowned."

Stephanie winced but pressed on. "It's not necessary that you succeed, Kyra. Just that you try."

I almost laughed, but my heart was too wrung out for my usual vitriol. "You really expect me to be able to do that?" *Please say yes. I could almost believe you, if you said yes.* "Live my life by a fortune-cookie saying? You forget what I do for a living."

"I don't know what a fortune cookie is," Stephanie said with a frown. "It sounds inane. But if you can't make a . . . living that way, then it's time to make one a new way. You've already begun to, with me."

"Yeah, and it's nearly gotten me—us—killed three times already!" The old me was down but not out, not yet. "This protector gig you've got me on is more hazardous than being a contract agent. What good is changing if it just gets you killed?"

"Everything dies, Kyra. Even gods." She shrugged. "Only you can decide if it's worth it." She reached her arms out. "Can you help me up?"

I found my feet and pulled her to hers. "You . . . make it sound easy."

Stephanie shook her head. "It's not. It won't be. Not ever. But it's the only choice if you want to be whole again."

Whole. With these things growing out of my head. There was the problem, the inescapable flaw in the plan. Stephanie's was a beautiful dream, but in the end, it was only a dream.

"I've done too many things I can't take back," I said, holding her arm as I steered her back to the car. "Made too many mistakes."

Stephanie stopped me as I tried to guide her into the passenger seat. She put a hand against my breast. "Our mistakes are what make us human, Kyra," she said. "They don't mean we're monsters."

I grimaced and took her hand away. For one long, last moment, I held it, savoring its warmth, its softness.

"Some," I sighed, "mean exactly that."

We'd been driving another ten minutes in blessed silence when it struck me that we were heading straight toward the city. I had planned to follow Route 20 until it fed us into 355; from there we'd work our way south until we got out of Illinois. The business with the Uber Bitch—as I now decreed she would hereafter be called until I dropped dead of old age—would have sent ripples across the fabric of the local continuum. That level of psychic and physical turbulence was sure to catch the eye of anyone scrying for unusual Mythic activity. The hunters would zone in on it. So it made sense to go in a different direction than the one we'd been heading.

Except—

I hit the brakes.

"Okay. Is this one of those things?"

Stephanie brushed her hair back from her shades. "What things?"

I turned to her. "Those karmically ironic things. Where I think I'm doing something of my own free will but, in reality, you're just jerking me around."

"What are you talking about?"

"We're on a boomerang course back to Chicago right now. Is that your doing?"

"I'm not the one driving!" Stephanie protested.

"No, but you're the one with her eyes on the threads and destiny and all that. Maybe you can put your, you know, fingers on them too. Make stuff happen."

Stephanie scowled. "If I was capable of that, we'd have headed right back to the city this morning. Or never left it."

Hm. Point. Still . . . "Maybe you can only affect people's brains if you touch them or heal them—"

"Oh, for God's sake, Kyra!" Stephanie threw up her hands. "Stop it! Stop putting the blame on everybody else for what you choose to do. Your decisions are your decisions, all right? No one makes them for you; not me, not the snakes, not anyone!"

I felt my cheeks flaming, and my ire instantly rose with it. "What the hell are you so mad about?"

And now all of a sudden she's crying. "Because you don't believe me! You didn't believe me when I told you we had to go back! And . . . and you don't believe what I told you about—oh, *Kyra*. You think I don't know? You've already given up! For a moment . . . back there . . . you were ready to try. But now . . ." She shook her head. "Kyra, I don't want to die."

How had this argument taken such a left turn? What were we even fighting about? And whoa, hold the phone—

"What's this talk about dying?" I said. "Look, we've only got to make it another nine hours, kid. And I know you said you're blind out here, but I'm sure we'll get someplace where you'll be able to—"

"No, it's not that." Stephanie swiped impatiently at her cheeks. "I thought so too, at first. That it was just about me being blind. I'd never experienced it like that—such darkness—I didn't understand what it meant."

Puppies and carrot cake? Unlikely. "What does it mean?"

Stephanie swallowed, seeming to gather her calm with an effort. "There are no threads out here because we're outside the tapestry. If we don't go back . . ."

I hated finishing sentences like this. But I was finally catching on to something. "We both die."

214

She nodded.

"The . . . threads you've been talking about. The tapestry . . ." I struggled to put my intuition into words. "You're talking about the weave of Fate, aren't you?" A car honked angrily as it passed, but I just gave it the finger, focusing on Stephanie. "You don't get visions of the future, like an oracle. You . . . you see the whole thing, don't you? You see the workings of the Moirai, the three Fates."

Stephanie bowed her head.

I felt a chill, as though a shadow had just bent over us, occluding the sunlight. Could this really be true? Was I actually sitting next to a fourteen-year-old girl who could see the machinery of the universe, who knew how and where everything fit together?

But if that were right . . . "Then nothing matters."

Stephanie jerked her head up. "What? No; that's not true."

"Oh, come on, Stephanie! If it's all there, the—the past, the present, the future, all written down like a book you can just read—then nothing I decide to do or not do with my life makes a damn bit of difference! All this talk about change and being something more is just a load of New Age, feel-good, hippie horseshit!" The car rocked as a truck rolled by, blaring its air horn in anger. I pulled my attention back to the road and hit the gas. Shouldn't interrupt my epiphany about the emptiness of existence with a car crash, right? "All of us—people, monsters, gods, if they even exist—we're all just puppets on strings, hopping around on the threads of Fate!"

"No!" I glanced over. Stephanie's face was streaked with tears, but I'd never seen her look so angry. "That is not true! You're doing it again: trying to justify giving up. You can't—!"

A loud siren startled us both. I looked in my rearview mirror and saw a flashing lightbar atop the vehicle closing in behind us.

"You've got to be kidding me," I muttered.

"What is it?"

"State police," I said, rolling to a stop on the shoulder. "Keep quiet and let's see what he wants." With luck, he'd just noticed us going too slow for traffic. If not . . . a nip from one of the snakes would put him out of action without killing him.

Huh. That was weird; I'd never counted on them as part of a plan of action before. Maybe I really was changing . . .

The trooper rapped on the pane. I lowered the window, turning up the wattage on my smile. A man in his forties wearing the khaki shirt and dark brown tie of the Illinois State Police bent down. Between his polarized shades and the shadow cast by his campaign hat, his expression was unreadable.

"Afternoon, officer," I said. "I guess we slowed down a bit, huh?"

"That you did, ma'am," said the trooper. "May I see your license, registration, and proof of insurance, please?"

"Here you go," I said. It wasn't my best work, patched together with my kit in the dead of night after we'd boosted the car. But if this really was just a routine traffic stop, it should suffice.

"Says here the car's registered to R. Sterling," said the trooper.

"That's my husband," I smiled. "He does all the bills. I'm just the one who does the cooking and cleaning." I brightened my smile until I looked like a happy lunatic. "I'm bringing his little sister to him as a surprise for our anniversary. He hasn't seen her in years."

"Mmm." He was being noncommittal. But there was no tension in his bearing. He wasn't on the alert, which meant he'd run the plates and they hadn't come up as stolen yet. As long as he didn't ask me to step out of the car . . .

"How about you, miss?" he said, looking toward Stephanie. "Everything all right here?"

"What?" Stephanie leaned across me to get within earshot over the noise of the traffic. Her bountiful golden hair was in my face. "What did you say?"

"You going to see your big brother?"

"Oh, no," said Stephanie. "I don't have a brother. I don't have anybody, not since this woman killed my mother. Aren't you going to arrest her? She's Kyra Anastas, a fugitive from Chicago."

I froze. Out of the corner of my eye, I saw the trooper draw his sidearm. I heard him shout for me to put my hands out the window. But the only words that penetrated were Stephanie's, as she slid past my ear back to her seat: "Wow. I guess I can make stuff happen, after all."

So . . . *that's* what guys mean when they say "kicked in the nuts."

The next few hours after that were pretty much a blur.

At first the state trooper hadn't believed what he'd stumbled upon. Until he frisked me, and found the makings of a small arsenal in my duster and Druison's satchel. The next thing I knew we were hip deep in white and gold–striped cruisers. For a while I sat in the back seat of one of their cars, cuffed to the riot bar, with two troopers watching me like a pair of hawks through the mesh of the cage while the others outside debated my fate.

Fate. Funny. We'd just been talking about fate. Everything came back around; everything was a circle, an endless, meaningless circle, a snake devouring its own tail. A roller coaster that just went round and round with only poor, dumb saps like me looking for it to actually take them somewhere.

As the sun crawled across the sky, I couldn't imagine why they weren't taking their prize back to the local barracks. Then I pulled my head up from staring at the floor long enough to notice that a black van had arrived on the scene. Stenciled in gold letters on its side were the words "Chicago Police Department—Special Prison Transport."

It looked like the headsman had come.

Two cops in black jackets were arguing with the troopers' ranking officer. Finally, they came over to the cruiser where I sat.

"Watch her," I heard one say as they opened the door. They pulled me out of the back, marched me through the crisp early-evening air to their van, then manacled me to the steel bench seat inside. Normally I'd have watched their faces, surveyed the weapons and gear on my captors, tested the gauge of my restraints, all the things I'd been trained to do.

Tonight, I just didn't care.

The joke was, I hadn't realized how much I'd come to depend on Stephanie's loyalty over the last twenty-four hours, her steadfast reliability. For her to have pulled the rug out from under my feet like that . . .

It was a joke, all right. Just not a "ha-ha" kind of joke.

Some of the cruisers were leaving the scene. We'd be getting under way then, the jurisdictional tug-of-war decided in the city's favor. When the shadow fell across the cargo hold, I thought it'd be one of the cops closing the double bay doors. Then Stephanie was sat down across from me. The cop fastened her to the ring set in the bench and left without a word. The doors slammed shut. A minute later, the van jerked into motion.

In an hour—maybe more, with commuter traffic—we'd be back in the city. And then . . .

I shook my head. What did it matter?

"I'm sorry."

I didn't want to answer her. I didn't want to acknowledge she even existed. But I couldn't help myself. All the crushed bitterness welled up in me at once.

"You got what you wanted, kid," I said, staring at the pattern of scuff marks on the floor. "We're going back to the city, to take our place in the Big Weave of Destiny. That should make you happy."

"It doesn't," said Stephanie. I forgot she'd been born without the Sarcasm Gene. "I'm scared."

"Well, maybe you could've thought of that before you turned me in to the cops!" I flared with as much anger as I could muster. Really, why were we even talking about this? I bit down on a whole host of retorts that were just lining up and looked away. No windows in the back doors. Just the screened slit between the cargo bay and cab with its sliding cover closed. No way to gauge where we were on our little journey.

"I really am sorry, Kyra."

"Stephanie, I find that I really don't care. This whole guardian angel gig has been one long fiasco after another. It seems . . . appropriate somehow that it ends with me being betrayed by the very person I'm supposed to be protecting." And now that I was wearing my special Betrayal Sensitive bifocals, something else was becoming clear to me. Like how the manticore had known to find us at the Center.

Maybe you should ask your handler that one.

Oh, I will, Uber Bitch. You can bank on that.

I felt the first stirrings of anger trying to beat back the numbness around my thoughts. I didn't want it to; I didn't want to feel anything.

"Kyra?"

"I'm not talking to you." You're just another betrayer, another liar, stabbing me in the back just when I . . .

It didn't matter.

"Kyra, please; we need to talk."

"No, we don't."

"Kyra, I had to do something! The threads were—"

"Do *not*." I growled. "Do not talk to me about your precious threads. I could care less about queuing up for my assigned spot in the Grand Scheme of the Cosmos, kid. It's been running fine without my willing participation up to now. It can all just play out without me jumping through the hoops like a good trained doggie—"

"No!" Stephanie brought her hands up, forgetting the chains. They snapped her wrists back and she almost toppled off the bench. I had to resist the instinctive urge to try to steady her; I couldn't have reached her in any case with my own restraints. And I didn't want to. I *didn't*. "You don't understand. That isn't how it works at all."

I put my head back against the wall and closed my eyes. "I don't care."

"Yes, you do. I know you do, deep down. You're just afraid of getting hurt again."

Here comes the psychobabble again. But I wasn't down on my knees this time. "Go analyze someone else, kid. Analyze yourself, why don't you?

Maybe ask yourself what kind of mother would lock her child away for fifteen years and then just abandon her? Spend some time thinking about that."

I could imagine Stephanie cocking her head even with my eyes shut.

"I know why my mother did what she did. She loved me."

I pressed my lips together. "Funny way of showing it. Maybe she just wanted you as a bargaining chip to avoid eternal damnation. Ever think of that? She'd had her fun, and now it was time to pay the bill. Unless you picked up the tab."

"You don't believe that."

"Oh, yeah, I keep forgetting; you've been in my head, haven't you?" I opened my eyes and hunched forward, gathering sweet outrage. "You went for a little walkabout in the wounded gorgon's mind while she was passed out, while you were so nobly healing me, and now you know me better than I know myself! So of course I should just go along with whatever you say I'm really thinking. Why should a puppet have any thoughts anyway? Seems kinda redundant to me. Major design flaw in the Plan—"

"You're not a puppet!" cried Stephanie. Tears were leaking from behind her sunglasses. "You have to understand how important you are: to the world, to me . . ."

It hurt to see her cry. So I closed my eyes again. "Why are you even back here? Why did they cuff you?"

"I told them that I was in on it. I said that I'd planned to kill my mother with your help, that we were working together."

"And they believed that? That a blind teenage kid helped me?"

"They didn't know what to believe. But I knew this way they'd keep us together."

"I wouldn't count on that!" I said heatedly. "Do you know what you've done, any idea what you've set in motion? Someone in the Chicago PD has framed me for . . . for a man's murder! When we get downtown, they'll lock me up! I won't be able to do a thing to protect you from a cell in the holding block." I blew out my breath. "If I even get that far."

"What do you mean?"

220

Her naïveté was maddening. "Stephanie, I'm not *human*. Do you think they're going to let me keep this pretty little beret when they book me? They'll take it off, and when they do, they'll see that I have live snakes *growing out of my head*. That is not something they're going to be equipped to deal with. Odds are fifty-fifty some rookie shoots me on the spot out of sheer panic." Unless I went on a cop-killing spree the likes of which Chicago hadn't seen since the days of Prohibition. Which would probably substantially impair any chance that Detective Druison would ask me out on a real date.

Ooh, why was I even thinking about him, about anything? Just too stubborn to know when the game was over, I guess.

"It was the only way," Stephanie said in a small voice.

"Yeah, yeah, I know," I said. "The only way to get back to the city."

"*The only way to save your life!*" Stephanie shouted. "Don't you understand?"

"No, I don't! This is how you save my life?" I couldn't believe how she was trying to be the one who was affronted in this conversation. "By handing me over to people who are going to put me in a cage for the rest of my life? Thanks for the thought, but you know what? All things considered, I'd rather be dead."

Stephanie shook that glorious mane of hair like an angry lion. "If you could stop feeling sorry for yourself for five seconds," she said, "you'd hear what I'm trying to say."

Most people who bickered like this had to go downtown for a marriage license first. Or at least know each other for more than a day and a half. We had to be setting some kind of record. "Fine. Speak your peace. We've got nothing else to do for a while." Until we reached the precinct, and the fun really began.

"You'll listen? Really listen?"

"Don't push it, kid."

"Okay." Stephanie drew in a deep breath. "What would you have done if I hadn't told the policeman who you were?"

"If you hadn't betrayed me? Ooh, I know this one. I'd have taken us east for a while longer, then headed south of the city, toward Indianapolis—"

"On a major road? Something that cuts through two great forests?"

"I—" I frowned, thinking. If I'd stayed on back roads, as I'd started to envision, we'd have come out above Route 355 along 290, and 290 ran south along the Busse Woods Forest Preserve and the Ned Brown Forest Preserve, two of the biggest tracts of undeveloped park in this part of the state. So, technically . . . "Maybe."

Stephanie didn't hesitate. "That's where it would have come upon us."

"Where what would have come upon us?"

"The last assassin," Stephanie said. "We would have been killed before we even knew what was happening."

Despite my determination to stay as pissed as possible, I felt a knot of dread creeping up in my throat. "How . . . how would you know that? I thought you were . . . blind and all that. Outside the tapestry."

"The closer we got to the city, the more the threads were becoming visible to me again. While the policeman was talking to you, I was able to see how and where the assassin's thread crossed over ours, how ours ended at that moment."

"But . . . if you can't change anything—"

"Finally," Stephanie said. "You *are* listening. The tapestry, the weaving of the threads . . . it's always changing, Kyra. With every decision, every action, every choice. You can change it utterly with as little as a word."

"But . . . what good is your gift then? If it's always changing, your foresight is only good moment to moment. Um, right?"

"Sort of," Stephanie nodded. "The patterns within the tapestry are always shifting. But they tend to flow in certain ways, like the rivers to the sea. Some are easily altered; others require a major influence to redirect them. I see where they are, and where they will be, unless something changes them."

I wasn't sure what I was feeling more as she spoke: I was uplifted by a sudden sense of possibility even as I felt the terror of screwing up landing squarely on my shoulders again. "So, when you got me . . . us . . . arrested?"

"It was a great enough change to reset the pattern," she said. "At least our threads in it. Now we don't meet him there."

"But we do meet him?"

"Oh, yes," she said grimly. "Our threads are bound together. I don't see any way of undoing that."

"And then?"

She shook her head. "I see his thread going on. Ours . . . depends."

"On what?"

"I don't know. Choice."

"What choice?" I asked. "Whose choice?"

"Yours, I think."

I would have chewed on my nails if I could've raised a hand that high. Instead, I had to content myself with worrying at my lip. "When?"

"Soon. Before midnight."

Yeah; of course. "You said 'his thread.' Is it a Mythic?" It had to be. "Can you tell what he is?"

"Something powerful," she said, shuddering. "And old. Very old. His thread goes back further than I can see."

Oh, great. Ancient and powerful. Just what I wanted to hear.

Of course, to kill us he'd have to get in line at this point. We still had the more immediate problem of being in police custody to deal with.

Speaking of which, the van had stopped. I felt the vibration of the engine cut out.

Showtime.

CHAPTER 12

The doors swung open, flooding the van with the level rays of the setting sun. I blinked, trying to make out the number of officers in the welcoming party. If Druison were there. . . . If I could just talk to him . . .

Stupid, Kyra. Lame. Just keep your head down and wait.

The van bounced slightly as one of the cops hopped in. He unchained me and guided me out into the dazzling golden light, one big hand crushing my upper arm just below the shoulder. Delgado could have told him that was a mistake, if Delgado had not been busy providing the groundwork for future beachgoers to enjoy Lake Michigan's western shores. I could sense the growing agitation under my beret and silently willed the snakes to stay calm; I had to see how bad the tactical situation was, if we were already through the fence, if we were facing cops in riot gear—

Abruptly released, I wrung the worst of the glare from my sight. I could still only make out two dim figures, the cops who had picked us up from the interstate, silhouetted by the sun. But all around us—

Uh, unless they'd done some serious redecorating...

"This isn't the police precinct," I said, more for Stephanie's benefit than anyone else's.

In fact, it wasn't even downtown Chicago. The smell from the South Bend of the Chicago River alone would have told me that. But the dead giveaways were the enormous concrete silos looming up on my left and the rusted grain elevator forming a partial roof over my head. A glance over my shoulder to the east confirmed my immediate impression as I took in the distant white spires of the John Hancock Center dominating the Chicago skyline: We were on the Lower West Side, at the Damen Silos.

The Silos were a former grain processing facility that had been empty for decades, becoming something of a Holy Grail for urbexers everywhere. Littered with crumbled concrete blocks and wild scrub that had taken root in every nook and cranny, the lot stretched away in both directions until the ground was lost in waves of rush grass. Moaning to itself as it crept along the curved silos and through the gaping windows, the wind huddled like a forlorn lover against the processing building that jutted out over the river's edge. The whole place reeked of abandonment as it waited patiently for grain barges that would never come again.

The perfect place to dump a body or two.

I repressed the urge to roll my eyes at the cosmos. Stephanie had said that the last assassin's appearance would be soon. In the heat of the moment, I'd momentarily forgotten that you always had to read the fine print in an oracle's pronouncements: I guess "soon" meant "imminent."

But...

These guys looked neither ancient nor powerful. And there were two of them, so...

"Okay, I give up," I said. "What are you guys? Werewolves? Vampires? Werevamps?" I threw a glance over my shoulder. "Hey, Stephanie, your ride's here."

The first cop stepped forward. "Where is he?"

I blinked at him. That was off script. "Where is who?"

226

"Delgado. Where've you stashed him?"

I couldn't help myself; the sensation of sheer relief that washed over me was palpable, demanding an outlet. I burst out laughing. "*Seriously?* This is about that stupid IA thing?" I waved vaguely. "Whew, you had me worried for a minute. Never mind, Steph; false alarm," I called behind me. "It's just two dirty cops trying to kill us."

"Try not to hurt them," her small voice came back.

This girl was really cramping my style. "Aw, c'mon; they've got guns and stuff. They probably plan to throw our bodies into one of the silos here after they're done torturing us for information." Not that I'd know anything about that, of course. I gestured for support. "I mean, help me out here, guys. I'm right, right?"

The cop with the big monkey paws for hands bristled. "Hey, funny lady. You think you're going to joke your way out of this?"

"No," I smiled. "Not really. I'm pretty sure I'm going to have to kill a pair of friggin' morons." Which was problematic, to say the least. Killing a cop—even a bad cop—would pretty much nix my chances of staying in Chicago; with that kind of heat, I'd be saying good-bye to the Windy City for good. Stunning them might do the trick, but I wasn't exactly batting a thousand in that department lately. If the Gaze either didn't work or exploded like a cannon again, I'd be worse off than before. Still, choices were looking slim here.

Monkey Paws had started forward, but his partner slapped a hand across his chest to halt him before he came within kicking range.

"Easy, Steve. The lady Fed can mouth off all she wants. It's just going to make the dyin' harder."

"Lady Fed?" They thought I was FBI? Then . . . they must think Delgado had been snatched by the Feds, that he was going to turn state's evidence, fingering the cops he knew were dirty. So they wanted to get to him first. Damn, it was almost funny. I'd actually done them a favor by killing Delgado, but instead of shaking my hand, they wanted to kill me.

Karma's a green-eyed, snaky little bitch.

A buzzing noise almost made me jump. The first cop fished out his cell then grunted and turned his back on us. "Yeah. Where you been? I've been calling you for an hour. No, we got her. Just unloading her at the old plant now. She wasn't alone, though. Got some crazy blind kid with her. You didn't say anything about that." His voice dropped to a whisper. He needn't have bothered; my hearing was on par with an owl's, so the words still carried clearly over the fluttering wind. "Well, what else don't you know? Hey, it's our asses on the line too, *Detective*." There was a pause while the caller spoke words I couldn't make out. Okay; maybe not an owl's. It was still damn close. "We'll have Delgado tonight. Oh, she'll give him up all right." He turned back to me with a grin in his tone. He hung up. "She's gonna give it *all* up."

Oh, brother. I'd be shaking in my boots if I hadn't had a few other things on my mind.

"Fine," I snapped. "You want Delgado? He's at our safe house, at the Center. There's a room in the underground level behind a door labeled 'Electrical Auxiliary Access.' Just go there and take him. I'm not dying for that scumbag."

The two cops glanced at each other, then the first drew out his cell again.

"Hey, Harry," he muttered, moving away again. "It's me. You working the Center tonight? Got a lead on our pigeon. Look into it. Take Fred with you and check out an electrical room in the underground level. Call me back when you get him."

"The door's password protected," I called. "He has to speak into the mike to get in."

The cop walked over. Ooh, now we were close enough to have some real fun. But I was still weighing my options here. "Aren't you the helpful little Fed?" he asked. I assumed it was a rhetorical question. "What's the password, sweetheart?"

Just once in my life it would be nice to have someone call me that who I wasn't about to send to the Great Hereafter. "Skorpios," I said. It's a real name; look it up.

228

"Our pigeon's password protected," the first cop said. "So you're going to find company there." He looked at me and smiled humorlessly. "Kick it in." He hung up and shook his head. "Think you're pretty clever, don't you? Giving us a password that will trigger an alert to whoever's minding the store. Well, my boys will deal with that."

His "boys" were about to have a lot more than that to deal with. The world was going to find itself short a Harry and/or Fred after they tried that particular door. But that didn't help with my immediate situation.

"Look," I said. "You didn't bring me out here to show me the glories of industry past. We both know what comes next." Well, I did, anyway. "Just tell me this: Who screwed with my gun? Who faked the ballistics report?"

"Put you in a bit of a bind, huh?" The cop sounded pretty pleased with himself, which was nice for a man who had less than three minutes to live. If I was any judge of the lengthening shadows, that was how long it would take for the sun to dip below the horizon and get out of my eyes. "That was the idea."

"Good idea," I said. "Yours?"

Now it was Chuckle Time apparently. "Still fishing?" He wagged his head. "Just like a Fed."

"C'mon, don't be that way," I said. "Pump me full of lead. Strangle me with some piano wire. Whatever's in vogue these days with you guys. But grant a dying girl her last request: Tell me who was behind that part. My bosses in DC already knew Delgado was still alive and kicking, so what was the point?"

"Thought you'd figured that out already," he said. "Get the bigger fish first before you come for the small fry and all that, right? That's how the Feds always work it, just to make sure you get the headlines. Well, that gave us a little time. We dug into the story you gave our guy and found a few holes, like how nobody at your art studio had ever seen you there. It wasn't hard to figure out who you were with after that, not with Marco disappearing the night he met up with you, just when things were gettin' sticky for him with his boss. If every cop in the city was hunting for you, thinking you'd committed murder, we knew we'd get you in the net quick. And after you gave up Delgado, if you had a little accident, say, if somebody overreacted when you reached for your badge . . ."

I made my impressed face. "That's actually not half bad," I said. I might have to use that some time. "Druison think it up?"

"Nah, sorry, lady. This ain't going down like you learned in Hostage 101 at Quantico. You go to your grave not knowing."

His cell buzzed again. Uh-oh; that was ahead of schedule. I still needed another half minute for a clear view. I glanced at his buddy. "You guys are dumber than a box of rocks," I said, shaking my head. "You just put your-selves behind bars for life. I can't believe nobody checked my hat for a wire."

Monkey Paws swore and grabbed for my beret. I didn't bother to dodge. But just then the other cop's cell phone erupted in a confused babble.

"What? What are you talking about?" shouted the first cop over the noise. "What do you mean he '*blew up*'?"

Monkey Paws had started to drag my hat off when he turned his head at the interruption. Calmly and distinctly, I articulated my will: "Get him, boys."

One snake darted out and nipped him in the corded muscle of his neck. He dropped to the concrete like a felled ox. So did my beret.

"Harry! Harry! What's going—?" The first cop caught the motion as his companion collapsed. He whipped out his sidearm and then froze as he saw the serpents rearing up over my head.

The sun went down.

"Mother of Mercy," he gasped.

"Not even close," I said, and showed him why.

A few minutes later, Stephanie's voice drifted out from inside the police van. "Kyra? What's happening? Are you all right?"

"I'm—peachy," I gasped, lifting the wedge of concrete block for another go at it. For such a little guy, the first cop was proving to be a real pain to break up into manageable pieces; I mean, I'd known he was dense, but . . .

"What are you doing?"

There were certain advantages to having a partner who was blind. "Just—getting my exercise," I said, dropping the block square on the belt line, which cracked the statue cleanly in half. That was more like it.

"What are the . . . the dirty cops doing?"

"Um . . . not much, really." I hefted the torso. Time for a swim, pal; your head's already down there waiting for you. I'd have preferred to reduce the remains to rubble, but there was simply no time for the usual niceties. If someone happened by while we were standing around like this, we'd be up to our elbows in cops. And clean bullets were just as deadly as dirty ones. "Back in a sec."

I know I don't work out like I should, but I'm still strong for my size. Nevertheless, by the time I waddled the last piece of statuary to the river's edge and disposed of it, I was feeling it in my shoulders. Untouched by the unnatural storm the Uber Bitch had used to follow us, Chicagoland was enjoying a hint of real spring today, and the temperature and exertion left me breathing hard and sweating as I climbed into the van and undid Stephanie's manacles.

She paused as I helped her climb down. "What's that sound?"

"Hm?" Oh, Monkey Paws was still hanging on, his breath wheezing out of his mouth in weak gasps. "That's just one of the cops. He'll be dead in a couple of minutes." I shrugged. "Some people just can't hold their venom. You want to ride in front?"

"He's dying?" cried Stephanie, pulling loose and stumbling toward the sound. "We have to save him!"

"Are you *kidding* me?" I said, catching her wrist and spinning her around. "Stephanie, these guys weren't innocent bystanders like those people at the motel. Don't you understand? They brought us out here to *kill* us! I did what I had to do."

231

"Maybe so," Stephanie said. "But he's defenseless now. If we can save his life, we have to. If we don't, we're no better than he is."

Who's looking to be better than he is? I nearly shouted. I just want to get out of this burg without coming down with a fatal case of lead projectile poisoning. But instead I found myself yelling: "Don't you lecture me on ethics! These two were dirty cops. Do you get that? They operate outside the law; no rules." I stopped; Elspeth Rougnagne had said much the same thing about me. I ground my teeth, made one last effort to steer this toward sanity. "Look; you heal this scumbag, he'll thank you by putting a bullet in your skull. We can't afford to let him live."

Stephanie shook her head. "You still don't understand," she said. "We can't afford *not* to." Pulling her arm free, she fumbled her way to the prone body and knelt down before it.

I stood over them, willing my hands not to curl into claws with some difficulty.

"He's fading too quickly," Stephanie said. "His breathing has stopped."

"Gee, that's too bad." That's neurotoxins for ya; an Agency lab tech had once told me the snakes had a lethal dose rating right up there with a death adder's, one of the world's most venomous serpents. Monkey Paws had probably gotten a good fifty milligrams of the stuff with that one bite, more than enough to send him into respiratory failure. I checked my watch. "Ready to go?"

"Help me," she said, her voice strained.

"No way," I said, shaking my head. "No. Way."

"Kyra!" Stephanie turned her head to look over her shoulder at me. Perspiration had beaded on her forehead. "You talk to me about having no right to heal you! You are responsible for this man's life. You have no right to stand by and let him die just because you are afraid."

"Afraid?" I growled. I crouched down next to her. "What am I supposed to be afraid of?"

232

Stephanie's lip quivered. I could see only myself in the dark lenses of her sunglasses. "Of not being a monster anymore." She turned back to the still figure under her.

I balled my hand into a fist and raised it over the back of her head. Then I hammered it down on Monkey Paws' chest. "We're—not—done—talking—about—this," I grunted between blows.

"I know," Stephanie murmured. Light bloomed under her fingers, sank into the body.

I couldn't believe I was doing this. At least she'd left the Uber Bitch to her own fate. Not getting to kill her had been bad enough. Now I was supposed to resuscitate everyone I had the snakes envenom?

No heartbeat. Swearing furiously, I pulled open the bastard's mouth and pumped air into his lungs, gagging at the foulness of his breath. I pumped his chest, my fingertips brushing against Stephanie's. There was a strange feeling of communion in the touch, a subtle sense of connection, though at that moment the emotion I was most conscious of was the desire to clock her.

When Monkey Paws suddenly shuddered and started breathing, we both fell back, panting. I didn't know if this was triumph or defeat. But Stephanie was smiling. With that I found I could be satisfied.

"Feels . . . good . . . doesn't it?" she gasped. "Preserving life . . . instead of . . . ending it?"

I scowled, though without much heat. "That's not a baby we just delivered," I said, standing up unsteadily. "Just a whole mess of trouble. When he wakes up . . ."

"You'll think of something," Stephanie said, extending a hand. "That's your gift."

"Really?" I pulled her to her feet. "And here I thought my gift was letting you drag me into one disaster after another."

"That too."

We both laughed. Monkey Paws groaned, stirring. I steered Stephanie to a seat in the van and came back. I hauled the cop up into a sitting position, then took out his cuffs and made him fast to a metal support. When he looked up, I gave him a friendly wave.

"Hi there! Remember me?"

The cop blinked blearily. "Yuh—you're the lady Fed . . . ," he said in a low, droning voice.

Interesting. I studied his face intently for a moment. There was something familiar about the way his eyes caught the light. Then it came to me. I'd seen this reaction before, when I'd been learning how to administer various serums to, ah, encourage cooperation. But to see it now . . .

Of course. The Agency had once proposed testing the venom's ability to suppress a recipient's memory and inhibition centers, but there'd been a profound lack of volunteers. I hadn't been too keen on it myself at the time. How pleased they'd be to know they'd apparently been on the right track.

Not that I had any intention of telling them. I had a different message in mind for that meeting.

"That's right," I said. I read the name plate on his shirt. "Your pal's bailed on you, Officer Pontano. He's gone, turned state's evidence to the FBI. Your crew's going down, hard. You don't want to be left holding the bag here."

"Don't . . . want to hold . . . the bag," he agreed.

"Good boy. So I'm going to give you this one chance, Officer Pontano. In about fifteen minutes, a call is going to be placed to the FBI regional headquarters on West Roosevelt. That call is going to make you a very popular man. In the five additional minutes it takes for the black vans to show up, I'd give some serious consideration to telling the Feds everything you know about what you and your friends have been up to with Marco Delgado and his boss. You don't want to be the only one holding the bag, right?" Repetition was key here.

Monkey Paws shook his head. "Don't . . . want the bag . . ."

"One more thing. You don't know me. You don't know anything about me. We've never met. Got it?"

"We've never . . . met . . ."

234

Could this actually work? If it did, I might have to actually start believing in luck.

"Sit and wait," I said, and left him there. Stephanie started in her seat as I hopped into the police van.

"Is he all right?"

"Sure," I said, guiding us out of the debris-strewn lot. We needed to put some distance between us and the Damen Silos and then find a pay phone. "You know, it's funny—"

"What's funny?"

"Just how Officer Pontano there managed to get healed enough to survive my snake's venom, but not enough to avoid it having an effect on his memory."

"That's not funny," said Stephanie, turning her face to the window. "That's just strange."

Maybe so. Yet, despite the strangeness, we were both cracking up as we rode past McKinley Park into the gathering dark.

While it was good to have wheels, a police prisoner transport was not my idea of inconspicuous. As soon as I'd finished with my pay phone call, I turned to the matter of ditching the van. Fortunately, we were still in a part of town where things could be made to disappear for a while.

I wended through the old rail lines that cut across the belly of the New City section of town, once the major artery for the Union Stock Yards back when Chicago was the meatpacking capital of the country. I tucked the van in a shadowed lane down a seemingly endless stretch of mobile trailers and checked what the police had left us. Surprisingly, no one had thought to dig through Druison's satchel. Otherwise, I'd be a poorer woman at this moment. I prized out the false bottom and counted the money: all there.

My weapons had been tossed in a separate bag by the Illinois troopers, but it only took a few minutes for a girl to feel pretty in her duster again.

And I had one other thing going for me, or *things*, to be accurate. Despite loosing their power against the cop, the snakes were still with me, coiling and rubbing against one another under my beret. They should have been dying by now, but it looked like all the old rules were out the window. And I had a feeling the explanation for that was sitting next to me in the van. Stephanie's healing aura was probably regenerating them, just as she'd healed my ankle simply by being in proximity to me.

That made sense, but I still felt strangely reluctant to bring up the subject. I told myself that it was just that we had enough on our plates at the moment. Y'know, like our heads. Besides, I had Stephanie on Thread Duty right now, watching if any sudden danger was heading our way. I didn't want to disturb her concentration—

"Where are we?" Stephanie asked.

"Back of the Yards," I muttered, looking out the windows as I made sure all my toys were in place. Whatever was coming, I'd at least be able to put on a good fireworks show. "Industrial park area in the southwest of the city. We should be able to score a new car from one of the employee lots."

"Then what?"

I blew out my breath. "That, Stephanie, is the sixty-four-thousand-dollar question. You're serious that we have to stay in the city to have any chance here?" I knew she was; I just wanted to hear it again, to see her certitude, since it was still the most tactically ridiculous notion I could have imagined. Somewhere, Sun Tzu was rolling over in his grave; in fact, the old Chinese general had probably been in rotisserie mode all weekend.

She nodded.

Well. That was that.

"Okay, then." I checked my watch. It was nearly eight-thirty. Three and a half hours to go till midnight. I should have felt relief at the thought: only 210 ticks of the clock. But all I could think was that this was way too much time to spend looking over my shoulder, trying to anticipate where and when the hammer would fall.

Stephanie had said that the assassin could have come upon us and wiped us out without us even knowing it. So either he was very stealthy or he had the ability to wreak wholesale destruction on a scale that dwarfed mine. If the latter was the case, then the only effective defense would be to get out of range. But Stephanie had ruled that out.

And when she knows, she is always right.

I grimaced. She'd better be, Elspeth. Or else your daughter's killed us both.

So, stealth. That didn't do much to narrow things down.

"Man, I could use that idiot Phil's help right now," I muttered.

"Who's Phil?"

"Just someone I'm going to k—um, contact later," I said. "My handler at the Agency I work for." Used to work for. It seemed they took the idea of a termination notice literally. "He would always give me information on my marks."

"You should call him then."

"Yeah," I snorted, "I doubt that would be . . . helpful—" I stopped, struck by a notion. A very interesting notion.

"Stephanie," I announced, "that is an excellent idea."

"It is?"

"Yes, indeed. Sun Tzu would be proud of you."

Stephanie cocked her head. "Who's Sun Zoo?"

I shook my head as I hunted for my cell phone. Kids, these days. How do you get to be fourteen without reading *The Art of War*?

"Phil."

"Kyra! I . . . uh—"

"I assume you got my position as soon as I turned my cell back on," I interrupted. "I just wanted to call you to let you know something: If I'm not dead by this time tomorrow, you and I are going to be getting together for a little chat. I'd get ready for that." I took a deep breath. Now for the plunge. "Let the assassin know we'll be waiting for him at the Pinnacle, on Superior."

"Kyra, I'm sor—"

I hung up.

Behind me, Stephanie sat on the concrete ledge before the decorative flowering bushes lining the front of the hotel. Stone Chinese dragons crouched on either side of her, their snarls frozen on their overlarge faces. Not my work; these had been born from the mind of an actual sculptor, though it was rumored there were one or two places in the Windy City that boasted statuary with a less savory origin. Poised a stone's throw from Chicago's famed Miracle Mile to ensure maximum shopping convenience, the Pinnacle catered to the rich and financially reckless. For tonight, at least, we qualified under both categories.

Stephanie was moving her head back and forth as though actually watching the tide of people going past her on the sidewalk as they blithely enjoyed the first balmy night of spring, clutching their precious bags from Cartier, Neiman Marcus, or Escada. With her dark sunglasses still on, she looked like a young, willowy Ingrid Bergman. Nobody should be allowed to look like a young, willowy Ingrid Bergman.

She tilted her head up as I turned around. Above us, the flags of the hotel fluttered and snapped in the wind. "The . . . Pinnacle? Is that where we are? Why did we come here?"

I smiled grimly. "Hey, if you gotta go," I said, taking her arm to guide her inside, "you might as well go in style."

CHAPTER 13

"Those skilled in war bring the enemy to the field of battle and are not brought there by him." Sun Tzu had taught that to his subordinates, some five hundred years before the birth of Christ. If the assassin was a Mythic who operated by stealth, then forcing him to come to the very heart of the bustling downtown district might neutralize his advantage, or at least take him out of his comfort zone.

It was a long shot. But so was everything else at this point.

Besides, I'd *always* wanted to stay a night at the Pinnacle. If this was going to be my last chance to do that, I wasn't going to waste it.

The concierge at the reservations desk regarded us dubiously as we walked across the immaculate marble floor. In our dusty clothes, I guess we didn't meet the usual dress code.

"Can I help you?" he said, implying he knew the answer.

"Oh, yes!" said Stephanie, before I could so much as open my mouth. "Can you tell me what that sound is? It's lovely!"

The concierge raised an eyebrow, then glanced over at me.

"My kid sister," I smiled. "She doesn't get out much. We need a room for the night."

"I see." Despite his air of diffidence, the concierge's eyes kept being drawn back to Stephanie as though her face was a lodestone. I had a feeling that was going to happen a lot if we stayed out in public. Elspeth Rougnagne may have been many things, I reflected, but a fool was not one of them.

"Hello," I said, snapping my fingers before his eyes. "A room, if you please. We don't have all night." God knows. We might only have minutes. I was getting those complimentary chocolates if it killed me.

"What kind of accommodations are you seeking?" he asked, reluctantly turning his attention back to me.

Got any panic rooms? "Your best," I said, sliding a thousand dollars onto the counter. "Have it ready in five minutes, and you can keep the change."

"Are there actual musicians here?" cried Stephanie in rapture. "I hear two violins and a . . . viola?"

The concierge seemed to finally grok that the gorgeous creature before him was blind. "You are correct," he said, smiling. The bills disappeared like a rabbit vanishing into its burrow. Money to burn, baby; money to burn. "We have live musicians each evening until ten, up there in the minstrel's gallery." He started to point, then reconsidered. "Perhaps you would like to meet them?"

"Oh, yes," said Stephanie.

"Some other time," I said, catching her arm. "We really need to freshen up, Sis."

"Oh. Of course." Stephanie nodded, bowing to necessity. As I was busy making up our personal information, a man in the uniform of a guest relations manager was being magnetized by Stephanie's charms. I kept one hand ready to draw my Glock in case this was more than another eligible bachelor. But at a murmured response from Stephanie, he didn't produce anything more dangerous looking than a pen and paper, with which he took down something she said in a low voice.

Huh. Well, it was either a request for popcorn to be sneaked up or a note that she was being kidnapped. Either seemed equally likely. I elected to let it ride. If I was going to keep my secrets from her, I guess she could keep one or two from me.

Without any luggage to carry, the bellhop didn't seem to know what to do with his hands as he guided us to the elevators. But I wasn't letting anyone touch Druison's satchel.

"So, what was that about?" I whispered. It didn't hurt to ask, right?

"Something for later," Stephanie said, smiling.

I shook my head. Such an optimist.

The bellhop extolled the virtues of the hotel the whole ride up.

"—from the deluxe suite on the twentieth floor give you a magnificent view of the city," he was saying to Stephanie, as oblivious as he was rhapsodic. "And if you haven't had dinner yet, the outdoor terrace on the fifteenth floor can seat your party up until eleven o'clock. Chef Huen prepares every meal personally. His creations have been featured in *Dining Chicago* twice in the last year—"

I counted twenty-two numbered buttons on the panel. "What's on the floors above ours? I asked for the best, you know."

The bellhop was too well trained to be provoked. "Yours is the very best suite we have, Miss. The top two floors are the indoor pool and spa facility. It closes at nine, but if you have special requirements, I'm sure that arrangements can be made . . ."

He droned on and on, obsequiousness raised to art form. By the time we'd come to the door of our room, I'd exceeded my Daily Maximum Allowance.

"Thank you," I said, plucking the key cards from his fingers and replacing it with a hundred-dollar bill. "We'll take it from here."

"I can show you the amenities—" he began before I shut the door in his face.

241

The room did not disappoint, elegance and comfort wrapping themselves around us in hues of cream and gold from carpet to chandelier. I threw the satchel on a chair and steered Stephanie around a coffee table bedecked with a fresh bouquet of flowers to a sofa.

Maybe it was just Captain Obsequious—or the fact that I was probably hours away from a horrible death—but I found that instead of relaxing me, the luxurious surroundings only made me feel more edgy. Trailing plumes of anxiety, I stalked over to the bedroom.

There were the chocolates, blazing red Pierre Marcolini truffles, shaped like little hearts and elegantly laid out on a fan-shaped dish atop the gorgeous mound of silken pillows, just as I'd imagined. I picked them up, trying to savor the sweet scent, and suddenly found I had no stomach for them.

"Here," I said, dropping them in Stephanie's lap. "You'll like these."

Stephanie's hands fell on the dish. "Are they better than popcorn?"

"Loads better," I said. "They're to die for." Maybe literally. I began pacing back and forth while she made short work of my treasure trove.

"Steph . . . I think this was a mistake," I said, scratching at the patch of scales on the back of my hand. "My gut is telling me we need to get out of here."

"But we just got here," Stephanie said around a mouthful of chocolate. "And you said Sun Zoo would approve."

Sun Tzu, I thought mordantly. Sun Tzu's head would explode if he knew I was boxing myself into a gilded corner with no means of surveilling the Enemy's approach.

"I may have been wrong," I said. "We're too vulnerable here. I don't like being so—"

"Blind?"

It didn't take a genius to hear the mild reproof. "It's not just that. I . . . I don't know what we're up against, so I don't know what may work against

242

it. If bullets don't kill it, I'll only have the Medusa's Gaze, and that's—" I shook my head. "This whole plan is crazy. I can't even trust the Gaze to work."

"What do you mean?"

"Ever since you healed me, the damn thing's been going haywire. Somehow you mucked it up."

"How could I do that?"

"How should I know? I'm not Destiny's Child or whatever. All I know is that all my life, whenever the snakes have let loose, they've all died afterward. Within hours. Every time. Like they die from shock or burnout or something. But not anymore! Not since you came along. Since then everything's gone wonky. Now when I try to use them to stun someone, nothing happens. Zip. Then, when I use the Gaze against the manticore, it goes berserk, chasing after Marty like a pack of hyenas until it brings him down. Maybe it was the mirrors, multiplying the effect, but I dunno . . . it seemed like something else was happening. Like the Gaze had become more powerful. It petrified that manticore in less time than it takes to spit."

"Good," murmured Stephanie. She wasn't above feeling some anger toward that particular monster at least. That was somehow comforting.

The Gaze had worked fine on Pontano's partner too. But that still begged the question of whether I could keep relying on it.

"Who did you try to stun?"

"Hm? Oh, uh . . . Detective Druison." Now what the hell was that smirk for? "Why?"

Stephanie shrugged. "Maybe he just has some natural immunity," she said. The smile widened. "Or maybe your heart wasn't in it."

"What would that have to do with it?" I fumed. "And I wasn't trying to hurt him, just put him out of commission for a while. I've done it before." But not often, truth be told. And there was always the risk that I'd use too much power and trigger the Change. I frowned: Had I been that afraid of hurting him?

"When you used your Gaze on the manticore, what were you thinking?"

That I was about two seconds from being a late-night snack for a socio-path. "Just that I was in trouble. That I needed . . ."

"Help?"

"Yeah." I wasn't sure I liked where this conversation was going.

"And you received it. From them."

I nodded stonily. She couldn't see that, but maybe she sensed it.

"And they haven't died since then," she murmured. "Since you used their power to save yourself, and me."

"Yeah? So? So what?" If I kept scratching, I was going to draw blood. With an effort, I kneaded my hands together behind my back.

"Have you ever . . . turned someone to stone by accident?"

My darling boy. His ghost seemed to be hovering close all the time now. "Just . . . once."

"So you control it? You have to will the Gaze to happen?"

"Yes!" I snapped. "Can we talk about something else?"

"Like what?"

Oh, God, I don't know. Like . . .

"Why?" I asked. If ever there was a time, I guess this was it. "Why did you choose me? What . . . made you think I'd say yes?"

Stephanie smiled, as though pleased. "Ever since I was little, and could understand what the threads were, my mother had me search them for certain patterns. She never told me why . . . just that she knew that some great calamity lay ahead. So I spent a lot of my time studying the Tapestry, learning the patterns, following where they led, seeing how different threads might combine or unravel. One day, yours . . . caught my attention. I saw your thread, once so bright, fading, going slowly into darkness. And I saw how, if it were woven with mine, it could be made to glow strongly again and become part of . . . of a greater pattern. So I brought you to me, and my mother offered you a choice. Your actions since then are proof enough of the choice you made."

244

I didn't make a choice! I wanted to rail. Your mother took my choices from me, during the soul-lock, when she threatened to annihilate me if I didn't do what she wanted.

But it was the only thing I had left to cling to, her misguided faith in me. "I'm not you, Stephanie." It was the best warning I could give her. "I never will be."

"I'm not asking you to be. I'm asking you to be a better *you*. The you that you were meant to be, that you still can be."

"The world doesn't work like that," I sighed.

"Then the world needs help," Stephanie said. "It needs healing."

I made a soft, scoffing sound. "That's a tall order for a teenage girl and one screwed-up gorgon."

"It has to start somewhere. We cannot live just for ourselves."

"That's easy for you to say!" I flared. "You've lived in a plastic bubble all your life! I've had to be out there fighting—doing—"

"Yes? Doing what?"

"You wouldn't understand."

"Tell me."

"You already know," I said. "You know the whole stupid story of my stupid life. You've seen it yourself."

"I haven't," she said.

"But . . . you healed me . . ."

"Ah," she said, nodding. "You think I entered your mind to do that. No. That's not how I cause a healing. I would never have invaded your privacy like that. When I healed you before, I felt your pain, your grief, but I didn't know what had caused it. Will you . . . will you tell me?"

"What's the point?" I sat down on the other side of the sofa, feeling oddly deflated. As mad as I'd been that she'd gone through my memories like that, I'd been sort of comforted by the fact that afterward she had still wanted to have me protect her, that she hadn't . . . "It doesn't change anything."

Stephanie sidled next to me and took my hand.

"Kyra, I think . . . I fear this is my last night on this Earth. Maybe for both of us. You've been the only friend I've ever had. I would like to understand what you've been through, if you'll allow it."

Her expression held a gentle entreaty I'd never seen on another person's face. There was fear there, but courage too. And suddenly I understood what she was doing, why she was asking. Stephanie believed in the necessity, the logic that had required her mother's death. But she still needed to understand why.

She needed to know *who* her mother's killer was.

I guess I owed her that. No matter what it cost me.

"When—" I cleared my throat. I had never talked about this before, not to anyone. But Stephanie was right. We were both probably going to be dead within the next few hours. What did it matter if one more person was disgusted by me? It's not like I would feel the hurt very long.

"When I was ten, my hair started falling out," I said. "I had no idea why. I was . . . upset, as you can probably imagine. But my mother was beside herself; she treated it like it was something I had done on purpose. I wasn't even allowed to talk about it. And then . . . when I started to grow these little green buds on my head, I was scared to death. I thought I was dying. My mother never explained what they were; she just started shaving my head every night. She used this big—it doesn't matter. I thought I'd done something wrong, y' know? Like I was being punished. And there was no one to explain it to me. My mother refused to discuss it, and there was nobody else; my father had walked out on us—" I recalled the face that I had so briefly glimpsed during the Siren's attack, the feeling of a connection being severed as it withdrew. Could that really have been my father? Did he stay long enough to see it was a monster being born into his household? Was that why he left us?

I shook my head free of the clinging image. "Anyway, this went on for a while. Then, when I was twelve . . . my mother sent me away. I'd done something . . . bad. Not me: the snakes." Old grief thickened in my throat, made each word halting, difficult. "There was . . . a boy. His name was Pietro

246

and we were in love. We'd decided to run away together. So we sneaked off and hid in the hills for a day while we made our way to a secluded bay on the other side of the island. We'd worked it all out, right? We knew my mother would head for the only port on the southern part of the island, so we figured that would give us extra time to get away. Only I hadn't shaved my head, see? I hadn't killed the snakes 'cause . . . 'cause I didn't *know*." Tears blurred my vision. "So I was stupid and careless and I . . . they . . . killed him, killed the boy I loved. I've wondered afterward if they were . . . jealous.

"When my mother found us, she made me throw the body into the ocean to hide it. I was wild, tried to throw myself in after him. My mother stopped me. When I wouldn't leave, she promised that she would put flowers in the sea for him, every year. I guess that made sense to a twelve-year-old, because I let her take me home.

"But I didn't stay long. My mother said I couldn't live there anymore after what the snakes had done. There was no point in trying to explain to the people of my village that what had happened was an accident. They were superstitious folk and would have hunted down the monster that had done it.

"So my mother said I had to go to America. She said people didn't believe in monsters there, only money. I would live with some distant cousins I didn't even know I had. They would meet me at the dock in New York City. There I could hide and be safe.

"Only nobody met me when I finally made it to the States. Nobody. I waited for days, until the authorities found me and arrested me for vagrancy. They called me an illegal immigrant and tossed me in with adults who supposedly came from the same place." I shook my head. "We didn't even speak the same language. Nobody knew what to do with me. I would get released and picked up again, over and over, until eventually I learned the tricks to staying out. When the Agency . . . rescued me, I'd been living on the streets of New York City for eight months, doing whatever I had to in order to eat, to get a roof or a cardboard box over my head for the night. Sometimes I would use the snakes to petrify rats for the butcher shops, and sometimes I'd do . . . other things.

247

"The Agency took me in, took me away from all that. They educated me and trained me in . . . you know, what I do."

"Killing people," Stephanie said softly. "For money."

"Well, when you put it that way . . ." But the joke died stillborn in my throat. It was the truth, wasn't it? "It's just a job," I muttered. "Nothing personal." But the words tasted like ash in my mouth.

"My mother didn't like you," Stephanie said, in what was probably the understatement of the week. "She said I shouldn't trust my life to someone like you."

I snorted silent approval; at least old Elspeth and I agreed on that much.

"But she researched you. She was always very thorough. She said one thing about you surprised her: that you always refused to take—contracts? Is that the right word? You wouldn't take contracts to kill people who were close to children. Tell me why."

Ah, God. All the scabs were coming off tonight. All the old ghosts coming home to say hello.

Or maybe this was good-bye.

I shook my head. In for a penny . . .

"Okay," I said. "One of my earliest . . . jobs for the Agency was to kill a man in Bahrain, a rich oil trader that someone couldn't negotiate with." I couldn't even remember his name now. What did that say about me? "He was a fat pig who had . . . let's just say some exotic interests. He lived on an estate that was like a fortified compound on the coast. The Agency sent three of us in to get to him. We were to work there as servants, living in the seraglio with the rest of the girls, until the objective was achieved. Danae was the one with the most experience; she was older than me—nearly fifteen. Brienne was only ten years old, but bright and clever. We'd trained and lived together for months. They were the closest thing I had in the world to friends." How vivid they still seemed, like a bright slash across my mind's eye—Danae's razor-sharp smile and stunning violet eyes; Brienne clutching the ragged doll she'd hide under her bed, crying each night when

248

everyone else was asleep. "Before we went in, we treated it almost like a game: You know, who would get him first.

"Only it went bad . . . real bad. One of us—Danae—got caught trying to slip poison into his wine. They tortured her for days, trying to find out who had sent her, if there were any more. Brienne panicked. Afraid that Danae would crack, she tried to get away. I refused to go with her, told her we had to finish the mission, that it was too dangerous to leave. I had a million reasons, but the reality was that I was just scared. I thought she'd listen to me.

"But Brienne went by herself. They shot her as she was scaling the wall of the compound. Her body hung there, tangled up in the barbed wire at the top, for a week. Every day the birds left a little less of her." My voice shook. "She was *ten*." Even all this time later, I could still see her body stretched out upside down, her dead mouth hanging open and her one arm thrown back, as though trying to point me out to the guards: *There she is—she's the other one.* I shuddered. "Eventually, the screams from the basement ceased. Danae had kept her silence to the last.

"The man went berserk. We all suffered for it. But eventually he went back to his pleasures. After a while, you'd think nothing had even happened. I waited. I never thought about trying to escape. Every night I went to sleep, dreaming of how I would kill the son of a bitch. He'd made it personal, you understand? I was going to see him dead for . . . for my friends. I waited a whole month to make my move. I'd carefully shaved my head every night as I learned his routine. When I knew I had two nights off, I let them grow out under my hijab. Then, when we were alone, and I was feeding him his dinner the way he liked, I tried to use the snakes to petrify him.

"I thought he would be easy, being so soft and fat, but on the inside he was tough as nails. He fought me like a tiger with his will; it was all I could do to finally lock the Medusa's Gaze. After I did, I was so exhausted that I let go of my hold early, before he was entirely gone. He could still use one arm. He got hold of a carving knife and opened up my stomach from here to here." I drew a nine-inch line across my belly. "Forty-five stitches. I did the job myself, right there, while his stone face watched and his spirit howled from Hell. I tried to sneak away, but I didn't get far before I almost passed out from blood loss. I made it to a closet and hid there, huddled against the cushions I'd used to sop up my own blood. I was unconscious, probably no more than twenty feet away, when the man's body was found.

"His retinue were old Persian stock. When they saw what had happened to him, they feared the wrath of the gods. Most took off, leaving the rest to face what they thought was holy judgment.

"The Agency knew something was up by then. They sent someone in to get us—me—out." I took a deep breath. "I was nearly gone by that point. But the Agency had been waiting a long time and needed a full report. So they used a healer to bring me back from the brink. To do that, he had to go deep into my mind . . . deeper than he should have. A few months later, when I was back up to speed, I went to find him, to thank him for saving me. I thought it was . . . the thing to do. Only I found out he'd—he'd taken his own life shortly after healing me. They said . . . before he died, he told them he saw things—terrible things—inside me. Things he couldn't bear to see any longer."

I tried to swallow the stone in my throat, failed. I stared at the plush rug, unwilling to look up. "I haven't let anyone heal me since."

And there it was. I'd finally said the things I'd been afraid for ten years to say to anyone. They say confession's good for the soul. But I felt nothing, not grief or dread, not even relief. Maybe Elspeth Rougnagne had been right all along; maybe I was already dead inside.

It was some time before she spoke.

"That's why you were so angry with me," Stephanie said. "And why you don't take contracts that will harm children. Because of Brienne."

I nodded. "Brienne. Pietro." Me. None of us had really been given a chance to live a normal life. Theirs had been cut short by death . . . and mine? Mine had turned into a living nightmare.

"Thank you," Stephanie said. "I think I understand now. . . . It's no wonder they die."

250

I frowned. "What . . . what do you—What are you talking about?"

She cocked her head. "The snakes."

My heart started beating faster. "I don't follow."

"And yet I'm the one called blind," Stephanie said, shaking her head with a sad smile. She took hold of both of my hands. "Kyra, you still don't understand. You're at war with yourself. You've been for years. You hate the death, the killing. Your guilt haunts you after every death you cause, but you don't know how to stop, and you hate that too. You try to pretend that you feel nothing, but your true feelings are eating you up inside, the pain consuming you. You want that pain to be gone, but you know deep down that there is a price for taking life, a price you've tried to pay by killing the part of you that you blame for doing it. Don't you see? The snakes aren't just attached to you; they *are* you, as much as your hand or heart is. They don't die from channeling the Medusa's Gaze; they die because you want them to, because you *tell* them to. They pay the price for your guilt so that you don't have to face it."

I yanked my hands free and stood up. "No," I muttered, backing away from her. "No, that's not true. It's not me—"

"But you can't murder guilt," Stephanie said. "It can only end when you accept it. Otherwise, as much as you push it away, it will always come back. Just as the snakes do. As they always will. Because they are a part of you too."

"No!" I snapped, appalled. Christ, why was she doing this to me? Didn't we have enough to deal with? "Weren't you listening to anything I said? They're the . . . ones. . . . The ones that do it. The ones that made me into a killer. If it weren't for them . . ." I'd have lived a normal life. I wouldn't be this freak! I'd still have a home, a family . . .

I wouldn't be alone.

"Kyra . . ."

I held up a hand. Dammit, it was shaking; I couldn't hit the broad side of a barn like this. Was she *trying* to get us killed? "Stop. Just stop. This was a mistake. I shouldn't have said anything." You're tearing me to pieces!

251

Can't—can't you leave me with anything? I grabbed my duster and made for the door.

"You stay here," I said over my shoulder. "If anyone knocks, don't answer. I need some air."

I yanked the door open. Stephanie said nothing as I closed it behind me. Thanking the gods for at least granting me that one small favor, I stormed down the hall, letting my boots beat my shame and anger out on the thick carpet.

I took the stairs in the hopes of avoiding running into any other people, people I might have to kill for looking at me the wrong way. I felt something primal and terrible building in my chest, scrabbling to claw its way out past my ribs. I just wanted to run out into the night and loose a scream that would never end, that would drive people to their knees, that would shatter glass—

Not very realistic, I know. But it helped to imagine these things while I tried to get myself under control. And the exertion of going down twenty flights of steps did its job, helping me to burn off the worst of my nascent hysteria. By the time I emerged—winded and sweating—into the lobby, the thing I really wanted was a cigarette and a drink.

I couldn't light up unless I went outside. And that would mean abandoning all pretense of maintaining a vantage point on the tactical situation. Fortunately, the hotel's spacious bar presented a partial solution: Its archway and bay windows looked out on the lobby, allowing me to surveil all points of access from one corner of the carved mahogany counter. And it turned out, the bartender knew how to make a bitchin' Manhattan.

I swirled the maraschino cherry around in the whiskey and sweet vermouth. Stephanie had been way out of line; she didn't know what she was talking about. They were the bad part, the thing that was alien, the . . . the monster; they didn't answer to me.

Except . . .

Except that over the last two days, when I'd asked for their help, they'd given it, not once or even twice, but three times. And when I'd had no will left to defend myself from the Siren, they'd gone on the attack to protect me; I'd sensed their anger at her too, their desire to harm her, to strike back against the one who was hurting their . . . what?

Owner? Mistress?

Friend?

Nah. No. No way. But . . .

I felt like I was stepping out onto rotten ice. The snakes had ruined my life, ended any chance I'd had at a normal childhood. They'd *killed* my love, for God's sake. I'd become what I was because of them. If they were anything but an enemy, then . . .

Then it was me. My fault that I'd done what I'd done, become the thing I was. Every death laid at my door belonged to me, and me alone.

The Uber Bitch had shoved the truth in my face, rubbed my nose in it. But it was Stephanie's gentle words that had made it impossible to deny.

After all, I was the one who used them, wasn't it? I who chose when to loose their power every time. They might have been built to deal death, but I was the croupier, doling out the cards to the unlucky players.

Except for Pietro . . .

He'd always been my answer when doubts had come gnawing, my firewall protecting me from accepting the fact that I was just a natural killer, a predator by choice, not chance. But if they hadn't lashed out at him out of malice, then maybe . . . maybe it really had been only an accident—an awful, avoidable accident as a young, feckless girl's hormones surged out of control, triggering a power she hadn't even known she possessed.

Was that really the truth?

I'd hated them for so long because of Pietro. It had become a reflex: hating them, wanting to punish them. I'd blamed them for costing me everything. And I'd punished them for it, hadn't I? Gods, I'd butchered them, over and over, loathing them with even greater ferocity each time they'd come back. Only—if Stephanie was right—in some weird, mysterious way, I'd just been hating myself.

There was an awful feeling of space before me, like a yawning chasm, and my thoughts were carrying me over the precipice without any brakes. The snakes had stopped dying when I'd given them free reign to help, when I'd used them to save us. When I'd stopped using them for murder.

When I'd stopped hating what I was doing with them.

I'd been too busy to see it up until this minute, but the evidence before me now was too damning to ignore. The manticore would have killed Stephanie—not to mention me—if I hadn't defended myself. Pontano's partner had been the same. When I'd used the Medusa's Gaze those times, it had been to preserve life, not just end it. And the snakes had survived. More than that; I'd felt the link between us growing stronger, as though—as though I wasn't fighting myself as much.

It fit. It made me out to be a world-class idiot not to have seen it before, but it fit. And it meant that there was a chance, a real chance to change—

I'd gotten too wrapped up in my own thoughts. As I stood drumming my nails on the bar counter, a hand came down over mine. The weight was not heavy, but the sheer force behind it pinned my hand as though it were buried under an avalanche. I turned my head, panic and fury rearing up, and then stopped dead as the nerves of my face felt the power washing over them. It was like opening the door to a blast furnace.

The man in the light gray suit standing there was compact in stature, probably only an inch or two taller than me, but he radiated heat and malice as clearly as a shout. The air around him shimmered faintly as though he were baking from within; it made his blunt features blur ever so slightly. He had a broad, crooked nose and a face that seemed to have been chiseled with imprecise blows. His sun-bronzed skin was weathered, crowned by short strands of snowy hair, combed back from a high forehead. A white stubble beard peppered with red and gold framed his small, colorless lips. Pale, unblinking blue eyes set under ruddy brows peered down at me intently.

Imagine you're at the zoo, staring at a tiger, with one of those thick plexiglass barriers between you. It's really awe-inspiring to be able to stand that close to one of nature's most perfect predators and know you're still safe, isn't it? You can admire everything about the creature: the beautiful striped fur, the sleek rippling muscles, the long, powerful claws, even the great, sharp teeth that could tear you to shreds in a second.

Now imagine that you wake one morning to find that same tiger crouching at the foot of your bed. And then you'd have a good idea how I felt at that moment.

A flush of fear unlike any I had ever known went through me. I knew at once what he was, and the realization froze me in place. The Serpent Imperialis. King of the Snakes. Basileus.

A basilisk.

Even among the Mythic, basilisks are rare, almost legendary. And for good reason: Deadly by gaze, deadly by voice, deadly by touch, their nature did not encourage company. I shivered despite the unnatural heat licking at my skin. Elspeth Rougnagne had made some bad enemies indeed if this was what they had called in to do their dirty work.

"You are the *little* one," the basilisk said in a wondering tone. He arched an eyebrow. "I confess surprise. When I heard of all the pandemonium a gorgon was causing, I expected it to be one of your sisters."

I licked my lips, unsure of what to say or do. If I provoked it, the basilisk could kill me with a glance. And I still couldn't move my hand, even though it felt like my fingers were being crushed.

The basilisk seemed to notice me wincing.

"Your pardon," he said, lifting his hand from mine. "No injury was intended. I merely meant to forestall any unnecessary . . . unpleasantries."

I massaged the back of my hand, which felt raw and tingly. "How . . . unnecessary?" I rasped, struggling to speak against the knot of dread in my throat.

The basilisk ignored the question. "I mislike eating while traveling," he said, as though we were discussing the weather, "even when a private jet has been provided. It detracts from the enjoyment of the meal, having to concentrate on . . . other things. As a result, I find myself quite famished. I've made dinner reservations at this hotel's charming outdoor terrace. I am assured the table will be ready shortly. May I count on your attendance?"

Even amidst the fear crowding my thoughts, I found a little room to be offended. "You think I'm just going to march Stephanie into the mouth of the lion? Forget it."

The ruddy eyebrows pinched slightly. "Steph—? Ah, the human. You misunderstand me. The reservation is for two. I thought we might discuss our situation privately, to see if a rapprochement may be achieved. Shall I see you at ten-thirty?"

"Cutting it a little fine, aren't we?" In lieu of actual bravery, I had to make do with sarcasm. "You've only got till midnight."

The basilisk just looked at me.

Damn. He was that sure of himself. And he could afford to be. I was nothing—less than nothing—to him.

"So," I said, "you're just going to let me walk out of here?"

"I bear you no ill will, little gorgon," he said gravely. "I intend to conduct my business as expeditiously as possible and take my leave of this place. Whether that becomes . . . complicated . . . is up to you."

"You won't try to follow me while I . . . freshen up?"

A slight smile tugged at the corner of the thin, colorless lips. "Are you looking for my word of honor?" He placed one hand on his breast pocket. "Very well. I agree to a . . . truce between us. I will not seek you or the human out while you . . . 'freshen up.'"

"Why?" Sometimes, I just can't keep my big yap shut.

"Two reasons," the basilisk said easily. "First, there are things I should like to discuss with you. Second, I have a great thirst after traveling so far. While you . . . prepare, I am eager to sample this barkeep's supply of single malts."

As though summoned, the bartender appeared. "What can I get you?"

"The Remy Martin Louis XIII," said the basilisk, pointing. He bowed decorously to me. "Until dinner."

"Yeah," I said. "Sure."

I couldn't help backing out of the bar. But the basilisk just settled into a seat and engaged the bartender in conversation, as though he'd already forgotten I existed. I bumped my hip, painfully, against the doorframe as I exited, and that finally brought me round. Then I took off for the elevators at a dead run.

CHAPTER 14

I came through the door so fast that Stephanie and I practically collided. She must have been standing near the threshold for some time, waiting for my return.

"Kyra! Oh, I've been so worried!" She hugged me like she was drowning. "I'm so sorry! I didn't mean to upset you—"

"Later," I said, catching her hands and disentangling myself. He'd given me a twenty-minute head start, and I couldn't afford to waste a second of it. "Get your shoes on. We're getting out of here."

Stephanie stepped back. "What is it? What's happened?"

"Whoever wants you dead just upped the ante." Big time. "I just bumped into the assassin downstairs."

"He attacked you?"

No. And that had been surprising.

"Not in so many words. If he'd attacked me, I wouldn't be here talking about it. He's a basilisk."

259

"That is . . . worse than you?"

At another time, I might have debated the grammar or tact of that question. Instead I scooped up my keys and grabbed the satchel. "Way worse. I haven't heard of a basilisk showing its face in centuries. Which is a good thing. Whenever one has appeared, towns tend to go missing from the maps."

Instead of reaching for my hand, Stephanie sat down on the sofa. "How do you defeat one?"

Tick, tick, tick . . . "You don't. They're not called the 'King of Serpents' for nothing. They're immortal and invulnerable. Even my Gaze won't work on him."

"There must be something that can stop one."

In another moment, I was going to start hyperventilating. "All I've ever heard of is folklore. Nonsense about weasel spit or urine. The crowing of a rooster. Making the basilisk see himself."

Stephanie clasped her hands together. "You'll find a way."

Hyperventilation Time had officially arrived. "Stephanie, unless you've got a magic rooster stashed in that little purse of yours, we are screwed. Our only chance is to make a break for it."

"Won't he expect that?"

I had been reaching for her hand, but that stopped me. Stephanie was right; he would expect that. First rule of the hunt: Flush the quarry out of hiding. Right now, secrecy was our only advantage. He'd narrowed it down to the hotel, but there were hundreds of rooms to choose from. If we could hole up here without detection until midnight, the basilisk's contract might be void. If I hadn't let my panic do the thinking, I'd have realized that at once.

But was hiding really an option here? I'd heard stories of basilisks destroying whole villages in their wrath. Fire and brimstone. Hell on Earth. Would this one really stint at wrecking one hotel?

I didn't think so.

"Maybe," I answered, deciding. "But we'll have to try. We're sitting ducks here. Come on."

260

Stephanie folded her legs under her on the sofa. "No."

"*Steph!*" Gods, this girl made me crazy. "We don't have time for this. That thing downstairs could eat ten gorgons for breakfast. You have to trust me."

"It's not a question of trust. I can't leave here."

I kept myself from shouting with an effort. "Why not?"

"Because this is where it ends," she said. "I've seen it."

This foresight thing was really kicking my ass. "You've seen it. Could you be a wee bit more specific? How exactly does it end?"

"One way or the other."

We'd been around this particular mulberry bush before. I wasn't going to get anywhere by berating her. Deflated, I dropped onto the other side of the sofa.

"So." I didn't know what to say. Absent the basilisk having a sudden and massive heart attack inside of the next hour, Stephanie had just put the final nail in our coffins. I couldn't outfight him, and she wouldn't let us run. We'd come all this way—suffered so much—for nothing.

Abruptly, I laughed. Well, what else did I deserve? I'd only gotten this far under false pretenses anyway. This was just the karma boomerang finally coming back to take my head off.

"What's funny?"

Except Stephanie didn't deserve this. She shouldn't have to pay for her mother's sins, or mine. The kid had done nothing wrong her whole life, except place her faith in a fraud.

"I'm sorry," I said. "It's either laugh or cry, kid. And monsters don't cry."

"What are you talking about, Kyra?"

I licked my dry lips. I was never going to hear her say my name that way again after this moment. But it was time to clear the slate. And maybe if she knew I'd tricked her, she wouldn't place so much faith in the dance of destiny's weave; maybe she'd actually run. That would be worth it. "I didn't—I'm not what you think, Stephanie. I—never have been. I didn't choose to help you."

"Of course, you did—"

"No." I shook my head. Was there a sorrier excuse for a person on the planet? "Your mother offered me a chance to choose this, to agree to protect you. But I wouldn't do it. I was . . . afraid, I guess; I don't know. I said no. So she forced me to. She put me in a soul-lock and said if I didn't promise to save you, she'd drag me down into death with her. So I promised . . . but only to save myself. It wasn't my choice." I closed my eyes. "My choice would have been to let you die."

I thought I heard her make a choked sound, like a sob. Then, in a small voice, she asked: "And now?"

"Now?" I opened my eyes, stared at the carpet. "It doesn't matter what I might choose now. All that matters is we're going to die here. Unless you let me take you away."

"I'm not leaving."

I let out a shuddering breath. Even this small bit of absolution would be denied me. "Then we're dead."

Stephanie said nothing. After a minute, though, she scooted over closer.

"If we are going to die," she said, "I would like to ask you for something."

Gods, this child. She should be weeping or screaming at me by now. Instead, she was asking me for a favor like we were equals, as though I'd not already forfeited all entitlement to decency or civility. "What?"

Her blind gaze went to my beret. "May I touch them?"

"Steph . . ." I began, going cold at the very thought. "That's not a good idea. They're wild, venomous. They could kill you."

"I don't believe that," she said. "You wouldn't let them."

"It's not up to me—" I started to say, and then stopped. I guess I was done with that lie too. And what difference did it make, really? Maybe, if she did suffer a nip, it would be a kinder fate.

"Trust me, Kyra," Stephanie said, raising her hand to my face. "Trust yourself."

The knot in my throat felt like it was strangling me. "All—all right."

Stephanie reached for my beret. I flinched as she touched my cheek. Her fingers grazed up my temple until they found the brim of my hat.

Slowly, almost reverently, she drew it off. Roused by the light, the snakes began uncoiling, hissing as they slid over one another. Every fiber of my being shrilled at me to shout a warning. In all my life, no one—not even my mother—had ever touched one of them and lived, not when they were full-grown like this.

Friend, I thought fervently, aching for them to listen, to heed. *She's my friend. Don't hurt her.*

Stephanie lifted up her hand again and rested her palm lightly on my head, on the heart of the nest. The serpents curled between her fingers, rubbing themselves against her skin.

Stephanie made a slight noise, like a whimper.

"What—?" I almost pulled my head back, but something in her face held me.

"They tickle," she said, and giggled. "I thought they'd be cold. But they're not. They're warm."

After a minute, she withdrew her hand and let me tug them back under my beret. They went quietly, but slowly, as though reluctant to go.

"Thank you," Stephanie said.

"I don't understand," I said. "Why . . . why would you . . . ?"

"I just wanted them to know they were loved too," she said. "To touch them once, before we said good-bye."

"Good-bye—?"

"Kyra Regina Anastas," Stephanie said. "I release you."

I snapped my head up. "What?"

Stephanie's face was pale but composed. "Your promise. To protect me. I release you from it. Go and save yourself."

My heart was beating hard against my ribs, in sudden terror or exultation. "I made that promise to your mother, not to you."

"That promise was made in my name, and I hold it now. You know this to be true. And I say I release you from it. I won't ask you to die for me. Go. Save yourself. Please."

For one mad moment, my limbs nearly took hold of the rest of me. I saw myself leaping off the sofa, racing down the stairs, fleeing for my life out into the night. I was going to live, to be free—

Except I wouldn't be free, would I? Not really. I'd have breath in my lungs, blood in my veins . . . and the memory of what I'd done here, tonight, forever.

"No."

Stephanie's breath caught. She shook her head in dismay. "Why?"

"Because . . ." But the words wouldn't come; they didn't belong to me, weren't said by things like me. "Because I'm stubborn, okay?"

Stephanie pouted. "That's not why."

"Just leave it be, Steph. Maybe I just don't want to give that son of a bitch the satisfaction of knowing he made me run with my tail between my legs."

"Kyra . . ." Stephanie's tone was reproving. "You don't need to sacrifice yourself for me. You can make a new path for yourself now. You aren't the same lost creature you were before. You are becoming something new—"

"Steph—!" I lurched up. She couldn't know how much it hurt, hearing this kind of talk. It was too much what I wanted to be true and now never could be. There'd be no time to walk down the path of possibility that had just opened before me tonight. The blinders had come off too late. "I'm warning you: I didn't promise your mother you would make it to midnight with all your teeth. So just drop it."

We enjoyed one of our trademark awkward silences. Finally, Stephanie broke it: "What did the basilisk do when you bumped into him?"

Now it was an awkward non-silence. I cleared my throat. "He . . . uh, he invited me to dinner, actually."

Stephanie cocked her head. Right there with you on this one, kid. "Why?"

I bit at my nails restlessly. "He said he wanted to talk."

"You should then."

"Should what?"

"Talk to him."

I blanched at the prospect. If given a choice between sitting down with a basilisk and sticking my head into a piranha tank, I'd have taken my chances playing kissy-face with the fish. "The hell I will," I said with feeling. "Why would I do that?"

She shrugged. "He could expose a weakness. Maybe you'll learn something. Or maybe he will. Isn't that would your Sun Zoo would do?"

I blinked, impressed. For such a sheltered kid, she was a quick study. And, unfortunately, she was right.

I checked my watch. Twenty after the hour already.

Oh, what the hell.

"Okay," I said, and cursed the quaver in my voice. "I'll go."

"Good," nodded Stephanie. She opened her purse.

"What are you doing?"

Stephanie winced as she produced a small bottle. "Well, since you're going, I have to say: You still smell like that creek we were at this afternoon. I thought you might want to do something about that."

I never knew if I wanted to hug her or brain her more. "I said I'd go to dinner," I said, putting a bite of iron in my tone, "but I'm not dressing up for the bastard."

They don't conduct exit polls of criminals who go to the gallows—for obvious reasons   but, if they could, I imagine the condemned would describe pretty much the same sensations going up the steps to the gibbet that I was experiencing as I walked into the hotel's Outer Terrace. My stomach was gamely trying to drop into my intestines, my fingers and feet felt numb, and I couldn't clear my throat no matter how many times I tried; it seemed I was making a noise like a strangled trumpet every few seconds.

265

Of course there were a few differences too. It wasn't a scaffold I was stepping out onto but an open porch made of interlocking ceramic tiles, with the John Hancock Center looming over it like an obsidian monolith. Open to the night sky, the restaurant still had an intimate atmosphere, as though it were being swaddled by Chicago's architecture on all sides. And instead of a hooded hangman standing next to a loop of hempen rope, I was greeted by a middle-aged Asian woman with her jet-black hair swept back into a traditional topknot that had been decorated with metal hairpins and a white-and-pink ribbon.

She bowed in greeting and escorted me through a maze of massive potted plants and high metal enclosures draped with red silk coverings like field tents. Most were unoccupied, though inside one I glimpsed a young couple huddled together on a divan heaped with cushions as they picked at a dish of crab Rangoon. Everywhere candles flickered in ornate holders on the low tables that had been scattered about with nonchalant elegance. Female servers dressed in tight red-and-black dresses moved like wraiths between the tents, carrying crystal decanters of water and silver trays of food.

My hostess stopped before the largest tent in the center of the terrace and gestured for me to enter. She needn't have troubled herself; the moment we came within twenty feet of it, the nerves of my face had told me what was inside. Making a final trumpet noise, I forced a smile onto my face and tugged the red curtain aside.

The basilisk sat with his back to the entrance, a glass of wine in one hand. Eschewing the soft pillows piled atop the sofas on either side, he had chosen a wicker chair for his repose. As I stood there on nerveless legs, he rose and pulled back a matching chair for me. Holding my braying fear in check, I let him seat me before the table, which was bedecked with red roses floating in clear vases. This close I could feel the concentrated hostility of his aura like sandpaper being dragged over my skin. It made the candles set around the interior of the tent seem pale and ghostlike, as though they were wisps before a blazing cauldron.

The basilisk smiled as he reseated himself. "Thank you for joining me," he said. "Sharing a meal is a luxury in which I rarely get to indulge."

I'll bet. "Yeah, well, this isn't a date."

"No? That isn't perfume?"

Crap; he'd noticed. Damn it, Stephanie. "It's not mine."

"Ah, your . . . client's, then. Well, we'll get to that shortly."

A procession of servers came in, bearing trays. They set them down before us and disappeared without a word.

"I hope you do not mind," the basilisk said. "I took the liberty of ordering for us."

I surveyed the cornucopia before me: pork dumplings, orange chicken, fried eggplant, piles of sliced beef shank, stuffed sugar beans with shrimp, all filling the tent with their savory scents.

This was a lot of food. I hoped the basilisk wasn't expecting me to split the tab. "Is the 101st Airborne joining us?"

A rumble of pleasant laughter shook the basilisk's chest. He was dressed in the same suit as before, but had added a silken handkerchief to his breast pocket. If anything, he looked even more refined, at home amidst the luxurious surroundings. "Since I was uncertain as to your preferences, I gave the chef free rein. I trust you will find something that satisfies."

That glass of wine looked to be a grand place to start. A broad and ripe shiraz, I nearly downed it in one gulp.

"Do you know why I wanted you to join me for dinner?"

I shook my head. Best to say as little as possible, let him draw himself out.

"Initially, it was for the reason you might surmise: I was simply going to offer you the chance to withdraw from this folly and thus purchase your life. But upon further reflection, I grew curious to talk with this oddity among Oddities, this monster who kills her own kind."

Was that an insult? If so, I found I could live with it. "Mythic have killed one another before."

"Of course. But always for gain: wealth, women, land. What do you gain by this, little gorgon?"

"You first," I said. If I let him stay in control of the conversation, I'd learn only what he wanted me to learn. If there was even a snowball's chance in Hell of us surviving this, I had to have more. "Give me some answers. What can a basilisk possibly want or need with money? Why are you doing this?"

A flicker of hesitation came and went in the blue eyes. He wasn't used to giving up information, and it disquieted him. That was nice to see; it made my fear settle down until it was more of a low, gibbering voice gnawing at the edge of my thoughts.

"I have an island off the coast of Minos that has always offered me solitude," he said finally. "Recently there have been . . . incursions. An investment in a new local authority will ensure that such intrusions cease." He shrugged. "I value my privacy."

I didn't know if that meant bribes or wholesale regime change. "And for this you'd kill an innocent girl?"

"The price is adequate."

"What is the kill fee on her?"

"Five hundred million euro. I would not trouble myself for less."

What? Someone was willing to pay half a billion euro for Stephanie's death? That was . . . insane. Who could possibly have that kind of capital? And . . . why? Why was it worth it to them?

"Who?" I sipped at the wine to clear my throat. "Who wants her dead?"

"I do not have a name, if that's what you are hoping for," answered the basilisk, turning to the beef shanks. "A private party secured my services, through an intermediary. That is how such things are typically done."

Had I always been so casual talking about murder? I guess so. "I just want to know who's behind all this."

"Why on Earth would you want to know that?" The basilisk seemed genuinely perplexed. In a softer, almost conciliatory tone, he said, "Listen to me, child: You won't know. You'll never know. Be glad of that. There are some knowledges that should not be sought after. There are Powers out there that could erase you from existence as easily as you might swat an irksome insect. Do not seek to swim up into their notice." He gestured toward my plate. "Try the chicken before it grows cold."

"Why is she worth all this trouble?" I asked, picking distractedly at the food. I was practically starving, and still I was too tense to eat anything. Tantalus himself hadn't been so tormented by a meal. "She's . . . gifted, yes. But why is someone so hell-bent on exterminating her?"

The basilisk shook his head. "I do not know. But I have heard certain whispers on the wind, as it were, and I have made my own guesses. Tell me, do you know why Ireland has been free of snakes for so many centuries?"

Whoa, that had come out of left field. "No idea," I admitted. "Saint Patrick?"

The basilisk grinned. "Christians. They are an inventive bunch, always coming up with something amusing. But it was something far darker than the Emerald Isle's patron saint that drove the serpents from its shores." Seeing he had my interest, the basilisk leaned forward. "Tell me, little one, have you ever heard of the *Mástiks para Teratos*?"

I shivered, without knowing why. The words were vaguely familiar, Greek for . . .

"Whip"? No . . . "plague"? And "teras" was . . . "monster," which was why doctors called any substance that caused birth defects a "teratogen": "monster maker." I'd always been particularly fond of that one. "I'm not sure . . ."

"The literal translation is 'Scourge of Monsters,'" answered the basilisk. "It is something of a myth among the mythical, you might say. What humans would call a bogeyman: the terrible thing that comes to destroy us all. There have been stories of such a thing over the centuries, appearing in Mesopotamia . . . Egypt . . . Hibernia. But now I hear the phrase being used again, in reference to this human of yours."

"Stephanie?" That was a hard pill to swallow, though I'd felt flayed open often enough by her during the past two days. Still, the only thing I'd seen Steph really destroy was a box of chocolates.

"And *that's* why you want her dead?" I asked. "Because of a fairy tale?"

The basilisk seemed affronted. "I don't *want* her dead; I don't want anything of the kind. We were discussing the motivation of other parties. I, however, am being paid to see that she *is* dead, before midnight tonight. And I do prefer to be punctual. My jet is refueling for my return flight as we speak, with a departure time of four in the morning."

I tried to swallow my fear, but it was too big. "Then it's down to you against me."

He gazed at me in mild consternation. "Little one, I am doing my level best to reason with you. This . . . quest you've set yourself upon can only lead to your destruction. Your older sisters cannot have approved of this course."

There was that idea again. But . . . "I don't know what you're talking about," I said. "I don't have any sisters."

The basilisk furrowed his brow. "Of course you do. You are born of the same enchantment as your twin sisters." He shook his head, as at a fond memory. "Those two were always getting up to mischief in one form or another in the mortal world. I had not heard of them in some time, though. Until tonight, I'd wondered if they were dead. Then I received word of a gorgon involved in this madness and thought that one of them must surely be at the heart of it." He had to have noticed me gaping, because he went on in a patient tone: "There are always three: the Two Who Are One and the One Who Stands Apart. That is the nature of the spell. Surely you were told all this by the human who bore you?"

Surely I was *not*. Was he—could the basilisk be telling me the truth? The Voice in the omphalos had called me . . . "Kyra Spellborn" and "The One Who Stands Apart." Did my mother know about this? Was this . . . was this something that had been *done* to me?

Did I really have *sisters*?

A host of questions leaped into my mind, but the basilisk held up a hand.

"Your turn, Medusan. I have been generous with my answers. Now, I think, it is time for yours. Why have you been protecting this human?"

My head was still spinning. I tried to focus again. This could all just be a smoke screen, camouflage, an attempt to disorient me.

Which, unfortunately, was working pretty well.

With effort, I put the idea aside. Later, I thought. If there is a later.

I glared at my plate. Two days ago, I would have had no answer for the basilisk's question. Now I had too many.

Because Stephanie's worth a hundred creatures like you or me.

Because if I'm going to die tonight, I want to go to my grave knowing that one person in the world thought I was beautiful, that I was worth being loved, that I was even a little bit good.

Because maybe . . . my whole life, until this night, everything I've believed has been . . . has been . . .

I shrugged. "Maybe I'm just tired."

"Tired?"

"Of being hated. Of being feared." I stirred my chopsticks through the dumplings. I'd once killed a man with chopsticks. "Of being a monster."

The basilisk frowned. "You cannot change your nature."

That wasn't what Stephanie believed. And . . . me? What did I believe? "Maybe . . . maybe you can. If you want it bad enough. If you really think that you can."

The basilisk shook his head. "Impossible. We are what we are. And the world does not forget. They will still hate you no matter what you do."

"Maybe," I muttered. "But maybe I can stop hating myself."

"Little gorgon . . ." The basilisk seemed at a loss. After a moment, he shrugged and returned to his beef. He chewed on it with gusto, then washed it down with half a glass of wine. I glimpsed a faint wisp of steam rising from the glass as he set it down, saw the slight deformation of its edge. Fire was another weapon reputed to be at the basilisk's command.

"May I presume you've had sufficient time to review your tactical situation? Would you care to share your thoughts?"

Maybe he assumed I wouldn't.

"You outgun me," I admitted. Somehow saying it aloud lessened the fear a little more. Go figure. "You can kill me by looking my way, by saying a word, or by just reaching over and touching me."

The basilisk smiled. "I needn't do even that."

"Right," I said. "The *Sapros Aer*." What the ancients had called the "Corrupting Air," some sort of mysterious destructive force that traveled with or around the basilisk, allowing it to transmit death even through intermediary objects. Medieval legends told tales of knights dying in their stirrups even as they struck down at a basilisk, death leaping into their bodies through their own lances or swords.

"Indeed," said the basilisk, tipping his wine glass decorously. "Everything is connected, the scribes tell us. Everything . . . even the smallest things." He glanced at the table between us, then back at me, as though—

I snatched my resting hand off the tablecloth. But the basilisk only grinned, as if it had been a joke, and went back to eating.

I felt slow and stupid. I was missing something . . .

"So, basically, I'd be a fool to try to stop you." When in doubt, blunder ahead.

He dabbed at his goatee with his napkin. "But you feel you must try. Very well. Proceed."

I recoiled. "You think I'm going to . . . expose myself in front of all these people?"

"Why not? Should you desire anonymity after, you have only to petrify the witnesses."

"I wouldn't do that!"

"Why not?"

"It's—" I struggled to put into words what I was feeling, but could only end lamely, "unprofessional."

"But you are not here as a professional, are you?" pounced the basilisk. "You are 'off the grid,' according to your Agency. They have even agreed to post a kill fee for your termination, though it is, frankly, an insulting sum."

"How do you know all this?"

"I have called your Agency, of course. In the past, we have had . . . dealings. They are older than you might think. They recollected me rather quickly. They say you are on an 'unsanctioned activity.' Tsk tsk; very bad for business."

272

"They told you that?"

"People do tend to tell me things. They seem to prefer to deal with me over the phone for some reason." He chuckled. "Perhaps they like the sound of my voice."

More like they wanted to keep the owner of that voice at a safe remove. I had no idea if a basilisk's voice was dangerous enough to kill over electronic lines, but in person it could be lethal. Small wonder Phil had given me up. Maybe I'd only kill him once.

"There are ways to kill even your kind," I said, trying to regain some momentum.

"There must be," agreed the basilisk. His insouciance was infuriating. "Otherwise, I should be supreme. Have you consulted the legends and fairy tales then? Procured the urine or sweat of a weasel, perhaps? My dear gorgon, if there was any truth to those old wives' tales, I'd have simply made arrangements to exterminate every weasel in every pet shop in the city. The truth is, that story stems from a confusion by the people of Persia between my kind and king cobras, who have as their natural enemy the mongoose. Those tales are all just myths."

"So are we," I said. "Yet here we sit, eating pan-fried pork dumplings in the heart of Chicago."

"Touché," he grinned. "As you wish, then. Is there a particular method you would like to try?"

"Just this," I said and snatched up the pocket mirror I'd been hiding in my lap. I pushed the mirror right under his nose so that his gaze instinctively fell upon it. The basilisk's blue eyes widened.

"Gods . . ." he whispered, startled, one hand going to his face. For an instant, I almost shouted with impossible triumph. Then the basilisk frowned. "Are those really crow's-feet? Well, live a few millennia and you must expect such things, I suppose."

He was screwing with me.

"I still have the Medusa's Gaze," I said defensively. "It can kill anything mortal. You're human enough in appearance. Maybe there's a little mortal blood in your ancestry. My Gaze could work on you."

The basilisk turned his attention back to his dinner, sampling the sugar beans. "A reasonable hypothesis," he admitted. "Would you care to verify it?" He steepled his fingers and rested his chin on them. "Why don't you use your Gaze on me now?"

He was baiting me, daring me to take my best shot. I tensed in my seat. I'd never get a better opportunity . . .

No. The game was rigged. I sat back and shook my head.

"Good." The basilisk actually sounded pleased, as though I'd passed some kind of test. "You demonstrate more sense than your sisters, at least. You might actually survive into the next century if you persist that way. Shall I tell you what would have happened if you had tried to employ your Gaze on me? My immunity to your power stems from the fact that mine is drawn from the same source, and I am much closer to that source than you, who have only had it given to you by others. Further, my visual field is selective, filtering out all undesirable elements. Do you comprehend?"

Not really. "You see . . . only what you want to?"

"Precisely. Then there is the question of willpower. I have had centuries to hone and perfect the exercise of my will. You have been alive . . . how long? Two decades? Three? Should you have used your Gaze, I would have been obliged to engage it and reflect it back to its origin. And then the only thing turned to stone at this table would have been you."

"So you say. But maybe you're not as tough as you let on. Maybe this is all just a bluff."

I was trying to provoke a reaction, but the only thing I got was an amazed stare that seemed almost admiring. It struck me that Druison had looked at me in much the same way.

"Gorgon . . . you are very brave. Almost you make me regret this. But do not mistake me; courage will not avail you here. No one and nothing is coming to save you or protect you."

274

It seemed I'd known that fact my whole life. "I'm pretty good at protecting myself."

"Doubtless this has been true. As immature as your powers are, they would present a considerable obstacle to many."

Just not me; he didn't even have to say it out loud. It just hung there between us, like a noose. But something else he'd said caught my attention.

"What do you mean, immature?"

"My dear child, you haven't even grown your wings yet! What is your Gaze capable of right now: petrifying a few mortals at a time, when you can hold their eye long enough?"

Wings?

"Isn't it enough that it kills?" I snapped. "What else do you think it should do?" It was ridiculous, but I felt immediately and irrationally defensive about the Gaze now, even though it was something I had always loathed.

"Why ask me?" smiled the basilisk.

"Well, who the hell else should I ask?"

He raised a hand. I tensed, but he only pointed a finger at my beret. "Them."

I felt a chill despite the closeness of the air. The serpents stirred, suddenly restive.

"What . . . what are you talking about? I can't . . . talk to them." But I had, hadn't I? In the past two days, I'd called on them over and over, even pleaded with them. Yet the idea of them communicating back made my stomach twist.

"You've never done a Lemurian Trance then," nodded the basilisk. "Never sent them out along the astral winds to do your bidding." He sighed. "Little gorgon, you make my point for me. You are too intelligent to fail to see the inevitable outcome of opposing me. Stand between me and this human and you will die. Is that why you are here, what you secretly desire? To end your unhappy existence?"

That was hitting a little too close to the mark. "I'm not that tired of living," I snapped. Not anymore. "And if that's what you're counting on—"

"Please. We need not threaten each other like schoolchildren in the yard. I am giving you this one, last chance: Turn aside from this path. You can't save the human, but you can save yourself."

I licked my lips. "Why warn me at all?"

The basilisk shrugged. "We are kin, after a fashion. Both children of Echidna."

Seriously? The Mother of Monsters? "Echidna's just a story."

He arched an eyebrow. "Perhaps," he said. He sampled another glass of wine with relish, nodding to himself, then turned back to me. "Where do we belong in the great scheme of Creation, little one? Did Eve do more than have speech with the Serpent in the Garden? How do you think monsters came into this world?"

Evidently by their mothers making some sort of sick, twisted magical deal with unknown others, others who were even now being added to my list of people I'd like to suspend over open coals. "I . . . don't know."

"You are honest," said the basilisk approvingly. "That is refreshing. But allow me to alleviate your confusion on the subject: We *don't* belong. Monsters have no place in this world. We are Nature's mistakes, the cells that have mutated and metastasized in the body of the universe, the cancers that walk and talk and kill. Small wonder the world has always tried so hard to eradicate us, to deny us. We are outside the laws of Nature, as we are outside the rules of men. By all rights, we should not exist."

Abruptly, as he was talking, I understood what I had been sensing intuitively from the beginning: The aura of hostility around the basilisk wasn't personal or even conscious; in fact, it wasn't even coming from the basilisk himself. Rather, what I had interpreted as malice was actually the environment's reaction to the basilisk's presence. Somehow his arrival had put a strain on the very fabric of reality around us. I realized I could almost hear the ground under my feet groaning as it strove to hold itself together while under this assault.

Worst of all, I sensed it was only the basilisk's forbearance that was maintaining even this fragile semblance of order. If he released his clenched grip on that restraint, chaos would erupt.

No wonder no one ever saw them anymore, why the legends spoke of their coming out from blasted, ruined, scorched countries, bereft of plants and animals. What other land could endure them?

"I'm sorry." The words slipped out unexpectedly, but I didn't regret them. The basilisk was going to kill us both . . . and still I pitied him. At least I'd been given a shadow of a life, for a while. I had something to lose. But the basilisk had nothing, had always had nothing . . .

The basilisk blinked at me. "What did you say?"

I shook my head. "Nothing. Forget it." What could my sympathy mean anyway? The basilisk was right. We didn't belong; this world didn't want us, had never wanted us. We had no right to be here. If I'd ever really doubted that, the proof was all around me, eager to be rid of us.

The basilisk had finished his dinner. He set his napkin down. "Leave, child." His tone was gentle, almost kind. "I have enjoyed your company. But the hour grows late."

"I can't," I said in a small voice.

"Why?"

"I . . . gave my word."

"To a human? What does that mean to creatures like us? Is your word worth dying for?"

I couldn't speak. Either answer damned me, doomed me.

"Ah, well. Pity. Remember: I did try, little gorgon."

"Kyra." I looked up, met his eyes. He was at least going to know who I was before he killed me. "My name is Kyra Anastas."

The basilisk stared a long moment, then inclined his head in a slight bow. "Kyra," he said quietly. "Go."

"I'm not leading you to her," I said.

"That hardly matters," sighed the basilisk, "now."

I heard plates crashing to the ground outside the enclosure. Sweeping the tent wall back with one hand, I made out the rest of the terrace.

All around us, the plants were collapsing, rotting in their massive pots, even as the pots themselves were crumbling. A glance at the party to my right showed their tent coverings had already disappeared in a shower of dust, the young couple disintegrating where they sat like ancient mummies. The servers lay scattered everywhere, struck down as the invisible tide of death rolled over them.

I staggered backward, out of the tent. In my wake, the metal poles started sagging like licorice in a microwave. Fissures opened in the tiles at my feet, began creeping for the walls.

Everything is connected, he'd warned me. The floor to the people to the walls themselves. Even the molecules of air touching one another. All carrying the *Sapros Aer* out from its source.

I spun around, hands reaching for my guns. The son of a bitch was just sitting there while the table melted in front of him like something out of a Dali painting.

He was going to kill her without lifting a finger.

"Tell her I'm coming," he said. "Tell her to make her peace."

I backed away, trying to stay ahead of the advancing rot.

"Too bad about the wings, really," he called, lifting his glass in farewell. "They might have bought you a little time."

CHAPTER 15

The Pinnacle was dying.

All around me, the tide of corruption spread outward, carrying ruin to everything it touched. The wallpaper blistered and peeled as I ran down the corridors. Plaster sifted down from rents in the ceiling in a thickening cloud. Statuary toppled as marble columns gave way to sudden internal stresses. It was as though the building's natural aging process had been accelerated a thousandfold and the entire structure was hastening toward its death.

I raced past the elevator banks, not daring to stop. I heard screams as one of the cars plummeted past. Behind me, the overhead lights began exploding, showering me with sparks, then plunging the floor into darkness. I found the stairwell door and shoved, sending it careening down the steps as it broke loose from dissolving hinges.

Emergency lamps were coming on, but even with their independent power source, they were already flickering. Twice I nearly lost my footing as I bounded up the steps. Once the rail snapped off under my hand in a spray of rust. The entire stairwell trembled; the load-bearing girders of the building were starting to bend under the weight of the basilisk's assault.

Should have shot him, I thought wildly. Should have tried something, anything. Instead I'd let him sit there and eat his supper like the King of Siam, while all the time he'd been sinking his unnatural influence into every nook and cranny in the building, setting it up for demolition. Stupid, stupid amateur—

In the uncertain light, I made out the sign for the twentieth floor. The door crashed to the floor as I plowed into it. The air reeked with the stench of ozone.

"Stephanie!" I yelled, nearly out of breath. It was so dark—how many doors down was the room? Was it left or right? Dammit, I couldn't remember—

"*Stephanie—!*" I howled.

"Kyra!"

Thank God. A faint glow was approaching. Stephanie was feeling her way down the hall, surrounded by a nimbus of light like a corona. I didn't have the wind or time to question her about it. I just grabbed her wrist and fled back to the stairs.

A glance down told me that escape the way I'd come was impossible. The stairs were disintegrating, huge chunks of concrete breaking off to spin down into the yawning abyss. I might have negotiated the way alone, but with Stephanie—

Then the nerves of my face felt it. The basilisk was on his way, his power reaching upward, mounting as he advanced. Streamers of fire licked the walls as the wiring began burning.

Up, we had to go up. Holding Stephanie's hand tight in mine, we stumbled up the shivering stairs to the next floor, coming out to the lobby of the spa facility. Through the bay windows on our left, I glimpsed the water of the indoor pool boiling and thrashing. A geyser of steam was rolling toward the glass.

"Get down!" I yelled, and threw Stephanie to the carpet, covering her with my body. As the superheated air hit the windows, they bulged and then exploded outward, sending shards zinging through the air and skittering over the back of my duster. I waited till the scalding hot mist thinned, then dragged her up. Through the haze, I made out the neon exit sign.

An alarm started blaring as I blundered through the emergency door. Stephanie coughed and stumbled in my wake while we reeled up another flight of steps. Cracks spread widening fingers along the concrete walls on either side. The building staggered and my ears were filled with the noise of tortured metal moaning like some great beast in its death throes.

We burst through the door onto the roof. The wash of cool air was a blissful sting of needles. I slammed the door shut. Keeping Stephanie close, I threaded a path through the air-conditioning units and HVAC ducts.

"Stay here!" I said, and roved the edges of the roof. On one side, the Chicago Water Tower loomed like a haven, close enough to touch but impossibly far away. No ladder, no fire escape. Only a narrow ledge on the north side of the building, two stories down, with a broader patio roof two stories below that. If I could lower Stephanie to the ledge, she might be able to then drop to the lower landing, make her way back inside. If I could hold the basilisk off for just a few minutes . . .

"Listen to me!" I said, tugging the belt of my duster off. "You need to hold onto this! I'm going to lower you down—!"

Stephanie shook her head violently. "No! I'm not leaving you!"

I dragged her to the edge of the roof. "Young lady, we are not arguing about this!" I wrapped the end of the belt around her wrist and knotted it. "You'll do as I say—"

"Kyra." Somehow her voice carried through the clamor around us. I raised my eyes to hers. Luminous tears were rolling down Stephanie's cheeks. She raised one hand and pressed her warm palm against my face.

"You've done more than I could have dreamed," she said. "If we're to die, I want to be with you."

Christ, now I was crying. "Steph . . . please . . ."

"Ssh," she said, smiling. "It's all right."

I grabbed her and hugged her hard, trying to crush her body into mine, to somehow make her understand what I was feeling. There was so much I wanted to say, and now we had no time left.

Time . . .

I looked at my watch and groaned aloud: eleven forty-five. Damn it all, we had gotten so *close*—

A sizzling sound spun me round.

Thirty feet away, the door was glowing red—now white—hot. After a moment, the handle melted off, dropping to the roof as molten slag. I thrust Stephanie behind me, drew out my Glocks. I shook my limbs for balance and battle.

"Just . . . had to be born at midnight, didn't ya?" I panted over my shoulder. "Couldn'ta been a preemie child of destiny . . ."

"Sorry about that," she said.

I laughed and bared my teeth in a predator's grin. The eyes; go for the eyes. If there was any vulnerable spot on the bastard, it would be there.

The door was no longer recognizable, just bits of liquid metal that flashed as they evaporated. And through the opening the basilisk strode onto the roof. He had grown darker, his face and form now like black coals, around which the very air itself ignited. The pressure of his active presence made the fabric of space ripple and whorl so that he seemed to be emerging from the center of a gathering cyclone. The panels on the HVAC units by the door sprang loose as their steel screws shook free. Even the asphalt under my feet erupted, flying upward into a spinning gyre of debris.

His eyes blazed with a piercing golden light, the fires of Hell come to Earth.

I aimed for those lights, loosing shot after shot. Eighteen .40 caliber slugs zipped through the tormented atmosphere, vaporizing as they struck the basilisk's aura. Then the barrels of my Glocks caught fire. I dropped the guns and fell into a crouch, slipping out my Ruger double-action revolver. But instead of shooting at the basilisk, I fired at the exposed condenser he was passing.

The pressurized refrigerant exploded, the blast throwing me backward with shrapnel zinging all around me. I collided with Stephanie, and we both tumbled to the ground. I felt blood streaming down my face and wiped it aside, trying to see if my desperate gambit had done some good.

The basilisk had been staggered by the detonation but was shrugging it off, advancing toward us. I pushed Stephanie to keep her down and climbed to my feet. The Ruger was nowhere to be seen.

"Gorgon," thundered the basilisk from the center of the whirling chaos. "Stand aside!"

"No!" I yelled. "I won't let you hurt her!"

I leapt into the heart of the maelstrom, clawing for his face. The basilisk caught my hands in his. As our eyes met, I threw everything I had—every ounce of power and passion I'd ever harnessed—into ramming my Gaze past his defenses. For a moment I felt the force pushing inward, seeking his ancient, unfathomable core. Then the basilisk's will surged against mine with redoubled force and the Gaze shattered into splinters. Under my beret, the snakes hissed and writhed in wounded fury.

"Kill him!" I shouted and, as one, they surged out like a deluge, like an avalanche, striking from dozens of outstretched mouths, burying their fangs into the basilisk's skull. The basilisk roared and one black and blazing hand reached up, seizing a bunch of the snakes in his fist. With a wrench, he ripped them out of my head.

In all my life, I had never dreamed a human being could feel so much pain and not die instantly. I screamed and went limp, nearly fainting in agony and horror. The ground rose up to meet me as the basilisk flung me away.

Black ichor and blood blinded me. I felt a terrible emptiness, a nausea unlike any I had ever known, as though a hole had been torn open in my soul. The surviving snakes jerked and shivered against my temples, searching frantically for their missing kin. I just wanted to lie down and die. But I could still make out Stephanie, prone on the roof, her one hand outstretched toward me as the shadow of the basilisk fell over her.

"Stephanie . . . ," I whispered. "I'm sorry."

283

With the last strength of my body and will, I crawled forward and threw myself on top of her.

"GORGON," boomed the basilisk, "STAND ASIDE!"

"No," I moaned. I squeezed my eyes shut, bracing for incineration.

"WHY?" roared the voice from above.

I dredged my head up. The thick lifeblood from the ragged stumps of my snakes was pulsing down my forehead, mixing with my tears. Through the haze over my sight, I could barely see the burning eyes of the shadow looming over me.

Fingers hot as brands seized me by the throat, drew me close.

"WHY?" demanded the basilisk.

I had nothing left. Nothing but the truth.

"Because . . . this is wrong," I sobbed, meeting his gaze. "It's *wrong*."

For a moment that seemed to last forever, I felt death closing in on me as the pressure and pain in my skull mounted. Darkness crept into the corners of my sight. All I could see were those eyes. Then, abruptly, the grip on my throat was gone. Released, I dropped facedown on the roof.

The unnatural heat and violence of the atmosphere seemed to collapse with me. A hush fell over the roof, broken only by the murmur of traffic from far below. Blind with pain and ichor, I realized my starving lungs were greedily sucking in sweet, cool air again. I sensed without seeing the basilisk standing before me. If I could have reached out, his shoes were close enough to touch. But he made no move to step over me.

I heard the scrunch of gravel as the basilisk bent to one knee. Fingers cupped my chin in his palm, swiped the blood from my eyes. Still gasping, I realized I could make out the basilisk's face, its darkness and fiery swirls fading back into the flesh even as I watched. The pale blue eyes regarded me from under the ruddy brows again. There was something in them I hadn't seen before—a strange, almost haunted look.

"So," he rumbled. "It would seem your Gaze is possessed of other dangers, Kyra Anastas. Perhaps the poet Virgil was wrong after all: Nature *can* change." A faint, sad smile tugged at one corner of his weathered lips. "You

284

have reproached me, little one. As youth will sometimes do to great age." He stood again, almost leaving my sight as I knelt there with my head bowed. "I take my leave of this place. The day is yours. But . . . I think it best we do not meet again. Fare you well."

I stared as his shoes turned around and crunched across the gravel back to the ruined doorway. The suited figure descended into the darkness there and disappeared.

I . . .

What?

Why . . . wait . . .

"What the hell just happened?" I croaked to anybody who might still be out in the real world where things made sense.

A sudden embrace from behind almost made me cry out. But it was only Stephanie, wrapping her arms around me.

"Kyra!" she said. "Oh, Kyra, you did it! You did it!"

"Did what?" I mumbled past my split and seared lips. What in God's name was she talking about?

"You saved us."

That got my attention. I still felt too sick to stand, but was finally able to force myself into a sitting position. Grinding the rest of the goop out of my eyes, I confirmed that it was no hallucination—the roof was indeed empty.

"What happened?" I kept blinking like an owl caught in the daylight. "Why aren't we dead? Where'd he go?"

"He's gone."

That dog just wouldn't hunt. It couldn't be. I levered myself upright with Stephanie's help. "Where?"

"I don't know. Back to his home, I suppose."

Some capacity for urgency reasserted itself. I stumbled to my feet, grabbed her hand. "Come on. He could come back at any minute."

Stephanie stayed me. "He won't."

"What makes you so sure?"

"He's been defeated. You heard him. It's over."

I gaped at her. "How? I couldn't stop him."

Stephanie smiled. "Yet you did."

"I don't understand."

"He was defeated the only way a basilisk can be defeated: He saw himself."

"No...." I shook my head. "I tried that. The mirror didn't have any effect."

"Not the surface image," Stephanie said. "That would mean nothing to him. The basilisk was used to seeing himself as a monster in other people's eyes. He could behave as one because he believed his nature justified it, even required it. By standing against him, even though you knew you had no chance of winning, by defending me when you yourself are what he would call a monster, you showed him that his true horror was in choosing to do evil. When he saw in your eyes an unwillingness to yield your principles even in the face of your own death, he saw his true self for the first time, stripped of self-deception and self-justification. That sight undid him."

That's not possible, I wanted to say. The world doesn't work like that. But it seemed the world had decided to ignore me.

I tried to laugh, but the pain throbbing above my scalp stopped me. Stephanie cocked her head.

"What's funny?"

"My Gaze," I said. "I finally did something good with it." I traced my fingers gingerly over the severed stumps, felt the survivors shivering in sympathetic pain. My poor little ones; they had been so brave.

Stephanie reached for them. "Let me heal you before I go."

Just being this close to her had already eased the worst of my pains. But I stopped her, shaking my head.

"But . . . why? You know I won't—"

"I know." I took her hands in mine, kissing them before letting her go. Maybe I was just beginning to get a handle on what they were—what *we* were—but I understood what they had done tonight. And whether they really were just some buried piece of me I'd denied, or had sentience on their own, I wanted to feel the weight of their sacrifice. I owed them that. So I just smiled and said: "But I think I . . . we . . . need time to grieve."

Stephanie nodded. "I understand."

The light around us was growing. I glanced at my watch. The face plate had gotten cracked, but I could still make out the time. "It's after midnight," I said, then realized the radiance was coming from Stephanie. "Wait . . . you're leaving?"

"Yes," she said. "My time has come."

She was looking at me with peace and a strange sort of serious joy in her eyes. I started. Her eyes . . .

"You can see!" I blurted out. Her eyes were no longer the milky white orbs of before, but a hazel flecked with gleaming gold.

"Do you like?" she asked. "I chose the color to remember you by. Not that I will ever forget you, my beautiful, courageous sister."

"Then . . . do you know . . . why you're here? What you're supposed to do?"

"Yes. At least I'm beginning to. More will become clear in time. But I understand the need for my creation now. When the power of the old gods waned, the Moirai faded with them. It had to be, but the Threads of Fate were left without a caretaker. And the result has been disorder, chaos. Now the process of restoration can begin."

I blinked. "You . . . are the Moirai now?"

"After a fashion. But I'm also Stephanie Rougnagne. More than that will—"

"Be clear in time," I said. "Gotcha. Well, uh, good luck with the new job, I guess. Try not to, you know . . ."

"I know," she said. "I will do my best to avoid 'mucking things up'—" she wiggled her fingers at me "—when I put my hands on the weave of the world."

"Smart-ass." But I was grinning. I couldn't help it. I kind of loved this kid.

Stephanie turned away, toward the center of the light that was spreading out around her, forming an archway. She seemed to be receding into it without moving. And I didn't want to let her go. "Hey . . . Steph?"

"Yes?" She glanced back.

"Happy birthday," I said, then grimaced. "Sorry I didn't get you anything."

Stephanie smiled like the sunrise. "My life was quite gift enough, thank you. Happy birthday to *you*, Kyra."

I frowned. "What do you mean? It's not my—" I stopped, understanding. "Yeah, okay," I said, nodding. It did feel like a rebirth of sorts. "Thanks, kid. Take care of yourself, will you?"

"I will." She lifted a hand in farewell. "Be good, Kyra. You know the way." Her voice faded as the light around her grew. "I'm so proud of you."

New tears were stinging my eyes. "Stephanie..." I began in a choked voice.

"I know," came back the whispered reply. "I love you too, Kyra."

Then the light was fading and all around me was night again.

It took me nearly half an hour to negotiate my way down the damaged stairwell to the lobby, stopping only to retrieve my satchel. Outside, the intersection of Superior and Michigan was choked with fire engines, ambulances, and police cars. Hundreds of injured people were scattered about, sitting on the curb or lying on stretchers. After waving off one EMT, I was largely ignored amidst the tide of greater need. Keeping my beret low and my head down, I wended my way past the cops hurrying to and fro. I was nearly at the cordon when someone touched my arm.

I froze, but it was only a young man in the uniform of a hotel clerk. His face was streaked with soot and minor cuts.

"Miss? Thank goodness. Your sister; is she okay?"

I smiled. "She's fine. She... went on ahead."

"Oh, good. She gave this to me. Said to deliver it to you after midnight. Sorry it got wrinkled but, well, you know..." He gestured around us.

I took the proffered envelope, comprehension slowly dawning. Stephanie's note. It had been for me. Something for later, she'd said.

I thanked him and opened the envelope. Through the backwash of strobing lights, I read:

He likes you. But he is not being honest with you. Be careful.

I frowned. The only other thing on the page was a series of numbers, written in the same hand: 10, 13, 14, 22, 52, and 11. And then the words: *For the trouble.*

"What's this—?" I began, but the clerk had already moved off. I stared stupidly at the sheet. Some sort of code? It was too many numbers for a combination lock. I shook my head; I was too tired to think. When a policeman with a notepad started working his way in my direction, I stuffed the note in my pocket and slipped away.

It took five blocks of hoofing it before I could hail a cab to take me back to Millennium Park. The Veyron was where I'd left it, gleaming under the mellow lights of the parking garage in all its midnight blue glory. I smiled wistfully; it was all that was left of the Rougnagne fortune, all that I could hold onto of Stephanie.

I needed to go. I was quits with the Windy City. That was another pang, one that ran almost as deep as the loss of my friend. But I could indulge that feeling at another time. It occurred to me that with nearly every cop in town converging on the Pinnacle, there'd never be a better time to grab a few of my personal effects from my apartment before hitting the road for good.

Twenty minutes later, I'd tucked the Veyron into a secluded spot and crept up the fire escape to my place. Through the window, I scanned the dark interior. Well, they'd tossed the place, but that was to be expected. Not that it didn't piss me off; it did—but my new, enlightened self just wasn't prepared to kill anyone about it.

I popped the latch and slipped inside. The drawers and cabinets in the kitchen had all been left open. On the tile countertop, the huge stainless-steel bowl still sat, site of countless midnight slaughters.

I'm sorry, I thought, grazing the rim with my fingers. *I was wrong.* About that. About so many things.

The bedroom—arguably the only room I'd have dared to call even semi-clean on a good day—had also been thoroughly gone over. But even before I moved the nightstand, I could tell they hadn't pulled the floorboards up. Bending on one knee, I wedged my throwing knife between the thin beams and prized open the hiding place. Sealed in an old shoebox was everything I'd ever managed to keep over the years that had any meaning for me. I'd go through it later when I'd gotten out of Illinois for . . . wherever I was going.

I started stuffing the shoebox into Druison's satchel, but there was just too much junk. Between my spare guns and ammo and all of the detective's bulky candles and cereal bowl, I could barely wedge the box halfway. I swore under my breath; why was I still carrying this man's trash around with me? For that matter, what kind of grown man traipses around Chicago with half a dozen scented candles and a stupid cereal bowl anyway? Was Druison one of those Sensitive New Age Guys? Ugh; maybe I was better off not . . .

I frowned, a thought coming unbidden from my memory: Druison had said he'd been looking all over town for me. But he'd never explained how he'd found me at Millennium Park. What was he doing searching for me there of all places, at midnight no less? The odds of us both being there at that moment had to be astronomical. Unless . . .

Unless he hadn't been looking for me at all.

Just then, my cell phone brayed against my chest, once. I almost jumped clear out of my skin. If I hadn't been so drained, I might have drawn and started firing at the shadows.

God Almighty, I *knew* I'd turned that damn thing off when I'd hung up on Phil outside the hotel. I must have accidentally pressed the "on" button at some point during the encounter with the basilisk. I fished the phone out of my breast pocket to turn it off, then stopped.

Thirteen voice mail messages. All from Phil. The oldest was dated Monday night, just before I'd gone to The Bean.

What the hell. I stabbed the play button, setting the cell on the floor, and turned back to the satchel. Picking out the cereal bowl, I surveyed it with a more critical eye. There, and there. In the grooves of the white surface, I picked out faint lines of scarlet.

Dried blood.

Under my beret, my snakes began hissing. Druison had come to The Bean for the same reason I had, to use the omphalos, to try to contact the spirit world . . .

He likes you. But he's not being honest with you. Be careful.

Phil's voice, tinny without speakers, rose from the floor: "Kyra, it's me. Listen, I know you're busy, but I've been doing some more digging, and you'll never believe what I found out about your two detectives, especially Druison. Get this: He's supposed to be a transfer from Albuquerque, New Mexico, right? Only when I accessed their database, I found that his records at their police department go back only two years. Beyond that, there's no record—anywhere—that this guy even exists. He's like some sort of ghost, completely off the grid—"

"There's actually a good explanation for that," said a voice over my shoulder.

"Yaah!" I snatched my knife up, spinning for a backhand stab. But a gloved hand caught my wrist and slammed me headfirst against the wall. Maybe he thought the blow would knock me out, but the snakes took the brunt of the impact, and I was able to hook my foot around his ankle and pull. We both tumbled to the floor. As we landed, I twisted, driving my elbow into his breadbasket. I heard him gasp as the breath went out of his lungs, then rolled on top of him, pinning his wrists.

"Detective Druison," I panted. "Fancy meeting you here."

Druison's face still had that puppy dog cuteness, but the eyes were narrow slits of balefire. "Anastas, listen to me—"

"Oh, I think we're done talking," I said. "In fact—"

"Ain't this sweet?" said another voice as the bedroom lights suddenly flared to life. "You two lovebirds all cozy on the floor."

I looked up, blinking, just in time to get a boot right against the base of my nose. Stars exploded across my sight and I tasted blood. Another kick shoved me against the wall, my legs still tangled with Druison's.

"Stan," Druison was saying, "what are you—?"

"Save it, *partner*. I know what you and the lady Fed here have been up to."

I couldn't clear my vision, but I recognized the voice: Detective Schober. Ah, God. What a night I was having.

And of course, to top things off, Phil was still rattling on from the floor: "—a few things about the other guy: Detective Stan Schober. Seems he's under investigation by the IAB for getting too friendly with the local drug kingpin—"

You could've led off with that, Phil! I wanted to yell. Then I heard the crunch of a boot stamping on the phone, silencing it.

"Couldn'ta left things alone, could you guys?" Schober growled above us. "So a few cops try to boost their lousy pensions with some of the stuff Delgado's boss leaves lying around after a coupla busts, and you have to go and make a federal case out of it." I heard the sound of a gun slide being pulled back. "I was on to you from the start, though, Druison. When the shit hit the fan because of Pontano, I got clear of the place and tailed you. I knew you'd lead me back to your contact, sooner or later. Shoulda known it would be her. Now we close the books."

I tried to throw my Gaze out at him but couldn't focus, I couldn't see him clearly—

Then Druison's gloved hand closed on mine. And suddenly I felt the power flowing out of me, not from my eyes but through our clasped hands. I heard Schober gasp, once, then the sound of his gun clattering to the floor.

Wringing the stars from my sight, I made out the petrified figure of the heavyset detective standing over us, an expression of shock now permanently etched on his stone features. I looked down at Druison, who was still staring up at his ex-partner.

"Wow," he breathed, glancing back at me. "You know, I really wasn't sure if that would work."

I snatched my hand from his and clambered to my feet. This was all happening way too fast. When Druison rose, I stabbed a shaky finger at him. "What—? What the hell is this? What are you?"

Druison raised his palms. "Easy there, Kyra, easy. I can explain."

"Yeah? How?"

"Like this." Druison tugged off one of his gloves, bared the back of his wrist.

It was covered with faint, greenish scales.

Like me. He was like me.

Kindred, Steph had said. *Like you.* Ooh, that little brat; I wouldn't have given her credit to slide one by me like that.

Except . . .

"Your hair. . . . You don't have snakes . . ."

Druison touched his wavy, black hair self-consciously. "Yeah, well, I told you my grandmother was from Greece, didn't I? She, uh, got involved with a cockatrice when she was young and kinda wild, so . . ."

A cockatrice? Seriously? He was one-quarter cockatrice? I couldn't help it; I burst out laughing.

Druison ducked his head, embarrassed. "We don't talk about it too much in my family."

"I'll bet." Who would? Cockatrices were supposed to have petrification powers of their own, not to mention the heads of roosters. Grandma Druison must have been wild indeed.

So, too diluted to trigger his own Gaze, Druison's blood must still have been able to use my power like a booster shot, channeling it through his eyes. And, if he could do that, that might mean he was immune to the Medusa's Gaze. Which would make him someone I couldn't hurt.

Well, unless I shot, stabbed, strangled, or did 111 other things I knew how to do to him, I mean. Still . . .

I set aside the possibilities with an effort. "But . . . that doesn't explain how you ended up on the Chicago police force."

"It's a long story," Druison said. Then he grinned. "Suppose I tell it to you over some coffee? Y'know, after we take out the trash." He gestured to the statue.

I shook my head. As tempting as that was. . . . "I've gotta leave town. There's a warrant out for my arrest, remember? And even if there wasn't, I disappeared from a prisoner van the cops were bringing in earlier. It's too much of a mess here for me."

"Funny thing about that prisoner transport," said Druison, tugging his glove back on. "Seems there was never an official request for it in the system. And Officer Pontano can't seem to recall who was in it, or even what happened. Though I'm told he's singing like a songbird about everything else."

"But the warrant—"

"Rescinded. Once Pontano admitted you'd been set up for Delgado's murder by Stan here, I was able to get it canceled. That's why I was staking your place out tonight. I was hoping you might come back here before you left town, so I could tell you—"

"Tell me what?"

Druison ducked his head. "That you could, you know, stick around. If you wanted to."

I gaped at him. A sweet dream. There was only one problem.

"I did kill him," I said. "I murdered Delgado."

Talk about your awkward silences; in fact, this felt like the Mother of All Awkward Silences. Finally, Druison frowned. "Well," he said, scratching the back of his head, "so much for getting my fee."

Fee? Sudden comprehension flooded in.

"You little shit!" I breathed in wonder. "You're with another agency, aren't you? Delgado was your mark too!"

"A double billing," nodded Druison. "It happens. Hard to be too surprised, really. Marco made more than his share of enemies. I got his name from a few families in East Pilsen that had people disappear because of our boy. You?"

"Vietnamese community."

Druison nodded again. "Sure."

This was officially the weirdest conversation I'd had all week, and that was saying something.

"So . . . you're not a cop, then?" I felt strangely let down. Despite the reprieve it meant for me, I'd found out my baby-faced prince had feet of clay. Just another one of the bad guys.

"No, I'm on the force. Graduated the Academy," Druison said. "With honors, actually. I just freelance once in a while when the job's right. My records were accidentally wiped by my agency two years ago; it's caused me no end of problems. But what can you do? My outfit's strictly bush league. Not like the one you're with."

"Was with." The realization struck me that I wasn't going back to that life, even if I stayed in Chicago, even if they lifted the kill fee on me. "I'm done."

"Done?"

"Done. Long story." I scowled. "So that's why you showed so much interest in me? To see if I'd taken your mark?"

"No." He looked honestly surprised, almost wounded. "Delgado *was* the key to an IAB probe. That's why I'd held off on taking him out for so long. When we came to your apartment, though, I realized what you were immediately. I figured you must have taken him out. But I didn't know who had hired you. You could have been trying to undermine the IAB's investigation. So I tried to learn more about you to see if you were . . . you know . . . a good gorgon or a bad one."

A good gorgon. I kind of liked the sound of that.

"So . . . that girl I saw. What happened? Did you save her?"

More like the other way around. "Yeah, she . . ." But there was too much to say there. Another time . . . maybe. "Yes."

"Is that . . . something you do?"

I started to shake my head, then stopped. Is this the way you change a life? One small decision at a time? A word can change it utterly, Stephanie had said.

And when she knows, she is always right.

Okay, okay. I didn't need *that* voice nagging me the rest of my life.

"Yeah," I answered. It felt scary to say it. It felt good. Most of all, it felt somehow . . . right. "It is."

Druison gave me a long, curious look, that gleam back in his deep gray eyes, the gleam I'd liked from the start. He shook his head and grinned. "You're a pretty interesting woman, Kyra Anastas."

"Flattery will get you everywhere, Detective," I said, and began hunting for one of my chisels. "But you're still paying for that coffee if you want to call it a date."

෬෬෬෬

Carved into a small, chaparral-covered hill that overlooks the Los Peñasquitos Canyon Reserve in Southern California is a quaint cul-de-sac of identical houses, each made of the same light earth-tone stucco and each sheltered from the sun by the same red-brown terra-cotta tile roofs. In one of these houses, an hour before noon, a young man with a mop of red hair and thick, wire-framed glasses was just trudging his way downstairs, rubbing the sleep from his eyes. Yawning impressively, he entered the kitchen and pulled the fridge open, then turned to sit down with a half-full bottle of orange juice in his hand.

Which was when he saw me, sitting with my boots propped up on the table.

"Hiya, Phil," I said. "How's tricks?"

The plastic bottle slipped from his fingers, splattering juice all over the floor. Phil staggered back, his eyes widening, until he was brought up short by the sideboard. He spun around and dragged a drawer open, scrabbling past assorted junk until he hauled out a long, single-action revolver that looked like something out of old Dodge City. Fumbling for control, he swung it in my direction.

Lord, he was making a hash of it. "Too high," I said, gesturing down with my hand. "You've got to lower the barrel."

Phil obediently dipped the gun until the legs of my chair were imperiled.

"No, no . . . you have to cock the hammer."

"What?" Phil cried.

"*Cock* it!" I snapped. "With your thumb! No, who are you: Wyatt Earp? You hold it with one hand and cock it with the *other* hand! C'mon, Phil! I'm gonna die of old age over here!"

296

"Oh, God," Phil groaned, dropping the weapon and clutching his temples. "Just get it over with! I can't stand it anymore."

Okay; I do love to make a good entrance, but this was just getting mean-spirited. I lifted my boots off the table and plucked the handgun from the widening pool of juice. Hell of a way to treat a vintage firearm.

I took Phil by the elbow and steered him into a seat, then fetched some paper towels from a lower cabinet. When I'd finished cleaning up, I sat down across from him.

"Relax, Phil," I said. "Good news. We've decided not to kill you."

"Oh, thank God," Phil said, sagging with relief. Then his freckled brow knitted. "Wait—'we'?"

I gestured to my hood. "The boys and me." I winced as I felt a nip over my left ear. "Actually, I'm pretty sure now a few of them are girls. We're still getting to know one another."

Phil's breathing was still unsteady. His eyes kept returning to the revolver on the table.

"Kyra . . . I could've *killed* you."

"I doubt it," I said. "I took out all the bullets while you were still snoring away."

"Oh. That's good. I guess." Phil nodded distractedly. "Um, don't change your mind or anything but . . . *why* aren't you going to kill me?"

Fair question. "I listened to your messages. You know, the one warning me about the detectives. And then the ones warning me that the Agency had disavowed me and that you'd gotten word of a Siren coming after Stephanie. And that there was a basilisk coming for us." I really would have to get better about checking my voicemail. "You took a big risk for me, Phil."

Phil's cheeks colored, bless the boy. "Yeah, well, it just seemed like dirty pool to me, so . . . " He shrugged.

"It's a dirty business we used to be in," I said with feeling. "Good thing we're leaving it."

"Um . . . we are?"

"Yeah, I've got something else in mind and thought you might want to partner up on it. A new business venture, you might say. Though first I have to settle up with the Agency."

"I guess you know that kill fee against you has been canceled."

"I'd heard about that." In the three weeks it had taken me to track down Phil, I'd heard a lot of interesting things, though I'd gotten no closer to learning who had bankrolled the contract on Stephanie. It would keep. She was out of harm's way. And snakes are patient predators. "That *your* doing?"

Phil nodded. "I guess the Agency reconsidered the wisdom of going after someone who could singlehandedly defeat a basilisk." He grimaced. "They still sacked me. In fact, I half expected them to send someone to take me out."

They had. The guy they'd given that unlucky assignment to was currently enjoying the view from the bottom of the local reservoir, tied up with his own tentacles. But Phil was nervous enough already; he didn't need to hear his fears confirmed. So I just grunted agreement.

"Um . . . so what's this business venture?"

"We can go over the details later," I said. "I just want to do something better, something . . . cleaner."

"Businesses need start-up money, Kyra," Phil said tentatively. "Capital. And, well . . ."

I tugged a small piece of paper out of my pocket. "Money's not going to be an issue for us. Not after you present this for payment."

"A lottery ticket?"

"Not *a* lottery ticket; *the* lottery ticket. Don't you watch the news, Phil? Look at the numbers."

Phil's eyes fell to the ticket. "Are these . . . ?"

"The winning Powerball numbers from a few weeks ago," I said, grinning.

"No one's come forward to claim that ticket," Phil said.

I waggled my eyebrows. "I know."

"It . . . was over three hundred million . . ."

"Not if you take it in cash," I said. "Then it's only a hundred and twenty-two million. Still, don't you think that would be enough to get us started?"

Really, half the fun was in watching his face. I hadn't realized how much entertainment I'd been deprived of over the years just talking on the phone.

"How . . . ?" he finally choked out.

"A friend," I said. "A really dear friend. Like you . . . partner." I stretched my arms over my head. My snakes were getting restless. This close to the ocean, they wanted to taste the salt air.

Patience, little ones, I thought. *We're going.*

I stood. Phil looked up. "You're . . . leaving this . . . with me?"

"Sure," I said. "I trust you. Also, I think it'd be best to keep my face out of the limelight, don't you? Collect the money, get things set up. I'll be back in a month or two."

"Where . . . where are you going?"

"Greece," I said. "My mother and I are overdue for a talk." Years overdue. It was time to clear the air, on both sides. "I'll call you when I get back."

"Okay . . . uh, partner."

I was at the door when Phil called after me: "Kyra . . . ?"

I turned. "Yeah?"

He shrugged his shoulders. "You're . . . I don't know . . . different somehow."

I smiled. It seemed to be getting easier each time I did it.

"I hope so," I said, and left.

I'm not saying I was practically skipping through the sunshine as I went down the street to the Veyron.

I'm not admitting anything.

Big Sur on a Sunday morning.

I sat on my blanket with the rising sun behind me, feeling it paint my shoulders and the back of my hood with glorious warmth. All around, the lush green slopes of the Pacific Valley mountains rolled steeply past till they fell into a wide, crescent-shaped beach of white sand below me. The wet kiss of the sea was in the air, forming a fine mist as it moved across the headland and swirled over the black rocks jutting up from the waves.

White foam gently fanned out across the deep blue waters, spreading like a stately procession of bridal gowns. High above, a hawk rode the ocean breeze, hunting for her breakfast. I closed my eyes and listened to the vast, slow breathing of the planet.

Are you out there, Stephanie? Can you see your big sister? Do you know what you did for me?

Half a country away, Chicago awaited my return. Maybe something would work out with Druison there, maybe it wouldn't. Time would tell where the threads of fate would take us. But I was content with today.

And, hey, forty-two days without a cigarette too. *Mirabile dictu*, baby.

My little ones were rousing with the light and warmth of the new day. No one was about. Standing up, I drew my hood off. I shook my head back and forth, encouraging the snakes to rise up into the dawn. Then I ran my fingers through them, luxuriating in their play.

You are as much a part of this as these blades of grass, she'd said, *as the wind in the sky, as the waves of the ocean.* I had a place here.

I didn't know what that place was yet. But for her sake, I was willing to look for it. I would hunt for it till I found it. Or until I made it.

So consider yourself on notice, I said to the wind and the waves. I won't go back to skulking in the shadows; I'm done hiding from you, from myself.

Gathering my things, I headed up the trail that would take me to the car, and the airport, and the future.

I'm here to stay, world.

Deal with it.

ACKNOWLEDGEMENTS

Thanks to the fine folks at When Words Count who helped me guide this story out into the light.

Big heaps of gratitude to my dear friend, Christine M. Eberle, for her selfless editing and enthusiasm for the manuscript. My Secret Weapon!

All my love and thanks to my first, and best, reader—my constant North Star, Kate. You always believed.

And much gratitude and affection to Joe Feeney, S.J., who long ago set my feet on the path.

301

ABOUT THE AUTHOR

David W. Burns began writing fiction when he was six years old, penning the tragic exploits of The Foolish Frog—complete with pictures—to amuse his mother. Since then, he has written several fantasy short stories, including one which won the 14th Annual Writers Digest Popular Fiction Awards Grand Prize, as well as a six-book series about humanity's last refuge against an apocalyptic vampire plague. By day (and some evenings) a trial attorney, David has spent years honing his story-telling skills before juries, learning through trial (and error) what themes and ideas people connect with. He lives in Marlton, New Jersey with his kind and very patient wife and three children and would likely enjoy many fascinating hobbies if he had any free time for them.